STORY OF MYTH AND LEGEND

IMMIXTUS

HOPE FORSMAN

Immixtus: A Story of Myth and Legend
First Edition
Copyright © 2023 by Hope Forsman

All rights reserved. No part of this book may be used or reproduced in any manner whatsoever, including Internet and social media usage, without written permission from the author.

This story is a work of fiction. References to real people, events, establishments, organizations, or locales are intended only to provide a sense of authenticity and are used fictitiously solely for entertainment. All other characters, and all incidents and dialogue are drawn from the authors imagination and are not to be construed as real or facts.

Cover Design by Angelee van Allman

Instagram: @hopeforsmanauthor
ISBN (paperback) - 979-8-9882592-0-6
ISBN (ebook) - 979-8-9882592-1-3

To the H's in my life
(Haley, Hannah, and Harley)

Contents

Chapter One	1
Chapter Two	11
Chapter Three	16
Chapter Four	28
Chapter Five	37
Chapter Six	47
Chapter Seven	54
Chapter Eight	66
Chapter Nine	75
Chapter Ten	84
Chapter Eleven	95
Chapter Twelve	105
Chapter Thirteen	119
Chapter Fourteen	128
Chapter Fifteen	138
Chapter Sixteen	148

Chapter Seventeen	154
Chapter Eighteen	165
Chapter Nineteen	173
Chapter Twenty	181
Chapter Twenty-One	192
Chapter Twenty – Two	203
Chapter Twenty – Three	209
Chapter Twenty – Four	220
Chapter Twenty - Five	228
Chapter Twenty – Six	235
Chapter Twenty – Seven	242
Chapter Twenty – Eight	250
Chapter Twenty – Nine	264
Chapter Thirty	268
Chapter Thirty- One	282
Chapter Thirty-Two	294
Chapter Thirty-Three	303
About The Author	311

Chapter One

THE WATER LOOKED LIKE teardrops as it ran down the window of the car and Cali leaned her head against the glass trying to guess which drop would win. Her phone had died about an hour ago and her mother insisted that she charge her phone as it was the one with access to the GPS for the drive.

Cali understood the feel of the rain as it began to subside. It left a deep heaviness in the air where the humidity pressed down; it felt sad. That's how she felt now. The trees whipped past; greens finally began to appear across the rolling hills as they left Athens behind. Greece was generally dry this time of year, so this fresh rain made for a rare occasion. Cali felt her annoyance fade, the miles between the family's car and her home continued to build. But she couldn't shake the feeling that something was missing, and no amount of vacationing would find whatever it was.

Her family was on their way to the summer cabin in the Foloi Forest, just over an hour outside of Athens. Her adoptive parents, Miriam and Aliax, spent the previous night reminding Cali of this being their final family trip before she goes to university in the fall. She had argued that she wanted to go to Rome, or Paris, or anywhere but the same place they went to every year. Her parents—or rather her overly anxious, safety-minded mother—had won out. Aliax had merely leaned back in his chair, shaking his head as he puffed smoke out of his pipe, a sure sign of victory on her parents' part. Cali had gone to her room without another word, slamming the door for good measure. So, here they were. Heading to Foloi Forest. Again.

An hour into the drive, not a word had been spoken between the three. The rain stopped as quickly as it had started. She continued to rest her forehead against the window, watching her breath fog against it and disappear. Her reflection stared back at her, distorted by the grey sky and streaks of water. She studied herself, the pale skin, the two different colored eyes, and the straight blonde hair, before closing her eyes.

"Did you hear me?"

Cali turned to look at her mom, her forehead squeaking against the window. Her mom turned to face her from the passenger seat, her eyebrow raised, and lips pursed. Peppery gray curls billowed around her face from the breeze of the cracked passenger window, wafting in the fresh smell of grass and rain. Eyes the same shade as a cloudy day waited patiently for Cali to respond.

"No, Mom, I didn't," Cali said her voice edged with sarcasm.

"You're half-deaf, not fully," Miriam said with a frown. "No need to get short with me."

"Sorry," mumbled Cali half-heartedly.

She brushed her fingers over the small thin scars that lined her left ear and traced them down to her eye. Three small reminders of a life she couldn't remember. Prior to her adoption, her biological parents were killed in a car accident, leaving Cali with partial deafness in her left ear. That wasn't so bad for Cali, it didn't hinder her hearing and life that much. But the look of the scars always bothered her.

Cali always noticed them first thing in the morning. The scars and her clear Scandinavian features made her stand out like a sore thumb among her peers in school. That hadn't been the only thing that kept Cali from making friends, though. There was that fight in her third year. The fight that caused her to be expelled, and that lost little Eugene Markos two of his teeth. After this 'incident' her parents chose to homeschool her. A novelty in Greece. Cali didn't mind that so much either, besides when the loneliness crept in. But she always told herself she was fine. She was definitely fine.

"I said we are almost there." Her mother looked her over, then turned back around to face the front of the car and fiddled with the GPS. "We need to clear the air so we can enjoy this trip. It will be our last for a while."

"Mom, once again, I'm starting with the University of Athena," Cali said, rolling her eyes and sitting up against her seat. "Just like you want." A smudge mark from her forehead still lingered on the glass and she wiped it away with her sleeve.

It wasn't that she minded the university. It was just that she went there nearly every day already. Her father had worked there for as long as she could remember as a senior main curator of arts and exhibits. She had seen him just that morning, working on the massive marble statue of Athena in the museum, and she used to find it interesting to sit and watch him, with his strange, multi-lensed spectacles, dusting and scraping away at artwork and history. Often, he would regale her with stories and legends, like Hercules, Zeus and Hera's love, Artemis and Apollo -- and so on. She knew the strange mythical stories more than she knew the factual history of Greece itself. He spoke of the gods and goddesses with so much pride and put that same amount of pride into his work. Nothing he did was ever without passion. It helped that he worked at the University, which gave Cali the ability to learn and dabble in many things that other peers might not have. It was like a second home to her.

But that was just it.

She had been to the university this morning. This fall she

planned to attend. Nothing would be different. And she wanted different. She *needed* different. *That's what's missing*. She crossed her arms—which she realized, as a seventeen-year-old girl, was immature to do—and looked out the window again.

"I don't see what the big deal is," Cali continued. "It's not like we'll even be far enough away from each other for me to miss you."

She winced and ducked her head as Miriam spun back to face her. "Anything could happen between now and then," Miriam snapped. "But it's good to know you feel so strongly about your own parents." Aliax's eyes shot to Cali's through the rearview mirror. He pushed his glasses up his nose. "This is our last real trip as a family before things...before things change." He patted his wife's leg, but her frown lines only deepened. "I want everything to be perfect."

"Dad says nothing is ever perfect. It's just a matter of perception." Cali traced a line in the glass through the fog. "Can we just get to the cabin and make it through the week?"

"I don't want you to be angry with me, Cali," her mother continued, her voice tight. "One day you'll know why I've been so strict. I used to feel the same way about my own mother as you do about me."

"Your mother was also impossibly crazy?"

"Watch your tone." Aliax's voice was low and soft, but the warning still took.

Cali mumbled an apology.

He added, "But Cali is right—not about you being crazy, Mir." Miriam scowled at him. "We will get through this week. We all need this vacation. Who knows what may happen? We may end up having a great time! Our entire life could be flipped upside down."

"Don't say that!" Miriam turned and glared daggers at her husband, but he just laughed. Cali sighed and rested her head back against her seat as her mother continued to chide her father on about his insensitive behavior. Her eyes drooped, and she let herself sleep the rest of the way.

***

They reached the cabin within the next hour. The small shack was just over 500 square feet. There were two small bedrooms and a dining room that doubled as a living room with a small toilet and sink in what was essentially a cupboard and an outdoor shower. The oppressive weather and their own gloominess had sapped their strength, so they simply unpacked, ate, and went to bed in silence.

The next morning, Cali rolled over and glanced at her phone, tapping it lightly. Nothing happened. She moved to her elbows and tapped it again. Still, black screen. Following the charger to the outlet, Cali let out a groan and leaned back into her pillow. The charger had pulled slightly from the wall. *This trip is really starting off with a bang.*

"Stupid phone," she muttered as she shoved it back in to charge and pulled herself out of bed. A glance out the small, round window told her it would be a sunny day, although there was a coolness in the late morning air. She slipped into her favorite faded jeans, a plain t-shirt, and her preferred ratty hiking boots that probably still held the dirt from last summer on them.

The smell of eggs and bacon wafted its way to her senses, making her stomach growl, so she followed it until she found Miriam was cooking over the small stove as in the kitchenette area. Aliax sat outside on the small patio with his black, leather-bound sketchbook that he always carried with him. A cup of coffee billowed soft clouds around his hand as he traced a finger over it thoughtfully, staring out into the forest. Her mother looked fresh and clean, her face holding a strained smile as she greeted Cali.

"Good morning, dear," she said in her soft voice, beckoning Cali towards her with her hand and giving her a small hug. "I'm sorry I was so off yesterday. I'll do better today. I know you thought it would be different—but I promise, we'll have a good time."

"It's okay," Cali said, picking up a slice of cheese from the table and munching on it. Just outside the open front door she could see her dad, his back to them, painting something out of sight.

"Good." Miriam tapped her spoon against the pan sharply. "What matters is today, moving forward, the future ... your future. Like any future, if you want to move into it, you must be a part of it."

Cali was used to how her mother turned her conversations into a lecture. "We aren't going to have the same conversation about me turning eighteen again, are we?" she asked as she watched Miriam stir the eggs. "I thought we already went over that yesterday."

They had. And the week before that. And the month before that. Over the past few months all Miriam could bring up was the upcoming birthday, how it would change Cali and how she needed to be ready for the future and this and that. Aliax didn't seem as phased or concerned, so Cali wasn't concerned either. In fact, she was excited—and nervous. But mostly excited. Still, Miriam's helicoptering was getting annoying.

"No, I'm not going to bring up your birthday," Miriam said. "Or that you'll be leaving us soon."

"Thank god," Cali mumbled between another piece of cheese.

"But," Miriam turned, one fist resting on her hip, "I do want to finally have the discussion."

Cali winced. The discussion. The one about her other parents. This had been something Miriam had brought them up more and more lately too. Never more than a mere snippet of information, nothing that gave Cali any idea of who they may have been. "You want to talk about my dead parents this early in the morning?"

"I didn't say right at this moment, did I?" Miriam snapped. "But it's important you know your history."

Cali snorted. "Why? Dad always says it's important to look to the future."

"The world is a dangerous place. It's just as important to know your past as it is to know your future," Miriam said defensively, pointing her spatula at Cali. "Early or not, you should know that."

"It's not like I actually get to experience anything remotely dangerous."

"So, that's what this attitude is about?" Miriam demanded, tapping the spatula hard against the pan again as she emphasized her words. The smell of burning began to fill the small room. "You *want* danger?"

"That's not what I said." Cali pushed herself from the table and crossed her arms. "But I'd like something other than," she paused as Miriam's eyes narrowed, "You know what I mean, Mom. You wouldn't even allow me to go with Dad on any of his museum visits to Rome. How *dangerous* would that have been?"

"If I realized Rome was so important to you, I would have...considered letting you go."

"You knew it was important," Cali shot back. "You taught me Latin and read me stories about myths and legends and fairy tales, creatures, and art—how is that preparing me for the real world? All I want is to be able to experience my own things and do things I want to do. But you only let me experience it through art or books! I want to actually live my life!"

"Where are you going?!" her mother snapped, slamming the burned eggs into the garbage bin.

"For a walk!" Cali stomped to the door. "Or am I not allowed to do that without my parents either?"

Aliax eyed her, one bushy eyebrow raised, as she came out of the cabin and onto the tiny slats of wood that made up the porch. His pencil stilled, poised in the air, just above the sketch of a bird, and his head was cocked to listen to their conversation. The glasses pulled low on his nose as he stared up at Cali with a solemn gaze. "A bit dramatic this morning, aren't we?"

"Me? What about you guys?" Cali retorted, the anger she felt needed to be directed somewhere, but she didn't want it to go toward her dad. Not now, not when he looked so peaceful. He just blinked at her slowly. "Sorry," she said with a sigh as she jumped from the porch to the gravel. "But do you really think that my entire life is just gonna flip upside down because I'm an adult suddenly? Things don't change that fast."

"Things can change in an instant." Her father continued to stare at her with his large, black eyes. Cali took a deep breath and turned to the woods and the familiar path she often took through them. "Perhaps it is bad timing, most uncomfortable things are. Life has a way of showing up when we least expect it. Adventures are not always what they seem in the moment. Even small simple ones. There is the old Norse saying: *Du skal kravle, før du kan gå.*"

"Does that mean mind your mother?" Cali glanced back inside with an eye roll towards her mom. Her father was fond of his sayings, just as fond as he was of saying them aloud. Mostly, they were just some proverbs meant to give Cali a life lesson. Through the years, Cali groaned at the constant use of them, but secretly, she wrote some down in her journal to remember for later.

"It means you have to learn to crawl before you can walk." Her father smiled and went back to his sketch. "As you can walk, why don't you follow the trail and come back around for breakfast that is not burned? There is also an old saying: let the angry woman be alone."

Cali laughed and made for the trailhead. "I'll be back for unburnt eggs in a half hour," she called over her shoulder. "Tell Mom I said sorry."

"Tell her yourself when you get back."

She shook her head, tossing her ponytail as she did, before she entered the forest.

***

"She shouldn't be out alone," Miriam chastised her husband as she shaded her eyes until Cali disappeared. "It's not a safe world, Al."

Aliax's hand hovered over the sketch in his hand. He took a shaky breath.

"The Collector stopped by."

The pan hit the floor, followed by the scattering of their breakfast.

***

Cali trudged along the dusty path, kicking at rocks and sticks as she stared absently into the trees. She had been down this trail many times in her childhood, alone and with her parents, so she knew her way. Growing up, her dad told her stories about Hercules, the demigod, who completed one of his seven trials in the forest. Miriam had never been particularly fond of these stories. *Stay on the path, Cali—don't wander in the forest*, her mother said. *Or the monsters might get you,* Aliax would add, a twinkle in his eye. Although Cali listened to her mother, it didn't stop her younger self from pretending there were goblins, fairies, and unicorns hiding in the forest. These imaginary stories became her friends in the summer. Now she had outgrown them, and she had no fanciful fairy friends, or unicorns, or trolls.

It was just her.

Alone.

I could be anywhere right now. She grabbed a flimsy branch as she walked and began to hit it against the trees and brush that she passed. *I wonder if this is how all parents feel about their children becoming adults. At least I'll be eighteen soon, then I'll have freedom.* A cold sweat broke out on her lower back. Many nights Cali lay in bed, staring at her cracked ceiling, both dreaming and dreading her future. Freedom sounded wonderful until she remembered one day she would be thrust into it. Would she be brave enough to claim her independence when she had the chance?

With few rental lodges in the area there were not many people in the forest, besides several elderly folks who would not go far. Cali soon grew accustomed to speaking to herself aloud as she walked. "It would be a lot more helpful -helpfuller? Helping if they would just say what they actually meant instead of sounding like some ancient wizards." She sighed. "I'd be better prepared for things. Being trapped isn't a way to live." She hit a low-hanging branch just outside the trail. "It's just not fair ..."

"*Life's not fair.*"

Chapter Two

Cali froze, her flimsy stick brandished in her hand like a useless weapon. It wasn't uncommon to hear some other visitor in the forest, taking a walk on the same trail she stood on now, calling out a greeting. But this voice had been in Cali's head.

"Hello?" she said, licking her too-dry lips as she squinted into the brush and branches around her.

Nothing.

Of course, it was nothing. Cali relaxed her tense shoulders and took a step forward, her hand still clasped tight around the stick. Her heart began pounding in her chest, and a cold sweat clung to her back as she took another step. *Get ahold of yourself Cali, it's nothing.*

But it was *something*. She knew it. Even as the shivers ran down her spine and the hair on her neck stood up. There was something out there in the forest with her. She tried to open her mouth again to speak but found nothing came out. The air shifted and she gasped. The forest was thicker in this area, and the trees and bushes pulled together much tighter. Little flickers of light poked through lush green leaves overhead, making shadow and sun shift in a strange dance. A childish feeling of panic crept over her. Like when she used to cry and run to her parent's room for fear of the thing she could not see in the dark. That fear was real then, and it felt real now. Cali turned towards the cabin, back to safety, anything away from this feeling. But to her horror, the trail was gone.

Instead, she stood deep within Foloi, in an area she had no memory of. Not knowing, or remembering, how she got there, Cali spun around and sprinted in the direction behind her. *I only took a few steps. How did I get so far off?* Abandoning the branch in her hand, she ran. Low branches hit her face and scratched at her arms, taunting her panic until she came to a small clearing in the trees where more sun peaked through. She didn't recognize the location but still paused. She took several deep breaths, doubled over, and rested her hands on her knees, feeling foolish for her panicked sprint. God, it was quiet - so quiet. She touched her good ear as she straightened. There was no sound of rustling leaves, or wind in the bushes, or even birds. She strained to listen. *Nothing.* Prickling sweat began to form across her entire body.

She looked up. Even the leaves were still.

A gust of wind rustled around her as leaves and brush pushed up against her legs, making her stumble forward. Cali did a slow circle before deciding to head north. Surely, she would find someone. The wind pushed her along as she began to walk, moving back into the forest. Slowly, her hearing began to edge back, muffled and static. From the corner of her eye, she saw darkness, harsher than the shadows among the trees, creeping through the forest beside her. When she turned her head, it was gone.

I know what you are. The voice again, soft and sweet and caramelly. And close.

Cali began to walk faster, facing forward. On either side, the mist grew, and each time she turned to face it, it was gone.

"Cali!"

Cali's heart leaped into her throat. That voice she recognized. "Mom?" She couldn't tell which direction it had come from.

Turning in a circle, and trying not to make a sound, Cali tried to listen. Everything in the forest seemed muffled and weighed down. Her own heartbeat sounded like a drum in her head and veins.

The feeling of the forest changed, shifting in on itself. The air froze, then pulled harshly in a different direction than before. Branches reached out to her, as if they were trying to grab at limbs and flesh and hold her down. Their leaves rustled in the wind that now had an edge of fog swirling about it. Everything was so muffled, so stifling.

She ran.

Her mother's voice still echoed in her head, calling out from somewhere in the forest. Tears of frustration and panic began to sting Cali's eyes, and she tried to blink them away. She dodged a fallen tree but then gasped as she pitched forward suddenly and hit the ground. Spitting out the leaves and dirt, she pushed herself to her hands and knees. Behind her, she knew it was there. Whatever it was that spoke to her. She slowly pushed herself to her feet even as the darkness curled like waves closer and closer, whispering through the branches and limbs like an unrelenting nightmare. Sweat made her shirt cling to her back as she slowly turned to face whatever it was.

Nothing. It was nothing. Or *something?* Cali took a shuddering breath as the black, shapeless form moved towards her. It shivered, faceless, as it moved closer. Cali simply stared at the shadow, a spectator in her own body, watching as it reached out for her.

She felt arms wrap around her waist from behind and begin to pull her back. Her instincts kicked in. Finally, she screamed and struggled. But the arms held tight even as the black fog moved in. She was pulled off her feet and drifted into darkness.

***

Cali blinked into the bright light. The warmth of the early summer sun radiated over her and made her feel safe. *It was just a dream.* She smiled to herself as the breeze brushed against her. *Just a dream.* The steady rock of her body told her she was being carried. As her eyes adjusted, she looked up to see her rescuer. The feeling from the sunshine vanished in an instant.

She shoved back against the bare chest that cradled her in his arms and, in surprise, the man let go. Falling hard to the ground, she looked up at the man who towered over her. Stillness settled between them for a moment. She blinked; her mouth half-open as she stared at him. He was no man. Or at least, not all man. From his waist up, he had the body of a male human, although his chest and arms were hairier than any Cali ever saw. Tracing her eyes from the waist down, Cali's throat went dry as she took in the four legs. Horse legs. Beside the half-man-horse stood three others. All staring at her. She shook her head slowly, then winced in pain. Reaching a hand up to her forehead, she drew it back and saw blood. *That makes sense.*

"Madam?" Cali looked slowly back up at her captor – the *Centaur*. She shook that idea away. *Head injury Cali, head injury.* A mange of hair wrapped his face, which was dark with large eyes that watched her every move. "If you please, will you allow us to continue on? It is not safe while the Furie is here."

"Safe?" Cali blinked. She swallowed several times to relieve the dry pain in her throat as she began to stand. "What—what do you mean? What are you?"

"I think you know what I am." Cali frowned. Wrinkles formed on his forehead as the centaur cocked his head. "My name is Arastoo, the son of Chiron. I am the protector of...well, let us just say I am a protector."

"What are you protecting?" Cali paused as her memory slipped back into place. *The shadow.* Even now, a chill ran over her entire body at the thought. She looked off into the forest as if it would appear at any moment. "What was *that*?"

Arastoo followed Cali's gaze, then turned back to her. "That," he said. "Is why we need to continue on." He held out a hand, but Cali didn't move. "Please, madam. James can only hold her off for so long. We must keep going."

"Going where?"

"To somewhere safe."

"Yes, but where is that?"

One of his companions shifted and stomped beside him, but the centaur waved him away. "I cannot say here—for who knows what whispers that shadows can bring to their master." Cali blinked at him, and Arastoo sighed deeply. "But I promise, once we get you safe, you will have your answers."

The trees around them shifted and danced, the shadows swirled between the bursts of sunlight. Cali shivered and lifted her hand, then hesitated. "My parents!" She jerked her hand back. "I..."

"Miriam and Aliax are safe," the centaur said, stepping forward. The kindness in his eyes moved into resolve as he looked down at her. "I apologize for the directness, but if you do not choose to come willingly, I do have to—ahem," he frowned. "Take you by force."

Miriam and Aliax are safe.

In a daze, Cali took the hand of the Arastoo. He bent one knee and moved her to his side. Her hands felt damp as she shakily climbed onto his back. As he rose to his feet, she barely had time to grab his mane before he and his companions lunged forward into the woods.

Chapter Three

They ran hard for five minutes, dodging trees and limbs and brush as they went deeper into Foloi Forest. Cali's eyes stung from the wind and unshed tears as she clung to Arastoo. Just over her shoulders, she could see ahead that they were approaching a thicket. It seemed to be some sort of natural barrier. Cali tensed. Arastoo and his company continued their speed and plunged into the brush. Her breath caught as a whir of dancing lights and shadows passed by. An instant later, they emerged on the other side into an open clearing. Here, Arastoo paused and caught his breath. Bending his knee forward, he allowed Cali to, unsteadily, dismount.

Her breath came out in ragged, fast gasps as she tried to steady her shaking body. Arastoo stood but kept close enough to Cali so that she could lean one hand on him for support. She felt his skin shiver beneath her touch, then he took several smaller steps forward, guiding her into the clearing.

In front of Cali stood what looked like a small farmyard. A tiny shack with faded and cracked paint stood slanted near the middle. On the other side of the shack were two larger square buildings, their wood faded from the sun. Between the buildings, at the center, was a strange, dead tree. It's branches still reached up, white and stripped of life, but still standing. Olive trees scattered beyond the shack and barns, almost extending to the other side of the clearing. Cali could see that the barrier circled around the whole space, like a shield, or protection. She swallowed hard as she focused back on the shack before her. Arastoo continued to lead her forward while a woman came out of the house and headed toward them.

Cali's heart pounded again. Each step brought her closer to the woman and the strange farm. From the corner of her eyes, she could see people—or what she assumed were people—behind the barns, running laps and ... Her heart skipped. She noticed the glint of silver before she heard the muffle clash of steel.

Fighting—they're fighting.

Pressure hammered her useless eardrum, and she brushed her fingers against the tiny scars. She hadn't realized she'd stopped walking until she felt a hand on her shoulder. She tensed but didn't pull back, staring up at the woman before her. The woman looked to be in her mid-thirties, and every part of her said 'warrior.' Her skin was darker than a Greek native, and her muscles glistened in the sun. Black and silver eyes matched her hair, which fell in several long braids down her back.

Panic mixed with the lack of substance from missing breakfast. Nausea swept over Cali, but she bit her tongue to keep from vomiting over the woman.

"You must be Cali," the woman said, giving Cali's shoulder a gentle squeeze. "I am Natasha, or Tash." She studied Cali with sharp, understanding eyes that matched the tone of her voice. "I am sure you have many questions, Cali. The two most important being why you are here and how I know your name."

"Where am I?" Cali couldn't take her eyes off the sparkle of weapons.

Natasha tilted her head to follow Cali's gaze, then turned back. "You are at the Farm," she answered. "This is one of the last safe havens for demi's and creatures of power." She put her arm around Cali's shoulders. "Those like us."

Those like us. "What?" Cali blinked at Natasha. But Natasha simply smiled and began to guide Cali toward the two-story shack. Beside her, Cali saw Arastoo detach himself and move away in the direction of the barns. She watched him go, silently begging him to turn around and come back. He gave her a small nod before swishing his tail and trotting away.

"It's going to be alright, Cali." Natasha was saying something else, but Cali was having trouble focusing. Blood and bile mixed in her mouth, and she dug her fingernails deep into her palms. "If you give me the chance, I'll explain it all to you."

They stopped at the white door of the shack. "First, let's get you cleaned up," Natasha said, opening the door with one hand and guiding Cali inside with the other. "Looks like James got to you in the nick of time."

They entered a small kitchen with a large butcher block table in the center.

"Here, sit." Natasha placed Cali in the closest chair and moved to a cupboard where she pulled out a tattered bag labeled *Første Assistant*. She poured a tall glass of liquid from a barrel on the counter and placed the glass in front of Cali. Then, she proceeded to dump the contents of the bag onto the table producing some salve, Band-Aids, and other miscellaneous medical supplies.

Cali looked down at her hands for the first time and saw the dirt, grime, and blood covering them. Crescent-shaped marks dotted her hands from where her nails drove into the skin. Her head still pounded from the wound near her forehead. She lay her hands, face up, on the table and allowed Natasha to dab gently away at the wounds.

Cali winced as the antiseptic reached the open skin. Channeling restraint served as the only mechanism to keep still and not pull her hands away.

"This will hurt a bit," Natasha said, her voice only slightly apologetic as she put the cloth away and pulled out some bandage. "Normally, I have one of our healers handle this, but that may be a little much right now." Her eyes flicked to the wound on Cali's forehead. "I'll get to that next."

Cali nodded. She studied Natasha's face as she concentrated on wrapping one hand. Then she looked at the room she was in. The kitchen was tiny. Open shelves held an array of haphazardly placed dishes and colorful jars. Dried herbs and flowers hung from the ceiling along with more aggressive objects such as knives, axes, and swords. The room was clean and comforting with a French-farm feel. Two doors led in and out on either side of the room. One additional door led deeper into the home to her right, where Cali could see a room with green paint. Faded, peeling wallpaper lined the walls of the kitchen. Cali's eyes traced each space before landing on the door. Her fingers curled as Natasha finished binding the first hand.

"How do you feel?" Natasha asked, crouched in front of Cali and still holding her wrist. Cali peeled her eyes from the door and met the silver gaze.

"I fell."

Natasha smiled and gave a small nod, but still held on to Cali. "So, I see," she said. "Not many come up against a Furie of Chaos and come out with so few scrapes and bruises." She licked her lips, her brows pulling. "You were lucky."

"I don't feel lucky," Cali replied. "I feel ..." She eyed Natasha's fingers as they tightened around her wrist. *She thinks I'm going to run.* Her gaze went up again. "I feel afraid."

The hold relaxed and Natasha gestured for the other hand. Cali held it out to her, and Natasha began to wrap it in clean, white gauze. "I don't understand why I'm here, or what that was, or ..." Cali trailed off and pulled her hand, half bandaged, away. "What am I doing here?"

The sweat began to build on Cali's lower back again. The door they came in was just behind her, and then there was the door to the back of the shack, too. Cali had never taken any type of physical education or done any sports, so she was pretty certain that, if she chose to run, she would easily be caught. Arastoo had said she would be safe, but she didn't feel it.

Natasha rocked on her heels; one hand braced against the table as she studied Cali. "You were always meant to come here, Cali," she said. "But this was a bit—well, earlier than we or your parents anticipated. We thought you would be safe. Aliax and Miriam never would have risked bringing you he ..."

"My parents?" Cali's heart plummeted to her feet, and she stilled. Even if she wanted to run, it would be impossible. "My parents ... my parents knew about this place?"

"Yes." Natasha moved to another chair at the table. She placed her elbows on her knees and leaned forward. "But we—well they decided it was best to keep this place from you until the time was right."

"And now is right?"

"To save you, yes."

Cali's eyes flashed. A strange confidence enveloped her, and she stared right at her captive savior. "I don't believe you," she snapped. "And I don't feel safe."

"That thing in the woods," Natasha said, pointing a finger in the direction of Foloi, "that was a Furie. She was sent to kill you." Cali blinked. Her head tilted, and she looked at her hands, now splayed in front of her on her shaking knees. The blood from her wounds had already begun to soil the bandages. "She would have succeeded to, if James hadn't been there." Natasha threw a look over Cali's shoulder. "Speaking of ..."

Behind her, the door opened, and she turned. A young man, no older than herself, filled the doorway. He was covered in mud and blood, but otherwise looked unscathed. Dark curls matted against his sweaty forehead. Cali flinched as his ocean-blue eyes landed on her.

"She made it," he said, stepping into the kitchen and closing the door behind him. "She looks awful."

Cali gaped at him in shock. Here he stood, her *savior,* who smelled and looked horrible, beside the way his sweat-soaked shirt clung to him, and the first thing he did was insult her.

"Well, you don't look very nice yourself, James." Natasha placed her fingers together, still leaning on her knees. Her eyes narrowed as she studied him. "How did it go?"

He shook out his dark curls, running his fingers through them, and stepping to the water barrel on the counter to down a glass. "She got away," he said, staring into the glass in his hand. He poured himself another one. "But it doesn't bode well that she's getting closer to the Farm."

"Bode well?" Cali repeated. It sounded like something her dad would say. She stood up, jostling the chair. "What am I doing here?"

James raised an eyebrow at Natasha over the glass at his lips. "You didn't tell her?"

"Well, it's a little hard to just come out and say," Natasha said with a sigh.

Cali glared down at her, Natasha ran her hands over her braids, visibly uncomfortable. "How about you just say it and let me decide?" she snapped.

James gave a small laugh, but Cali kept her eyes on Natasha. With another deep sigh, Natasha straightened in her chair. "Sit down, Cali."

Cali remained standing and crossed her arms in emphasis.

"Or remain standing, that's fine." Natasha crossed her own arms and licked her lips. "You're a demigod Cali."

Cali stared.

"More specifically," Natasha continued, her eyes turning almost black as she spoke. "You are the daughter of Freya." Cali still said nothing. "That is why you're here."

"I don't understand what you're saying." Cali rubbed a hand over her face, then winced in pain from her wounds. Her fingertips brushed against the open wound near her temple, and she pulled it away and stared at it. *Freya ... Freya?* She rubbed her forehead as it began to ache.

Natasha watched her. "You are aware of what a demigod is?"

"Of course, I know what it means—what they are," Cali snapped. "But—you have it wrong. I am not one of them." She gave a short laugh. "This is crazy. I'm not one because they aren't even real. They're stories."

"They're as real as the centaurs who brought you here," Natasha said with a knowing smile. "And as real as the threat that you faced in the woods."

Cali stared at her. She couldn't argue about the centaurs. Arastoo had brought her here—*hadn't he?* She looked between James and Natasha helplessly. There was no lie behind their eyes. They believed what they were saying. And the tales and stories and legends. They were all...

"Can I go home?" Cali asked after a moment, knowing the truth even as she said the words aloud.

James made a noise of discomfort and ducked his head at Natasha's glare.

"Can't I?" Cali demanded, again.

Natasha stared at her evenly. "No."

"Why?"

"It's not safe."

"It's not safe?" Cali repeated. "But I thought James ..." She gestured wildly at James, who remained impassive against the counter. "My parents. They'll be worried. I have to—"

"They will be worried, yes," Natasha agreed. "But you can't leave Cali. There are dangers in this world that—well, that we can only keep you safe from if you remain here."

"No—no." Cali wanted to laugh, or scream, or cry. *This isn't real.* "No," she repeated firmly. "This isn't real—for all I know you've ... you've drugged me or something," she gestured to the empty glass on the table, "Or I hit my head and I'm bleeding out in the forest, and someone will find me and—no, this isn't real."

"No one is coming to find you, Cali," Natasha said, her voice even. She leaned back in her chair. Sympathy and traces of annoyance lined her face. "And I think you know that what I'm saying is true."

Tears threatened the corner of her eyes, and she blinked them away. Even with the pain in her palms, she bunched her hands into fists. This woman, these people, knew her name, and her parents, and that she had been in danger in the woods. Her eardrum pulsed against her skull, and she thought it might explode. Her entire world shifted. She turned to the door, but James, still posted at the counter, gave a small shake of his head as if to say *don't even think about it.* Grabbing the chair to her right, she sat back down and continued to stare at the door. Natasha was saying something, but through the pounding in her head, Cali couldn't hear.

"You said others like ... me, like us," Cali said, not caring that she interrupted whatever Natasha had been saying. She kept her eyes fixed on the knob of the door even though she knew she wouldn't move for it. "Out there," she jerked her head toward the door. "All those people I saw. They are all demigods too?"

"They are," Natasha said, her voice clearer as she stood and came up beside Cali. "Although they prefer the name demi's these days." She rested a hand on Cali's shoulder and squeezed, firm and resolute. Cali looked from the hand to the face, tears tracing down her cheeks. "It's going to be okay, Cali. I promise you; you are going to be okay."

The kind smile almost reassured Cali, but still, she couldn't quite believe Natasha. A flash just at the door to the green-colored room, drew Cali's attention. She peered around Natasha and saw a man leaning on crutch in the doorway. A blonde and white streaked beard covered his face, but his features seemed young. He was hunched over, but built well, besides the one leg that was cut off completely at the knee. He looked at Cali with piercing crystal blue eyes and she shivered, unable to break away from his stare. Natasha looked over at him and gave a quick shake of her head. The man, who had just moved his one good leg to enter the room frowned, then disappeared back into the room, and round the corner, out of sight.

"Who was that?" Cali asked, still staring at where the man had been.

Natasha moved in front of her. "Not someone we need to worry about now." She grabbed Cali's chin and tilted it up. "So, you'll stay?"

Cali glared at her. "Do I have a choice?"

Natasha's lips formed a thin line and she let go of Cali. "I'm sorry," she murmured. "Truly, I am. And before you can say it" — a flicker of remorse crossed her face — "you're right, it isn't fair."

***

James led Cali around the corner into the green room, where a wide stairway led up to the second floor. At least, it should have led to the second floor. As Cali followed him up the stairs, with the flickering sconce lights every several feet, she tried to understand how it was possible for there to be so many steps. At the top, they reached an open hallway that stretched farther than what should have been possible, given the smallness of the shack. The dark green walls were barely illuminated by the golden lights between each door. And there were many, many doors.

Cali opened her mouth to speak but then gasped as James turned to face her. She collided with him and, in a swift move, he grabbed her shoulders and forced her to step back.

"Sorry," she mumbled, unable to look at him directly. He smelled like mud and forest, but the worst part was the coppery scent of dried blood. Her hands clenched into fists as the scent invaded her nostrils and then her mind.

Letting go of her shoulders, he pointed to the open door to their right. Cali could see inside that the shelves were lined with books and plush chairs and sofas. Two windows peered out onto a drizzly day, which Cali thought was strange given she got here an hour ago and the sun had been shining.

"That is the common room," James said, then pointed to two doors on the opposite side of the room. "That is Tash's room, and that is Auto's room. They are, as you would understand it, *in charge.*" She could tell he was looking at her, but she still didn't meet his gaze. His condescending words were grating on her, even though his tone was not unkind. "You're allowed in the common room as much as you want, but if you need Tash and Auto, ask me—or one of the other leaders" He paused. "You'll meet them later, so for now, just ask me."

Turning back on his heel, he marched up the hall and stopped at the fifth door on the right. He crossed his arms and waited for Cali to trail him there. She looked between him and the door expectantly.

"And this is your room." With a sigh, James swung the door open.

Behind it was a small, square room with eggshell-white walls. A simple cedarwood dresser sat next to another, smaller door near the left corner of the room. Above the dresser was a round, cracked mirror with gold engravings of leaves encircling it. A single window, with cream-colored curtains, opened to a sweet-smelling, summer day. A soft-hued quilt wrapped around the bed in the four-post frame. Cali swallowed back the tears that welled up in her throat as she recognized the single suitcase on the bed.

My suitcase. The suitcase which she had brought with her on vacation, one filled with her own things. That she had left with her parents.

"How did that get here?" she asked, her voice barely coming out as she stared at the luggage at the end of the bed.

James shifted awkwardly beside her. "I, um ... I did." Finally, she looked up at him, her fists clenched. "Not to add wood to the burning fire inside you, but ..." he rubbed the back of his neck and looked away. "I knew your father, Aliax, before ..."

"Before ..." Cali echoed. "Before now, you mean?"

"Yes."

Cali found it hard to breathe, let alone hold back the tears in her eyes. James cleared his throat and stepped back; one arm still outstretched, as if to guide her into the room.

"I don't want to be here," Cali said, her voice breaking.

He studied her. "I know." He reached into his pocket and pulled out a folded paper, then handed it to her. "Aliax asked me to give this to you."

Cali took the paper, not caring that her hand shook as her fingers closed around it.

He continued after she took it, "He wanted to let you know that he was sorry and that he..." James cleared his throat again and looked down the hall as a door behind Cali opened. He stepped away from her, his face becoming unreadable. "We allow new demi's three days to adjust. Then you'll be assigned to a group, and you will begin training."

"Training?" Cali repeated the word but stared at the delicate sketch of the bird on the paper she held. She sensed James step around her and grabbed his forearm, digging her fingers into his muscle. "What do you mean?" she demanded; her voice sharp. "What training?"

"Let go," James said, his voice dropping several notes as he looked down at her. She hesitated but then released him. He jerked his arm back, revulsion covering his face. "Don't ever do that again," he growled.

Without another word he stalked back down the hall to the stairs. Confused and afraid, Cali heard the door behind her slam shut, and she shivered. *None of this makes sense.*

Alone in the hall, she looked back to the stairs, then up the length of the hall to where it seemed never to end. Her parent's letter in hand, Cali took a shaky breath, stepped into her room and closed the door.

Chapter Four

Cali fell asleep crying that first night. She woke up the next morning with a severe headache and a crust on her eyes. She rubbed them clean and stumbled to the bathroom where she drank from the faucet and splashed water on her face. Blinking and dripping wet, she studied her puffy-red eyes. She hadn't showered yesterday. Hadn't even taken off the clothes she wore. If she didn't get up and get cleaned soon, she would begin to stink. But the effort to pull herself from bed seemed too far away.

Not bothering to lift the quilt over her, she lay back on the bed.

The paper James had given her lay open on the quilt. She sprawled across the covers and picked it up, re-reading it although she already had it memorized.

Cali,

In all our lives together, I never thought I would get to the point where I would be writing this letter to you now.

I understand you will be afraid and, have questions, and maybe

receive very few answers, but know that with your world being turned upside down, there is still hope.

Your mother and I should have told you—and we will always regret that.

But what I will tell you now is this: do not believe everything you hear,

do not trust everyone who claims to be a friend and has the answers.

Beware of the darkness.

Learn what you can—but never stop questioning.

Know that your mother and I have always loved you—and will always

love you. In any place in time, in any Realm, you will always have our

love.

Dad and Mom

Over and over again she had read the letter until—between the tears and nightfall—sleep filled with nightmares, waterfalls, and monsters found her. Sometime in the night, she was jolted awake, right in the middle of a nightmare that had her going over an ice-covered waterfall. In a panic, she scrambled to the window and looked down. The ground beneath the sill looked blurry in the light of the half-filled moon. She had reasoned that the shack was barely two stories high. Which is why she had tried to climb down the side of the house. Her hold had slipped and, in a jolt that both pulled and pushed her, she landed back in her room, just below the window. The feeling had been so jarring that she crawled back into bed and wrapped herself into a ball.

In the strange light of day cast by the window, Cali felt a bit lighter. Her head and damaged ear still throbbed against her skull, but life didn't seem so hopeless. She threw a wary glance at the window, where a breeze rustled the curtains. *I won't be trying that again,* she thought with a shudder.

Folding the letter, she stood just as the door to her room opened and a beautiful young girl entered, holding a tray of assorted bread, meat and cheese. Her smile radiated across her whole face, which was accented by lovely, perfect gold curls. The crystal blue eyes danced with mirth as she trotted over to the bed and placed the tray on the quilt.

"I'm Griffin," she said, her voice clear and sweet. "Tash said I could bring you breakfast this morning, if you're up for it that is." She gave Cali a quick, sympathetic once-over. "Seeny—she's a fire nymph—will come and bring lunch, then I can bring dinner again. If you like, that is … you can ask Seeny to, that's fine. I don't mind."

Cali stared at Griffin as she spoke. She looked so at ease—so normal. Besides being maybe one of the most stunning people Cali had ever seen. Griffin began to worry about the breakfast she chose to bring, prompting Cali to snap back into focus.

"No, it's okay," Cali croaked out. She cleared her throat. "I mean, this is fine. I'm not really all that hungry, anyway." She stared at the food on the tray, ignoring the pains in her stomach.

"I can imagine this must be really hard for you," Griffin said after a moment. "Some of the others were saying that—"

"Others?" Cali looked back at Griffin, who flushed. "Is—are you a demi?"

Griffin gave a charming half-smile and nodded, her curls bobbing. She looked like she wanted to say more, but the door behind her opened again. *Once again, interrupted before I can get real answers.* Cali frowned as Natasha strode into the room.

Any appetite disappeared, and Cali stiffened. Natasha crossed her arms and looked between the two.

"Thank you for bringing Cali her breakfast, Griffin."

Understanding the dismissal, but still smiling, Griffin said a quick goodbye before leaving the room. Natasha said nothing for a moment as she surveyed Cali's clothes and made bed.

"You need a bath," she said.

Cali frowned. "I need answers first."

Natasha's lips twitched. "Then let's give you some." She

turned on her heel and made for the door. "And bring your food with you, Cali. You'll need it."

***

Cali dug her fingernails into the lush velvet of the armchair in Natasha's room. Everything in the room, the plants, the greens, the smell, made it feel like a rainforest. The space was furnished in deep and exotic colors. Red satin covered a canopy bed, and while pulled back, revealed a plush bed decked in an assortment of pillows. Rich, green plants of all different sizes lined the shelves and floors. The two largest—nearly trees—were on each side of the bed. Pillows in all colors covered the room, both on the bed, the chairs, and the window seats. Two large dark-green chairs sat on either side of a still fireplace. Cali sat in one and the one-legged man perched in the other.

She tried to focus on the items on the coffee table in front of her to avoid staring at the man, or his leg, or his piercing, knowing eyes. *I should have eaten something.*

"Cali, this is Autolycus, or Auto." Natasha nodded in the direction of the man. She leaned on the end of her bed and looked between them. "He helps me manage the Farm."

"James told me that," Cali replied, looking at her nails. "He told me that he knew my father too, before all this." She turned her gaze to Natasha. "And that I have to train."

Cali didn't know how far questions would get her. Her father's words still rang in her head, but she still needed to know *something*—anything about this place—about what she was, and about what she was meant to do here.

"You're afraid."

Cali's eyes darted to Autolycus. Smoke filled the air around his face from his pipe, but she could still make out his eyes watching her.

"Of course, I'm afraid."

He laughed, jostling the clouds. "Not nearly enough."

"Why do people always say that?" Cali snapped. "How much more afraid should I be? I don't even know what's going on!"

"Enough." Natasha raised her hand, another rested fingers between the bridge of her nose. Cali tore her glare from Auto back to Natasha. "Now is not the time for that, Auto." Auto harrumphed but said nothing else. "You want to know who you are – why you're here. Of course, that's understandable."

Cali leaned further back in her chair.

"Did your parents ever tell you stories about myths or the Realms?" Natasha paused, but Cali said nothing. "Magic?" Natasha recrossed her arms and frowned. "You're telling me the curator of the University of Athena, and former historian to Olympus, never shared any stories of myth and legend with you?"

Cali's throat tightened. "He …" She licked her lips, trying to ignore the sudden urge to panic. "He told me stories when I was young, but … they were just stories." *Or at least, I thought they were just stories.*

"The usual, I assume," Auto chimed in through his smoke cloud. "Zeus, Poseidon, and the ever-popular drama queen Hercules." Cali nodded, silently. "What about the monsters?" There was a flicker between the wafting smoke where she saw his eyes flash. "The dark and evil gods?"

This time, Cali shook her head. A chill ran down her spine as Auto stared at her. "Like the darkness in the woods?" she said, her voice soft and quiet.

Natasha inclined her head. "That was just a whisper of what's coming," she said with a heavy sigh. "And although I would once again like to remind Auto to be less dramatic, there are real monsters out there, just as the demi's here at the Farm are real."

"What was that ... thing out there?" Cali questioned, looking to the window. Behind the pane she saw the deep jungle and could smell the humidity in the surrounding air, cut through by the scent of tobacco. "Was that a monster?"

"Of sorts," snorted Auto.

Natasha shot him a look. "Three hundred years ago, the original ..." she paused, and her eyebrows pulled together as if she struggled to find the word. Eventually, she straightened and continued. "The original monster, Chaos, used her followers to stir up dissension between the Realms. Then, she sent them after the demi's. First to kill them, thinking she could end the god's bloodlines. She would provide tests and temptations to lead those to ruin. Aliax may have told you about some. Achilles, Hercules, Actaeon?" Cali stared at Natasha, open-mouthed, and Natasha gave a grim smile. "After a while, she grew bored of playing with the forgotten children of the gods and turned to killing them. And after that, she found a worse torment."

"What's worse than death?" Cali snapped her mouth closed. From the other chair, she could hear Auto shuffle. She felt her face grow warm as she tried to avoid looking at where his lost limb should be.

"Many things," Natasha said, as if reading her thoughts. "She took most of her slaughter to the Middle Realm, here on Earth, before turning on her own creations." Pushing herself from the bed, Natasha walked to the plant at the end of her bed, picking the dead leaves. "But she created too well, and she couldn't destroy them all. But she tried. And they tried too. They almost succeeded. Instead, during one of the final battles, nearly three hundred years ago, the Realms did something far more ... unbelievable."

"What did they do?" Cali asked.

"They worked together," Auto scoffed. "In thousands of years, I've never seen it."

Natasha moved, so that she stood near the coffee table, towering between them both as she spoke. "They did," she added. "And they succeeded in binding her with the help of what they called the Silent Treaty."

"The Silent Treaty?"

"Yes," Natasha said, dusting her hands as if to finish the tale. "It bound Chaos to Tartarus, along with the vilest of the monsters. The Realms were safe, and so they promised each other never to set foot in the other's land again."

Cali frowned. Her knees knocked against the coffee table, and she gently maneuvered the edges of the book in front of her. "So, if Chaos is trapped," she began, staring at the book. "Why was I attacked by that monster thing and why am I—or anyone else—here?"

"That's where it gets funny." A smile could be heard through Auto's words.

Cali glared in his direction; almost having forgotten he was there. But he just smirked at her.

"Seventeen years ago, Chaos began to—well, for lack of better words let's say— 'wake up,'" Natasha said with a sigh. She dropped to her haunches beside the coffee table and rearranged the books that Cali had moved. "She's not free, but she is close. Which is why the Furie attacked you in the woods. She's becoming stronger, summoning an army—"

"An army?"

Natasha nodded. "An army bent on destroying the world of humans."

"How come now?" Cali asked. "Why not, like, a hundred years from now or—"

"Because she's taking souls and demi's and creatures from the Realms and either killing them or turning them to her cause,"

Natasha snapped; her cool demeanor gone. It quickly adjusted back to impassivity as she sat on the coffee table and faced Cali. "It was always meant to be. Chaos was always going to be here, in this time, and this was—all of it—was meant to happen."

Meant to be? Cali leaned forward so that she was on the edge of her chair, her eyes trained on Natasha. The story sounded like something her dad would have told her as a child, something Miriam would have chirped about being too violent or fantastical. The thought of them, and the secret they kept from her, made Cali's stomach twist. She stared for several long seconds at the books on the coffee table. "And you know this war," she paused, "this war is going to happen? No matter what?"

"Yes," Natasha replied.

"And that's why you're training us here?"

"Yes."

Cali met her gaze, blinking back tears. "And you know—you're sure—I'm one of you? A demi?"

Natasha's eyes softened with a mere flicker of compassion. "Yes."

"I'm not special," Cali whispered.

"There is no doubting that you are the daughter of Freya, Cali."

From behind Natasha, Auto rose, a bit unsteadily, from his chair. Cali could hear muffled curses in Latin beneath his breath, along with other things, before he grabbed his crutch and swung himself towards the door. Natasha eyed him as the smoke trailed behind until he left.

"He's rather sensitive about this topic," Natasha said once the door slammed. "But know this Cali." She placed her hands on Cali's own, bandaged and sitting in her lap. "You were also meant to be here."

She patted Cali's knee, thoughtfully, before standing. "I think that's enough for today." Cali stood, more on instinct than on listening to what Natasha was saying. "Get some rest. Use these three days to adjust, to mourn, whatever it is you need," Natasha said as Cali made for the door. "I'm here if you need anything, Cali."

Without another word, or look in their direction, Cali flung the door open. She stalked past a goat-looking person who gawked at her as she passed. When she reached her room, she slammed the door behind her. She barely made it to the bathroom in time to throw up.

Chapter Five

Cali spent the next three days self-confined in her room. She did not unpack her duffel bag but had finally showered and changed clothes. She woke up on the second day to find her formerly dirty clothes clean, but she didn't dare ask about that. The afternoon of her second day, she ventured into the hall, only to be greeted by a chiseled, half-dressed minotaur. That kept her in her room for the rest of her confinement. Griffin brought breakfast, the nymph brought lunch, and Natasha would come with history books and dinner at night.

Every day Cali heard the constant clammer of feet and voices streaming up and down the hall. Laughter, curses, and jeers made her cringe, making it harder to pretend this place wasn't real when humor was involved. Sometimes the curious would peek their heads in as Natasha left. But a sharp word drove them away. Griffin would normally stay longer in the mornings, talking about life on the Farm, the hamadryads magic that kept them safe, how the hamadryads created the barrier and the halls, and many other things Cali couldn't keep track of.

Cali felt strangely calm around Griffin until she lightly grazed Cali's arm with her own. Tingling warmth radiated through Cali at the sudden touch. It made her queasy and made her emotions feel muddled. Still, Griffin's kindness, and the way she would enrapture herself in a conversation, made it hard for Cali to be put off by her intrusion.

"I honestly cannot imagine what you must be feeling." Griffin sat on the quilt and fiddled with a loose piece of string. It was the third morning and Cali, although hungry, was finding it hard to eat the fruits and scones that Griffin brought up. Outside the door, Cali could hear muffled foot and hoof falls as everyone made their way to training. Trying not to dwell on the sound—or the thought of what training would bring tomorrow—proved difficult. "Many of us here knew what we were getting into when they brought us," Griffin continued. "But to know nothing about this world besides the myths...it's strange your parents never told you."

"Yeah, strange." Cali toyed with the blueberries on her plate. "The others here ... are like ... us?"

"Well, some of them," Griffin replied as she slung her legs up and sat cross-legged beside Cali. "There are two types of demi's. Prominent's and Eminent's. The Eminent's have more almost naturalistic gifts. They aren't so ... evident, even though they're demi's. And the Prominent's—well, that's mostly in the name, I suppose." Here Griffin sighed and looked out the window. The sun sparkled against her clear, blue eyes. "Mostly, everyone has come from different places you'll find. I suppose that's the easiest way of putting it for now. I don't really want to make you dizzy with the time and space continuum nonsense Maechon goes on about." She laughed, but Cali just stared at her. "But all of them are either demi's or hold ancestral heritage."

"I have no idea what you're talking about," Cali said with a noncommittal laugh. "But I'm sure I'll figure it out."

Griffin threw her arm around Cali's shoulder and squeezed, sending shivers down Cali's spine. "Of course you'll figure it out," she said. "And you'll have loads of help. Most everyone is willing."

"I still think they have it wrong."

"Tash and Auto wouldn't have risked James' open collection for nothing." Griffin pulled back and tossed her hair. "The Hunter wouldn't have risked coming for you in the woods either if you weren't special."

"The Hunter?" The darkness from the wood shuddered over her like a blanket.

Griffin's lips twisted. "Yeah—she's part of the reason we have the barrier. She's a Furie, one of the last—there were three," she added, seeing Cali's confused look. "They used to be impartial, between Realms, until Chaos turned them."

Cali shuddered. The shadow from the wood still crept into her nightmares and the feeling it gave echoed in her bones like a cold wind.

"James got to the Hunter before she got to you, but just barely," Griffin continued. "He distracted her so that Arastoo could bring you here." She looked at Cali. "You heard about him and your parents, then?"

"Yeah."

"Don't be angry with him," she said quietly. "Or them—your parents I mean."

"I'm not ... really." Cali looked at her feet. "I don't know if I feel much of anything right now." Her fresh bandages crinkled as she flexed her fingers. "Besides fear."

Griffin laughed softly. She placed her hand over Cali's and immediate warmth radiated up through her arm and to her shoulder. She stiffened but couldn't move away.

"I know this isn't ... ideal," Griffin murmured. "If you just give it—"

Griffin's hand pulled back as the door to the bedroom flew open and Natasha strode in. Her tall, foreboding figure filled the room with crackling energy. She wore fitted black clothes and emanated power; the woman's bedroom differed from her dark, everyday look. The bulk of muscle her body held, and tattoos inked into her arms, in no way negated the beauty of the goddess. Cali's eyes narrowed as she tried to quell the impressed look that dared to cross her face when she looked at Natasha.

"It's been three days." Natasha's voice remained cool, but the severity of her words lined her face.

"I have given you as much time as we can afford," she continued. "You have to start your training if you are to be safe in this world. Also, it will also provide you with a healthy distraction from delving too deep into your feelings." Her eyes looked between the girls and narrowed. "Griffin, since you're here and you're in her omáda, you can bring her down and introduce her."

"Okay!" Griffin bounced up, beaming expectantly at Cali.

Cali stared dumbfounded between them.

Natasha shook her head and turned to the door. "Be down in fifteen minutes or I will send James up to collect."

Training must begin.

Any calm Cali felt dissipated with those words. Over the past few days, Natasha and Griffin talked to her about the Farm, the layout, the training ... the training. The scars that littered Natasha's chest and arms told Cali it wouldn't just be gym class. Their training was to protect, or so Natasha liked to say. Griffin held more romantic views. She considered it a comradery of family and community building. Cali hated both ideas. *I want to go home.*

Still, her legs managed to move her to her boots, then follow Griffin out the door of her room.

They left safety behind and entered the Farm.

***

Cali blinked into the daylight as she took in the fresh air. The 'trick' window of the hamadryads did not have the same feeling of warmth and life against her skin.

So far, everything in the air around her felt normal until she heard a deep voice greet them as it walked past. *A faun.* Cali remembered the name from her phase of reading only fantasy books. This faun looked nothing like how she pictured it in her head. It stood on legs as thick and hairy as Icelandic cows and the top half was a man's frame (although there seemed to be more joints in the arms). He would have been almost naked if not for the vest. Cali's eyes followed the creature as he continued toward one of the barns. Groves of olives and fruit trees spread out across the field to the left of the barns and Cali saw more fauns and people collecting the harvest.

From beside her, Griffin grabbed her by the elbow and nudged her forward. "Come on, I'll show you around. Here ..." She pointed to the two barns across from the shack. They headed in that direction. "Essentially, there are the Greek-demi's and the Norse-demi's. Mostly, we have just Greek instructor's, our teachers, but there are some Nord instructor's as well." Griffin pointed to a figure that walked like a man but was covered in thick, brown hair. "Like Bearoque, he's the son of Beowulf." Cali nodded, staring at the man as he stalked past to one of the barns. "You have the instructor's, and the centaurs mostly quarters there, and then the food barn on the right here. That's the barn where all the meals take place." Cali followed Griffin's pointing finger again. "There are shifts dictating who help prepare, clean, and do essentially all the chores. Oh, there—Arastoo!"

Cali felt a mixture of relief at the recognition of her savior, and bitterness surprisingly accompanied it. The centaur's coppery-brown mane ruffled around his face as he waved them over to where he stood. Behind him, Cali eyed the other centaurs, humans, and creatures that raced laps around the oval field. Each looked just about—or around—her age. It should have brought her comfort. But it didn't. She tried not to think about it as she surveyed the rest of the field. Everyone was alive with action. Some demi's had long sticks and swords that glinted in the sun. Others pulled weapons from what seemed like thin air with a flash and hiss. Each one of them carried some sort of weapon, a spear, shield, or sword.

Cali grimaced as the sound of steel rang in the air. *Just get through this, just get through this ...* she repeated. *And then what, Cali?*

"Hey." Griffin nudged Cali's elbow with her own. "I asked how you're doing—you okay?"

Cali nodded. "Yeah—yeah, I'll be ..." She took a deep breath. "I'll be fine."

"It's a lot I know," Griffin said. "We'll try and take it easy to get to know everyone. Here ... let's go see Arastoo." She looped her arm through Cali's and began to pull her toward the field. "He is our instructor. The group we're in is a small one, but we work together really well. The newest one to our group, well, to the Farm really, is Maech. He's been here about five months, I think?"

They reached Arastoo, and he gave them a tight smile and nod, then turned to the field. He slammed the long staff he held onto the ground and several mismatched demi's detached from the training and headed toward them.

Cali's pulse quickened and sweat began to form along her neck and lower back as they stopped in a circle around Arastoo. There was an awkward silence as the group—filled with demi's no older than Cali—stood there, staring at her. They all seemed to be waiting to see if she would run or fall apart. Griffin pulled her arm back and prodded her forward a bit. Arastoo shook out his mane before he tied it back, his staff crooked in his arm. His glassy black eyes surveyed his group with cool strength.

"Cali of the Nord, I offer my sincerest apologies for my behavior on your arrival," he said, resting a hand on his chest and bowing his head. His voice rumbled low and deep; in any other situation, it could have been a soothing sound to Cali. "Truly, if I could have made your transition here easier. I would have. I hope that it does not trouble you, being placed in my omáda?"

Cali shook her head in mute shock. Fear of throwing up or crying made her silent.

"Very good." He turned to the rest. "Omáda, let us welcome our newest demi. Cali, of Freya and the Nord."

Mumbled hellos passed over the group of watchful faces.

"We will treat her as our equal, we will treat her with respect, we will treat her as our family."

"I hate this family," a sullen voice of a young woman said from beside the cyclops.

"Blythe," Arastoo said, his eyebrows drawn together in reproach.

Blythe scoffed and stuck her tongue out. Her mousey brown eyes continued to bore into Cali as Arastoo spoke. Cali tried to avoid meeting the girl's hate-filled gaze, as well as avoid staring at the scars that riddled her face, neck, and down her chest.

"Let us do some introductions first. I am the instructor, the leader of this group, or omáda. We split all omáda's into five to six demi's each. You already know my name, and may recognize that of my father, Chiron." He bowed his head and placed a hand on his chest at his father's name, then continued. "This is Maechon, the son of Hebe. Blythe, daughter of Hephaestus. Ottomubus and Oscatonus, the satyr twins, grandchildren of Silenus—stay still you both or I will send you back to the kitchens! Garwin, the grandson of the Great Arges. You have met Griffin, who shares your Nordic heritage. Her father is Loki of Asgard." Here, he paused and took in Cali's face. Her heart hammered in her chest and she wayed as she stared at the demigods around her. "I do not expect you to remember their names but remember the faces as this will be the omáda you will train with, and mission with if that time ever comes."

Cali had studied each person's face vaguely as Arastoo gave their names.

All eyes were on her. Their expressions all seemed to mirror her thoughts: *What am I doing?*

Cali turned and walked, without a word, to the edge of the forest where she came in. No movement came from behind her. No one would stop her if she ran.

So, she did.

Lights sparkled in front of her through the brush and trees. Her breath came out in gasps as her lungs screamed at the sudden exertion, but it didn't take long for her to reach the barrier, and the promise of danger beyond. The lights sparkled faster, brighter. She halted, teetering on her feet, at the edge. Glows from the trees winked at her like the eyes of a monster in the darkness of night. The lights subsided to see if she would now try and come through. It felt like a dare. But even in her fear, her terror, and confusion, Cali did not move forward. She remembered her fear and terror in the woods. Her parent's smiling faces. The darkness in the forest …. Instead, her knees buckled, and she barely braced herself with her hands before she face-planted into the ground. Her fingers dug into the soil as she knelt on the ground, hands planted in front of her, facing the barrier.

"I don't belong here," she whispered.

Nobody responded as the lights resumed their intricate dance between branch, leaf, and shadow. *I don't belong here*; she repeated it to herself. But another truth whispered to her. *But Cali, you don't belong out there either.* She could almost hear her mother's soft, reproachful voice saying the words—always full of reason and logic.

"Are you okay?"

Cali didn't need to turn to see who spoke. Even though his voice was muffled by the sound of blood pulsing in her skull and eardrums, she knew it was James. He stepped close, just beside her.

"What do you think?" Cali asked through gritted teeth.

His boots shifted beside her as if contemplating whether he should join her on the ground. "I know it's difficult to have your world turned upside down," he said. He remained standing. "But you are one of us, and you do belong here. Whether you think it or not."

"That's easy for you to say," Cali said with a bitter laugh, pushing herself up so that she knelt upright. "Griffin said most everyone knew they were meant to be here." Her fingers dug into her blonde tangled mess of hair, and she cursed. "I was taken against my will to a place that shouldn't exist with people that ... shouldn't exist ... I shouldn't exist! None of this makes any sense."

"It's like the Mona Lisa."

"What?" Cali stared up at him through her hands and hair. She blinked at the sunlight that flickered around his face as he stared down at her. "What the hell is that supposed to mean?"

"Just because we don't understand it doesn't make it not real."

Cali sat there in silence. She felt a twinge of bitterness at James' words—because they were familiar. She had heard them before. From her father, Aliax. Her father and his love of proverbs, riddles, and words of wisdom. Tearing her eyes off him, she blinked back the hot tears as stared back into the trees, baring her teeth to keep from screaming. She brushed her hair back from her face.

"Why didn't they tell me?" She raised her hand. "And don't

tell me it was to keep me safe—because that ..." *Makes the most sense, Cali.* She frowned at her own common sense.

"Perhaps they wanted to steal you away from your true mother, Freya, and raise you as their own."

Cali's frown only deepened at James' words. *That also makes sense in a demented way.* She wished she could ask her parents. She wished that her mother had just come out and said what she meant at breakfast or the day before, or the months before, when Cali was truly safe.

James held out a hand to her, but she swatted it away and stood on her own.

"Mir and Aliax were trying to do what's best for you," he said, crossing his arms. "Whether you believe that or not, it's the truth."

Her throat squeezed, and she swallowed the sob building there at the mention of her parents. She almost forgot he knew them. *So many secrets I still don't know.*

James grabbed her by the shoulders, and Cali blinked. She had begun swaying, her eyes unfocused, but then she leveled her gaze on his. The ocean blue eyes narrowed.

"Get ahold of yourself," he said stiffly as he let her go. "Think of your stay here however you like, but you're here now, so get it together."

She glared at him. "I think I'm beginning to really not like you."

"I think I'm beginning to see that."

Without another word, Cali spun on her heel and shakily stormed back to the field.

Chapter Six

Arastoo agreed to allow Cali one day of observation, with the expectation that she would be back with them in the morning to begin her full regime. He'd also hinted at wanting to see Cali's *gift*. Cali had no idea what that meant, and she was too afraid to ask. Her mind buzzed with all the words being said and the conversations of the groups of demi's around her. Some of her own group tried to ask her questions, but they gave up when she only provided one-worded answers. Griffin never seemed to tire of trying to get Cali involved. Cali may have appreciated the effort if she didn't feel so overwhelmed.

There were eight omáda's under an instructor each. They trained in the large, oval-shaped track that ran behind the two barns. A dirt track marked the outline, and looked like someone was always running it. The inside of the track held a field that contained a wide assortment of dummy weapons, dummies, and real steel tipped blades on racks and shelves. Cali began to wince less and less with each clash of a blade as she stood and took in everything around her.

"There is a system," Arastoo was explaining as Cali continued to stare at those locked in combat around her. "Where we will work with you and the level you are at. But for now, Blythe, Garwin," he gestured to two long spears with dull wood ends, "you will spar together. Observe, Cali. Watch to see what you may learn."

Cali nodded, even though she had no idea what to watch for, and then jumped as the one-eyed cyclops, who was at least a foot over his opponent's height, leaped at Blythe. Their spears connected, and Blythe remained on her feet. Cali watched in amazement for a minute, enraptured by the way they attacked and lunged. Then a spark caught her eye to the right. She blinked, and the sword that had just appeared in the faun's hand several feet away, disappeared. The faun lifted his hands up, his face contorted, and brought them together again. The sword reappeared in a flash. Cali gaped at him. Something inside her sparked to life—an excitement, an anticipation. Like the kind she would get as a child when her dad told her stories of these places and people.

"Pretty cool, huh?" Griffin asked, her voice muffled as she spoke from Cali's left. Cali tore her eyes away from the faun and back to Griffin and nodded. "It's an elemental gift. That's what Arastoo was talking about before."

"I don't think I can do that," Cali murmured, glancing back at the weapon.

"Everyone has their own gifts," Griffin said with a laugh and a toss of her curls. "Like I said, some are Prominent, and some are Eminent. Who knows what you'll have!"

Cali nodded absently, her eyes brought back to the sparring of Blythe and Garwin. Blythe stood over the cyclops, one foot on his neck, the other wielding her snapped spear close to his pulsing artery.

"Yes, that's quite enough, Blythe," Arastoo said with a steady clap of his hands. "Allow Garwin to go to Becca and Iolo for healing before he loses an eye." The centaur flushed and coughed into his hand at his poor word choice, before turning. "Griffin?"

Griffin nodded, eagerness bubbling over in her smile. "I love a good challenge."

Cali said nothing as Griffin tied back her hair, took the spear offered to her by the ever-quiet Maechon, and went for Blythe.

***

After training, which went all day with a brief lunch break outside, Cali got to have her first experience in the Barn. Of the two barns, one was used for meals, and the other housed the centaurs and other instructors of the Farm. Cali followed her group warily through the double doors into the large space. The smell of roast chicken, potatoes, and smoke filled her lungs and made her stomach growl. She covered it with her hand and ducked her head as she weaved between those milling around trying to find seats. Two large, long tables stretched on either side of the walls, with enough space for both sides, and either end, to be filled. At the opposite end of the door, there was a counter lined with plates and an assortment of foods. Steam pushed out from a door to the left of the counter.

Cali remained quiet as she trailed through the line and filled her plate. She followed her group to the table, Griffin already falling into conversation with two girls closest to her, the fire nymph who had brought Cali food before, Seeny, and another girl with snow-white hair and eyes. The others in Cali's group either kept to themselves or talked to the other demi's around them. Cali poked at the mashed potatoes on her plate. *Take a breath and eat something, Cali.* Someone nudged her from under the table and she looked over to find Maechon staring at her.

"I sa-said you should e-e-eat." He nodded to her food before ducking his head back down into his book.

She eyed the food, then felt another nudge from Maechon's elbow. She began to pick at the chicken on her plate with her fingers and ate it in small bites.

"What—um, what are you reading?" she asked, unable to stay quiet while so much conversation happened around her.

Maechon's head shot up, as if he was surprised someone spoke to him. Cali might have laughed at his comical appearance, the frizzy hair that stuck out in all directions and the round, owl-like glasses that kept sliding down his nose, but he already looked so uncomfortable.

"Sorry, I didn't mean to interrupt ..." She grimaced. "Sorry.'

"D-don't be." Maechon's cheeks began to flush pink. "I-i-i'm reading *Paradise Lost*. H-h-have you...have y-y-you..." He trailed off and his cheeks grew red.

"I haven't, no," Cali answered, trying to make him feel more at ease. She ate more of her chicken as they sat in several more moments of silence.

"A-are-are you doing okay?"

Cali gave a shrug. "I suppose," she replied, poking at the vegetables on her plate that she grabbed when her eyes were bigger than her stomach. "I suppose it's not every day someone gets told they're a demigod, gets attacked by some shapeless shadow, and then is brought to train for a war that may or may not come."

"It h-h-happens every cou-couple w-w-weeks here," he said, his brows pulled tight and serious in concentration. "You were j-joking?" Cali nodded, giving him a half smile.

His mouth opened and then closed again with a snap, and he ducked back to his book. Griffin stood in front of them, Seeny and the pale girl on either side of her.

"We're heading back to the library," Griffin said, smiling with her entire features emanating warmth. "Want to come?"

Cali gave a weak smile. "I, um, am going to finish eating."

The crystal blue eyes flicked to Maechon, before dropping back on Cali. "We'll see you later!" She spun around, and the two girls followed. Cali watched until she disappeared behind a large faun that carried stacks of plates. *Charming friends.*

"I can't believe this place is real," she muttered, more to herself.

"Y-y-you'll get u-u-used to it," Maechon said, blushing crimson again as he averted his eyes and cleared his throat. "I can help." He flipped a page in his book, holding the paper between his fingers. "W-w-will you ... will you t-try to run away a-a-again?"

Cali frowned. She didn't know what she had been thinking when she went to the barrier. *Had I been trying to run?* She had considered it for the briefest moment. But it wasn't just the thought of getting lost in Foloi and having the shadow Furie find her and do, gods know what ... it was something more. She wanted to stay; she wanted to see what she was, what her purpose was here. That scared her, and she didn't know why.

"No, I won't be trying to leave," Cali said after a moment. "At least, not till after dinner."

Maechon laughed, jostling his glasses down his nose. He pushed them back up and studied her. "I-I-I am glad yo-you're staying."

"At least one of us is." Blythe slammed her fists on the table, making them both look up. "Mixie," she gave Cali a nod and look over before turning her attention back to Maechon. "And you need to start sparring more, Maech, otherwise you'll fall behind."

Maechon turned pink and then white, unable to meet Blythe's dark gaze. Cali felt her dislike of Blythe grow as Maechon struggled to find his words. The scar-faced girl pressed her palms onto the table as she studied them.

"I-I don't ... I d-d-don't like f-fighting."

Blythe looked at Cali. "What about you?" she asked, a feral smile pulling at her lips. "Do you like fighting?"

Well, I haven't fought anyone since grade two, so no. "No," Cali said aloud.

"Too bad," said Blythe. "At least Maech here will have someone at his level."

"Why are you being so mean?"

Cali felt strangely protective over Maechon against this wild-looking girl. Blythe and Maechon were about her age, but two completely different people. Blythe oozed confidence and strength, while Maechon seemed more at ease within the pages of his book.

Blythe's eyes narrowed. "Because Chaos isn't going to be destroyed by *kindness*," she sneered. "No matter what that curly-headed idiot told you."

Chaos. The noise in the hall began to shrink as the tables began to clear. *And to think I was just beginning to feel normal.* Blythe rapped knuckles on the table and straightened, offering a smirk. "Don't be too worried, Mixie," she said. "It gets a lot harder each day."

Okay, so I'm Mixie—probably some curse in some mythical language. Blythe said nothing else as she turned and stalked out of the barn, her brown braid flicking with each step. There were still some demi's around, cleaning up the hall. A stout goat-like man scooped up left behind dishes from the table Cali and Maechon still sat at, muttering about how 'some people are too lazy to walk a few extra steps to drop their dishes off.' He trotted away toward the kitchen behind the door.

"Well," she muttered, more to herself than to Maechon, who was hurriedly shoving his book into a backpack that was filled with more books. "If Chaos is anything like her, then this really is going to be an adventure."

She winced at her word choice. *Adventure.* That's what she

said to her mom in the kitchen when ... She shook the thought away and stood with Maechon. He laughed under his breath at her as he walked his dishes to the far-end counter. Cali followed.

"I-I-I can p-promise ... I can promise y-you it w-w-will be an ... be an adventure," he said with a half grin as he dumped his plates into the bin.

Cali did the same, and then together they headed for the shack.

Chapter Seven

CALI WOKE UP WITH a headache the next morning. Not from crying. She was beyond that. But the same nightmare she had been having for days haunted her dreams and every morning, even though the details were fuzzy, she could never quite shake the feeling. As she slipped into the hand-me-down stretchy active wear after her shower, she tried to remember. All that came to mind was the waterfall, and ice, and cold ... *eyes? Maybe?* If she thought too hard on it, the memory would drift away.

Pulling on her boots and surveying what she could of herself in the mirror above her dresser, she sighed. Her blonde hair was pulled back into a braid down her back, loose strands already fell on her forehead. The white shirt was hers, the activewear from Griffin—since all Cali brought was Yoga pants that she only wore for lounging—and then her boots. She also had on her light brown jacket, with its many pockets. *I guess this will have to do.*

She weaved past two fauns laughing outside the common room, finished a quiet breakfast with Maechon—who was reading a different book this morning—by her side, then they followed their group to the field. Two other omáda's were already practicing with both elemental and wooden sword. Cali's fingers began to tingle as she got closer. Arastoo waited for them just at the edge of the loop.

"Good morning," he said, looking at each one in turn. "Today, we will begin at the beginning." Cali's lips twisted to hide her confused look as the rest of the group moaned. "Have you forgotten, so soon, what it was like when you first arrived?" Arastoo chided. He tapped his staff on the ground and gestured with it toward the track.

Cali's stomach flipped. *Running—the beginning is running.* She had never been much for working out, and the only sneakers she ever wore had been used for simple walks around Athens. But she hadn't packed those. She looked from her boots to Arastoo as her omáda began to take their places on the track.

Arastoo raised an eyebrow and nodded his head for Cali to follow.

"I'm not wearing the right shoes," she said, knowing it was a lame attempt to get herself out of running.

"An attack by the enemy may not always have you wearing the right shoes, daughter of Freya," Arastoo replied. "You must learn to work with that which you have."

Right, okay. Cali nodded and gloomily walked to the track. She watched the others as they stretched and moved their bodies, and she tried to mimic their movements, even though she felt incredibly self-conscious.

"I'll run beside you," Griffin said, coming up beside her with one hand on the arm she stretched behind her head. "We'll set a good pace—I promise, it's gonna be fine. Come on. We'll walk first."

Cali said nothing as she stepped in beside Griffin, who began walking the track. The others in her omáda had already set a steady pace ahead of them. Then Griffin picked up into a slow jog. Cali tried to control her breathing as she ran beside her. She could see Blythe's sneer that she threw over her shoulder. *Just keep going, just keep breathing, just keep going.* By the first lap, her lungs were screaming, and her legs felt like Jell-O.

"Good job!" Griffin said. She gave Cali a pat on the shoulder as Cali doubled over to catch her breath. Shedding her jacket, Cali tossed it away and tried to straighten. A pang shot through her side, and she grimaced. "You'll keep getting better with each lap."

"Unless I die right here," Cali groaned, clutching her side.

Griffin laughed. The wooden staff of their instructor came down, and he commanded another lap. Cali looked helplessly at Griffin, who shrugged and gave her a dazzling smile.

"You can do it!"

Cali shook her head but let go of her side and began to move alongside her new friend as they circled the track.

***

Half a dozen laps, a brief explanation of weapons, then muscle training at the end of the day before dinner. Cali chose to eat in her room, alone, and covered in sweat. The first day of training flew by and her whole body ached. Never before had she known her muscles could stretch or pull in the ways she had made them do today. A quick glance in the mirror showed her beet-red face reflected back at her, with her hair sticking to the side of her neck and face. *I have never looked better and never felt worse*, she thought, laughing to herself. Her hand shook as she brought her fork, piled with chicken and potatoes, to her lips. The strenuous workout brought her appetite back, and she finished the entire plate in minutes.

Groaning, she stood from her crisscross position on the bed. She used the bedpost to keep upright, began shedding her sweat-covered clothes, and staggered to the shower. The bathroom adjoining her room was tiny, barely containing the toilet, sink and glass-sealed shower, but she was grateful that it was just hers. Standing beneath the warmth of the pounding water for what felt like an hour, sighing with relief, before she dragged herself out of the warmth and dried off.

Her enchanted window, which followed the actual day outside, began to edge into darkness, with just a streak of purple left.

Flopping back on her bed, Cali pulled the quilt over her head, not even bothering to put clothes back on. She fell to sleep almost instantly and, for the first time since her arrival, no dreams or nightmares found her.

***

Three weeks passed with the same routine of training. Sometimes the day would consist of strictly physical, and other times one of the older centaurs or even Natasha would come and provide a brief history lesson on some monster, weapon, or person from myth.

Bruises littered Cali's body after training, causing pain and stiffness that slowly began to build into strength. It was still fragile, as she was nowhere near the strongest of the fighters, but even she was surprised by how fast she adapted. Her muscles became defined, and her senses seemed heightened. But no 'gift' or power showed itself; much to the disappointment of Arastoo. Cali tried to ignore his subtle disappointment and focused on learning the terms of the fighting styles of the Greek and Nord. Words like *dory*, *hoplon*, *kopis*, *xiphos*, and more jumbled together in her head as she tried to both maintain her physical and mental health. Even though they were all the words for different weapons, Cali stuck to what she knew: spear, shield, sword, dagger. She felt a sliver of jealousy any time she saw one of the demi's who could create their own elemental weapon, but she wasn't quite sure why. With little experience with weapons, Cali wondered at her own desire to hold one in her tingling grasp.

Through the weeks, she began to learn to wield wooden duplicates of various weapons and found, to her surprise, she liked it. She liked the weight and the feel of each weapon, especially the swords.

Today, she would get to practice against Maechon. She tried to hide her enthusiasm as she swung her blade lazily in her hand, rolling her wrist with a swift motion. She wondered what the weight of real steel felt like ...

"Cali—focus."

Cali paused mid-swing as Arastoo stomped one of his hooves.

"Last week, you bested Maechon on luck, not strength." The words stung, but Cali knew he was right. "Today, you need to remember the training you have learned. It should be instinct and skill—you know this."

"Sorry," she mumbled, avoiding the smirk from Blythe as she moved to her place opposite Maechon.

They were inside the track today, near the edge of a small, rundown part of the grass. The barrier, which was closer to this part of the track, shimmered with the little sparkling lights that were the Hamadryads. Maechon already stood several paces away from Cali, his own wooden sword raised and ready, although his face did not reflect his posture. Still, he came close to beating Cali last week because, even though he hated fighting, he had more training. Arastoo was right, she got lucky, and she needed to do better.

She brought her sword up and waited for Arastoo's command.

"Begin."

A scream shattered the air. Cali lurched to a stop, sword raised. Maechon's eyes were huge as he dropped his weapon and stepped back. Another scream came from Cali's right. *From the barrier.*

She turned slowly and faced the thick trees. They shook and rattled; the lights flickering faster and faster. The wood of the hilt felt clammy in her grip, but Cali kept it raised, as if it would do any good to whatever came through the trees. All activity around the track stopped. Everyone stared at the forest. Waiting.

A man burst from the overgrown hedge, one arm hanging limp at his side, the other clutching his chest. From the several yards between them, Cali could see the deep gashes and blood that poured from the wounds where his hand was.

In a flurry of hooves and brown fur, Arastoo bolted around her and toward the man. Several other centaurs, and the Nord trainer Bearoque, rushed the man just as he collapsed on the ground. They surrounded him, blocking him from view. But that didn't stop the demi's from surging forward and following their instructors to the victim.

"Cali—wait, don't—"

But Cali ignored Griffin and sprinted toward the man. She skidded to a stop just as she reached the huddled circle of bodies. Her chest heaved and her heart thudded in her chest as adrenaline bubbled through her. Arastoo and another centaur knelt near the man and gently, they rolled him over.

Arastoo's paled and his eyes shot to the demi's that began to murmur around them.

"Back—everyone back," he roared.

A quick gesture from him to the standing centaurs created a small barrier around the wounded man. But Cali still caught another glimpse. There was so much blood. She covered her mouth as her stomach flipped. She recognized the man as the half-faun from the Barn who always worked in the kitchen. His entire chest was ripped open with deep, brutal scars all the way to the bone beneath. *What could make wounds like that?* Something knocked into her shoulder, and she staggered into the rump of a centaur she stood next to.

"James!" Arastoo said, relief and stress tight in his voice and face. "How …"

James dropped to his knees beside the man and lifted his head. Between the shifting centaurs, Cali caught glimpses of him and the man.

"What happened? Luca?" James held one of his hands over the wound, although it did nothing. Dark red leaked between his splayed fingers as they pressed against the man's chest.

Blood spurted from the man's mouth as he tried to speak. "Shadow …"

"What?"

Cali saw James' shoulders stiffen before they were blocked from her view again.

"Shadow … coming …"

The rest of the man's words were lost to her, even as she cocked her good ear to hear. She noticed Griffin beside her, her face pale and eyes wide. Each demi echoed the look and exchanged glances of fear.

"Send them back to their rooms." James' voice rose above the beginning rumble of questions and worry rising from the demi's. "You—Bear, with me. The rest, bring them back to the shack."

"And Becca?" Cali heard Arastoo ask, his voice muted.

"She won't be needed—he's dead."

The standing centaurs turned to their trainee's and began to herd them back to the shack, using their bodies as shields against the dead faun on the ground.

"Come, come," the centaur closest to Cali said, gesturing

forward. "Griffin, Blythe – you do not need to see this now." Cali's feet stumbled forward, Griffin at her side. "Come now, we will have answers in time. Back to the shack ... come now."

The same strained, comforting words continued as they were ushered back to the shack and into their rooms. Most of the demi's went without struggle, although many threw looks over their shoulders at the scene they left. Cali did the same. She saw James rise from the body and, with two centaurs at his side, dart into the barrier. He disappeared into the trees. Turning back to the shack, she released the strain of her fingers as they clenched into fists.

***

The whole of Cali's omáda sat on the side of the Barn near the willow trees. Blythe was silently working on sharpening a forks spike, Garwin lay splayed on his back asleep in the sun, the two satyrs were off harassing another omáda wood nymph, and Maechon sat curled beneath a tree with a book in his hands. Everyone remained in their own world after dinner, but they also remained close. The sun began to hit the edges of the trees. Everything seemed so normal—almost peaceful.

"I thought no one could break through the barrier?" Cali picked at an orange on her plate as she spoke.

She couldn't stop looking back at the place where the dead faun had been. The body had been moved by lunch and the only remnant that anything out of the ordinary occurred was the feeling left behind. The instructor's, led by Natasha, gave a brief speech about the importance of remaining vigilant, about the threat to their lives, and emphasized that although they were safe now, they may not always be safe in the future.

Then, life continued. Training. Sparring, Laps. Stretches. Up till now, Cali convinced herself that the only way of surviving the Farm was to get through each day. With routine came complacency, and she had forgotten the reason they were here. Forgotten and not truly, really believed. But the man had said *shadow*. Cali shuddered. *The shadow is still out there and that ... that could have been me.*

Griffin sighed from beside her and rested her head against the side of the Barn they sat alongside. "Only if it holds," she said. "Between the Totem and the Hamadryad's, we should be fine."

"But what was he doing out there?" Cali asked. "And why ..." *Did he die?*

Griffin turned her head so that she faced Cali, her eyes filled with sorrow and worry. "He was a Collector, like James," she replied. "He was most likely sent to help a demi in crisis and bring them here."

Cali looked back at the barrier, her appetite completely lost at the thought of James and the centaurs out there, looking for the shadow Furie and perhaps a demi who had met the same fate as Luca.

"Will James be okay?" she asked.

Griffin gave a small laugh. "He generally is."

"Yeah, lucky him." Blythe snorted from her spot on her stomach in the grass near them. "Bet Luca would have really liked it if he could have ..."

"Enough, B," Griffin snapped. Heat surged from her, and Cali looked her friend over in surprise. In her weeks at the Farm, Griffin had never used a harsh tone. Cali had found it almost annoying how optimistic and kind she was, but the flash of anger in the crystal blue eyes made her uncomfortable. Griffin blinked. "James is at risk as much as anyone. Don't be such a ... just don't."

Blythe snorted. "I'm sure James would appreciate his girlfriend defending his honor."

Girlfriend ... oh. Cali's face grew warm. She toyed with the end of her braid. "What else does James collect?" she asked, trying to change the subject.

Blythe looked up from her project with a smirk. "Oh, he doesn't say, does he Griff?"

"You know he can't, B," Griffin shot back.

"Oh, he *could*," Blythe retorted. Mischief danced behind her brown eyes, and Cali shifted uncomfortably beside Griffin. "You could just *persuade* him to—"

"Enough Blythe." Griffin shot to her feet, her curls bouncing around her face, which turned red with rage. Cali stared up at her in surprise at the sudden burst of emotion. "Stop being so mean – we're supposed to be a team, we're supposed to ..." Her lips quivered, and she brushed the stray hair from her face. "I ... I'm going back inside. I'll see you later, Cali?"

Cali nodded. "Yeah," she replied, but Griffin had already turned toward the shack and began to walk quickly away. Turning back to Blythe, Cali's eyes narrowed. "What the hell was that about? Why are you so rude all the time?"

Blythe shrugged.

"She c-c-can't ... she can't control the p-power, Blythe," Maechon said, barely looking up from his book at them. "Y-y-you know ... you know that."

Cali looked between them, but neither of them seemed to think more explanation was needed. "What do you mean, her power?"

Blythe dug her knife into the dirt. "Oh, you know, the whole touchy-feely thing," she said, kicking her legs in the air behind her. "It's her special little gift."

Cali gaped at her. "Her power—her gift," she said slowly, trying to wrap her head around the idea still forming there. "She—"

"She can emotionally manipulate people," Blythe answered with a short laugh. "That's her power—she's a *Prominent*." She caught Cali's confused face and laughed again. "You know what that is, right?"

"Well, yeah," Cali said, scowling at Blythe's smirk. "And ... no. I was told a lot of stuff my first week here and I don't really, remember—understand it all."

She felt her face get hot and pulled her knees to her chest to rest her chin on them. Blythe seemed pleased with her discomfort.

"Prominent's have higher more ... visible powers, like the ones who create the elemental blades, or Seeny with her fire magic, Becca and Iolo, the Healers, or Griffin," Blythe gave a nod in the direction of the shack, "with her power of manipulation."

"And James," Maechon added. He forgot his book to listen to their conversation, although it still remained open on his lap.

"James?" Cali asked, unable to stop her gaze from going back to the forest's edge.

"Yeah, him too," Blythe said. "His is invulnerability, both physically and emotionally if you ask me." She snorted at her own joke, even though no one joined her.

Cali couldn't help but wonder where her own power—if any—might lie. *Is that why I stayed here?* She brushed her fingers over her ear and scars there, pushing the hair back. "And you guys?"

Blythe looked at Maechon, who twisted his lips. "We are Eminent's," Blythe said, a twinge of bitterness in her voice. "Which means our gifts are less defined or *impressive* to the gods." She slammed her fork into the ground and Cali watched in awe as it melted beneath scar-flecked fingers. "We're still their children, but we just have to work harder." Blythe rolled to her back and draped an arm over her eyes.

"Blythe can m-make ... can make any we-weapon," Maechon

said, blushing crimson as he spoke.

Cali could see Blythe's small smile beneath her elbow. "And Maech is a genius."

Maechon's flush ran all the way down his neck at her words.

"Does everyone get one?" Cali felt foolish for asking, but a part of herself wanted to know—wanted a power. Part of it may have been to fit in in this world, but another part wanted something to help her feel in control, too.

"Feeling left out?" Blythe mumbled. Cali glared at her, uselessly as Blythe still covered her eyes with the crook of her arm. "We all got something—that's why we're here."

"But—"

"Don't overthink it, Mixie. If it hasn't happened yet, it will."

A loud, obnoxious snore woke Garwin, who sat bolt upright, drool hanging from his mouth. Blythe and Maechon laughed. Shaking her head, Cali tried to laugh along with them, but it came out forced. She looked at her hands, now healed from her fall in Foloi in her first week. Besides the small crescents she continued to dig into her palms, and the bruises and sore muscles, she was fine. *So, not invincible.*

She looked back from the barrier to the shack, then back again. She wondered if a power like that could stop a goddess like the Furie. She curled her fingers into fists as the image of the dead faun flashed through her mind.

Chapter Eight

"Yield, I yield!"

Cali tried to pull her face from the grass and dirt. Blythe was on top of her, her knee pressing into Cali's spine. With a final push forward, Blythe pulled herself off Cali, who rolled over and wiped what remained of the grass from her mouth. Blythe grinned down at her but didn't offer a hand as she sauntered away.

It had been two weeks since the demi-faun, Luca, came through the barrier. Two weeks filled with whispers between the omáda's and unanswered questions from Natasha and Auto. Yes, they provided *some* answers. But Cali had the feeling they were hiding something; or just trying to keep the young demi's from panicking. Natasha seemed to have forgotten about her, or just had better things to do than worry that Cali was having trouble adapting. For her part, Cali tried to keep her head down and just keep training. She felt lost in the sea of demi's who knew their purpose and knew the reality of their situation. Each day brought more questions, and more confusing answers. All the other demi's knew their purpose, some even knew their god-parentages, and they all recognized Chaos as being a real threat. Cali hadn't until she had seen those wounds … those gashes in the demi-faun's chest.

So Cali kept training. And found that she not only enjoyed

it but was also rather good at it. She mastered the wooden sword, and her footwork was getting much better. Though she still struggled with the spear, and handling anything more than two weapons, with every day, she grew more confident. Her hearing—or rather partial lack-thereof—made it a bit more difficult to anticipate certain moves; especially with the closeness of the other omáda's in the field. A lifetime of adjustment in an able-bodied world had at least prepared her for one aspect of the Farm. She learned to tilt her head, focusing. She learned to center herself and her breathing. Still, she had a long, long way to go. Something that Blythe loved to remind her of any and every chance she got.

"Very good Cali, Blythe," Arastoo said from his post beside the flattened grass that made up the sparring ground. "If this had been a real fight, Cali would most certainly be dead."

Thanks for the ego boost. Cali limped off the field to where her omáda's stood. She knew Arastoo was disappointed in her; it showed on his face every time she failed as if he expected something *more* from her. But Cali gave it her all every day—and still, no gift, or at least no *Prominent* gift, produced itself.

"You'd think being the daughter of Freya would get me something," Cali had muttered offhandedly to Griffin one day.

Griffin had grown quiet. "Power isn't everything, Cali," she had said.

But it's something, Cali had wanted to reply. *It could keep me safe, and it could help keep others safe.*

Rubbing her jaw, she stepped in beside Griffin on the outskirts of the sparring circle. Two other omáda's mixed with their group today, each taking turns against the other. That was one thing Cali noticed since the death of Luca. Training became more intense and combat more brutal. Chaos's whisper of death brought by her Hunter still hung over them.

"Nice try!" Griffin said as she patted Cali on the back. She drew her hand back at Cali's wince, mouthing an apology. "You kept your sword on you much longer this time."

"Thanks."

"Y-y-yeah," Maechon said from the other side of Griffin. "You're do-doing ... you're d-doing great."

"Tell that to the grass, Mixie," Blythe snorted. "Even with a real sword, you'd never stand a chance."

Blythe gave a dramatic, and skilled, loop of her wooden blade before stalking around to stand beside them.

"Why does she keep calling me that?" Cali growled.

"I have no idea," Griffin replied, rolling her eyes.

"Panthos, Garwin, center." Arastoo clapped his hands for attention. Cali ignored Blythe's taunting grin to look back at the two massive creatures about to face off in the field. Arastoo and the centaur instructor from Panthos' group stood close together, watching with intent, wild eyes. Garwin was the only cyclops left of his kind, so Cali heard, and Panthos, well —he may have been a faun, but he was twice the size of the rest at the Farm. Watching them fight gave Cali chills. Even though she'd seen them spar before, Cali still jumped as they lunged and slammed into each other. Because they had the Healers, any move that didn't bring death was fair.

Wincing at the sound of snapping bones, Cali looked away. Just over her shoulder, she saw someone standing at the edge of one of the barns, watching. James continued to look in the direction of the fight and then, even at the distance between them, Cali felt his eyes on her. *I wonder if he saw me lose.* Strangely, the thought embarrassed her more than she felt it should have, and she looked away. *Get a grip Cali—what does it matter if he sees you win or lose? You don't care what he thinks.* By the time she threw another quick look back over her shoulder, he was gone.

***

"Come on! We've been training for months, you for of couple weeks." Griffin held Cali's wrist and pulled her from the door of the shack. In the cool, just-before-nightfall air, Cali could already smell the smoke of the bonfire.

It had been Natasha's idea to provide a bit of relief after a six-week heavy stint of training. Already, the young demi's could be heard laughing and singing where the blaze burned. Cali had promised Maechon she was going to learn about the difference between myth and folklore in the North. She was hoping to find out more about her birth mother, Freya, and maybe find out what her power might be, or become.

"No—Maechon can wait." Griffin didn't relent. She ground her feet in and pulled again, her smile growing as Cali rolled her eyes.

"Gods forbid Mixie actually tries to enjoy herself while she's here," Blythe muttered, shoving past Cali towards the fire.

Cali spit her tongue out at Blythe's back. "As if you even know what the word fun means."

"I don't like agreeing with Blythe ever," Griffin said, "but I *do* think she may be right that you need some fun! It'll be good for you!"

"Fine, fine, I'll go," Cali said with a final groan.

Griffin let out a squeal of delight, and Cali couldn't help but smile. Cali's smile—one that soon faded as they reached the circle around the fire. Nerves took the place of excitement. Suddenly, something about socializing seemed more daunting than learning to fight. There had been children growing up in her neighborhood in Athens, many of whom invited her to birthdays. But she didn't go—whether by Miriam's refusal or Cali's own shyness. Soon, the invites stopped all together. This smoke-filled wonder, with dancing mythologies howling at the half-mooned sky, made her heart skip a beat. It was hard not to get wrapped up in the moment. A faun started a song on his lute, several others began to dance. Even the enormous Garwin moved in loping movements around the fire. Seeny continued to pull and manipulate the flames as the music continued.

Cali swayed with the sound of the flute and drums. The heaviness of her life at the Farm, the finding her place, momentarily suspended as she allowed herself to laugh along with the rest. As quickly as it came, the feeling was damped by a sudden off-ness. Looking up from the flames, Cali saw James's silhouette just behind the jeering satyr twins. Cali could see his eyes were trained on her. *Why does he keep staring?* Something about his stare made her uncomfortable. He looked troubled, haunted, as if he held some terrible secret or weight.

"Hey—Cal."

Cali tore her eyes away from James and looked at Griffin's outstretched hand.

"You're leaving already?" Cali asked. "You just told me to come out."

"And it's been over an hour already!" Griffin laughed. She gestured for Cali to rise, still smiling, and seemingly oblivious to her boyfriend's intense gaze on her friend. "Come on—I want to show you my favorite spot."

James became lost behind the lumbered movements of Garwin as he danced in circles. So Cali stood and followed Griffen through the willows and olive trees, to the edge of the forest hedge where the wood nymphs danced. Before she could ask, Griffin plopped herself down on the ground and lay back. Cali stood over her for a moment.

"Um?"

Griffin patted the ground beside her. Shrugging, Cali followed suit and lay back on the cool grass. She was immediately struck by the stars and how dazzling they looked flicking in the night sky. It was so vast, and so far away. She nearly forgot that she was still trapped in this marvelously strange and sometimes horrible place. Were the gods looking down on her now? Freya, that parent who abandoned her long ago—was she watching Cali suffer here on Earth? Or laughing as she remained safe in the Vanir Realm? *What the hell am I even thinking about? Realms? God, I wish I was just crazy.* Cali's eyes squeezed shut as the memory of Miriam's peppery hair flitted through her mind. *It would be so much easier to be clinically insane right now.* Griffin, clearing her throat, brought her attention back to Earth.

Cali turned her head so she could hear her better, only to find Griffin staring at her. Something about the way the moon sparkled against Griffin's eyes made them seem wild—like a spark before it burst into a dangerous flame.

"What?" Griffin asked, brushing a golden curl from her forehead.

Cali responded with the same question. "What yourself?"

"Why are you looking at me like that?"

"Didn't you—I thought you asked something?"

"I did," Griffin said, laughing. She rested her hand in the crook of her arm. "I just didn't expect your face to look horrified."

"I wasn't horrified!" Cali protested, still laying on her back. "What did you say?"

"I just asked what you were thinking about."

"I guess home?" Her eyes went back to the stars. "Wondering what my parents are doing now? Why didn't they tell me? Why I'm here?"

"So, just the normal stuff," Griffin said.

It was the first time Cali had said her fears aloud to someone besides Natasha. They were the feelings she pushed down deep and away; hidden behind the door she always kept closed inside herself. There was more, but Cali bit the inside of her cheek to keep from talking. Some parts she would keep to herself. As the tears threatened to push to the corner of her eyes, she shot a look at Griffin's hands. They rested comfortably in their place by her side as she listened to Cali talk. *I wonder if she can still manipulate my emotions without touching me?*

"I mean, it's not really something you just come out and say, I guess," Cali said. "Like, 'Hey, you know how we adopted you and said your real parents died in a car crash? That was a lie. You're a demigod, or more classically put, *demi*. Now go live on a Farm ...'"

Griffin laughed at Cali's attempted mockery, and Cali couldn't help but smile along with her. It had been a long time since she really laughed—it felt good.

"I've always wondered if ..." Griffin suddenly trailed off and looked away, embarrassed.

"What?"

"Actually, it's kind of dumb. I shouldn't have ..."

"Just ask, I'll decide if it's dumb."

Griffin pursed her lips. Her dimples pulled on her face when she did. "Well, when I was a child, I found out on accident about my Prominent power," she said slowly. "I didn't know what was happening at first."

"How did you know you had done anything?" Cali wondered how a child would discover they could manipulate emotions. It wasn't exactly a visible power.

"I was upset about being scolded in class and cried," Griffin said softly. "I made the entire class cry too. Mother Henriet always had it out for me—finding out I was 'possessed' made it even more fun for her to torture me."

"Mother Henriet?"

Griffin's finger toyed with the grass. "At the orphanage. Before I went into foster care." She licked her lips.

"How old were you?"

"Eight. I didn't find out about Loki being my father until I was ten and that was by accident when I heard one of the nuns talking about it being nonsense. I suppose if demon possession could be real—why couldn't the other gods?"

Whoa.

"But then Tash found me, and I came here. I was one of the first, two years ago," Griffin said proudly, her stunning smile erasing any sign of sadness the memory drudged up. "She told me that a lot of times, demi's who don't initially know about their powers start to flex them based on big emotions. Most of the time, unfortunately it's negative emotions that trigger it."

Griffin looked at Cali expectantly, still twirling her hair between her fingers. Cali knew what Griffin was hinting at and she pulled her eyes back up to the stars, pretending to think.

"I don't ..." she paused and moved to her elbows to lean on them, clenching her fists to keep her fingers from shaking. "I can't think of anything where I didn't act totally norm ... human."

"Well, who knows what could happen," Griffin said with a sigh, staring up at the sky. "At least you've—well, come into your own here, I guess."

"You mean I'm not so afraid?"

Griffin laughed. "You know what I meant," she hesitated, "you are doing okay, right?"

"Up till now I've just been ... surviving here, each day," Cali said, staring at the sky. "A part of me," she blinked back the tears in her eyes, ashamed, "a part of me wanted to stay because I thought *what an adventure*. Like it would prove to my mom that I could do it – or prove to myself, I guess." Her hand brushed the corner of her eyes. "But that demi, Luca ..."

"It made it real," Griffin finished for her.

Cali nodded. "So much has happened since I arrived here," she said after a moment. "I just kept telling myself one more day, one more day. But one more day to what?" She paused, "Chaos is really, really out there, isn't she?"

From the corner of her eye, Cali saw Griffin nod.

"And she wants to destroy the gods—and demigods."

Griffin sighed. "Pretty much."

Sitting up Cali watched as the nymphs flitted between the olive and willows. Even the hamadryads, sparkling in the barrier, seemed more alive than usual. Cali laughed, feeling slightly hysterical. She kept laughing until tears streamed down her face. Griffin sat up and stared at her, but Cali didn't care. *I'm definitely losing it.*

"Sorry," Cali said, wiping a hand across her face. "I don't know where that came from but … you know, I realized I'm really happy that, even with all the unanswered questions and the threat of war any day, and impending doom and all," she turned to Griffin, "I'm glad that I have you as a friend in it."

Griffin caught Cali's free hand and squeezed. Cali returned the gesture, a sign of trust, of friendship, and smiled.

Chapter Nine

For the past two days, the sun and heat made training unbearable. Still, each day, Cali and the other demi's sparred, ran laps, stretched, learned weapons, or did some other sort of horrible physical exercise. With the weather came emotions, mostly anger, frustration, or fear. The last one bothered Cali the most. Natasha did her best try to and keep the peace, but everyone was on edge. Although there was no breeze, Cali could almost feel the shift in the air. Something was coming—something had changed.

Finally, the heat broke. With it, the demi's of the Farm were allowed a single afternoon without training. Granted, they all were encouraged to find something productive to do. Cali found herself a willow tree and hunkered down against the base, a book in hand. She always liked reading. However, the book that Maechon recommended to her was not really her style. Still, he said it was important.

"Good book?"

Cali groaned quietly to herself and folded the top of the book down to look at him. She scooted her back against the tree and looked up at James. He stood near her feet and stared down at her; his arms crossed against his chest. She couldn't tell if he was angry or intrigued. As unreadable as ever.

"Riveting," she responded.

"*Euripides*. Light reading."

"Of course, Maechon gave it to me." Cali rolled her eyes. Maechon was always recommending some outlandishly educational read. "But it's apparently the easier version. I'm still having trouble getting through it." *Did he just laugh?* "Are you laughing at me?"

"Hardly." His lips twitched, and he cleared his throat. Distant sounds of screams and laughter filled the air, and he looked over to the field where most of the demi's were enjoying their afternoon off by playing what Cali assumed was an old relic version of soccer. "How's training?"

"Well." Cali rested the book on her lap and stared up at him, her head cocked. "I haven't tried to run away again, if that's what you mean."

He looked at her. "I meant, how are you? I didn't mean for it to have you overthink it."

"Sorry," Cali muttered. "It's been a long week—well, weeks really." She gave a short laugh. "You know with impending end of the Realms and all."

His brow furrowed, as if he wasn't sure how to react. "You seem to be getting on with your omáda."

"Yeah, Maech, Griff, and Gar are great. Blythe, not so much." Cali rubbed a lingering bruise on her forearm. "I think she hates me."

"She hates everyone," he said. His arms relaxed, and he shifted his stance. "But she's the best fighter and the most loyal person here. I'm glad she's on our side."

"Our side," Cali echoed. Her fingers toyed with the edges of the book in her lap as she considered the word. "A month ago, I didn't even know there were sides, and now ..."

"Now?"

She sighed. "I mean, I barely understand my own place in this world," she confided. "People keep telling me I'm a daughter of

Freya, and I'm meant to be here, and us demi's," she gestured broadly, "are going to help save the Realms. But it's kinda hard to, I don't know, believe it, focus ... keep up?"

He made a sound and she stared at him. *Now he really is laughing at me. Great.* Frowning, she pulled herself up against the tree and stood.

"Thanks for the encouragement."

"Hey, even Herakles had bad days," James muttered and pointed to her book.

Herakles —*that's how you say it!* She looked between him and the blue-bound paper. *You and me, Herk, have no idea what's going on, but we keep going.*

"Yeah, well as long as he gets his family back and they all get happy endings, that's all that matters," she said. "You know, with all the bad things, there has to be something good right?" His eyes flickered like the sea, and she had trouble meeting them. She clutched the book to her chest.

"*Come back. Even as a shadow, even as a dream.*"

She gaped at him, stunned. "Is that in this book?"

"Yes, later on."

Something to look forward to. "Don't spoil it for me."

He laughed. A short, real laugh that faded as quickly as it came. "I wouldn't dream of it."

Shaking her head, she began to walk back to the shack, and he stepped in beside her. "This is maybe rude, but I didn't picture you as a reader."

"Well, you don't know me."

"Well, maybe if you spent more time talking to me instead of just staring ..." Cali trailed off, her face suddenly feeling too warm. Beside her, his step faltered. "Sorry, well no, I guess I'm not sorry but these last few days you've looked so ... I don't know, it just seems like you know something you're not telling me and that ..." Her heart skidded in her chest, and she froze.

She felt his hand on her elbow and heard his muffled voice asking her if she was okay. Slowly, she turned to face him. "Is ... is it my parents?" She could barely say the words. "Are they ... are my parents ..."

"No, no, gods no," James said, his face going from confused to realization in moments. He let go of her elbow as she took a deep breath. "Miriam and Aliax are fine," *well, he sounds confident,* "I didn't mean to scare you. I ...well I suppose, like the rest of us, I am wondering when your gift will reveal itself."

Well, keep waiting. Cali shook too much to respond as they kept walking past the gnarled Totem tree, to the shack. She could tell he wanted her to add something. He kept glancing at her, waiting. But she didn't know what to say.

She almost ran into Griffin when trying to beat James through the door to avoid him pushing further. Griffin looked from James to Cali. A radiant smile crossed her face. "You guys are just who I wanted to see," she said, looping an arm through both Cali and James' arms as she led them, awkwardly, into the house. "And you're becoming friends—which is even better to see."

"What's going on, Griffin?" James demanded, an edge in his smooth tone.

Cali looked between them. But if Griffin realized her boyfriend was annoyed, she didn't let it phase her.

"Auto and Tash have called a meeting." Griffin paused at the base of the long staircase, still hooked between them. "And you're both invited."

***

Cali stared up at the ceiling of her room. *Did that really happen?*

She had been laying still since she woke up two hours ago but found it difficult to get out of bed yet. The conversation yesterday between James, Natasha, and Auto had not gone well. Squinting, Cali tried to remember the details. They were fuzzy, edged against the memory of another nightmare she woke from this morning, but she could recall most of it.

Natasha and Auto were in Auto's room, along with Maechon and another instructor who Cali couldn't remember the name of. Griffin ushered James and Cali through the door, gave a quick wave to Cali and planted a soft kiss on James' cheek before she closed the door. Cali tried to pretend she didn't see as James clenched his jaw.

"This is a bad idea," he said before he or Cali made it any further in the room. Cali looked at him, an eyebrow raised. *You know what's going on?* He didn't look at her as he stepped to the high-back chair that Maechon sat in. "We have it under control."

"I'm sure Luca would beg to differ," Auto snorted. Cali tried not to look at him. Every time she heard him speak; she felt a wave of ice in her veins. She rubbed her arms. "Clearly, we need a little extra help in the field."

"Leave Luca out of this," James snarled. Heat radiated from him, and Cali took a step away from him and toward the fireplace.

Auto's room was pale and gray, with deep black curtains that barely covered windows that displayed dismal days. Snow battered the glass, and the panes were edged in ice. The only furniture was the bed, where Auto leaned on one side and Natasha stood at the other, the two black leather chairs, and a coffee table that held one, single book. The table and chairs sat closest to the shiny black mantle, where there was no fire lit. The whole room felt cold, beside James' snap of anger.

Auto raised a hand. Coldness creased his face. "We've all lost things, boy," he hissed back. "Don't think that this decision is easy."

"They aren't ready!" James protested, rounding the chair and leaving Cali looking helplessly alone beside Maechon and the empty fireplace. She caught Maechon's eye and gave him a questioning *what are we doing here?* look. But he only gave a small shrug.

"What has been the point of training these past two years if they aren't ready now?" Auto retorted. "If not now, when?"

"Someone will get hurt—"

"Or we could all die," Natasha said, raising her voice above the others. "This isn't ideal, James, but we are running out of time. The Totem won't—" Auto coughed into his hand and nodded in the direction of Cali and Maechon. Correcting herself, Natasha continued. "Keipelle, Arastoo, and Bear have all lead successful missions in the past There is no reason to think this won't work out."

"There is every reason to think this won't work out." James took a step closer to her and Cali could see the muscles in his shoulders spasm with anger. It seemed to her James was doing his best not to explode in anger—but just barely. "That was for artifacts that meant nothing—this is for a person. A demi! If the Hunter …"

"It always would come to this, James," Natasha snapped. "This is happening. Do not question it."

She straightened to her full height and stared down at James. Cali could almost see the darkness radiating from her rage as she dared him to challenge her again. Cali looked to Auto, who seemed unphased by the confrontation. Natasha rubbed the bridge of her nose as James cocked his head and stepped back a pace.

It really feels like I shouldn't be here. "Um, I'm sorry to, well, interrupt, but," all eyes turned to her and she could feel her face grow warm, "well, why am I," Maechon looked up at her, "are *we* here?"

James ran a hand through his dark curls and shook his head. Rage still rippled out of him, but he stood silently and waited for Natasha to speak.

"A demi has been located that is in need of extraction, or, as we put it, collection," Natasha began. A shadow seemed to shimmer over her body as she spoke, her entire posture exuded power and command. *This is serious.* Dread washed over Cali.

"I thought that was"—*you're about to ask a dumb question, Mixie.* She ignored Blythe's voice in her head and asked it anyway— "I thought that was the Collector's job?"

From his post near the wall, James let out a short, bitter laugh. "You'd think," he muttered.

"Normally, yes," Natasha continued, ignoring him. "But unfortunately, that was when time was on our side. Time is not on our side anymore."

"And what does that have to do with Maech and me?"

"We used to send trainees into the field to bring in demi's before we assigned the Collector's," Auto said. He watched Cali carefully as he spoke. "It gave them the opportunity to use their skills and see the world. We stopped it about a year ago after two demi's died in a kaoti attack in Greece."

"Kaoti?" Cali asked, her mind spinning with the new information. "What is that?" She jumped to her next question before anyone could answer. "Wait, no—wait are you saying that we," she pointed to Maechon, her, and then James, "are going to rescue a demi?"

Natasha sighed and stretched out her shoulders, rolling her neck. "Two demi's, in fact." Her voice sounded strained and tired as she began to relax. "You'll be going with your group, led by James, and Keipelle will lead his. We asked you and Maechon here as you are the two newest to the Farm. The demi you will be collecting is in Varsna, Italy." Natasha paused and looked pointedly at Cali. "Varsna 1427."

Natasha continued to stare, but Cali only stared back. "You don't have any questions about that?" Natasha prodded.

"Why would …" *1427… 1427….* "1427," Cali repeated. Her legs suddenly felt like they wouldn't hold her. "Like, the … the year 1427? That's …"

"Impossible?" Auto suggested. Cali blinked at him and, as if embarrassed by her stare, he ducked his head.

"So, Maechon has yet to talk to you about the formidable world of time travel," Natasha said with a slightly wicked gleam in her silver eyes. Cali grabbed the back of Maechon's chair, and he tilted his head to see her, his eyes as wide and as apologetic as ever. "But I won't rest that entirely on him, of course, but we had hoped in buddying you to together for the Realms collective histories, that you would get there soon. I thought it would be easier to learn from your peers about some things."

Cali said nothing. *Time travel, time travel … I mean, of course, right? Why not?*

"Time travel?" she said aloud. "I … how?"

"With this."

Natasha pulled something from her pocket and held it up.

"A key?"

"Yes."

Cali frowned. "And so we just open a door and …?"

"It's a tiny bit more complicated than that," Natasha said with a grin. "This key can be used to both open and lock, time and place between our own Realm, which falls under Olympus. With it, we can go nearly anywhere where the mark of the gods has been. Which is how we've been bringing demi's here to the Farm."

Cali nodded slowly. "Why here? And why now?" she asked, trying to understand. "I mean, I'm alive in this century." *I think.*

"Are all the demi's here not ... from here?"

"It's complicated," Natasha said, putting the key back in her pocket. "We have only been able to collect demi's from the last five-hundred years, and only if they are in our Realm at the time in that span. We can't use this key to cross the other Realms—only within our own. But regarding now," she exchanged a quick look with Auto, who turned away and looked out the window at the snowstorm, "We have utilized the oracles try to locate demi's in need, but everything seems to stop with you."

"What do you mean?" Cali asked, her stomach curled into knots.

"She means you are the last of the demi's," Auto said, his voice so faint Cali could barely hear his words.

The last of the demi's—what does that mean? Cold sweat broke out on her lower back. She released the chair and began to back to the door. "I don't know if I can help with this mission thing," she stammered. "I don't think I ..." *I don't think I am brave enough to.* She stopped talking and looked at her feet.

Natasha gave her a sympathetic smile. "I get it Cali," she said. "You're afraid. That demi out there, Ophelli, she's afraid of the same shadow as you. And we're her only option. If we don't save her, she'll die."

Chapter Ten

Cali mumbled a silent curse as she pulled the scratchy, cotton dress over her head. The beige fabric dropped to just above her ankles and hung loose around her body. She scowled at herself in her mirror, taking in the unflattering look. Her braid had been expertly tied back by Griffin and the end rested across her shoulder. Thankfully, she was still able to wear 21st-century underwear, but it didn't help the itch of the dress on her skin. She wrapped the tattered orange belt around her waist and slipped on the too-small sandals that Griffin had brought her. Wriggling her toes, she winced beneath the stretch of the leather on her feet. *I am definitely going to have blisters after this.* Cali tried not to think about the fact that she may have worse than blisters on her feet after this rescue mission.

Although Natasha insisted in her speech to the two groups departing that day that each extraction would be simple and quick, Cali couldn't shake the feeling of impending doom. She missed breakfast because she chose to lie in bed and do nothing, which she was now regretting as her stomach growled at her. Natasha said they would arrive in Varsna 1427—*time travel*, Cali reminded herself—in midday. This specific day was chosen as there was a record of an earthquake occurring that afternoon. They needed to choose a time with some sort of natural distraction, or disaster, according to what Maechon told her after their meeting in Auto's room. "Any t-t-ti ... any time a p-portal is o-o-open, it cau-causes a break," he had told her as he trailed her to her room. "The gods do-do ... don't like p-portals being r-r-r ... re-opened."

With a final deep breath, Cali swung the door open to her room.

"James."

He stood; a hand poised as if to knock. In his other hand, he clutched something close to his side. Cali almost laughed as she took in his appearance. He wore similar attire, but the male version was much ... shorter. He also had a brown-leather vest and matching belt. Attached to the belt on his left was his sword, the silver hilt barely visible beneath the cover of the oversized vest. She imagined the awkward size vest hid other weapons beneath.

"You look ... interesting," she said, covering her mouth with her hand to hide her grin.

His brows pulled into a frown. "We look like we belong in Varsna," he replied, dropping his hand. The other shifted at his side. "Are you ready?"

No. "Yes."

Throwing a glance up the hall, he took a step closer, and Cali instinctively stepped back. His frown deepened, and he stopped just inside the doorway. The hidden hand revealed a sword with a simple bronze hilt, which he held out to her. Cali stared at the weapon, then at James, then back at the weapon.

"We aren't supposed to have weapons," she protested, but a tickle of anticipation ran through her fingers as she looked at the sword. She had not been allowed to train with real weapons yet, only sticks and spears without heads. As she always thought herself rather pacifist, Cali was surprised at her own desire to take the weapon. She licked her lips, sweat stinging her hands. "I've never held a real weapon before—I don't know how ..."

"It's just like a dummy weapon." He kept his voice low. "But a bit more lethal. Let's just pray you don't have to use it."

Cali's eyes widened as she looked at her reflection in the steel.

"Take it," James insisted. "If it's any comfort, I suggested against it, but Auto wanted you to have it, just in case. Keep it hidden for now. Blythe would kill me."

Yeah, really comforting. Gently, she placed her fingers around the hilt. She tried to keep her hands from shaking as she slipped it beneath the folds of her dress, the coolness pressing against her thigh.

"Now, are you ready?"

Cali nodded and, still shaking, followed him down the hall.

***

Cali's group stood near the door at the very end of the hall. The light was much dimmer at this end, which Cali assumed is why she never noticed the black carved wood before. She threw a look at the demi's she trained with, each wearing their own version of Italy 1400s clothes. Garwin was missing, due to what Maechon suggested, was essentially cyclops racism of the time. Instead, two other half-human demi's took his place. Mauricio, the son of Thor, and Roro, whose specific heritage was unknown but is said to be the granddaughter of Zeus himself. They had been 'in the field' before and, being some of the only demi's who had seen real battle, would serve as an extra layer of protection.

"As I said." Cali pulled her attention from the group, and the cold sword that pressed into her skin made her look back at James as he spoke. "You stick either with Mauricio, or with me. I do not want anyone getting left behind, lost, or killed. This is not a sightseeing trip. We get in, we get out."

Without waiting for a response from his group, he turned to the silver-knobbed door. Cail saw the glint of the key in his hand as he pressed it to the lock.

"You doing okay?"

Why does everyone keep asking me that? Cali tried not to let her annoyance at Griffin's question show on her face. Griffin looked amazing in her dress. She kept her blonde curls tucked beneath a shawl over her head.

"I'm fine," Cali replied, not taking her eyes off the key in James hand. "Overwhelmed, but fine."

Griffin handed her something. "Here." A scarf, faded blue. "You'll need it to cover your hair. We'll stand out here."

Cali murmured a soft thank you as she took the scarf and wrapped it awkwardly around her head and shoulders. There was a soft click, and she turned back to the door just as James pushed it open. Light flooded the hall and Cali gasped as she took in the buildings, people, and town of Varsna.

***

They stepped out of the door to a quiet street near the front of the village. Large, cracked pillars marked the main entrance where a gate used to be. All that remained were rusted hinges. Cali looked at the door they walked through in wonder. It looked like any other run-down door, held together with pieces of wood with a simple handle. She pulled her shawl around her face as she stood close to the wall, her eyes wide as she took in everything around her. The rest of her group filed in alongside her and waited for James' instruction.

"We're going to split up so we can cover more ground in case something does go wrong. Arastoo wanted as many of you to experience as much of this as possible." James pointed to the street tucked to the left. "Mauricio, you take the twins, Maechon, and Blythe. Griffin, Roro will come with me."

The village was small, with tiny, patched-up buildings scattered inside the crumbled walls. Up the street to the right, Cali could make out people as they rushed the streets with baskets of food, berries, nuts, and olives. Villagers loitered on the roads, talking to each other. A man sat without legs begging at the side of one building. Several small children screamed and chased and played. Sheep and goats pushed through a narrow street, hustled away by a scraggly man. Cali may not have believed what she was seeing if it were not for the intense mixture of smells in the air. A tap on her shoulder made her turn.

"This way." James nodded down the street between vendors where Roro and Griffin walked ahead.

Cali noticed Mauricio had led the others down the alley to the left and disappeared behind a bend. She was about to ask why they split up when she noticed James was not at her side. She caught up with him. He walked quickly, looking down every so often at a piece of paper in his hand. They weaved between some villagers as they made their way through the street.

"Do you ... do this a lot?" Cali asked as she kept trying to take it all in. The village sprawled out with narrow streets shoved with carts and vendors trying to sell. She saw a basket full of shiny, red apples and immediately felt the urge to take one. Her fingers tingled, but she walked past.

"Yes." James put the paper back in his pocket.

"You don't think anything bad is actually going to happen, right?" She tried to keep pace with him as they weaved around two women with baskets on their heads.

"I try to prepare for anything," he replied, his voice low. "Every mission has its risks, so it's important to be ready."

"Which is why I have a sword?"

He checked his pace and looked down at her. "Which is why you, and everyone else on this mission, have a sword. Besides Maechon."

"Oh." Cali didn't know why she felt a little offended by this. "I thought—"

"Demi's who've been training for less than three months are not allowed to wield blades, unless it is their own elemental weapon," he said, as if reading her thoughts. He stopped looking at her as he picked up his speed. "But I don't want anyone on my mission getting hurt because they couldn't properly defend themselves." When Cali said nothing, he paused. "You'll be fine. I'll make sure nothing happens to you."

Cali nodded, then screeched as she pitched forward. A wheel from a cart stuck out in the street and she caught her foot, causing James to instinctively reach out and grab her.

"Watch where you're going," he snapped. She felt a shiver through her body as his fingers pulled away. A rumble under her feet made her almost tumble again.

"What was that?" she asked, dread at knowing what it was already coursing through her.

"That's not good," he muttered, looking around. "Quick ... come on."

Griffin and Roro waited at the center of the village where a dilapidated statue of Athena stood in a dried-up fountain. They both looked worried, but Griffin's features edged on irritation.

"Did you feel that?" Roro demanded. James gave a tense nod. "It's early."

"We gotta get this done," Griffin added. She looked between Cali and James, her face tense beneath her shawl. "Is everything okay?"

"It's fine—let's go." James turned down another street and stopped in front of a door on his right. Looking both ways, he knocked. Cali's anxiety spiked as the door opened. The house shuddered and dust rippled through the air around them as they stepped inside.

"Griff." James shot a glance over her shoulder. Griffin caught her cue. Her eyes flashed, but she turned, departed down the side of the street, and disappeared behind a building.

"Where's she going?" Cali asked.

"She's getting the others."

Cali blinked several times before her eyes adjusted to the dark room. She could make out a small table, several cupboards that were empty, and an almost bare secondary room, save matt made of straw. In front of her, James was just visible, his shoulders tensed, and beside him Roro, her silent gaze searching the room for signs of trouble.

"Ophelli?" James asked.

A quiet and fearful voice came from the kitchen. "Yes."

A young woman, no older than Cali herself, lingered in the shadows of light. Even in the stifled dark, Cali could see Vitiligo patches of brown and white across her body. Dozens of plaits wrapped her hair tight against her forehead and her large eyes stared at them in a mixture of wonder and fear.

"It's time." James took a step forward, his hands out as if to prove they came in peace. "Do you have what you need?"

"Yes, I suppose," the girl, Ophelli, nodded. "Postverta said I would have more time—"

"I think perhaps she misjudged that," James continued. Roro glanced anxiously at the window of the house that were shuttered. Dust shook from the frames as they rattled. Cali felt a pit grow in her stomach. "I don't think—"

"I know," Ophelli said, her voice quavered as if she would cry at any moment. "I saw."

"Okay." James drew the word out slowly as if what Ophelli said changed things. *She must have a gift, too.* Cali peered at the girl over his shoulder as she stepped into the small kitchen space. She remembered Maechon talking about oracles and their children who held the gift of foresight. *She must be one of them? How can she be so powerful but so scared?*

"So, you saw this happening—it doesn't matter. We still have *some* time before the earthquake is scheduled." James turned to Roro. "Roro—go find Griffin. She should have found Maurcio by now. Get to the door. We're leaving—"

A loud crash from outside caused the entire house to shake. A shelf dropped from its place, shattering jars and dishes. Ophelli squeaked in fear, her large eyes growing bigger. Her hands flew to her mouth to cover her scream. The shutters on the window shook vigorously, one snapping beneath the pressure.

"That did not feel like an earthquake," Cali muttered, stepping closer to James.

"Roro—go now." James' voice strained as he jerked his head towards the door. Without a word Roro ran out the door, sword in hand. James stepped to the window and looked out. "Of course," he mumbled.

Cali felt a jolt of fear as he rested his hand on the hilt of his sword. *What is happening? What is it?* He caught her stare before turning to Ophelli. "She'll be here any minute; we have to go. Now!"

"Who? What are you talking about?" Cali asked.

From her place near the table, Cali couldn't see out the window but could still hear several crashes mixed with what she could only assume were screams. She had experienced small tremor earthquakes in Athens, nothing that rendered this reaction. James crossed the room and looked out the door. When he turned, his face was grim. There was something else there. It frightened Cali.

"It's the Hunter." He snapped his finger at Ophelli to move. Cali's skin went cold. James drew a hand through his hair as he looked out again before turning to her. "You still have your weapon?"

"Yes, but, James—"

"Be ready."

"Ophelli"

Ophelli let out a yelp, hitting herself against the edge of the table, and pitched forward. Cali instinctively stepped to catch her as she fell. "Thanks, I ..." Ophelli's voice faded as her cold hand grasped Cali's arm for support.

As if pulled into a dream, Cali found herself standing outside her own home in Athens. The relief she may have felt evaporated as she took in the scene in front of her. The place her home used to stand was nothing more than an indent and rubble littered the ground. The sky glowed red with fire; fear and smoke transparent in the air, making it thick. Panic gripped Cali as she tried to open her mouth to call out, but she couldn't make a sound. Something on the ground around the apartment building caught her eye. A body. She staggered slowly forward, forcing her feet towards it, knowing before she saw the face who it was. She gasped for air, tears burning in her eyes and smoke burning her lungs. Unable to look away, she stared at the face in front of her. *Close your eyes. Close them.*

In an instant, she was staring back at Ophelli, who ripped her arm out of Cali's steely grasp. They stared at each other with wide, horrified eyes.

"I'm sorry," whispered a panicked Ophelli. "I'm so sorry—"

"What was that?" Cali demanded, her breath coming out in gasps. James took a step towards them. The vision had been only an instant and worry creased deeper against James' face. "What ... was that real?"

"Please," Ophelli pleaded. "Please, I can explain."

"Cali, we don't have time for this." James took another step toward her, his voice strained.

"What *was* that?!" Cali ignored him, even with the rumble of noise outside the door. Nothing mattered but the truth. Nothing mattered but answers.

"Cali, we don't have time …." James grabbed for her arm, but she shook it off. He stood his ground. The house shook as the thundering earthquake began to take effect on the village. "Whatever you saw just now, it wasn't real. Come on."

"No." She jerked her arm away, trying to shove James back as she continued to question Ophelli, her voice raising to match whatever madness happened outside. A shaking explosion made James' grip loosen.

"Are they dead?" she hissed out the word, barely able to say it. "You see the future—that's your gift. Is it real?"

"I don't know, I don't know!" Ophelli began. Tears formed in her large eyes as she looked from James to Cali.

"Cali!" Cali could feel the rage emanating from him. He grabbed Cali from behind with one arm, pinning the arm that gripped her blade. Cali strained against him, cursing. She couldn't focus—her brain wouldn't let her calm down. "Ophelli, let's go!"

"Please, I don't kno—" A strange expression crossed Ophelli's face, and the house stilled in an eerie quiet. James and Cali froze as well, his arms still wrapped around her.

The demi girl blinked several times in confusion. Tears trailed down her face as all eyes went to the silver tip of a blade protruding from her chest. It glinted in the sparse light of the room, driven in so clean blood hardly clung to it.

"I …" Ophelli said, her unfocused eyes looking between them.

The breath left Cali's lungs as the sword slowly withdrew as if it was being pulled from her. She kept Ophelli's gaze as the girl sank to the floor, hitting with a thud.

The chaos outside was a soft buzz humming in Cali's ear. A feeling, unlike anything she'd felt before, crawled across her as she stared at the lifeless form of the girl they had come to save. The seconds seemed to last for hours. Finally tearing her eyes away from Ophelli, Cali followed James' gaze to the bearer of the sword.

A tall, dark woman with white hair cropped short to her chin stood staring at them coolly. She wore all-black clothes mixed with sheers and solids that clung perfectly to her muscled frame. A cloak, the hood dropped back to reveal the face, wafted in the warm breeze. Behind her stood two figures that Cali felt could only be the things of nightmare. Their bodies were almost human but contained a gargoyle-esque horror in their dead eyes and flayed, patchy skin that pulled across and away from their bones.

James' arms were still wrapped around Cali, and she felt them tighten as one of the creatures let out a gurgled wail. He began to lift Cali off the ground as she remained stunned in place. Cocking her head slightly, the woman studied Cali with a flash of interest crossing her brow. She was about to take a step forward when the house collapsed in on itself, the roof caving inwards. Cali was unsure how her bronze-hilted sword made it to her hands, but she felt herself embrace the coolness of it with vehemence. James shouted something but she couldn't understand it over the sounds around them.

Releasing his hold on her, he reeled around as one of the creatures breached the ruble and made for them. It buried its fingers in James' arm and Cali gasped. No blood came from the claw marks as James buried his weapon in its head.

Cali stumbled back, her own sword hanging useless at her side, and her body began to shake. The last thing she saw was James bringing his weapon around to the woman, and then Cali's head connected with a wall.

She allowed herself to succumb to the darkness she deserved.

Chapter Eleven

Light streamed through the window, and the heat from the sun warmed Cali's eyelid as she woke. Her chest rose and fell painfully with each breath. She would hear her mother call shortly to tell her to get up and start the day. Cali would open her eyes, see the splintering crack in her ceiling, then bring her feet to the floor. She would be home. She would be safe.

You'll never be safe again.

Slowly opening her eyes, Cali focused on the ceiling. There was no large crack there; this was not her room. This was not her home. She blinked, trying to remember how she got here. Her head throbbed painfully, and both ears buzzed. The open window let in a soft breeze. She turned her head to watch the curtain ruffle in the soft gusts of air. Her mind raced back to another window. The window in the house in Varsna. That noise ... Her breath became rapid, and she tensed as her mind brought her back to reality with a painful jolt. She shut her eyes, squeezing them as tight as she could as she pressed her palms to them. This only made it worse as the horrified face of Ophelli flashed in the darkness there.

"No, no, no," she whispered. Her body curled inwards on itself. She wrapped her arms around her head to hide from the feeling. The weight slammed into her like a large elephant on her chest. "No, no ... please." She rocked back and forth, opening her eyes, hoping for tears to begin.

"You don't get to hide from this." a low, muted voice spoke from behind her.

Cali stopped rocking and slowly unraveled herself. Ignoring her stiff muscles, she sat up on the bed. She pushed her blonde, matted hair out of her face and turned to face Natasha, who stared back at her with impassive, silver-streaked eyes.

"Ophelli." Cali's voice cracked as she said the girl's name aloud. With the name came the face that haunted her vision.

Natasha studied Cali's face with her cunning eyes. "She is dead."

Cali nodded and stared across at her own reflection in the mirror above the dresser. Dark circles were beneath her multicolored eyes and her blonde hair appeared matted against her face. She looked like a ghost. Her eyes seemed to see past herself and see who she had become. Seen the deed she had done.

"James?" she asked, still staring blankly at the mirror.

"He's fine. They all made it back before the earthquake took the city.

"He ... he tried to ..." Cali looked down at her hands.

"He told us," Natasha said, leaning forward in her chair to be as close to the bed as possible. Her hands folded into a tent before her face, resting on her lips. "Cali ..."

"It's my fault she's dead," Cali choked out.

"In a way, yes."

Cali didn't know what else to say. The guilt was overwhelming her, and she wanted to curl back up into a ball. Wanted it to crush her—to overwhelm her and drag her soul to the underworld.

"You were afraid of what you saw," Natasha continued, watching Cali's struggle from her chair. "And it made you blind. You'll have to live with that knowledge for the rest of your life and there's nothing anyone can do about that. But only

James, Auto, you and I know what happened in that house in Varsna ..."

"I killed someone."

Natasha leaned back in her chair as if trying to find the right words to say. Her brow furrowed for a moment as she thought, but then she sighed. "That's a matter of perspective," she said slowly.

"A matter of perspective?" Cali spat out. "I—James told me we needed to leave, that we didn't have enough time, but I ..." Sobs choked out her words and she covered her mouth. "It's my fault she's dead."

"Well, that may or may not be true," Natasha said with a frown. "But Cali, this is not just all on you. I take full responsibility for—"

"For her death?" Cali hissed, facing her. She dug her fingers deep into the quilt, her body shaking. "You weren't there! It was my fault—my fault ..." The whole bed shuddered beneath her grief. "I can't live with this." *I can't breathe.* "I can't ..."

"Enough of this, Cali—or I will have Griffin calm you down!" Natasha's serene voice, like honey, changed to steel as sharp as a knife. "Whatever guilt you feel, whatever rage, you will quell now. This is not on you. This is on Erinyes."

Erinyes—so, the Hunter has a name. Cali could still see the mad black eyes staring back at her, the silver blade and the blood ... Her breath shuddered and rattled as she inhaled and then let the air out slowly.

Natasha studied her for a moment. "You do not get the luxury of suffering like this for long. There is an old proverb: *Nu är sagan all.*"

Cali turned her red-rimmed eyes to her mentor. "What does that mean?"

"*Now the fairytale is over,*" Natasha responded.

They sat in silence for a moment.

Tears ran down Cali's face. "Nobody will trust me ... I don't trust me."

"There are some things that are best to keep at bay, not as secrets, but as protection," Natasha said. "As your own parents did for you."

"And look where I am now," Cali said bitterly. She pulled her arms around her knees, digging her nails into her palms. "Essentially a murder." She gave a shuddering breath. "My parents would be so proud."

"You are very much like your ... mother, Freya," Natasha said but caught herself on the last word as if she was about to say something, or someone, else. "You have a big heart, but you do not always think with the mind you were given. We cannot change what has been done, we can do what we must move on. I suggest, for now, you begin with a shower. Set the passion of guilt aside and we will go from there."

Cali brushed her hands up to pull her disheveled hair back from her red, puffy face. No more tears came—she felt empty. *All my fault.* She nodded to Natasha without looking up to meet her eyes again.

Natasha stood and walked to the door, where she paused.

"What we have done in the past does not need to define what we do in the present." Her voice sounded sad, as if she was speaking to herself as well. "We can rewrite ourselves at any time ... we have to. And Cali—your parents, Miriam and Aliax—they would be proud of you."

Natasha disappeared through the door. Taking a long, deep breath of her own, Cali crawled out of her bed and into her small bathroom, where she stood in the shower, fully clothed, and tried to wash away her shame.

***

"You awake, Cal?" a soft voice followed the knock on the door and Griffin's blonde curls popped around the corner of it.

"Yeah." Cali sat on her bed and ran her fingers through her damp hair, prepping her braid. Griffin stepped into the room, her face full of sympathy and her hands holding a plate with a sandwich. It reminded Cali of her first week at the Farm. *How long ago was that*?

"I know you missed breakfast, and lunch," Griffin said as she sat on the bed beside Cali. She passed the wilted sandwich to her. "I had to wait until Natasha was busy before I could sneak up; that's why it's kind of soggy looking. Sorry."

"No, this is great, thank you." Cali left her hair alone and grabbed the sandwich. Her stomach gurgled in reprimand as it reminded Cali it had not been fed for some time.

"Don't eat too fast." Griffin laughed as Cali began devouring the food. She scooted herself behind Cali, placing her hands on her head. "Do you mind?"

Cali shook her head.

So Griffin showed off her impressive skills as she quickly and efficiently tied back all of Cali's wispy hair into a braid. Although a braid was the most efficient hairstyle in battle for a girl with long hair, Cali always felt her head looked large and bald with her hair pulled so tight against her scalp. She frowned as she stared at her pale face with flushed cheeks in comparison to Griffin's curly, blonde hair that always fell right into place.

"Thanks." Cali finished her sandwich and licked the tips of her fingers. "And thanks for the food, too. It's almost too annoying how nice you are."

"Don't say that!" Griffin laughed, shifting herself to sit beside Cali. "I just want to be helpful, that's all. You seem to be healing pretty well." She paused and looked at Cali with a sickening sympathy that made Cali's bones ache. "How are you?"

The face of Ophelli flashed in front of Cali, and she stiffened. Griffin's hand rested on Cali's and Cali shifted hers as the intensity of the touch rushed through her arm. Still, the effect of Griffin's power soothed the sudden rush of guilt that flooded her.

"I ... I mean I ... I guess I'm awful," Cali said, turning her eyes from Griffin's. "It was the worst thing I've ever gone through."

"I believe it. Seeing death, it's awful." Griffin paused, taking a labored breath. "Do you want to talk about what happened?"

Cali looked back up at herself in the mirror and could see Griffin staring at her face in the reflection. Griffin's voice echoed the same pain Cali felt as Cali knew her life had been difficult at the orphanage before, but the haunting look in her eyes made Cali wonder if there was something more to her past.

"I ... I don't know what happened," Cali said quietly. "What did James say?" Only James knew that Cali had lingered far longer than intended and that Cali had pushed far too hard for answers for the vision than the moment allowed. There was no time, and Cali knew it, and she had pushed anyway.

Griffin sighed. "He didn't say anything. But he wouldn't. Has he come to check in on you?"

I wouldn't be surprised if he never wanted to see my face again. "No. But I wasn't counting on it." Cali blinked back the stinging tears. "It's not like he failed..." she trailed off, thinking of Natasha's warning about sharing the truth of what happened.

"Hey—it's okay," Griffin said, giving Cali a reassuring squeeze. Heat from where Griffin's touch had been still pulsed beneath Cali's skin. The false calm that warmed her mixed with her own true emotions, making Cali dizzy. "I'm sure you didn't fail. You should talk about it. Let me help you..."

"I don't need your help."

Griffin's hand pulled back and her eyes widened in surprise. Cali stared back at her, equally surprised at her own overreaction.

"I didn't mean it like that," Cali said as Griffin stood slowly from the bed. "Griff—please, I ..."

"It's fine, Cali, really." Griffin pushed her curls onto one shoulder but kept her gaze on her feet. "You've been through a trauma. You're reacting to it, not me."

"Griffin ..."

Griffin looked up at her with a strained smile, hurt still shimmering in her crystal blue eyes. "It's really alright Cali," she said. "Get some rest—you'll come down to dinner, right?"

Cali nodded and then watched as Griffin spun on her heel and left the room.

Why did you say that? Cali covered her face with her hands and shook her head. *Idiot. Griffin is your only friend, and this is how you treat her?* Sitting up, Cali dropped her feet to the floor and stood. "Get a hold of yourself, Cali," she muttered through gritted teeth. "Get a hold of yourself."

***

Cali waited for the footfalls of the others to fade down the hall before she got the courage to poke her head out the door of her room. She took a deep breath as she stepped into the hallway. The black door still stood at the end, almost covered in shadows cast by the low lights. The darkness shifted. Cali's mouth went dry, and she stared at the tall woman who detached herself from the wall.

The woman's head cocked, like a beast assessing its prey before an attack, and she smiled. Cali was immediately struck by how beautiful and slightly horrifying she was. The woman wore a simple cream-colored tank with loose brown pants and sandals. A belt looped around her waist and across her chest at the right shoulder, each space holding pouches or daggers or what looked like small animal bones. Gold bracelets adorned her biceps on each side and Cali could see the muscles flex as if anticipating a threat at any moment. The long golden-brown hair wisped lightly across her face and down her back in a long, loose braid.

"Artemis."

Cali didn't know how she knew the woman's name, only that she *knew* it was her. Artemis took a step forward, like a curious deer, wondering how Cali would react if she closed the space between them.

"What are you doing here?" Cali breathed, wondering for a split second if the goddess knew about Varsna. *How though?* Cali reasoned. *She's not the judge of souls, she's ... a hunter.* Her heart skittered in her chest as Artemis took another step.

"I am not here for you, child," Artemis said, her voice cool and smooth. The dark eyes flicked behind Cali. "I am here for them."

Cali turned slowly, keeping her eyes on Artemis. Auto stepped in front of her, blocking her from Artemis' advance. He braced himself on his crutch as he tried to raise himself to his full height and shield Cali.

"Don't come any closer." Cali shivered at the dropped tone Auto took in addressing the goddess. His blonde and white streaked hair remained as unruly as ever, and his outdated clothes gave him a homeless look, but at that moment, he emanated power. Cali realized she never knew if he himself was a god or what his power was. She made a mental note to talk to Maechon immediately after she got out of this situation.

"Oh, Autolycus," Artemis purred. "It has been far too long."

She looked at his lost limb, then at his face. "Much of you is missing."

"Why don't you dive over a waterfall and tell me—"

"Auto." Natasha strode down the hall from the stairs. With each step, the incandescent lights flickered and dimmed, as if she pulled the very shadows after her. Cali looked between her and Auto, unsure of what to do. Natasha stopped beside her, but her eyes remained on the goddess in the hall. "Artemis—what are you doing here?"

"You know why I am here," Artemis said, with an almost laugh in her voice.

"We need more time."

"You don't have it."

"They're not ready."

"Tash." Auto interrupted the two women before they went physically toe-to-toe and threw a quick, meaningful glance at Cali.

Natasha frowned and crossed her arms.

"Your Totem is dying, whether you chose to believe it or not," Artemis said. "What little protection you have from the Hamadryads and their barrier will not quell the Hunter's thirst, or the general's drive to destroy all those who stand against Chaos and her plan for the Realms."

"And you know what those plans are?" Auto asked. He shifted his weight on his staff and Cali winced as he staggered into the wall. "I'm fine," he snapped, brushing her hand away and turning back to Artemis. "What is she going for?"

Artemis watched him warily. "She wants the gifts."

The gifts? Cali kept silent between Auto and Natasha, but she tried to think back to anything that Maechon or her training had told her about gifts.

Natasha's frown deepened. "She cannot find them, not without—"

"The Map of the Void?" Artemis said, eyebrow raised. "Yes, well, that's been located, love." The deep brown eyes shifted back to Cali. "And in the most interesting place." She took a step forward, ignoring Auto's growl of warning. "So," she said, almost in a whisper as she paused before Cali. "This is the girl?"

Cali unclenched her hands and wiped the sweat on her pants, unable to pull away from the stare. Sweat trickled down her forehead, but she remained still. *What girl?*

"Leave her alone," Auto growled. "You've caused enough damage ..."

"Oh, and I could cause so, very much more old man."

Artemis turned on Auto and matched his bared teeth with her own. He tried to place himself between Cali and her again but found it difficult with his crutch in the way. Gently, Natasha pushed Cali back and stepped forward.

"Enough of this," she said, her voice even and calm. "Clearly, we have bigger issues. If Chaos is after the gifts, the gods should intervene."

"They won't," Artemis scoffed. "They gave you the Realm key to stop that from happening."

"But you're here?" Cali pointed out, finding her voice.

Artemis grinned. "Am I? Really?" Cali pursed her lips. "You're on your own with this, Tash. I can't intervene unless I'm—"

"We get it, you're on a leash," Auto hissed. "You've said your peace. Now leave."

Artemis looked from Natasha, to him, then back to Cali. No one spoke for a beat. "I know when I'm not wanted," she said with a wink at Cali. "We'll meet again, little one."

"No you—"

But Artemis had already stalked down the hall and, in a swift motion, left through the black door.

Chapter Twelve

News of Artemis' arrival spread rapidly due to the satyr twins, Ottie and Ozzie, secretly watching the entire impromptu meeting from the stairs. They had been given clean-up duty in the barns by Arastoo for culpable behavior, not that either of them cared. Whispers grew with training; dread and fear mixed with sweat. The Totem's already dying limbs began to rustle and break. Cali had learned her first week that the Totem was the first line of protection against gods on either side. They couldn't enter the farm while the tree still stood. The barrier of the hamadryad's merely kept them invisible.

Cali tried to focus her thoughts on her training. After Varsna and Artemis' warning, it was increasingly difficult.

"Cali," Arastoo's voice broke through her reverie. She stood, staring into nothing, on the grassy field for training. "Do you need to take a break? We are all here to learn and grow cohesively together. We are here for you in this, if you need ..."

"I'm fine," Cali said, a bit harsher than she intended. She lifted her chin, driving the point home.

Thankfully Arastoo didn't seem to catch it, or care. He nodded and continued his talk about the benefits of weaponry being at your less dominant side and the reasoning for the daggers at their left side. It had been two days since the incident at Varsna and the visit of Artemis. Word spread of Ophelli's death, but there was nothing known about Cali's involvement, just as Natasha had promised. Not that it made Cali feel any better.

The trainees would approach her with a bit of awe that she had survived against Erinyes, last of the Furie's, Hunter of demi's. It made Cali sick that her unknown failure was being perceived as some sort of twisted turn of fate. No one knew if any effort was being made to find him. Natasha was serious when she told Cali to keep herself in check and not let the truth of what happened at Varsna cloud the hope of the demi's. The sudden arrival and departure of Artemis had turned the tides of gossip through the Farm. Natasha also found it best not to talk about Artemis' warning, instructing Cali to follow this order to the letter. *And the secrets continue.* Cali's lips formed a grim line as she stared off into the forest again. To make matters worse, Cali had found out this morning that Maurico had been captured in Varsna. *If you had just listened to James ...*

"Hey Cali." Garwin poked her shoulder, his one eye gleaming at her. "This is Huratio, he's Panthos' cousin, brought on the other day. He is from Turkey. Huratio, Cali ..."

Huratio nodded in acknowledgment of Cali but said nothing.

"He's training with our omáda since Ophelli died." The cyclops' ability to have no emotional connection to anything unnerved Cali. She knew that, as Maechon had told her, cyclops were known for their to-the-point wording, but it still stung. Cali tried to keep her face even as the guilt pushed to her throat.

Cali studied the faun. He clearly had been training all his life for this moment, his muscles thick and ready. Blythe sauntered up beside them and surveyed the monstrous faun with unimpressed eyes. New scars, bruises, and stitches covered the exposed skin of her face, arms and chest, matching those that were already there. She seemed to revel in the discomfort her tank top gave Cali in showing her wounds. Maechon trailed her to the edge of the group; his wide eyes twitched at every blow of a blade.

"And with that, use of the weapons will strictly remain under the watch of your instructor's. We do not need to overwhelm the healers on the first day of you using steel against each other." Arastoo tapped the butt of his spear into the earth. "Blythe, you will continue to partner with Cali."

Blythe narrowed her eyes at Cali as she stalked forward. Today would be the first sparring with real steel, at least for Cali's omáda. Others were much farther ahead, but since she and Maechon held the least experience, their group was considered 'behind.' Cali rested her sweating hand on the hilt of her bronze-hilted sword as it rested against her hip.

Arastoo continued to divvy out partners. "Garwin and Huratio. Maechon, with Griffin. Cali, this will be slightly different from battling with wooden weapons. Huratio, I know you came from a battle already, so this should be no different. Although this is training, you still may be injured so I would ask that you all take this seriously. Please stand in your positions."

Blythe took her spot opposite Cali, the others followed suit, standing about six or so feet from each other taking their practice combative positions. Cali held her sword in her hand as she did with her wooden one. The weight of this real blade James gave her was the same, but the hilt felt less comforting than the smooth handle of the practice weapon. She tried to will herself to stop sweating and stood opposite Blythe.

Blythe's own blade, *Nordfos*, seemed to reflect every piece of light. There were few weapons Blythe could wield without feeling the intense pain in her body—or so she claimed—due to the gods cursed gift on her heritage. Her father, Hephaestus, had been the skilled craftsman of Olympus. She took after his skill and looks. With the skill of crafting elaborate weapons, Blythe carried the weight of his curse. It was said she could wield the weapons she made, but the pain would be excruciating with each blow. A gift from Zeus to his least favorite child, Griffin had told Cali once. But Blythe was nothing if not resilient.

Their eyes met. Blythe's face was lit with a dark rage that made Cali's hands clammy against the cold hilt of her blade. Cali's fingers thrummed with excitement that hadn't yet reached the rest of her body. It confused her, but she focused on Blythe. Arastoo gave the signal to begin. Blythe would practice offense and Cali defense.

Cali blocked the first blows from Blythe with relative ease. Blythe's face remained passive, unchanged as she continued to stare Cali down. Each swing ricocheted up Cali's arm, but Cali held firm.

"Switch!"

Blythe pulled back her blows and allowed Cali to step forward on her. Cali's swings felt less enthusiastic than Blythe's as she brought her blade around. Blythe danced back, expertly blocking each blow.

"Cali, you have to take this seriously," Arastoo chided, driving his spear into the ground to make his point. "Blythe can take the hit and respond in kind. Garwin ... you would not be nicked by the blade if you held it properly. If you cannot stand the scratch, go see the healers."

Cali moved her feet with her sword, driving Blythe back to her starting position, bringing her blade around a bit harder each time. Echoes of steel against steel rattled in the air. Something in Cali overcame her guilt as the ringing built between them. Although having never used her sword as a real weapon before that moment, Cali felt it as an attachment of her limb. The thought startled her—but also triggered something in her that made her alive. Her training must have paid off because her blows became surer.

Blythe stepped farther back, even as Arastoo called to switch again. She continued to block the blows Cali dealt, even with Arastoo's second pointed command in their direction. Cali ignored them. Whatever it was that made her feel the attachment to the weapon, pulled at her soul—making her vengeful and ... excited. All her senses heightened, and she narrowed her focus.

A sneering smile crept across Blythe's face. She caught the change and switched her tactics. She threw herself at Cali with fervor that drew Cali back to reality. Cali stepped back quickly in surprise, her volleying blows turning defense as Blythe railed on her.

"Blythe ..." Arastoo's voice faded as Blythe continued to bring her sword down on Cali again and again. The once unity Cali felt with her weapon faltered. Her training took over as she ducked to barely miss the singing of the blade near her good ear. Blythe was like an animal, ignoring Arastoo's demands to fall back.

Cali's blade hit Blythe's hard, shuddering paint to her shoulder. Cali slid it down to the hilt, clipping Blythe's knuckles which started spurting blood. Blythe didn't seem to realize this, but Cali was taken aback at her own actions and faltered. Pulling her sword back to herself with both hands, she opened her mouth to apologize, but Blythe came at her again. Cali blocked the blow directed at her face. Blythe stood right in front of her, inches, as she pushed her sword up, pushing Cali's with it. Cali gritted her teeth and glared at Blythe, trying to push back down with her weapon. Their faces were inches from each other.

Blythe's smile grew wider, and she winked.

"You had this coming, Mixie."

A cold feeling rushed into Cali's stomach, followed by a surging, horrible pain in her side. Looking down in delayed horror, Cali saw Blythe release one hand from her sword and dug one of her daggers deep into Cali's side. The bronzed hilt slipped from Cali's grasp as Blythe stepped back, leaving her dagger in Cali's side and drawing her blade back to her.

A collective gasp and murmur broke out among a small crowd that gathered around them.

"*Blythe*!"

Arastoo's rage filled the air. Cali swayed as the dagger stuck from her side. She looked up at Blythe, but she had already turned back towards the shack, parting the small circle of onlookers. Her knees buckled, but Arastoo and Garwin caught her before she hit the ground.

"Bring her to Iolo. Now!" Arastoo demanded, handing Cali to Garwin as the blood began to flow from the wound. He snapped his fingers at the two other centaur leaders who stood with their groups. "Everyone else, back to training. Chear, Hok ... now!" Arastoo's tail flicked behind him as he raced after Blythe towards the shack. Cali tried to stagger from Garwin's arms but pitched forward, only to fall back into them. He picked her up just as she began shaking and rushed her to the healer.

***

It took Cali the rest of the week to heal from her Blythe-induced injury. In that time, Natasha had upped training regime, and James and Auto remained unseen by everyone. Cali was quickly mending thanks to the skills of the healers, sisters Iolo and Becca. They were the twin daughters of Asclepius, the healer of the demigod's cursed with mortality. Although not able to heal as efficiently as their revered father, they could still mend wounds and injuries in triple the time natural or modern medicine could.

Blythe was sent to the Hamadryads as punishment, which

Auto insisted was not a severe enough punishment. Cali felt no punishment had been needed, especially as her own feelings of guilt had abated the moment the dagger struck its mark. Maechon and Griffin took turns sitting with Cali as she recovered. Griffin insisted the punishment for Blythe was not so harsh and was confused as to why she would have hurt Cali in the first place. Maechon on the other hand brought practicality. He insisted that he would bring books to help Cali understand her history, the history of the Farm, and as much as he could fill in between. There was some light history training that the oldest centaur, Chear, and faun, Moriander. There were even some translated stories from the Hamadryads; although Cali never understood what they were saying in their wispy accents. Cali had a hard time keeping up with the information—there were too many names, too many places, and in general far too much of it all together. Not that any of it mattered now.

"Thanks for putting this together, Maech," Cali said as they sat on her bed together and delved into one of his books. "I doubt I'll remember any of the names, but it's still nice to have a face to a name."

Maechon sat at the end of her bed, flipping through a book of crudely drawn images that he'd put together to simplify the history and family ties of the Greek and Norse Realms. Of the Realms, these two had the longest history of rivalry. Cali studied the book's drawings and names, tracing the face of the Norse goddess on the page. *Freya*, the name below read.

"I-I-I ..." Maechon took a deep breath," I'm not a goo-good artist. I w-w-want to help if I ... if I can."

"I think it's easier to understand this than Chear's droning on and on." Cali flipped through some pages till she landed on several sketches of crude, gargoyle-esque creatures. *kaoti.* That was their name. Cali remembered Auto saying it at one point, but she didn't understand what it meant. What *they* meant.

The dead army of Chaos: her stolen souls, her soldiers. The horrifically dilapidated creatures that flanked the Furie, Erinyes in Varsna. Cali's fingers tightened on the paper, but she relaxed when she noticed Maechon's worried expression. "You seem to have captured them nicely."

Maechon nodded. Cali flipped back through the book for him, landing on the name *Hebe*. Below his name were the words: *Servant of the gods.*

"Your dad?" Cali said, studying the drawing that was done with a bit more detail than the rest. Maechon nodded again, the pink returning to his cheeks. "He's very good-looking." Maechon turned crimson, and it was Cali's turn to grin. "He also looks very kind—I suppose you take after that."

She continued to flip through the pages. "Lots of ... promiscuous behavior happening between these guys." Maechon gave a side-eyed-knowing glance. "Makes you wonder why they made the rule of fraternizing with the humans in the first place since they just broke it."

"R-rules ar-r-re ... rules are m-meant to be b-b-broken?" Maechon grinned. "I j-just hope it h-h-helps ... helps you un-understand who you are." He paused. "I kno-know how c-confusing it can be." He began to shove some unfinished drawings into his bag, his shoulders hunched as he kicked his feet absently. "W-when I came, after M-m-marseille. I wa-wa ... I was afraid and n-nobody u-understood me."

"That hardly seems fair."

He shrugged. "I d-d-didn't understand anyone else either."

"Were you ... afraid when you came here?" Cali asked, pulling her legs into a crisscross on the bed, wincing from the wound. She had found out about Maechon being born in Marseille, France, in 1720. He was told only several weeks before, by his dying mother, that he was the son of a god. He was *collected* right after her succumbing to the plague by James. She wondered if it was easier—the knowing. Or if any of the demi's who found out about their heritage had tried to escape it. The thought of what awaited them, that Furie's black stare ... *to safety or to death.* She had also wondered about the time aspect of it but, after getting a very lengthy, confusing response from Maechon, she decided she didn't really care so long as it made sense to someone.

"I-I-I am always a-afraid."

Cali absently fanned the pages of the book. "I get that. But at least you know what your gift is." She gave a small laugh. "I know, I know you're going to say it's Eminent because you're just super, super smart and retain any information given to you—but that's something. And at least you know."

"You shou-shouldn't c-c-c ... compare. W-w-we are all afraid at some p-p-point. W-we c-can be together in that!"

Cali rolled her eyes and stopped on a sketch of a trio of women. *Moirai.* The goddess' of fate and destiny. The ones feared by the gods almost as much as Chaos; or so it was said by the demi's who liked to tell haunted tales around the campfire. Cali felt no one could be as fear-inducing as Erinyes, especially three weaving women supposedly connected by a string. Flipping the page over, she studied the inscription just below the sketch.

"What's an *Immixtus*?" She looked up and noticed another person standing in the doorway. Her skin prickled with an iced rage.

"Look at you two getting all cozy." Blythe leaned against the doorframe, watching them. "Figure out anything exciting about ourselves?"

"Come to finish the job, Blythe?" Cali challenged. Maechon shifted uncomfortably as he clutched his backpack to his chest.

"Hardly." Blythe peeled herself from the frame and stared them down, still not crossing the threshold. "I did what needed to be done. Besides." She raised an eyebrow. "I know just as much about the Immixtus as Maech."

"I didn't ask you," Cali snapped. She shut the book. "Get out."

"So, you aren't interested knowing that they are the god-children of Zeus and Frigg?"

Cali shot a look to Maechon, whose face verified the statement.

Blythe smirked. "The *Moirai,* or the Faytes as some call them, are the reason for the last great battle among the Realms."

"Why?" Cali asked, unable to stop her curiosity from showing, even with her annoyance at Blythe.

"Because the Moirai were created by the ... well, let's say *intermingling* of gods from two of the Realms—two different Realms."

Cali frowned. "Why would that make a difference?"

"Because they didn't know what kind of power a child of mixed Realms could have," Blythe snorted as if it was obvious. "At least in their own Realms, whatever twisted fantasies they played out with the mortals there, they could track and control any power created."

"So, is that why our portal key only goes between our Realms?" Cali felt a twinge of pride in herself for thinking this through and looked at Maechon for confirmation of her assumption. He nodded, beaming. "So, we can go between our own Realm's timeline—but what stopped the Realms from going between each other?"

"After the Realms trapped Chaos, they imposed the Silent Treaty—"

"I know about the Treaty," Cali snapped.

Blythe raised an eyebrow but continued. "Well, miss know-some-things, did you know that the Treaty barred any gods from setting foot on another Realm? That it effectively stopped demi's from being created?"

"So, that's why Chaos trying to kill them?" Cali asked.

"She d-d-doesn't," Maechon replied solemnly. "Normally."

"Normally?" Cali's gut twisted, and she looked away from Blythe's withering glare. "Is she an Immixtus?"

"N-no. Sh-she is the first of us."

Blythe picked at her nails. "At least that's what they *say*." She threw a feral smile in Cali's direction and Cali dug her fingers into her sheets to keep from springing at the girl. "She's supposedly the very first god, there at the beginning and all. Which means she couldn't be an Immixtus."

Cali let out a low breath. "So, the Immixtus are just as dangerous as Chaos?"

"Maybe," Blythe scoffed, "but they haven't been seen for centuries. Some say hidden, some say dead. But I doubt it's the latter." She gave a feral smile. "Not that they could be taken down by a blade, like some people."

"I hav-have to ... have to go to- to t-t-training." Sensing trouble, Maechon shot up from the bed, disrupting the books as he stood.

Without looking back, he said a hasty goodbye and fled the room. Blythe gave a final smirk before disappearing behind a wall of demi's that made their way down the hall. Cali was left at the edge of her bed, the door to her room open, feeling too lazy to get up to close it. Closing her eyes, she dropped back onto the pile of papers and books. "Ouch," she grumbled, rubbing her head that hit the edge of a cover.

"You're recovering well."

Cali cursed as she bolted upright. James stood in the doorway.

"Sorry." He looked unsure if he should enter. "I didn't mean to startle you, I just wanted ... I'll go."

"What do you want?" Cali demanded. Heat rose to her cheeks, but she wasn't sure if it was from anger or from seeing him looking freshly showered. *His hair is still wet ...* Shaking her head she decided to tap into the anger emotion instead.

He had been avoiding her since Varsna, and for good reason. She was more upset that she *wanted* him to be angry with her; she wanted him to be the one to stab her. *Blythe was right, I had it coming.* He stood emotionless in the doorway, staring at her with his cool blue eyes, waiting for entry.

"I wanted to see that you were alright," James said evenly. "But you seem fine, so I'll—" "Wait," Cali almost yelped and then closed her mouth. James stepped into the room, leaving the door ajar. "Wait, I ... I want to talk to you."

"We have nothing to talk about."

"Are you serious?"

James remained at the door, closing it a bit more as he kept his eyes on Cali.

"You ... are always there in my life when things happen, and I don't know why ... .and I just can't take it anymore!" Cali's heart pounded against her chest, staring him down. "I just ... I just need someone who understands."

"I don't know if I can be that person," James said, his voice low. He walked over and flipped through the book of Nordic gods Maechon left on the bed, landing on one whose strong jaw and hair whipped around his face in braids. A deep scar ran across the man's face, almost erasing his nose. *Balder, the god of light, purity, and sunshine. Deceased.*

Cali blinked and looked up at him. "Did you ever get to meet him?" she asked carefully, knowing some of them were lucky enough to know their god-parents and their human parents. Some of the demi's, mostly fauns, even had the opportunity to train with their parent before being rushed off to the safe zone of the Farm and sheltered away from the noise that was Chaos.

"No," James shook his head, still studying the chart, and then switched to look at the Greek family tree. "He died when I was born; killed, actually. By Loki. Several hundred years ago."

"Loki is Griffin's dad ...." Cali intended to say, *'how could you be with someone who killed your dad?'* She bit her tongue instead.

"It's not always that simple."

Cali thought about Griffin's gift of touch. *Griffin wouldn't ...*

"And it's not like that," James said as if reading her thoughts.

"I didn't ..." Cali flushed and snapped the books closed, wincing as she pulled herself off the bed to place them on her dresser. "Griff said your talent was invincibility."

James gave a half grin. "Invincible?" Cali rolled her eyes. "But, no ... I can't be hurt."

"Okay." Cali drew out the word and raised an eyebrow at him. He pursed his lips and stepped away from the bed as she came back to where he stood. "Like ... emotionally?"

"Physically. I can't physically be injured in battle with the weapons of ... humans and most gods."

"That must come in handy." Cali patted her future scar. "I know we can't pick our gifts, but it would be nice to have at least one. Maechon said that everyone has *something*. What's the point of being a demigod if I don't get any powers, even if it is Eminent?"

"Having power isn't everything. It won't change—shouldn't change—who you are." He turned on his heel and made for the door. "Besides, you'll have time to figure it out."

"Now I have time?"

"I guess." He shrugged.

"Blythe said I just need to not overthink it."

"Well, Blythe is the one who stabbed you."

Don't say it. "Like you haven't thought about it?"

"Maybe once or twice." He looked over his shoulder at her and Cali could have sworn he was actually, truly smiling. It infuriated her. Everything he wore made him stand out as this handsome, charming man. *Perfect for luring unknowing teenage half-gods to a fate worse than death*, Cali mused, digging her fingernails into the palms of her skin. "But if I wanted you dead, Cali, you would be dead."

"Great, wonderful to know," Cali muttered. She whipped around and began straightening the rumpled duvet in an attempt to keep her hands distracted. "And here I thought we were finally becoming friends ..."

"Griffin."

"What?" Cali placed her hands on her hips and turned. Griffin poked her smiling head around the door, ignoring the fact her boyfriend and friend were standing alone in her friend's room. "Griff—hey. What's up?"

"I'm glad I found you both at the same time!" she said, without missing a beat and nearly singing out the words. "Tash is looking for you."

James grabbed the handle and moved to pass Griffin's beaming figure. She placed a pale hand on his chest, stopping him.

"Both of you."

Chapter Thirteen

"No!"

Cali sat silent and shocked between James and Natasha. The former stood face to face with the leader of the Farm. Rage and firm resolve emanated from both.

"That is the stupidest idea I've ever heard," James growled.

"It's not really in your nature, or position, to question an order," Natasha said, staring James down. They matched each other's height and could give a death glare like none other. Cali wondered who would win in a match between them, but another part of her didn't want to find out. "Blythe has it out of her system, and from Iolo it sounds like Cali is almost completely on the mend. There's really no reason that this won't work."

"You're basing this off the word of a goddess who wouldn't even stand by you when it mattered." Cali realized James must be talking about Artemis. It had been eight days since the goddess walked through the portal. Cali hadn't been sure *how* she had, or if the gods of Olympus held keys of their own, or perhaps, the goddess had been right and the Totem tree was truly dying which meant anyone, threat or not, could come through the barrier.

"Artemis has no reason to lie," Natasha snapped back, her voice losing calm. "And if we do not get the map now, Erinyes will, or it will get lost in time again and we will spend centuries looking for it ... *again.*"

James rolled his shoulders, but Cali sensed he was far from defeated. "She shouldn't be allowed to go."

"No, she shouldn't," Auto agreed from the chair opposite Cali. Cali watched as his foot tapped the floor. *He's nervous.* She tried not to let that thought affect her nerves. In her study of Maechon's more simplified version of history, Cali discovered Autolycus' heritage as being the son of Hermes. Auto had tried to live up to his father's role as messenger, but instead fell into using his gifts for more nefarious purposes. Thievery. The former god of theft didn't take his eyes off Cali as he spoke, and she shrank beneath his stare.

"Cali is the only one who knows the grounds," Natasha insisted, crossing her arms.

James shook his head. "You know I know the area way more than Cali does—she's never even been!"

Been where? Cali bit her lip as stared between them.

"She'll know where to look."

"I met Aliax there many times—she shouldn't have to go."

Oh no ...

"She's going with," Natasha said firmly. "End of story."

James' lips curled into a silent snarl, but he stepped back. Rubbing his forehead, he stepped back and leaned against the chair Cali sat in. "What is this really about Tash?" he demanded; hand still mangled in his curls as he frowned back at the leader of the Farm.

"There is no double meaning to her going," Natasha replied, her eyes narrowing. "I truly believe she will be the best help in finding the map."

The map. "What map?" Cali said, finding her voice. They all looked at her. "The map Artemis was talking about? That's what we're getting?"

Natasha nodded solemnly.

"Why is it so important?"

"That's not important right now," Natasha replied, interrupting Auto's attempt to speak. She relaxed her shoulders and lowered her arms to her side. "What is important is that it is retrieved and brought back here."

"So, you won't tell me." Cali frowned and matched Natasha's glare. "Fine. But why can't the other gods, like Artemis, just go get this precious, secretive map? Why does it have to be us?"

Auto laughed, bitter and quiet. "That is the question, isn't it?"

"The gods and goddesses are unable to intervene with the course of mortals, or demi's since they are half-mortal," Natasha said. "Unless one of their own higher deities, like Zeus, allows it." She stroked her chin thoughtfully. "There are only a few portals even still left in the Olympian Realm, fewer keys to open them, so we are on our own in this."

Several questions jumped into Cali's mind at once. *What happened to the other portals? To the keys? What happens after we get the map?* But by the look on Natasha's face, Cali knew she would get vague answers; if she received any answer at all.

"So," Cali said after a moment, stretching her fingers out from their tightened fists. "Will you at least tell me where we are going?"

A mischievous smile played across Natasha's lips. "A place you have always dreamed of going." Cali's stomach fluttered. "To Rome."

***

First steps.

Cali stood against the wall just near the black door that would lead them to Rome. Roro and Blythe stood opposite her, both silent as they waited for James to come with the key. Blythe kept staring at Cali, but Cali refused to give her the satisfaction of seeing her fear.

Thankfully, the sweat only clung to her lower back, and the long coat she wore draped over it. She leaned her head back and closed her eyes, thinking of her father's words. She had always imagined her first trip to Rome would be with him—to one of the museums he partnered with. Or that she would have gone alone, after graduation, before school. Never in a million years did she imagine she would be going covered in weapons to search for a mysterious item with the help of demigods. *And to think, you're one too.*

She brought a finger across the small dagger that rested in its place against her left side, as was the custom of Greek fighters. It curved slightly and pressed awkwardly into her side. She barely had training with her real sword and was not as good with daggers as the others, but she liked the fact that she now had something there in case she needed it. Her other hand rested on the sword at her side. Each finger tapped it lightly, in rhythm, as she waited with the others, her breath matching each beat.

"Scared?" Blythe sneered.

Cali lowered her chin and met Blythe's mischief-filled eyes. "No."

Blythe laughed and beside her, Roro shook her head but remained silent, eyes closed. Blythe stepped across the hall and stood in front of Cali; her head cocked like a predator. "Is this your good ear, Mixie?" The hair on Cali's neck stood on end as Blythe leaned forward and whispered in her right ear. "Because you know what? I think you're terrified."

"Why do you keep calling me that?" Cali demanded, her fingers finding a rest on the sword at her side. It lay hidden beneath the long coat she chose to wear, but it was still there.

A strange comfort rippled through her arm at the contact. *And what are you going to do with that? Kill her?* Cali bristled at the idea.

Blythe's gaze flicked to Cali's hand, and she stepped back with a sneer.

"Don't even think about it," she hissed.

"I get it, you hate me." The wound in Cali's side hummed as she glared back at her. "Then why not just leave me alone?"

"Leave it be, Blythe." Auto growled as he moved in beside Cali. Blythe turned away from Cali and went to her post beside Roro. She shoved the dagger she'd silently slipped into her hand back in place at her side. Auto shook his head, eying Blythe warily as he stood beside Cali. "I'm sure she wasn't intending to use that." He didn't sound convinced at his own words.

"Sure," Cali muttered. She looked down at her shaking fingers as they hovered over her blade.

"Cali," Auto said, his voice quiet, but earnest. Just over his shoulder Cali could see Natasha and James walking towards them in the flickering shadow of light. "I need you to promise that you'll listen to James. So that you make it back ... here ..."

"Of course ..." Cali said, a bit taken aback at the urgency behind Auto's cold blue stare.

"Promise."

Her skin prickled as if burned. "Yeah, I'll ..." She heard the muffled sound of Blythe snort in laughter and her face heated. "I promise, I'll behave." She ground out the last words.

Auto frowned. "That's not what I—"

"Are we ready?"

Natasha dusted her hands together and looked between them, her eyes lingering on Auto with an unspoken question. But he didn't meet her gaze. James stood at her shoulder, the muscles in his jaw tight.

"Cali, Roro, Blythe—yes?" All three girls nodded. Natasha's

lips formed a thin line as James moved past her, key in hand, to the black door. "You will have two hours upon arriving in Rome to find the map. After that, the weather is predicted to turn rough. This will drive many tourists away and draw more unwanted attention to you – as well as your weapons."

"Do you think we'll have to face any kaoti?" Roro asked, her dark eyebrows pulled together as she listened to Natasha.

Kaoti. Cali shivered at the mention of their name. She gripped the hilt of her sword to stop her hand from trembling and stuck the other in her pocket, where it brushed against the piece of paper—the letter—she kept there.

Natasha squeezed Roro's shoulder. "I truly hope not," she said. "But I would suggest preparing for anything."

There was a soft click to Cali's right. James looked over his shoulder at her, then at the rest of them. "Ready?"

She nodded. Although she knew he was asking them all, she felt his eyes go back to her.

"Ready."

The black carvings shifted as he turned the handle and pushed the door open. Without another word, the four stepped through to Rome.

***

For years, Cali had begged her father to take her with him on his trips to Rome. He had often gone to other places in Europe for curating or collecting items for the university's museum. But Rome always tugged at Cali's heart. Year after year, he refused. Now it took everything in her not to cry as she stepped through the door.

As soon as she was through, Cali knew where she was. She

gaped in wonder at the crumbling rock, still noble and standing in a rounded structure. At the bottom of the stadium there were pillars and stones, what remained of the hypogeum—the place that contained the monsters and men that would fight and die before those that watched.

The Colosseum.

Behind her, Blythe closed the door labeled *Staff Only*. Before Cali could take in any of the site further, a group of tourists, led by a boisterous man with a heavy Italian accent, stomped down the hall in their direction.

"And this is the perfect view for those of you interested in how the lions were kept from mauling the adoring fans." The tour guide pointed down and around him. "If you listen closely, you may even hear the echoes of their roars hidden in the ..." his voice was lost behind the shuddering of cameras snapping pictures of everything. Cali grimaced but felt a hidden desire to stay and hear what else the man had to stay. It felt so ... normal.

"Come on."

James strode down the opposite hallway, passing a group of frantic girls that Cali pegged as American. Roro and Blythe flanked him, both of their hands resting close to their weapons that hid beneath the folds of their jackets. With the tourists crowding around the site, there was almost no reason to keep them hidden. No one even looked in their direction. With a sigh, Cali pulled herself from the view of the immense piece of history and followed. He led them down a side flight of steps towards an almost hidden exit at the side between some rocks.

James surveyed the curved streets on either side as they exited. He paused, a frown pulling lines across his forehead. On either side of the Colosseum streets lined with the beautiful architecture that was Rome, there was a steady stream of buildings to their left, and a thin forest to their right. Hordes of cars and tourists circled the Colosseum in endless traffic and noise.

Rome in the early 2000s—*I'm a baby out there somewhere in the world right now.* Cali tried not to think of this aspect of her current reality. Her brain struggled to keep up with the basic functions of the real world of gods and demons, she did not need to know if there was another version of herself running around in time. *But I mean, is there?* She made a mental note to ask Maechon about this at some point.

"The one on the left." James pointed towards the sidewalk. "Natasha gave us two hours; I want this done in one. We need to get in and get out."

Roro and Blythe headed in the direction he picked towards a blur of houses and streets and restaurants. Cali stepped in beside James, but he didn't look at her as they crossed the busy street and down another. From the corner of her eye, she could see James' shoulders pull and then loosen, as if he was trying to relax.

"Everything okay?" she dared to ask.

He didn't look at her. "You shouldn't be here."

She almost tripped over her feet and mumbled a quick apology to an annoyed passing tourist as she steadied herself. "Why? I mean, I know why…I know you're angry at me because of what happened in … to …" Cali couldn't say the girl's name. She blinked several times to block out the flash of memory of her face. "I'll listen to you this time."

"It's not about …" He paused at the corner and ran a hand through his hair. Roro hesitated, throwing a wary look over her shoulder at them as Blythe continued down the next street. He turned to face her but didn't meet her eyes. "You aren't just here to figure out where Aliax hid the map, Cali."

Cali's mouth went dry. "What…what do you mean?"

He shook his head, his lips forming a thin line as his jaw tightened. As if he debated what to say, or how to say it.

"Why am I here?"

"They want to find out your gift," he said after a moment.

Cali blinked. "What?" He didn't say anything. "Is something going to happen here?"

He went rigid. "Nothing—forget I said anything." With a shake of his curls, began to cross the street.

Cali rushed after him, breathless. "What do you mean, never mind? You can't just say that and ..."

"I shouldn't have said anything," he muttered, more to himself it seemed than her. Irritation radiated from his body. As they reached Roro, who gave them a curious look but said nothing as they trailed the street Blythe went down. "Nothing is going to happen because we are getting in and getting out."

Cali opened her mouth to protest, to demand answers, even as her veins surged with anger. But she stopped short at the sight of the massive building encased in glass windows in front of her. She recognized it at once, even before she read the sign. *Museo della curatela.* Her father's curating office was behind those doors. She kept silent, beside her pounding heart, as she followed James and Roro to the side door where Blythe stood.

"Took you long enough," she said with a smirk.

Removing a small dagger from her belt, she snapped the badge lock in two and the door jolted open. Grinning, she turned to the others, pulling the door wide. The pride on her face froze when the alarm began to sound.

Chapter Fourteen

"Why the hell did you do that?" Cali demanded.

Blythe shrugged and began waving her hand to get them through the door. They filed into a large gray hallway. Blythe's smile grew as she crossed the hall and pulled the fire alarm. Lights began flashing and chaotic noise filled the hallway they stood in.

Cali threw her hands in the air. "Stop doing that!"

Doors opened, and employees began to stream down the halls in confusion, heading to the exit markers and stairs. Blythe shrugged as she hid her knife away. "This will allow for the safety of the staff in case of trouble."

"Yes, but this isn't just any building, Blythe! It holds priceless artifacts." Cali side stepped a frantic woman who made her way to the door they had just entered. "If the fire alarm goes off, if any alarm goes off—"

"The units would lockdown." James caught on and glared at Blythe in frustration. "We have to move."

She ignored his look as she made her way up the hall, dodging employees and keeping her head down.

"Buddy, you told me this would work," she insisted as they trailed her. "Since this is your secret mission, why don't you tell me what to do next?"

"Now," James looked up one set of stairs and down the other. "Now we move quickly." He stopped and turned to Cali. "Where would he keep it?"

Distracted by everything around her, Cali ran right into him. He grabbed her shoulders and moved her away with a frown.

"Who?" she asked. "What?"

"Who do you think, dumbass?" Blythe snorted from beside her. "Your father. Why d'ya think you were here? For a charming vis—"

James raised a hand to silence Blythe before she could continue. "This is why you're here, Cali." He ducked his head as a man passed by. He caught her eye and gave a small shake of his head, a silent plea for her to ignore his earlier comment.

I won't. She glared at him. "Where would he keep something ... valuable?"

"Haven't you been here before?" she hissed, crossing her arms.

He matched her stance. "We don't have time for this. I only know the layout of the building. I've never been in it. You're here to find it."

"We don't have time for this," Roro snapped.

She's right, Cali, get it together. "If it was ... historic ...important," she stumbled over her words, arms still crossed as she avoided James' glower. "He would keep it either in his office, upstairs." Blythe began to leap up the stairs. "Or," Cali said, holding up a hand, "It could be in the curators room, which is in the basement with the Greek statues. If it's important, he would keep it on the shelves of Athena ..." She cleared her throat as the at memory of her father talking about his treasured possessions. "That's what he called his work in-progress shelves."

"Great." Blythe rolled her eyes. "So, we split up ... again. Mixie comes with me."

"There is no way in history that's happening." James lowered his voice as two round men in suits pushed past him down the hall and through the exit. The hallway was empty now, save for the blaring siren and the red and orange lights blinking in tandem. "You and Roro will go to the curators room; Cali and I will check the office."

"Don't have as much fun as last time without me," Blythe snarled. James stepped between them before Cali lunged at her.

"Blythe let's just go," Roro insisted from her position on the stairs. Her eyes danced with an edge of fire that made Cali's stomach churn. The impending feeling of dread began to creep over her skin.

Before she could dwell too much on the feeling, James grabbed her elbow and pulled her up the stairs behind him. Employees still streamed down the stairs, some that, to Cali, held a familiarity behind with them. James' vice grip on her arm yanked her up to keep from tripping on the stairs.

"I can get up the stairs myself," she said, pulling her arm away.

He didn't look at her as they reached the landing. The siren still blared every few seconds and lights flickered.

"I was just trying to help," he said, surveying the floor for any stragglers.

"You could help by telling me what you meant before?" Cali winced as her side spasmed. Thank whatever god we are at the top. Even with the side pain, she couldn't help but push a little more. "Do they really think throwing me into this is going to...I don't know, trigger some gift?"

"I don't know."

She caught up with him as they started up another set of stairs. "But you know *something*," she managed, grabbing her side. "Why is it so important that I have a gift? What if I'm just an Eminent demi or nothing?"

"You're hardly nothing." He looked at her as they made it to the next landing that stretched into a hallway. "But you are very annoying."

"So are you."

James rolled his eyes, but Cali caught the hint of a grin on his face as they rounded the corner to the hall of offices. She almost choked on her breath as she took it in. They were just as her father had described them. Large, glass-paned rooms with wood paneling made the office spaces seem like they were enclosed in display cases. Each room had its unique look. Some were tidy and clean, while others were strewn with large paintings, fabric, sculptures, and other random items.

"Cali?"

"Hu ... what?" Cali said, stunned.

He nodded to the halls. "I asked which office."

"Oh—um, the first one between the second hallway." Cali pointed as the lights of the fire alarm flashed on the now-empty office floor. The sound on the floor cut, but the lights continued to flash. "We don't have much time." They walked forward through the offices. There were few who still had an artist or two sitting and working as if the world could end around them and they would still salvage the art. Her father would have been like that ... her father. Cali bit the inside of her cheek.

"What exactly did you and my father do together?" Cali asked, trying for a distraction.

James' step hesitated. "Some items he found were stolen from Olympus or artifacts from our history," he replied. "I was assigned to collect any items he found that were worth the gods time."

"And you never met him here?"

"Not here, no," James said, his blue eyes wavering. "Often at the Colosseum. Or further down at a café. He wanted some things...private. Away from you and Miriam, to keep you safe in case...something went wrong. That's why we never met in Athens."

"For how long?"

"That depends on how you think of time." She scowled at him. "Before I began collecting demi's two years ago," he gave her a strained half-smile at her confused expression. "So, maybe five years. Time is tricky."

Five years. Cali knew, based on what Natasha said, that Chaos had been waking up for the last seventeen years. Beginning with killing, then turning the demi's she found. For the past two years the Farm had been built to shelter those outsides of her reach. A safe place for demi's all over time and the Realm. "Where are you from?" she asked, her head tilted as she studied him.

He shook his head, almost smiling. "That is a story for another time." His head inclined to the waiting hall before them.

Cali nodded and blinked several times, trying to avoid his piercing gaze as she turned back to the hall. "It should be right here …"

James grabbed her arm and pulled her down behind the corner of the first office, hiding them behind the tall bookshelf. She could feel his heart beating against her back as he held her close, a single finger on his lips. But it was too late. Three men exited the office, and the one with his face toward the window, caught Cali's eye, and held it.

"Nothing, it was nothing … let's go."

Cali's heart jumped to her throat at the unmistakable, familiar voice that spoke. All three men drifted down the hall in the opposite direction, led by the speaker.

"Come on," James whispered close to her right ear. He peered around the corner before stepping into the cleared hall. Cali remained crouched and hidden; her eyes wide. "Cali—we don't have time for this. Remember what—"

"I remember." Cali was on her feet in an instant.

"I didn't mean that."

I know what you meant. "Let's go." Cali hissed, ignoring his strained attempt to catch her eye.

They passed the first office with the bookshelf and opened the door to the adjoining room. This office was like the rest, with high glass for walls. But the desks, artwork, and a closet shielded most of the room from outside view. The desk sat at the other side of the room, in the middle of large canvases and many, many books on bookshelves. Crossing over to it, she drew her fingers across the items on top. It was scattered with unfinished sketches, notes, notebooks, pencils, and miscellaneous creative utensils.

James had already begun searching the place, but Cali fixed her gaze on the small, family picture facing the swivel chair. A man, a woman, and a small, golden-haired baby with one blue and one brown eye. Her chest began to ache.

I have to get out of here.

"Where would he put it?" James said, his voice muffled at her left. She shook her head and looked at him, dazed.

Papers and books still in hand from the closest shelf, he paused. "Cali, I realize this is hard, but we really—we don't have time right now."

"I know, I ... I know." Cali pulled her focus around the room, searching. "Somewhere obvious. It was his way of showing that people overthink the simple things. Like a joke."

Desk, bookshelves, artifacts, art... She did a quick scan before her eyes rested on a small, single book. She couldn't read the title from where she stood, but it looked familiar.

They both tensed as the doorknob jangled. The door was the only part of the office made from wood, making it impossible to see who was on the other side. James stepped close to Cali and his hand briefly brushed against hers as he gestured for her to get behind him as the door opened. *Not this time.* She wrapped her fingers around the hilt of her sword and threw a wary glance around the room. *Although, Dad will kill me if I break anything.*

And then he was there.

Standing in the room with them.

He didn't turn to look at them as he stepped in and crossed to his desk. Cali wasn't even sure if he saw them, standing together in the middle of the room, staring and silent. Mumbling under his breath, he went to the bookshelf just behind his desk and pulled out the first one on top. The one Cali had seen. She could just make out the title. *Common Sense*, an American book. Even in her heart-pounding anxiety, she almost laughed. He flipped through the book until he came to a folded parchment.

His fingers traced the edges and then he put the book back, all without raising his eyes to see the intruders. As he rounded his desk, he placed it at the center as he made for the door. James' hand closed around hers as they waited anxiously for what would happen next. Cali gasped as Aliax turned his gaze to her. The round glasses slid from his nose, hiding his glistening eyes, before he pushed them back in place. He looked younger, but not by much. *His hair isn't so white...* Cali tried to remember to breathe.

Aliax nodded, thoughtful and wordless, then left the way he came.

***

"Sheesh, who died?" Blythe asked.

Cali scowled at Blythe as she reached the bottom of the stairs in the middle landing. Alarms still flickered, but silence filled the halls. It broke when the doors began to open, and the employees began to file back into the building.

"Enough B," James snapped. "Let's concentrate on that not

happening."

"Whatever. Did you find it?"

"Yeah, we got the stupid map," Cali shot back for James. Blythe raised an eyebrow but said nothing else as they turned to their exit door. Workplace life was about to resume, and they needed to leave.

"Hey, does Dr. Claude know you took weapons from the safe?" one of the employees said as they passed.

"Dr. Claude can shove—"

"Blythe!" Cali and James hissed at the same time, nearly dragging her away from the gaping employee as they made for the exit.

Behind her, Roro hid a smirk behind her hand. "Let's play nice a little longer, girls," she said.

"Blythe started it—"

"Well, I'm ending it—" James' words were cut off by a thunderous crack that reverberated through the building. Screams followed. Hollow, death-filled screeches just beyond the door. Cali recognized the sound at once. She'd heard it only once before—in Varsna. The sound of those creatures—those kaoti—coming at James.

"Dun, dun, duuunnn," Blythe goaded. She pulled her glimmering swords out from where it was barely hidden by the jacket tied around her waist. "Looks like Mixie's friends are back."

Panic racked Cali's body as she frantically grabbed for her sword, but James stopped her.

"No. Blythe and Roro are here for this," he said, nodding to the two warrior women to his right. "You and I need to make it back to the Farm."

"And leave them to die?" Cali demanded. She felt a spurt of annoyed courage.

"Thanks for the vote of confidence, Mixie," Blythe sighed as they reached the emergency exit. Roro rolled her eyes and followed Blythe as she slammed into it. "Woof—it's already gnarly out there—"

"I didn't mean—"

Chaos from the streets silenced Cali as they burst through the doors. Storm clouds built fast in the sky, pulling wind from all directions. Lightening crackled like veins in the sky, followed closely by thunder. From their left, dark mist began pouring out of the sparce forest, hedging the city. Locals and tourists alike stared up at the sky and pointed, many exchanging angry glances at the turn of the weather that would ruin their day. Cali hoped that would be all it ruined.

"To the Colosseum! Go!" Roro jerked her head in the direction of the building across the street as she drew her blade. Blythe hissed as she spun to face the darkness.

The screeches of the kaoti filled the air. Rain began to pelt down. Mayhem launched at the same time. Tourists and locals rushed from the sudden downpour into the safety of buildings and underpasses. Some pointed in the direction of the darkness, others just trying to escape the rain. The historic streets reverberated with the sounds of the screams, both from humans and kaoti. Windows shook and telephone poles swayed dangerously in the shadowy wind.

Cali watched as it crept forward and enveloped the surrounding streets in darkness. From the corner of her eye, she saw the stealthy and fast figure of Roro moving toward the monsters, tearing through the street like a dark tornado. Blythe followed, a gleaming sword in her hand. They moved so fast that Cali hardly realized they had left her and James' side.

She gasped as James grabbed her forearm and yanked her to follow him. "I said I can—"

"Then move, Cali," he shouted, his voice barely reaching her over the sound of the wind and screams in the air. "We have to get the map out of here."

Something in Cali snapped to life. As if in slow motion, she took a step to the malady before her, as if she knew what she had to do and exactly how to do it.

She felt it in her then—the yearning. The desire for the fray. She was made for this—

A crack ripped up the street, and Cali looked over her shoulder to follow its length as it crept through the Earth. It stopped just in front of Roro and Blythe's feet as the kaoti reached them. A deep crevasse formed that crawled up the side of the building and swallowed the first two creatures that reached it.

"James ..." Cali watched in horror as the earthquake rattled the buildings around them, shattering windows, and cracking walls. Cali had no memory of her father ever telling her of such an event happening when he was there. *Her father.* Fear rippled through Cali as she looked to the curator's building. Windows had shattered, but it stood. From the corner of her eye, Cali saw Blythe grab Roro from toppling into the cracked street.

"Keep moving!" James shouted at her.

Cali turned from where the two demi's stood at the crumbling street, slaughtering the kaoti, and followed James. More kaoti lashed out of the blackness towards them through the trees. The sky cast darkness over Rome, and the rain made it almost impossible to see where they were running. Cali tried to ignore the pain of her sword slapping against her soaked thighs. They reached the staff door to the Colosseum and James yanked it open. Cali hesitated, looking back for a split second, before he grabbed her arm and pulled her through just as a kaoti lunged for her.

Chapter Fifteen

An announcement garbled over the speakers as they staggered back into the Colosseum. James straightened and began to search the pockets of his coat, his sword still in hand. Heart hammering and breathless, Cali brushed strands of hair from her face and faced the door.

"We have to help them!" she said as the door rattled with the impact of one of the beasts.

"We have to get the map out of here," he replied. "Where is—here."

Cali turned to face him, then side stepped into his path as he went for the door, key in hand. "We can't just leave them," she growled, surprised at herself. "Those things will kill them."

James' face clouded and rain dripped down his forehead as he stared down at her. "This is what we've been training for Cali—what they've been training for."

She blinked, stunned. "We can't just—"

He shook his head and made to move around her, but she grabbed the arm with the key. "Cali, don't do this again."

Don't do this again. Guilt and rage built up in her chest. *Yeah, Cali, don't do this again – you don't even like Blythe.* She let go of his sleeve and released the too-tight grip she had on her sword by her side. *That doesn't mean she should die.*

His eyes flicked to the door and then he ran his fingers

through his hair with a heavy sigh. "Cali, we—"

"Hey! Hey, you there, you two!" A security guard began weaving through the pillars, a finger pointed at them. "You cannot be here. Evacuation—"

On the other side of the round Colosseum, Cali saw two other security guards look their way.

"Down. Get to the next level."

James was moving even as he spoke. He hoisted himself over the study ledge of the main floor and disappeared behind the rock. Cali followed him. She grunted as she hit the unstable ground. Opposite where they stood, she saw a larger half-cut clearing of stone, and an observation deck to the pits below. James stopped at the edge, ducking down to hide below the ledge as the guards rushed past. He gestured for Cali to do the same.

The ledge they stood on was slick from rain and the gravel loose. She slipped in the mud and James outstretched hand was too late to keep her from falling back into the gladiator's pit.

***

Stars floated around her eyes as she gasped for breath. The rain felt like hail on her skin and her ears sang a silent, humming whine in her head. She squeezed her eyes shut as she tried to focus on the barely audible voice calling to her. Her chest spasmed; her mind tried to remember how to take in air.

"Cali?! Cali, are you okay?" James' face became clearer behind her dazed vision. She gingerly pulled her arms up and touched his face. Her fingers still tingled from her fall. As he came further into focus, Cali could see him wince beneath her touch. She pulled back. "Are you hurt?"

"I—It hurts," she rasped out as his whole face and voice became clear. She pushed to a seated position and patted herself down, still breathing a bit shaky. "But I ... I think I'm okay."

James stood and put his hand out and helped pull her to her feet. She swayed for a moment, and she felt his muscles stiffen as he braced her from falling. As she pulled her focus back, she took in the pillars of stone around them where brutal history unfolded centuries ago. It was breathtakingly eerie—like the feeling you would get walking through a graveyard at night. Cali shivered from the feeling and the rain. The rolling thunder covered the screeches of the kaoti outside. If Cali hadn't known better, she may have assumed their screams were just the sound of the storm.

"You good?"

"Yes, yeah." Cali brushed her matted hair from her face and nodded. She met his cool gaze. "James, I'm sorry, I should have..."

"Don't. Just—don't." He began weaving through the columns on the ground level. "There have to be stairs out of here."

Cali put a foot out to follow him and then yelped. He whipped around to face her, his eyes looking everywhere around them for danger. "What? Can you walk? I can—"

"No, it's just ... my sword. I'm going to have a massive bruise ... everywhere tomorrow." Cali shoved down the pain ripping through her side and followed him. The rain seemed to be letting up, but the muddy damage was done as they trudged forward. "Do you think Blythe and Roro will be okay?"

"Let's focus on us being okay, shall we?" James snapped.

I deserved that. Cali still scowled at his back as she followed him around another corner. They met another dead end. He paused and looked up and down the Colosseum's fighting floor with furrowed brows. Rain dripped through his hair and down his face.

"This way."

"Are you sure?"

"Just stay close."

Cali nodded and remained silent as she stepped in beside him. They weaved through the pillars to the opposite end they initially had tried to reach. Cali, who had been taking in the site, ran into James' back when he stopped.

"Somethings wrong," he muttered, more to himself than to her. The crease between his brow returned, and he ran a quick hand over his curls to push them from his face.

"What?" Cali asked, and she looked around as if she would somehow find the answer.

"We went in a circle."

"We went straight."

James turned to face her and pointed in the other direction. "We should have found stairs by now. And this thunder," he glanced at the rolling clouds and the lightening that flitted through them, "these didn't just come from nowhere."

"So, what does that mean?" Cali dropped her fingers to the hilt of her sword.

He frowned and began to walk toward the stairs again. "It means we could be trapped down here for a long time."

Trapped? "What do you—ugh." Cali barely caught herself as she slipped in the mud beneath her boots. As she steadied herself, Cali caught a glimpse of something—someone—who stepped out from behind a pillar. "James."

Beside her, James froze. His body went rigid; ready to pounce and attack. A girl, no older than Cali, and maybe even younger, stood in the drizzle of rain. She stared at them with an unreadable look and dark black eyes. A yellow baseball cap covered her loose, straight black hair. With her jeans, faded t-shirt, and sneakers on she looked like a lost tourist. But there was something about the way she held her chin up, how her shoulders rolled back as she stared at them, that made goosebumps crawl up Cali's arms.

"There are worse places to be trapped than here," the girl said, her voice carrying to them easily over the distance between them.

"Are ... are you lost?" Cali asked, side stepping James before he could stop her. "Did you get separated from your group or parents?"

"Hardly," the girl said, taking a small step forward. Cali hesitated. "But I have been separated from well ... something."

She continued walking toward them. James stepped beside Cali, so close their shoulders brushed. She looked at him from the corner of his eye and saw a strained muscle feather in his jaw. *What is it?* She wanted to ask. Dread began to form in her chest. It mixed with a dark feeling inside her. Something pulled in Cali as the girl flicked her eyes over her. It felt dark and powerful but remained silent. Something behind a door just waiting for Cali to open—

No. Cali pressed a hand to her chest, her other resting on her sword.

The girl tilted her head and smiled.

"A sword won't stop me, son of Balder."

Beside her, James had his hand on the hilt of his blade and nearly pulled it out but stopped. She stopped, leaving several feet between them. "I mean you can try, little boy, but it will just make a mess that I do not have the time to clean."

"Chaos."

Cali shivered at the dangerous growl in James' voice as he said the name. *This is Chaos?* Cali stared at the young girl in front of her in a mixture of fear and confusion. Cali was certain that if they were in a crowd, she would be easily overlooked. *How is this Chaos?*

The black eye turned to her. "Chaos comes in many forms, little one." Chaos' frame shifted and shook, as if she would disappear with a gust of wind. *Is she here?* Cali wondered. "If you prefer, I could become something else entirely—perhaps a little more like what you would expect?" The body of Chaos shifted like a dark cloud and nearly became the vision of Erinyes, then another face, darker and more defined, then returned to the young girl. "But I think not. At least not now, anyway."

"How are you here?" Cali surprised herself with her own question. "I thought—"

"She's an Echo," James murmured. Cali looked up at him. The face of the Collector and savior of demi's had grown pale. *He's ... he's afraid.* The thought made Cali's breath hitch.

"He's right," Chaos agreed. She twirled a loose strand of hair between her fingers. "I'm here—but not all here. After centuries of being trapped, it is nice to have a little freedom these last seventeen years. Even if it is just a shadow." The goddess sighed, then adjusted her hat and looked directly at Cali with her jet-black eyes. "Do not think for one second, being a reflection of myself here, does not make me less powerful, child. All this," she gestured loosely to the sound of thunder and stifled madness outside the Colosseum, "is because of me. Because of me and for me."

"Why are you here?" Cali whispered, already knowing the answer.

Chaos' eyebrows twitched. "How disappointing." She sighed again. "I'm here for my map."

"No." The sword at James' side rang against its sheath as he pulled it out. "As you said, you are not at your full power here – so you can't have it."

Just at the edge of Cali's vision, the world began to shiver and bend. It looked like the darkness and shadows between the rocks of the Colosseum were being pulled. Manipulated. *They are being pulled.* She stepped closer to James – so close their arms bumped. Her fingers brushed against the pocket of her coat and closed. Inside was the only reminder of her past life, of her parents. She stuck her hand in with the letter, her mind working fast as the darkness flickered in her vision.

"Brave little boy," Chaos purred. "I can see how the little Furie of the Farm values you so."

Cold fear clenched over Cali's stomach. *Furie? At the Farm? What is she?*

Chaos took a step forward, scattering Cali's thoughts. James' muscles tightened as he gripped his sword in both hands.

"No," he repeated, his voice coming out like a blade.

Cali moved in front of him before Chaos could take another step. She grabbed his coat tight and stared up at him with wide, pleading eyes. "James, don't." Cali darted her eyes to the shadows that danced in her peripheral. They stayed just there, always at the edge of sight. She let James tense beneath her hands on his chest and she fumbled her grip on him. "Just let her have it—it's not worth dying over."

"It *is*—"

"James!"

He met her stare with rage as she pulled back from him, the folded piece of paper in her hand. "Don't." he snarled.

She winced at the anger rippling across his face as she slowly turned and, with shaking fingers, held the creased paper out to Chaos. Chaos took it with a small smirk and, without looking at it, shoved it into the back of her faded jeans.

"Good girl," she said, her voice shifting into a serene tone that made Cali's hair stand up. "And good boy." She patted the pocket as she stepped back, and the darkness clouding Cali's vision faded. "You make quite a pair. I would stay longer, but," she threw a glance at the grumbling sky, "I think Zeus is a bit angry with me overstaying my welcome. And, as hard as it is to admit," she sighed dramatically and adjusted her hand again, "I am a bit spent."

"You have what you want," Cali hissed. "So, why don't you go back to the hell you came from—"

Chaos was in front of Cali before she or James could react. Her fingers clasped cold and hard around Cali's face. She squeezed, her nails digging into the skin. The longing in Cali built again. It stretched so tight inside her that she thought she would explode.

"You," Chaos whispered, her face inches from Cali's own so that their noses almost touched. "You're not like the others." James brought his blade around in a flash, but she grabbed it with her free hand. Blood seeped from it as she held the sharp edges. James stared, frozen in his spot, appearing unable to pull his sword away. "And I don't mean in an ironic, not-like-other-girls way." Chaos' eyes danced madly. "You're no demigod."

"What?" Cali's breath caught in her throat.

Lightning sizzled around them and snagged against the wall. A crack formed, then spread rapidly down to the muddy Earth and reached for them. Chaos eyes followed the crack as it built and then strained to a stop at Cali's feet. She tilted her head with an impish grin. Her eyes darted back to Cali.

"How *very* interesting." She mused with dancing eyes. "I wish I had time to catch up, child, but we've wasted so much time already. And your poor friends at the Farm are just dying for...well, just dying I suppose is the best way of putting it." Her lips brushed against Cali's cheek, sending shivers down Cali's spine. "Till we meet again, little one."

She vanished. The feeling of her fingers was the only sign she had been there at all.

The rain almost subsided as Cali swayed in place. "James—"

He was already moving. Sword in hand, he bolted to the right where Cali could see a small staircase leading up. The crack that began at the top of the wall stopped as it reached the ground. Not wanting to wait and see if the Earth would open and swallow them, Cali turned and followed James. They raced up the thin stoned stairs into the main hallway of the round building.

James whipped around and caught Cali as she ran. He pulled her back hard into a dark hallway just beyond the door to their escape. *What the ...?* She cursed and pushed back, but James clamped a hand over her mouth and held a finger up to his own. A raspy scream pulled through the Colosseum and Cali's eyes widened. Her hand pulled on her sword. James shook his head as they stood, face to face, still soaking wet. He removed his hand slowly and reached for his sword. She could feel his heart, his breath against her, and, in looking up at him, could see the wild fear in his eyes.

"What did she mean?" Cali breathed, knowing he could hear her. "Chaos. What did she mean about me? About the Fu—"

"What happened outside, Cali?" he interrupted, his eyes searching hers. "And down there just now?"

Cali frowned, her brows pulling together as she stared at him dumbly. *What?* Her heart hammered and, although she didn't understand the question, she felt she *knew* the answer. "What do you mean?"

"The cracks?"

"I don't—what are you even talking about?"

"Cali, you have to control it."

"Control what? What are you talking about?"

"Later." He pushed himself from her and whirled around with a low growl. As if on cue, a figure stood in the dim light coming into the hall they stood in. She was covered in mud and blood, in her element, and stood with a sly smile on her face.

"Ugh, gag me with a spoon. Am I interrupting something?"

James turned to face Blythe as she surveyed them with mischief-filled eyes. "Blythe, they're at the Farm."

Blythe's sneer faded. "Then let's get the hell out of here."

Chapter Sixteen

Even before Cali stepped over the threshold into the hall, she could smell the smoke. It curled up the stairs and beneath the doors to the bedrooms. The smell of flame and fear filled her nostrils as she stumbled into the hall with James and Blythe. James didn't even hesitate as he yanked the key from the lock and bolted down the hall, Blythe at his heels.

Cali staggered against the wall and braced herself with her hand. The other hand clutched the pocket of her jacket. Dizziness washed over her, and she felt weak. Something had drained her. She rested her cold sweat-covered forehead on the back of her hand as she took a shuddering breath. *Breathe, breathe.*

A muffled scream made her jump. In seconds, she pulled her bronze hilt from its sheath and raced past the rooms and down the stairs.

Smoke and soot filled her lungs as she burst from the small shack. Darkness covered the Farm. An unnatural and heavy dark pushed against her as she stumbled forward.

Kaoti, vicious and lithe, clashed against the demi's. The screams of the soulless ripped through the night as they scratched and tore their way across the Farm. They poured in from the shadow and dark of the trees, outnumbering their prey. The cool weight of Cali's bronzed hilt felt like a sad comfort in her hands as she lunged forward. Fire exploded and sent sparks in all directions as one of the barns caught a flame. The olive grove, including the pale, dead Totem tree, crackled with fire. From where she stood, she could see two of the demi's she knew had the Prominent power of ice and water attempting to save the beyond-damaged Totem. Together, the demi's moved, as if dancing, trying to stop the fires from spreading.

Within the light of the flames, Cali saw a large kaoti grab a faun and throw it into the air, into the darkness, as if it were nothing. Another kaoti went for the thin ice-powered demi. Cali staggered forward, already calling a warning, but a cry came from behind her. Before she could turn or react, she was lifted off the ground and thrown back hard.

Her shoulder jammed into the Earth, but she kept a hold of her sword, even as pain coursed through her bones. The kaoti who tossed her towered over her. Up close, Cali could see the traces of humanity behind the dead eyes. But that was a far reach as she stared at the massive deteriorating creature towering over her. The skin was patchy, pale, dark, and stretched unnaturally across the muscles and protruding bones. The rest of the face was smeared, with no nose, no cheekbones, a hollow representation of a mummified corpse. The bloody teeth snarled at her as it reached out, a sickle in hand. The arm was coming down towards her. *This is not how you die!* Instinctively raising her own arm in defense, Cali brought her sword up into the creature in front of her. It met its mark, but barely.

The kaoti reeled back, its screech filled the air as it came at her again. Cali scooted back, unable to stand up to face it, and felt her hand touch something soft. She glanced down and her throat caught. It was the arm of one of the satyr twins, Ottie. His eyes closed as blood ran from a gaping hole inside his stomach. The sight of him paralyzed Cali for a moment. She recovered just in time to block the blow from the sickle with her arm. She matched the scream of the beast with her own cry of pain. Her grip on her blade wavered as the pain shot through her body and blood spurted from the gash the blade created.

The kaoti again pulled the sickle back to strike, but then froze. The head lolled back, dropping to the ground. The body followed in a heap on top of it. James stared down at Cali through a blood-covered face, his eyes manic and shiny in the yellow light.

"You need to get out of here," he said as he reached down to help her up.

Cali grabbed her bleeding arm and pushed herself to her knees, her eyes catching the still figure of Ottie again. She allowed James to help navigate her to her feet, using her sword as a brace.

"And go where?" she demanded. His response was a raised sword, but Cali beat him to it. She whirled so fast that when her blade connected with the kaoti behind her, she found herself covered in blood. The creature's face contorted, and Cali thought she saw pain behind its eyes before it faded. She tried to ignore the pit in her stomach, and the realization that she had killed someone. *Something, not someone. Something, not someone.*

From the corner of her eye, Cali saw Maechon swing a backpack through the air. It connected with a kaoti, that went down. Behind him, Cali saw Blythe finish the creature as Maechon sprinted over.

"Cali!" he cried, clutching the backpack.

"Maech—are you alright?" Cali asked. He nodded, eyes wide through his cracked glasses. "Where's Griffin?"

Before he could respond, a blast burst through the air. One barn teetered, engulfed in flames. The fight became more visible with the fire. The kaoti had engulfed the Farm. They picked off demi's one at a time, either killing them or pulling them into the dark. Natasha stood near the crumbling barn, a black sword and an axe in her hand. Her opponent matched her height and strength. Even as the two danced between the shadows and light, Cali recognized the rival Natasha fought. *Erinyes.* Cali's blood went cold. *But how? How did she get here? How did any of them get here?* The black blade in Natasha's hand shimmered, sparking at each connection, and seemed more smoke than steel. It looked so like the weapon in her opponent's hand that Cali for a moment thought Natasha had disarmed Erinyes. She could only see their shadows as they drifted, performing a horrifying dance of flame and violence. Her brain felt like it was on fire, and her ears thundered in her skull as she tried to focus.

She lost sight of Natasha as a scream from behind caught her attention. She looked in horror at the face of a kaoti, who grabbed Maechon. It dragged him by his backpack across the ground. Cali pulled her blade up with her good arm in a swift movement and brought it down on the kaoti's arm, surprising herself and the kaoti with the blow. Maechon cried out as he struggled to free himself from the still-attached arm of the kaoti, He stumbled back as Blythe drove her blade into the kaoti's back.

"Into the forest!" James roared.

"Maech, go! Run!" Blythe screamed, spinning to slice through another kaoti.

Maechon, a small axe in hand, began to make his way to the tree line.

A kaoti rushed Cali and brought its sword back around to her stomach. She pulled back to avoid it and slammed her blade up. The injured arm shocked her to her shoulder, and she almost dropped her sword. She bared her teeth and instead pulled the blade back moving her feet as she had been trained and plunged it forward deep into the kaoti's chest. It let out a hiss that made Cali's skin crawl. Yanking the sword out, she repeated her action as the kaoti fell backward, a blank expression on its face.

She spun to follow Maechon, but he was gone.

"Maech?!" Cali screamed. The light from the fire helped with the weight of the dark. Maechon lay several feet away, the thin fingers of a kaoti pierced his skin as it dragged him across the dirt. Cali took a step toward him. She spun her sword round, cracking the jaw of a kaoti as she dug the blade. The injured arm screamed in pain once again as someone slammed into it from behind, making her stagger against the blow.

Blonde curls flew behind Griffin as she made her way to where Maechon lay, her own sword flashing silver in the night. From somewhere, Cali could hear Blythe's muffled curses and screams. She heard Macehon's name but wasn't sure if Blythe screamed it or if the voice was her own. As Griffin reached the kaoti she severed its head before her body went rigid.

Erinyes suddenly held Griffin's arm; her fingers wrapped tight. Griffin's blade dropped. If she was standing here, was Natasha ...?

No. Cali straightened. *No—*

"*Bedre lykke neste gang.*" The voice was soft and smooth. *Better luck next time.* Erinyes eyes burned with embers of hate and rage as she pulled Griffin back. The voice, so similar to Natasha's, made Cali's hair stand up.

"Run!" Maechon choked out.

"Cali—!" Griffin cried, desperate against the strength of the goddess holding her throat.

Cali could feel the hot breeze in the air. She felt fear and guilt and she stared down the goddess, but she also felt anticipation. That desire. She knew what to do now. It called to her. The gnawing in Cali's chest felt like it would burst if she didn't do something.

Erinyes cocked her head, a predator assessing its next victim.

A crack, like lightning, resonated through the air. It brought a light as blinding as the sun as it shot through the dark and pierced the dark. The noise of slaughter halted instantly.

Something in Erinyes' eyes shifted as she looked beyond Cali. *Fear—she's afraid*. Cali risked a look over her shoulder and saw a tall woman now standing in the field and bow with a quiver of arrows made from elements around her flying in the air, hitting each mark.

Artemis had returned.

Erinyes hissed, drawing Cali's attention back.

"No!" Cali stood up too fast and swayed. Her ears rang to the point where she thought her head might explode. But she still lurched forward with her sword dripping blood between her fingers. It made no difference.

With a snap of her fingers, Erinyes and her kaoti army, along with Cali's friends, disappeared into the night.

Chapter Seventeen

"We have to go after them!"

Cali stood at the end of the makeshift table that had been created out of the door to the destroyed centaur's barn. The edges were singed black, and it creaked as she leaned against the wood and stared down across the table at Natasha. She could feel Auto's ever-present, watchful gaze on her from his post at the head of the table. James had informed them all of Chaos' attack in Rome, and that she had taken the map. Cali wasn't sure if he informed Natasha and Auto the reasoning she was able to take it. By the glint in Auto's eye, Cali didn't doubt he knew. She felt no guilt for her actions in Rome, however. Besides the guilt that dug into her gut when Maechon and Griffin had vanished into the shadows with the Furie Erinyes.

Now, hours later, as the smolders of the fires still licked for the morning sky, Natasha had decided to leave the Farm behind. There would be no rebuilding, they would hardly have time to bury their dead. Or at least that is what Artemis said. She stood at the other end of the door-table, all traces of her elemental weapons gone, surveying the destruction with cool, calculating eyes.

All around them the echoes of the battle—*slaughter*, Cali reminded herself—lingered. Many of the instructors were directing those that remained, a little more than half of what had been at the Farm when Cali arrived, to build pyres and bury their dead in the way of their Realm or custom. Songs, low and deep, moved through the survivors. Sad songs filled with pain and sorrow, and maybe a little bit of hope. The centaurs sang the farewell of their people, the Nordic their song of Valhalla, the Greek sang the song of the dead. But mostly, fear still filled the small clearing that once provided safety and a home.

Any illusion that Chaos was not a present threat had been shattered the night before. Cali almost wished she could go back to the days of not believing, of not seeing. *Nu är sagan all*: the words Natasha had once told her had never rung truer. The fairytale was truly over, and now she had to survive a world infested by shadow and nightmare. She could no longer hide behind the strength of her friends or even the magic, and what was left made Cali angry. It provoked the unfamiliar feeling inside of her that was awakening.

"Bold sentiment from someone who could barely handle their first few weeks here," Auto murmured.

Cali faced him. "A lot can happen in a month." She scowled as his eyes continued to twinkle with some unknown emotion. "I don't think that has anything to do with helping the others."

He nodded and fell silent. Natasha shifted in her chair, one that had been brought from the caved-in kitchen of the shack. The rooms and hall remained unharmed for the most part, due mostly in part to the lingering magic of the Hamadryads. The ancient wood nymphs grew as silent as the rest of the open space, besides a small sparkle of light now and then between the shattered tree line. To Cali's right stood Becca, who finished tightening the bandage across Cali's forearm. The muscle was sore, but the healer's power already began the tickling sensation of repair. Becca's face was tight and wan. Iolo, her twin, was one of the seven dead. Several others were still seriously injured. Twenty demi's were taken. Twenty *young* demi's.

"I understand that it may be seen as cruel to, what you may consider, abandon our people to Chaos," she said, picking each word slowly. "But with Chaos taking Roro and the map in Rome —Cali cringed as Natasha spoke— "and with the destruction here. We are not safe. Even if ..." Natasha raised a hand to pause Cali from speaking, "Even if she was just an Echoe of herself. She was there and she took exactly what she needed."

And you let her. Cali didn't know if that was what Natasha meant, but by the cold that leaked into her stare as she stopped talking, she could guess it was. Keeping her chin up, she braced herself against the table and looked at the former leader of the Farm. Becca patted Cali's arm and Cali returned the gesture with a nod.

"Thanks," Cali murmured to the girl as she stepped away. "And Becca I ..."

Becca didn't look directly at her as she shifted to face Cali. She merely nodded, with dulled eyes, and walked to the single-standing Barn where the rest of the wounded lay.

Cali slipped back into her jacket and turned back to Natasha. "It's not right," she said, crossing her arms.

Natasha sighed and ran a hand over her plaited hair. "Be that as it may, we need to regroup." She turned to face Artemis, who remained motionless. "Poseidon is willing to give us the island?"

"Barely," Artemis said with a small sneer. "He will allow a single portal to be created to enter the island only in this century—more specifically, he only wants it within the last seventeen years. He does not trust anything outside of this current of time, especially after Chaos's arrival in Rome."

"He's afraid, you mean," Auto snorted. "That sea urchin is only offering because he thinks he'll lose his powers if he doesn't."

Natasha bridged her fingers in front of her. "Of course he is," she said thoughtfully. "He knows the prophecy as much as any of us ..." she trailed off at Artemis small cough and darted, quick look in Cali's direction.

Prophecy? Cali nearly groaned aloud. One thing she remembered from her father's bedtime stories that covered myths and fairy tales was that there was always, *always* prophecy.

"What prophecy?" she asked, looking at them.

Auto frowned but no one answered. Instead, Natasha stood with a heavy sigh and looked over Cali's shoulder. "Arastoo," she said to the centaur who came up beside Cali. "How do they fare?"

Arastoo shook out his mane, deep lines of sadness tracing his face. "The dead have been buried," he replied, his voice still and quiet. "Those that remain are gathering their things and will be ready within the hour."

"Very good."

Cali looked between the leaders of the Farm, and the goddess Artemis. *So, it's been decided*, Cali mused. *Run away and keep more secrets.* Seeming to guess her thoughts, Natasha turned her silver-streaked gaze back to her.

"This is not a debate, Cali," she said, her voice rumbling low. "And it is not defeat—not yet anyway. Gather your things."

"But—"

"We leave in an hour."

Arastoo placed a tentative, comforting hand on Cali's shoulder. She understood their reasoning, with the songs of sorrow and mourning fading into the soft crackle of flames from the pyres built for the dead behind her. But it didn't make it easy. *Not much that is right is easy.* Cali could picture her mother, hands on her hips, as she lectured her for something or other. A small, sad smile almost pulled at Cali's lips as Arastoo gave a final squeeze and then turned back to the remaining demi's scattered over the ruins.

Natasha crossed around to Artemis and began to speak to her

in low tones, but Auto continued to stay in his spot at the table, his gaze on Cali unyielding.

"What?" Cali demanded, a little harsher than she intended.

He raised an eyebrow, and a faint smile broke into his face. Something about the look annoyed her—as if he knew something that he wasn't saying. She tucked her left hand into her pocket and pursed her lips as she stared back at him. "What?" she asked again. She could feel Natasha's eyes flick back to them, even though she pretended not to listen.

"Do what you have to do, Cali," Auto said and rose from the table with a stifled groan. His sharp ice-blue eyes pierced her. "Do what you have to do."

Cali swallowed the dread building in her throat, unsure of what to say or what he meant. Not that it needed explaining. *Do what you have to do*. Without waiting for him to explain further, or give another riddle, she turned on her heel and stalked toward the crumpled door of the shack.

***

Cali leaned against the door to her room, her head tilted back as she stared at the ceiling. She wasn't sure how long she had been standing there. Auto's words still rippled through her. *Do what you have to do*. She ran a quick hand over her face, under her eyes, to brush away the stray tears. Her muscles ached, especially the one in her still-healing arm. A large crack rippled through the ceiling, not unlike the one in her old room back in Athens. She tried to think what Auto could have meant, what emotion played behind his eyes as he said the word. A challenge? A command?

What I have to do. She sighed and pushed herself from the

door. *I'll deal with it.*

"Nobody else is dying because of me," she whispered, glancing at her shaking, bloody, dirt-crusted hands. Overall, the hamadryads magic had held the structure of the rooms in almost perfect order. Cali tried to ignore this painful fact as she cleaned herself up in her bathroom. Then she grabbed some things and hastily shoved them into the small bag Garwin had given her in her second week. It was just a small brown leather backpack, but it would work for what she needed. *What does someone bring on a spur-of-the-moment rescue mission?* She shoved in an extra shirt, socks, underwear, and toothbrush and tied the top with a shrug.

She slipped into a pair of jeans and a simple white cotton shirt then pulled on the frayed jacket. Finally, she hooked her sword to her belt and surveyed herself in the shattered round mirror above her dresser. She almost laughed. *What would my parents think of me now?* The thought was meant to be a bitter joke, but it jarred her. Clenching her fists, she turned away from the view of herself as a mangled, 21st-century warrior and left the room.

The only things she knew about the evils of humanity were from podcasts on murder she had listened to in zeal for the last two years, but she was not dealing with the evil of humanity so she could not imagine what pain her friends might be suffering. If Natasha and Auto would do nothing—she would do something. Chaos would still be trapped in Tartarus, and she wouldn't expect just one small demigod to do something as stupid as a rescue mission.

But you're not a demigod, a voice whispered to Cali. She shuddered and dismissed the thought as she took a deep breath. Her fingers traced the small, wilted parchment that sat in her pocket next. Her dad's letter was still etched in her mind.

She took a step outside her door and gasped as she ran right into a wall. *Not a wall.* James stared down at her impassively, his arms crossed.

"Shit! You scared the crap out of me," Cali snapped. "What are you doing?"

"What are *you* doing?" Dark, sea-blue eyes bore into her. Even though he still had a bit of scruff and looked immensely tired, Cali was annoyed to notice that he smelled clean. She frowned at him.

"What are you talking about?" She shoved past him and began walking down the hall. "We're all leaving for Poseidon's secret island."

"You know what I mean, Cali." He kept an easy pace beside her. "Let me tell you what I think."

"Please, do," Cali muttered.

"I think you're about to do something stupid."

"Well, I generally do, don't I?"

From the corner of her eye, she saw his scowl deepen. "I think you're going to try to go to Tartarus on your own, like an idiot, and attempt a suicidal rescue mission."

Cali paused mid-step. Her hand levitated over the railing. "Why would I do that?" she asked tentatively, looking up at him.

"Because you're not really one to listen to reason."

A burst of rage rippled through her, and she clenched the rail, swaying. She clamped down on the feeling of unhinged power that began to gnaw at her chest. *Calm down Cali.*

He tilted his head. "Or it's because of guilt."

Without a word, Cali turned away and stomped down the stairs. She wouldn't look at him —she wouldn't give him that satisfaction. James followed her down. The magic that held the shack together felt untethered, and the stairs creaked under their weight. "Saving them won't take away what happened in Varsna—"

Cali knew he had quick reflexes, so she was shocked when he

didn't move away from her slap. Her hand stung with the impact. They both stared at each other. His expression remained neutral, but darkness flickered behind his eyes. *More guilt to add to the pile.*

"I ... I'm so sorry." Cali retracted her fingers and pulled them to her chest.

"Do you feel better?"

"No."

He reached the bottom of the stairs and turned. She followed; her hands fisted at her side. The quaint kitchen in front of her was caved in beyond recognition. It was strange to think just several weeks ago she sat there wanting to leave this place. Now she would leave—but not in the way she would have ever anticipated. James made his way around the strewn cabinets and herbs to the back door. His tall figure was shadowed by the brightness of the day as it creaked in the wind. Cali could just make out the bristling forest hedge of the now unoccupied barrier.

"Are you coming?"

Cali froze halfway between the front and back doors. "What ... what are you talking about?"

"You really think you could just walk into Tartarus by yourself?"

James's hand rested on the frame as he looked over his shoulder at her expectantly. Cali felt the impulse to turn around and run back into the house and hide under her bed upstairs. It was a childish impulse, but it was the only comforting thought in her head. Instead, she met him at the door.

"I ... well." Cali cleared her throat. "I wasn't going to just walk right in."

He raised an eyebrow at her.

"Well, you do have the map, so I suppose it does give you a small advantage."

Cali stared at him in shock. He almost smiled—*almost*. "You didn't think you were that clever, did you?"

Dammit. Cali frowned. "You knew I took it?"

He nodded.

"And ... and you didn't tell them." She jerked her chin in the direction of the front door opposite them. "Why?"

Darkness filled his gaze as he studied her. "As soon as I saw Chaos, I knew she would have already found a way to breach the Farm," he said, his voice strained. "Our Totem tree was already dying, the barrier hardly strong enough—and after Artemis ..." He sighed and ran a calloused hand through his curls. "It was only a matter of time before she struck."

"But why not tell Tash, or Auto?"

"Because they have enough to do with making sure the demi's that remain are safe and prepared for any other attack," he replied. "As long as Chaos doesn't have the map, that's all that matters."

Cali nodded slowly. Then dared to ask the next question on her mind. "And where exactly does the map lead?"

He cocked his head at her. "You were willing to go to the depths of Tartarus with one of the most powerful artifacts in the history of the Realms and had no idea why?" Cali frowned as amusement lit behind his eyes and they stepped outside. On this side of the shack, closer to the edge of the once strong barrier, it was quiet and still. As if nothing occurred to disturb the peace. "This is why I'm going with you."

Cali opened her mouth to protest but was interrupted by a brittle voice.

"Well, well, well, what have we here?"

Blythe leaned against the cracked wood just on the other side of the door, a mischievous grin on her bruised face. The look showed she had heard the entire conversation.

Cali groaned, but it only made the smile grow.

"Blythe," James said, his voice low in warning as Blythe detached herself from the doorframe and sauntered up beside Cali. Blythe ignored him as she surveyed Cali from head to toe.

"So, our little Mixie had the map all along." Blythe let out a low whistle. "Who would have thought you could think on your feet like that?"

"What do you want?" Cali snapped, shouldering her bag higher as she scowled at the demi girl.

"How'd you do it?" Blythe asked, cocking her head, ignoring Cali's question.

"I ... traded it."

James frowned. "For what?"

"Your soul?" Blythe snorted.

"My parents' letter," Cali mumbled. She clenched her fists as her eyes dared Blythe to push the subject. Cali knew how childish it had been to hold on to the letter through training, through meals, through the life she lived on the Farm. But it had given her comfort— a hope. Anyway, it had come in handy. *And now, I have nothing more to remember my parents by*. She shook this thought away.

"And you don't know what it does?" Blythe pushed, a goading smile on her lips.

Cali stared at her, but Blythe merely laughed. "You don't know!" she crowed and silenced herself, only barely at James' warning look.

"I assumed it was a way for Chaos to get out of Tartarus," Cali growled, shoving a hand into her pocket and turning on her heel to the barrier before she reacted any more to Blythe's taunting smirk. "If it was worth her destroying Rome and killing the ... demi's, then I assumed it would be important."

"But you don't know how it works."

Cali glared as Blythe began to walk beside her. James took up her other side, throwing a last look over his shoulder the closer they moved to the edge of the barrier.

"No, I don't," Cali snapped. "You don't have to come." *Please, don't come.*

"Oh, I'm coming, little Mix-a-lot," Blythe said, grinning as Cali groaned aloud. "Sounds like a *really* stupid plan with very little thought process involved, so you'll definitely be needing me."

"Before you two kill each other," James interrupted as Cali retorted to Blythe's taunt. "I agree that Blythe should come with." Cali stared at him in horror. "You can take offense if you want, but we need her."

"Yeah, you need me." Blythe threw an arm around Cali's shoulder, which Cali immediately shrugged off in disgust. "You idiots ready for this?"

Cali looked at James as they paused at the brink of the barrier. No lights flickered in the wooded area, but Cali could sense the eyes of the Hamadryads on them. There was no need for their protection anymore, for there was nothing on the Farm left to protect.

A muscle in James' jaw twitched as he looked between Blythe and Cali, then back at the forest. *Am I ready for this?* Cali tried not to let the uncertainty show on her face as James straightened his shoulders and stepped into the forest. Blythe let out a heavy sigh and followed him in.

With a final look behind her, Cali turned and left the Farm.

Chapter Eighteen

THEY WALKED IN SILENCE for the better part of an hour after they passed through the barrier and into Foloi Forest. Sunlight flickered through the leaves and branches overhead, and the soft chirp of birds and the rustle of small woodland animals made everything seem – for the briefest moment—peaceful. Cali wondered what month it was, but guessed it was late in the summer. She had been taken to the Farm in the middle of June and at least several weeks had passed since then, if not months. She trudged along between James and Blythe as they wandered deeper into the forest. James seemed to know where he was going, leading them East. Cali didn't mind. The folded parchment still rested in her pocket, untouched.

"How do you know where we're going?" Blythe asked, swatting blindly at some flies as they buzzed around her face.

"Chaos is held in Tartarus," James began. "Or at least part of her is—"

"We already know this," Blythe groaned.

"I don't," Cali retorted, ignoring Blythe's annoyed eyeroll. "What do you mean, *part* of her?"

"Well, most of her really," he continued, ducking as he moved aside a low-hanging branch. "Chaos was too powerful to be all contained by one Realm alone. Which is why, at the beginning of the Treaty's signing, there were three gifts given between the

Realms."

"Gifts?" Cali asked skeptically.

"Yes gifts. And not just any items either. Three of the strongest Realms bound themselves together and trapped her in Tartarus with the help of the items. The strong magic between the deities helped bind her there. Then, after they trapped her, they scattered the gifts between the Realms."

Cali frowned. "Why?"

"Because of the *curse*." Blythe emphasized the last word with a look of mock-horror on her face.

Cali grimaced. But to her surprise, James nodded in agreement.

"She's telling the truth?" Cali asked, incredulous.

"Hey—I do that a lot," Blythe whined.

"It was more of a prophecy." James gave Cali a knowing side-eye, even before she groaned aloud at the words. *A prophecy? Really?* "When the gifts were used to bind Chaos, she summoned the Faytes, the first Immixtus, to fulfill a bargain she made with them centuries ago." Cali's eyebrows raised but she kept quiet and listened. "She made them summon a prophecy for her to be released when the time was right."

"And ...?" Cali waited but James just shrugged. "That's it? Do we know when the time is right? What did the prophecy say?"

"I don't know what the prophecy said ... for sure," he admitted with a furrowed brow. "But," he stopped and looked back at her, "I do know, that map you carry is the key to finding the gifts—any place, or any time."

"Tash sent us after the Map of the Void?" Blythe asked. "Damn."

"How do you know all this?" Cali peaked over his shoulder at the still invisible contents.

He shifted away from her. "Your father told me."

Cali stiffened and stepped back. Her skin felt tight. The leaves of the forest crunched beneath her, but she could barely hear them over the thrumming in her head. Blythe was saying something, but Cali turned her head away.

Map of the Void. Cali shoved her hand into her pocket and drew her fingers over the map. James' sharp eyes followed her movements, but he didn't ask to hold it. Instead, he dragged a hand over his sweaty brow as he looked around and stopped them in a sparser part of the forest. Leaves covered the ground, and the trees did not cling so close.

"So, you're saying this wouldn't have gotten me to Tartarus?" Cali pulled the map out slowly and waved it in the air. Blythe looked at it hungrily—as if the very parchment held adventure.

"Maybe," he replied. "But one does not just walk into Tartarus. Especially with a map that powerful."

"You've been to Tartarus before?" Cali almost thought he winced as she asked.

"We aren't going to Tartarus," he held up a hand to stop her and Blythe's poised questions, "not yet. First, we have to find the way to get in."

Goosebumps rose on Cali's arms at the drop in his voice. Beside her, Blythe looked more annoyed than anything at James. She crossed her arms and again swatted at a fly that buzzed around her face.

"So, where are we going?" she demanded.

Cali watched as she caught the fly between her fingers. "And what do we need to find?"

James let out a heavy sigh. "We have to find the first gift," he said slowly. "But for that, we will need the map."

"What's the gift?"

"A key—The Key of Ymir." Clearly seeing Cali's bewildered look, James continued. "It's similar to the key we used to get between our Realms, but this portal key can allow access to any Realm, any time, any reality."

Cali kept quiet, so he explained.

"As you maybe know, we demi's, we are able to go between the North and South without issue." He pointed towards the trees and began walking. "Let's keep moving—this way."

Cali and Blythe exchanged a look before moving in tandem to follow him through the forest again.

"The gods do not have that luxury, and neither does Chaos, for now. The key is one of the gifts that bound Chaos to Tartarus. If she is able to get her hands on all the gifts in the Treaty, she won't need to use her demi's or kaoti to jump between realms and time – through *all* eternity. The dwarf brothers forged it …"

"They prefer the term *little people.*"

James glared at Blythe, and she made a move to pretend to zip her lips.

"The brothers, Brokk and Eiti, created the key by melting down the sickle used to kill Cronus and Ymir. They forged the key as an all-powerful access tool for Chaos to walk across Realms freely and unchecked."

"Um, what?" Cali vaguely recalled the sickle used to cut off Cronus' prized parts and made a face. "So, we are going to find a mystical key used to open time and space that was made from the weapon that cut the creator of time's junk off that is now binding one of the most powerful gods' … power?"

"Eloquently put," James said. "And yes, that is essentially what we are doing."

"Why do we need the key—can't we just go to Tartarus?"

"Since I gave the portal key to the Olympian Realm back to Tash," he replied. "We need some sort of … fast escape if things go badly."

Cali could almost hear Blythe say *things will go badly* even though she didn't even speak.

He paused. "Also, the only other access to Tartarus that I

know of is through the Underworld. That's where Chaos has been leaching her souls."

Cali shuddered at the flash of memory that brought the eyes of the kaoti. She dropped her hand to her sword. James moved around a larger brush, holding it back for the girls to pass. They circled the last trees and entered an opening in the forest. The opening contained a cracked, paved road. A car zipped by, and Cali almost choked on her breath as she stared after it. She had been gripping her sword during their walk. It grounded her. Now it made her feel starkly out of place. In traveling across times, even in the trauma that haunted her at night from Varsna, it felt like a dream. This was the 21st-century though—this was her century. The reality made her heart race.

She still held the parchment between her fingers and didn't pull it back as he took it. Unfolding it, he scowled. "Shit."

"What?" both girls said in unison as they came up alongside him and stared down at the map. Cali squinted, but all she could see were fuzzy characters and letters and shapes. "What does it mean?" she asked, trying to angle her head to see if that would help the images focus. It didn't.

"It means I know where we have to go," he hissed, his fingers tightening over the frayed edges of the paper so that it wrinkled beneath his grip.

"You can read it?" Blythe asked, looking between him and the map, unconvinced.

"It shows what the bearer needs to see," he said, his jaw still set tight.

"And it's showing you where we need to go?" Cali prompted, looking from his white knuckles to his face. He caught her look and loosened his hold.

"Yes," he replied, folding the map again and handing it to her.

She shook her head. "Keep it if you can read it." He turned around. "Where are we going?" Cali asked as she and Blythe stepped in beside him.

"To Hell."

He gestured South, towards the coast. Cali rolled her eyes as she walked beside him in the direction he pointed. "No, but really."

"Actually, the Underworld. The map says: *to find the Key of Ymir, you have to find the holder that can set a done life free.*"

"From that, you're getting the Underworld?" Cali asked, unconvinced. "Can't the map just have an X marks the spot on it like a regular map?"

James put it in his jacket pocket. "This isn't a normal map. And Pluto is the only one who can allow someone's life there to go free."

"Okay, so how do we get there?"

"We have to find the Cave of Erebus," said James. "If we find him, he can get us *in* to the Underworld."

"Erebus," Cali recalled the name. "Maechon said he is the god of darkness, the ..." *The direct son of Chaos.* James nodded grimly.

Blythe grinned. "Gotta hand it to you Mixie, you really know how to pick adventures."

"Shove it, B," Cali snapped, throwing her hands up, suddenly aware of the ridiculousness of the flimsy plan, the elusive Map of the Void, and the fact they were walking on a road to the god of darkness. "Are we just planning on walking there, then?"

A van lulled its way around the bend and rolled to a stop after it passed them. Blythe and Cali exchanged a look as James slowed his step. All three cautiously watched as the car's hazard lights blinked. As they approached, Blythe moved up to the driver's window, passing James, who made the move first. She waved at whoever sat beyond the open window.

"Hello there," Blythe said in a voice that matched more Griffin's than her own. "We were hiking and got lost in the forest and now we were hoping to get a ride back into the nearest town. We'd call a cab but, ugh, all our phones are dead."

Cali and James made their way to stand behind Blythe as she spoke with the driver. Cali took in the woman behind the wheel. She was a very old, wrinkled Greek woman that could have been between sixty or a hundred. Cali was both impressed, and disturbed, that the woman and her trembling hands was out on the road driving. The woman nodded as she took in Blythe's words and pushed some large, round glasses up her nose to look through them at the group.

"Fine, fine," the old woman said. She pushed a button on her side, releasing the locks on her doors. "That's all fine. You seem like very nice children, tired nice children. Come on in."

"Thanks, we super appreciate it," Blythe said in her singsong voice. She turned to make a gagging face at James and Cali before trotting around to the passenger seat. "You don't mind, right? Carsick, you know." Cali rolled her eyes but clambered into the backseat. James hesitated at the door.

"You're sure it's no trouble?" he asked, his voice edging suspicion. "You don't know us."

"I don't know many people," the woman replied. "But I am a very old lady who has lived an old life—What's the harm in doing good?"

James mumbled something under his breath about no-good-deed, but he moved into the seat beside Cali. The car was small and dusty. Lace doilies lay across the back seat headrest and there was a faint smell of floral in the air, lilac.

"Fine, fine." The wrinkled hand reached up to adjust her mirror where a small stuffed owl swayed in the breeze. She caught Cali's eye. For a moment Cali almost swore the woman winked at her, but at the risk of sounding alarmed for James, she quickly looked out the window.

"I go as far as Katakolo," the woman said as the car lurched forward. The soft hum of the car made Cali's eyelids feel heavy. Her body seemed to melt into the seat, exhaustion rippling her through her bones and muscles. They had been walking for who knows how long—and it had been even longer since she slept. Even with her stomach grumbling for food, the tiredness was winning out.

"Katakolo?" Blythe gushed. "That's the coast. That's exactly where we need—"

"We don't expect you to bring strangers all the way with you there," James interrupted, he poked Blythe's shoulder from behind.

Blythe let out a dramatic yelp, but the woman didn't seem to care. Cali shook her head as she looked out the window. *What am I doing?* Her forehead dipped so that it leaned against the pane, and she watched the trees and hills of Foloi rush by. *Doing what needs to be done.* She almost laughed at her own self-confidence as she let her eyes droop.

"Oh, that's fine, fine," the woman said. She tapped Blythe's leg as she spit her tongue in triumph at James. "It's no trouble, no trouble at all. Everyone wants an adventure. I had a few in my da ..." the woman's voice trailed off as Cali nodded to sleep.

Chapter Nineteen

She stood at the edge of a frozen river. The overhang looked off into a large, dense forest that seemed to go for miles. The trees had a fresh blanket of snow—she could smell it in the air.

The forest was still, almost peaceful. But there was an eeriness to the place. To her right, she heard a low rumble.

Her boots left soft imprints in the snow as she followed the river upstream and to the source of the sound. It bent around curves and disappeared out of sight. Cali peered over the edge of the fall and the steep drop below. Snow covered the ground at her feet. The air chilled as it crept across her skin.

Familiarity—haunting and cold—crawled over her as she stared at the place. Pain made her left ear throb and fill the space with silence. This side of the falls was a stark contrast to below. The trees stood like skeleton needles in the white landscape, almost hidden by the fog that enveloped them. The mist became so thick that Cali felt her breath catch.

Out of the mist came the shadow. Slow and calculating, it made its way down the river, as if seeking something. Cali soon saw what the shadow followed.

A man burst from the dark. He ran at an abnormal speed straight toward her.

Shadow and man were still yards away, but they would be on her in moments. Cali stood as frozen as the world around her. Her heart hammered in her chest, flooding her head and thoughts. She could hear the water rush behind her. Her body forgot its most basic functions and her breath became shallow.

The man's simple tunic and leather-strapped feet would have provided no warmth in this climate. Across his chest sat a bulky mass of furs. He clutched it with one arm as he sprinted up the river and towards the edge.

Several paces more and they would be on her.

A loud crack ruptured through the air. The forest shook and a flock of birds exploded from the safety of their branches. His pace faltered for a moment as the ice shifted; blood ran down his feet, leaving a faint trail. Trees pulled around them and the weather changed like a gasp of cold air. The river cracked and began to shatter beneath him as he reached the ledge where Cali stood, rooted to the spot. The forest clung together, and a dark mist seeped through the branches, blocking out the sun and what little sky was visible.

"Enough."

A low, dark voice moved through the forest on all sides. Cali wrapped her arms around herself and squeezed, but she couldn't tear her eyes away from the darkness.

"I said enough!"

The runner stood on a single shard of ice. His eyes darted around as he searched for a landing of ice big enough to help him escape to the shore. Stiff, frozen fingers clung to the parcel in front of him. Cali knew, even if she tried, she could not help him. The shadow took no solid form, but it did not stop Cali from knowing the voice. The man kept his back to the shoreline as it approached. Would the shore be any safer than the icy river if he made it there?

"You used to be much faster, and cleverer, than you are now," the shadow grew larger, pulsing. "Running in the open instead of the coverage of the wood. You thought this would make your path straight, but you are not as fast as your father, and your panic has

made you slow."

The voice hovered near the runner, its shadow becoming murky. The man was losing his footing; the blood running from his ankles made it hard to balance. They both stood so close to Cali that she could smell his sweat and blood. All hovered near the precipice.

"Just let me have it and we can both calm down and go on our way," the shadow said, its tone smooth as silk. "This is no business of yours. Just let me have it."

The roar of the falls beside them grew and Cali's whole body ached with the knowledge of what would come next. What had to come next.

"You are right, I am a fool," the runner said, his voice clear and confident. He looked down at the small package strapped to his chest, almost smothered in wool and fur. "And I don't know how to swim, yes..."

The runner made up his mind.

"But I am a fast learner."

"No!" The darkness lunged but was too slow as the runner plunged over the waterfall. Cali's whole body lurched forward, as if she would follow him down.

The shadow formed into a cloak-shrouded figure and drifted to the edge of the falls, so near to Cali that she held her breath. "Stillhet!" Cali's hands went to her throat, as if to stifle a scream. "Vi ses i helvete, min venn ... I will see you in Hell."

The figure did not seem to notice Cali as it turned to the mouth of the river. But then, the eyes turned back, looking over their shoulder at her. Those dark, familiar eyes ... she had seen them before. But where? The shadow reached for her.

"Cali."

Instinctively, Cali took a step back and felt herself fall.

"Cali!"

***

"Cali!" James hovered over Cali's. One hand cupped her chin, and the other gripped her shoulder as if to shake her. Cali blinked, and he released his hold. She saw, over his shoulder, the old woman's face turned and staring at them. "Are you okay?"

Cali choked on air as she struggled to sit up and wipe the sweat and drool from her face. "Sorry. Bad dream, sorry."

"Fine, fine," the old woman said. She clicked a button that unlocked the doors, and Blythe bolted out. "You slept right through my stories and all the way to the coast."

James gave Cali another questioning look, but Cali just glared at him.

"I'm fine," she growled. He raised an eyebrow but didn't push. "We're here," he said, then exited the car on his side. "Thank you, Merta."

Cali opened her door as he made his way around the trunk of the car to where Blythe stretched outside. She winced as she caught sight of Blythe's blade and wondered if Merta thought anything about it besides 'fine.' Before she could maneuver herself from the vehicle, the bony hand of Merta shot out and stopped her.

Cali stalled, surprised by the suddenness of the movement of such a fragile-looking person. She looked from serious eyes to the open palm before her. A single gray feather lay there. "Dreams can be many things," the old woman said Her voice seemed to lose its age as the tone grew serious. "Many things, but *never* real. This is real."

"Okay," Cali said. She felt the sudden need to spring from the car and run. "Sorry—thanks again. We really appreciate it."

"Take it." Cali looked from it to the woman's face, to her companions. James was saying something serious to Blythe, who looked bored. Cali took the feather and exited the vehicle. She gave an awkward smile to Merta as she shut the door. "Thanks."

"Fine, that's fine," the woman's soft voice continued as she touched her rearview owl and moved her car forward, away from the three.

"Thanks again, Merta!" Blythe called out as she waved to the slow-moving vehicle. "Weird, weird lady."

"She was kind enough to bring us here," Cali retorted as she stretched her own shoulders out. The sweat-inducing nap did little to rest her sore muscles.

"I meant you." Blythe smirked.

"I'm fine," Cali said. But she could still feel the effects of the nightmare on her skin. "It was just a bad dream."

"Ah, poor baby Mixie."

James placed himself between the girls before Cali leaped on Blythe. "Can we leave the killing of each other till after we save our friends?" Cali glared daggers at Blythe, who just spit her tongue out. "Unless you want to turn back now?"

"We're fine." Cali snarled.

"Well, you may have gotten some sleep, but I want to get some before we go take on Erebus and the Underworld." Blythe pointed to the sleepy costal town they had arrived in. A few people trudged around the streets, mostly locals Cali assumed as the town was not for any Greek tourist. "There." She pointed to a small sign that read *Sleep and Meal*.

Cali looked out to the sea and fading sun. The last bit of the sunlight just began to kiss the ocean and the two lampposts in the town gave little light in the dark. "We don't have time to wait," she murmured. Her mind drifted to her friends, to Griffin and Maechon and the rest ... where they were, what might be happening to them. She shivered.

"Sleep first," Blythe said in a sing-song voice as she headed toward the motel. "Our friends are getting tortured; we don't have to torture ourselves with lack of sleep."

Cali stared at Blythe's for a moment, clasping and unclasping her fists. "What the hell is wrong with her?"

"Many, many things," James said. "But I have to agree with her on this."

Cali whirled to face him. "But Maech, Griffin—your girlfriend, they could be—"

"I know what could be happening to them," he growled, not meeting her stare even as he looked at her. "I've been doing this much longer than you have and I know what threat Chaos poses. But I also know," he stepped in front of Cali as she tried to pass him, "I know she won't kill the demi's she's taken."

"How can you know that?" Cali seethed with rage. Her pulse pounded in her head as she stared up at him. Ophelli's face—pale and scared—flashed in her mind. *Breathe, breathe ...* "You can't know that."

"I do," he said, his voice low and eyes on her. "If she didn't kill them on sight, then she'll have Erinyes bring them to General Nyx." He paused; his throat bobbed. "She won't kill the ones she's kidnapped because it's more fun if she breaks them."

She peeled her gaze from his and looked to the sea as the light faded and threw crystals across the waves. Her heart still skittered in her chest, but she listened to the voice in her head—coaxing her to breathe. She did.

"It's going to be okay."

"You keep saying that, but I don't see how anything will ever be okay again. It's just this idea of going to save these people I've only just met a couple of weeks ago—"

"Otherwise known as friends," James interrupted with a knowing look.

She paused and drew a ragged breath. Her eyes stung from the salt spray of the ocean and her own unshed tears. *No more crying, Cali.* "I know this was my idea. My stupid, impulsive idea to save my *friends*, but it just seems so overwhelmingly real now."

"Much more real now that you're in it."

Cali nodded. "Before, with the map, you said it shows what you want—desire. I *do* want to help them. I mean, I want to help myself too, but ... is it that complicated? Why didn't it show me? Why can't I do anything right? Why can't I just calm down and listen?"

"Maybe you wanted me to come along the whole time."

Cali shot him a look and couldn't help but share his half-smile with her own. "That sounds like something Blythe would say."

"You don't have to do this alone, Cal." His voice remained low as he studied her. "We're all in this fight now. Together. I said I would protect you and the others, and that's what I intend to do." A tense smile pulled on his mouth as he turned back to the motel. "And don't think you need to always listen to me."

She didn't return the smile. Something behind his eyes made her want to trust him, but there were still too many unanswered questions. She watched as he walked away. "What Chaos said before, in Rome, about me ..." Cali trailed, hoping he would fill in the blanks. He stopped but didn't turn back to her. "What did she mean when she said I wasn't a demi?"

He hesitated before replying. "I don't know."

"Could Auto and Tash have been wrong?" Her fingers trembled at the question. "Could I just be an ordinary, boring human?"

A mixture of hope and despair made her not want to know. She had gone through so much in these last several weeks. What if Chaos was right? If she wasn't a demi, then she didn't belong. But deep down, Cali knew if that was the case, she would always have the longing to be a part of this life. She waited.

He looked over his shoulder at her. Even in the dim light of the lamp closest to them, she could see a flicker of blue in his eyes but couldn't place the emotion. "Even if you were a human, you wouldn't be ordinary, and you'd hardly be boring. But Cali, I don't have these answers."

"I don't know if I trust you." She added after a moment, "You're lying."

Without another word, she brushed past him and made for the small motel building, and whatever dreams awaited her that night before dawn.

Chapter Twenty

"I don't think you know where we're going."

Blythe stomped her foot in impatience as she surveyed the rocky crags around them. The first two times she had made this observation, it annoyed Cali. This time, Cali wanted to second the opinion as it seemed they were walking in circles around the deserted dunes. Bottles, plastic, wrappers, and garbage were strewn between the rocks and water. The smell of dead fish was overwhelming in the air and Cali's stomach felt tight. She had barely swallowed the granola bar that Blythe had 'commandeered' for breakfast. Now, it took everything to keep the small amount of food from coming back up. She tried to focus by holding on to the cool hilt of her blade.

"I am reading the map!" James snapped. He flicked the edge of the map as he looked between it and the rocks. "It shows one of these caves belonging to Erebus. But I can't tell because there is a damn riddle here, too."

"You said that already," Cali grumbled.

"Aye, Aye, captain, but the tides a'comin in so we gotta find this fast." Blythe grabbed for the map, but James pulled away.

"If she can read it, let her," Cali begged. "I think she wants to help."

James begrudgingly handed it over to Blythe. Her face quickly turned to disgust as she studied it.

"Well, this explains nothing." She squinted as she studied the yellowed parchment. James was about to grab it back, and then her eyes widened. "Oh, *that's* why! Okay, we need to go there." She pointed towards a small section of the rocks several feet away, in the opposite direction they were in.

"How did you ..." James looked over her in disbelief but then leaned back with a nod. "Okay fine. Let's go."

"Maybe you just didn't want it bad enough," Blythe said. James held his hand out for the map, and she toyed with him before handing it back.

Cali rolled her eyes. She tried not to show the disappointment of Blythe's successful map reading reflected on her face. *At least we're getting somewhere*. They crossed the sand and jutted rocks to where Blythe pointed.

"Okay, so that horrifying cave that we are all now just seeing," Cali said as they took in the opening of a large crevasse in the rock.

It didn't look like a normal cave entrance. It was more of a large crack in the side of the rock face, barely big enough to fit one person at a time. People walking by would only notice if they'd been looking, and maybe not even then. The smell of dead fish and sewage was stronger here, deterring any passerby. The overhangs and surrounding rock made for an almost illusion feel to the face of the cave.

"Yup." Blythe wrapped her arm around Cali and peered into the dark hole. "Highway to Hell, baby."

"Okay, we all have to remember what we are doing," James said. He grabbed the map back from Blythe as Cali shoved her away. "We have to stick together. The entire time. Can we manage not killing each other until we get to Hell?"

"Question."

James gave a heavy sigh. "Yes, B?"

"If we killed ourselves, would we get there faster?"

Instead of responding, James turned to the thin crack in the rock.

"What is wrong with you?" Cali hissed at Blythe, who just smirked.

"So very, very many things, Mixie."

"Ladies, if you're ready?" James pushed himself with some difficulty into the crack. His shoulders scrapped against the rock face, but then the darkness swallowed him from sight. Blythe and Cali followed close behind.

As soon as she entered the cave, Cali felt a shift in the air. It was too dark. It was heavy and clammy, like the feeling of a wave pulling you down to its depths. It felt like the surrounding air was pulling her forward. But there was no breeze, no other sounds. It reminded her of that day in Foloi Forest. She shivered and took a deep breath, mostly to ensure she could still do that.

The space grew so that she could almost walk side by side with Blythe. For the first time, Cali felt grateful, knowing the confident, cocky nemesis was close by. She tried to adjust her eyes, but it seemed impossible. Instead, she just moved forward. There was a soft clicking sound, and a very low beam cut through the darkness. She jumped.

"Guys?" Cali's voice felt muffled and flat. *I do not like this.* She dug her fingernails into her palms as she tried to quell the fear in her chest. Already the Earth seemed to be tilting below her, shifting and rocking...

"What? Do you see something?" James whipped around, the low beam of the flashlight only showing his hand.

"No," Cali said sheepishly, as she blindly grabbed at the rock to brace herself. Her foot caught a crack, and she tripped forward. She caught herself on Blythe, who shrieked. "Sorry! I just wanted to make sure you guys were still there."

"We're still here," Blythe grumbled, pulling herself from Cali. "How far in do you think we have to go?"

"We've been here about the same amount of time as you, B," James' voice sounded from before them. "I can't see the map enough to know where we are."

A few minutes of bated breath later, Cali realized they had moved into a larger portion of the cave. As her eyes adjusted, Cali could make out James and Blythe nearby. The flashlight tried its best to cut through the darkness, but all it could provide was a faint beam showing more rocks. The darkness of the room shifted again. It was a sensation Cali thought felt like passing out, but she patted herself down and realized she was still standing.

"I'm assuming we're close?" she whispered.

Blythe shrugged. James was about to step forward when he froze. Cali felt her heart stop with him.

"What reason has brought you here?"

The voice that spoke was as heavy as the darkness around them. Cali looked around for the speaker, but the voice seemed to echo around the cavern on its own, using the shadows as its body.

"Erebus." James growled. Cali could see, even in the dark, that he had gone for his sword.

With a jolt, Cali started as a hand seized her own, realizing just as suddenly that it was Blythe. The hand retracted as quickly as it reached out, but Cali still felt the heat of Blythe's body nearby. She strained through the dark to see and was able to make out two large shapes that stood as black shadows against the cave to the right. One of the shadows shifted, detaching itself from the mass.

"Three ambitious travelers; alive I see," Erebus purred, each syllable coming out long and smooth. The shape moved with his words. It never quite took the shape of a man but grew larger as it detached itself from the other shadow and made for them. "Many your age choose to take their own life for the feat of getting to the Underworld; maybe this is your way of doing that. For why else, would you be so foolish to come here?"

"Well, clearly, we didn't come here for you ..." Blythe cursed as Cali elbowed her.

"We came to see Pluto," Cali said. "But we appreciate that you are just as powerful as the Master of Hell."

"Kiss ass," Blythe mumbled under her breath.

Cali shushed her. Even though Blythe was right, if there was one thing Cali had learned and retained from her father's many stories of legend, the gods *loved* flattery.

"You think flattery will save you from what awaits you in the end?" The strange voice spoke, its whispers drifted around the ears of the listeners like the tickle of straw it floated about. Cali's stomach sank. "Although I must admit, upping that little prig of the deep—that would do wonders for my darkened ego. Ah yes, it's a tempting thing, having two demigods and ... what's this?" the voice hissed.

It felt like it was directly in Cali's good ear, and she had to tense her body to not swat it away.

"Something else entirely." A clouded face appeared out of the shadow, pale and haunting. "You girl. You are not possible."

Sharp chills rushed over Cali's back and she whipped around. But only Blythe stood next to her, eyes wide. "Okay, that was spooky," she breathed as the air again shifted and Erebus pulled away.

"What do you—"

"You know why we've come, Erebus," James interrupted Cali, his sword raised. Cali glowered at him but bit her tongue and waited. "What is your cost?"

The pale, taut face turned on James, the eyes shimmering white.

"Cost?" Erebus sneered. His lipless mouth pulled back, revealing razor sharp points for teeth. "What price can you pay, son of Balder?"

Cali jumped as Blythe brushed her arm. She shook her head and then darted her eyes towards the shadowy object to their right. By squinting, the outline became a bit clearer. *A boat?* Cali glanced at Blythe, who nodded. *She can't be thinking what I think she's thinking.* As if she heard her, Blythe flashed a feral smile.

"So, you'll do it for nothing." The flashlight in James' hand flickered before it snuffed out.

"I will not do it at all, boy." Erebus snarled. "I admittedly am fascinated by the boldness in coming here, especially one with your unique heritage. It will be a shame to lose someone so handsome as yourself."

Even as Cali edged with Blythe through the darkness to the shadowy boat, she could feel James' tension. The black form focused on him. A bone-white hand brushed James' face. "I too lost much in the last war. The darkness is all that I have." The shadowy voice grew sad and faint, like a whisper. "And all that I want." Erebus paused.

Cali and Blythe froze. The boat was less than two yards away. The brief thought crossed Cali that she could make it if she ran. *Then what?*

"We fell out, long ago, mother dearest and I—but perhaps I could make a deal and provide what it is that brought you here to her. She did for my sister, yes. That little darkling bitch. You did come here to me after all, and many things go wrong in the darkness. Chaos would bring darkness—such darkness the world would never know."

"Go!" Blythe shoved Cali forward in the direction of the boat. Cali moved her legs to keep from pitching forward. Over her shoulder, she could see Blythe had retrieved her prize possession, the only sword she could wield under the sight of the gods: *Nordfos*. It illuminated Blythe in a steady stream of lights.

Greens, purples, and white floated about her as she stood with it drawn in her hand.

Erebus' shadow halted. Retracting from James, he spun on her. Cali backed up to the more defined outline of the boat. She blinked against the suddenness of the light.

"That is not the *Angurvadal* blade." Erebus laughed, but Cali caught apprehension behind it. "That blade was destroyed long ago by Nyx; that has no power here."

"Ah, but not all the pieces were destroyed." Blythe's face twisted with an edge of madness in the light, accentuating the scars and bruises on her wild face. Her eyes flicked over to Cali, and she jerked her head towards the boat. From the corner of her eye, Cali saw James already moving in the direction of the dark shape. "Perhaps a skilled blacksmith found a piece and made it work for her?"

"That's not how the blade works." Erebus sounded exasperated, but his shadow dimmed as if unsure.

"Why don't we find out," Blythe sneered, and placed her other hand on the blade. In an instant, the entire cave filled with light and a roar of anguish from the shadow as it melted underneath its strength.

James gestured at Cali as he backed towards the vessel. Cali moved. As she raced to the boat, she could hear the splash of water beneath her feet. The light drew shadows and shapes in the cavern, but even with it, Cali saw the water beneath her was black. She reached the boat just after James. He leaped in and then held a hand to her. "Come on!"

Beneath her fingers, Cali felt the coolness of the wood of the vessel. Shadow still enveloped the rig, swallowing her hands in its darkness, but she hoisted herself up and tumbled onto the solid floor. She pushed James' hand away as she scrambled to her feet, her eyes landing on Blythe. The darkness in front of them pulled closer and shook the cave.

"Blythe!" James shouted. "Let's go." He was already at the end of the boat, using a long oar to shove off from the rocky shoal.

Cali moved to help him, and they both heaved against the weight of it.

"Blythe, come on!" she shouted.

Blythe ran, sword in hand, shining less now as the shadows began to crawl around. She leaped in the air and landed easily on the deck just as the dark water pulled them forward. When she landed, she turned. *Nordfos* hummed in her hands, brilliantly sending the murkiness into retreat. Curses filled the air, echoing around them.

The boat jerked forward into further darkness. It moved fast through the current. Looking behind them, Cali saw the dark figure of Erebus standing on the shoreline.

"You'll never make it back!" he roared. Unable to cross the water, his black shadow raged like a flame around him. "You may make it to the Underworld—but he'll never let you leave!"

The darkness swallowed him from sight.

They drifted forward without the assistance of oars and with James at the rudder. Mist-like smoke still lingered over the dingy, but in the light of *Nordfos,* the shape took form around them.

Cali pushed her stray hair behind her ears before tightening her braid. "That did not go well."

"Nope," James agreed. He leaned against the edge of the boat, one hand on the rudder, another through his hair. "I hardly expected it to, but Blythe always has something up her sleeve, so I knew she'd pull through."

"I don't get it. Why did *Nordfos* freak out a god?"

"Maybe it was me who freaked him out?" Blythe challenged.

Cali rolled her eyes. "Oh, you're right, that makes more sense."

Blythe snorted, flipping the sword round in her hand. "My father, Heph, found the pieces of *Angurvadal*, the flaming blade of the Norse, after Nyx had destroyed it. Thought it might come in handy, so I took the pieces and forged something new."

"But the light," Cali stared around them, "Maechon said the *Angurvadal* blade was made of fire." She gestured to green and purple lights. "How are there so many colors?"

"It's the *Aurora Borealis*, the Northern Lights." James looked almost reverently at the beauty around them. "I used to stay up at night and watch them when I was a child on Faroe Island."

There was a moment of silence after he spoke. Both girls, surprised at this uncharacteristic sharing, exchanged a look between themselves. James himself seemed a bit surprised and turned to look out into the water.

Cali cleared her throat to break the awkwardness. "Do we think this will draw too much ... unwanted attention?" she asked, still a bit breathless from her sprint and the beauty of the rippling light.

"Don't worry, I also have a more subtle weapon." Blythe grinned as she patted a small dagger at her left.

"Maech told me your father's bloodline was cursed," Cali continued, ignoring the familiar blade and the phantom pain in her side. "That it's hard for you to wield a blade. Is that true?"

"My father taught me few things," Blythe replied. She ran her fingers down the length of the blade with a grin. "He did teach me weapons, though. He was stationed in Asgard, with the Valkyrie, where he maybe stole some of their light and sent it back to me as an apology for being a dick. Never saw him again. He did also give me his stunning looks though, so there's that."

"But that doesn't explain why you can use it."

"Would it help you understand if I told you it hurt like a mutha every time I wielded a blade?" Blythe snarled. She pointed *Nordfos* at Cali, the tip inches from her face. Cali didn't flinch. "Every gift has its price, Mixie. As does every passion."

"So, you are passionate about weaponry. Which is why you do it through pain?"

"I'm passionate about killing."

Cali batted the sword away as Blythe laughed. James just shook his head. She looked out over the water, her mind ticking back to the cave, to Erebus' deathlike face, and their escape. "You knew he wouldn't help," she said after a moment. "And that we'd have to steal the boat the whole time."

"I mean, it wasn't my plan," Blythe said with a shrug. "James said I should just be prepared for anything today because Ruby-boy is an a-class-moron."

"Oh." Cali felt a slight, and surprising, twinge of hurt at the thought of a plan being developed that didn't involve her. James didn't owe her his trust, and she hadn't really done anything to deserve it. But still, this rescue mission was *her* idea. And when they talked yesterday it seemed like they were friends again. She trailed her fingers through the mist of darkness at the rail of the boat.

"I would have told you," James said, as if reading her thoughts. "But since Blythe has more real-world experience, I though—"

"It's fine." Cali waved her hand as if to dismiss it. "We're here now, going to Hell, going to rescue our friends." She swallowed hard. "That's all that matters."

James frowned, unconvinced.

"Well, glad you came around quick," Blythe said. She turned and dug the tip of her blade into the deck of the ship as she stared up. "Because I think we may have just entered the gates."

Cali and James followed her gaze to an awning. Intricately carved gargoyles, bones, and monsters covered the overhang; dead eyes seemed to watch from the vacant faces. The water moved faster now, but Cali could still make out the description above the door before they passed beneath: *Θανάτου μόνον ουκ έστιν επανόρθωμα;*

Only in death is there no remedy.

Chapter Twenty-One

The atmosphere of the cave changed after crossing the threshold of the Underworld. No one spoke for some time as they sailed down the dark river. Blythe put away *Nordfos* and sat at the end of the boat, maneuvering down the black river with the back rudder she had commandeered from James.

Cali watched the water beneath the ship and crouched beside the hull. It lapped heavily against the side, unnatural in its rhythm. She shivered as the sad wind kissed her face, and while reaching up to brush it away, her fingers stroked her scars near her ear. She thought about what Blythe had said before, about gifts and power. Right now, the only powers she felt she'd received from her real parents were these scars and the silence behind the ear. *You're no demi.* She traced each scar as she considered the words. She didn't feel any different from how she had when she thought she was just a *mortal*, but something in her knew—*felt*—that she was something. *If not a demi, what am I?*

"You okay?" James asked. He looked across the small space from his position opposite her. His hands rested on either of his knees as he sat there. She noted the map, folded in his grip.

"Yeah, yeah, of course." She tried to ignore the gnawing feeling of anxiety inside. It bubbled up, wanting to ... *wanting to what?* With a shudder, she brushed the feeling away. *Calm down—focus.* She shifted around to face him, sitting on her butt with her back against the rail. "Does the map show where this river leads? Are we even heading in the right direction?"

"Pluto's lair is in the middle of the rivers. We should know it when we see it."

"Lair?" Cali scoffed. "What is he? A dragon?" She paused. "Wait - he's not a dragon, is he?"

"No."

Cali didn't feel as relieved at his answer as she hoped. Especially given his face remained grim and a bit uncertain in his response. "Maech said there were five rivers." Cali tried to recall exactly what Maechon had said about this place. Again, there was too much information to sift through. What was a myth and what was a truth? "Which one do you think we're in?"

"Hate, fire, misery, forgetfulness, and wailing," he listed. Cali raised her eyebrow. "Yes, surprisingly, I know things, too." His lips pulled for a moment in a half smile. "It isn't the fire or wailing—"

A screech from the dark made them both jump. James was on his feet, sword in hand, before Blythe's laughter broke.

"Blythe!" One hand gripped the side of the boat as she struggled to stand, and the other clutched her chest. "What the hell?"

James rolled his eyes and replaced his sword.

"That wasn't funny, B." Cali leaned against the rail and took deep breaths.

"Someone could have heard," James agreed.

"Eh." Blythe shrugged. "Don't wake the dead, I suppose."

"She's insane," Cali mumbled, more to herself than to James.

"I'm just glad she's on our side," James said. He raked his fingers through his curls, making them stick in all directions as he leaned back against the hull of the boat. "Blythe – put *Nordfos* away until we're sure we aren't being tracked."

"You think Pluto already knows we're here?" Cali asked,

alarmed as the green and yellow lights dimmed around them.

James nodded. "He most certainly does. I just don't want to make us a sitting target." Cali looked out across the bubbling black water. Her eyes could barely adjust to the shift in the darkness. The waves rolled over each other and as she watched, she felt the nagging in her chest again. "When we get there, it's important that you listen to what I say." Cali's grip tightened on the wood rail, and she slowly turned to face him. "I've been here before; I know how Pluto works. He is almost as good as Loki when it comes to manipulation. He'll use whatever he can to get to you."

"I get it, listen, do what you say without question, got it."

James' eyebrows raised at the force behind Cali's words. Cali blinked but kept her back straight against the rail. *What does he think I'm going to do, just freak out again and ruin everything?* Another part of her understood the concern that danced behind his eyes, but she still didn't find it entirely fair. "You don't have to get angry—I'm just trying to make sure we all get out alive."

"This time." Cali almost choked on her own words. *What am I saying? Stop, Cali, stop.* But she couldn't—or wouldn't. She wasn't sure. But she felt a bitter spark flicker through her as she glared across at him.

"That's not what I meant," he replied, slowly, not taking his eyes off her.

From the stern, Cali could hear a muffled laugh from Blythe, but she ignored her.

"I know what you meant," she snapped. "You don't trust me—I get it. I messed up and someone died," the words poured out and she hated them and herself for saying them, "You think I don't feel guilty about that every single day? Because I do. But you know what else I feel? Angry—really angry. Angry that I was brought to this," she gestured around, "life where everyone claimed I was one thing but then tells me I'm not. I'm sick and tired of all these stupid secrets and—"

"You're angry?" James went rigid, speaking over her. "You? Aliax said you always talked about wanting some great, big adventure in your life, and here you are—"

"That's not what I mea—"

"—making sure everyone knows how much your life sucks," he continued. He stood and, in an instant, Cali was on her feet too, inches from him. "When all your parents ever did was try and keep you safe with everything Auto and Tash have done for you at the Farm—"

"This is not what I wanted!"

His lips pulled into a sneer as he stared down at her. "And what is it you want? Because I don't think you know." Cali matched his glare but said nothing. "I think you got exactly what you wanted in life, adventure and mystery and a life away from your hovering parents, and you realized you're just a coward."

"Well, I think you're an asshole."

A beat of silence drifted between them, save the sound of their breath.

"*Acheron*, I bet," said Blythe and they both turned to face her.

"What the hell are you talking about?" Cali snapped. Blood pooled at the base of her nails, but still she dug in. If she let go...*why am I shaking? Stop shaking!*

"The river," Blythe responded coolly, with a shrug in the direction of the water. "It's *Acheron,* for sure."

James groaned, and he took a step from Cali. He ran his fingers through his hair, cursing.

"Of course," he said. "The river of woe and misery."

"Yeah, and you sucker's fell right into it. Misery loves company," Blythe snickered. "Not me though—I hate both of you."

Cali unclenched her jaw and wiped her hands against her pants. She knew Blythe was right. But still, the pain, the guilt, all of it built too much, and she felt she may burst. She swallowed hard, trying to quell the ripple of anger in her chest. James didn't look at her as he stepped to the edge of the boat, still cursing.

"So, why aren't you affected, then?" Cali demanded; arms crossed.

"I'm always miserable," said Blythe with a small shrug. She stood up suddenly and pointed. "Dead ahead. Literally *and* figuratively. Woof, good thing there's fire burning because we never would have seen it."

Blythe's sarcasm fell flat as all three stared up at the fortress. It seemed to have appeared from the gloom in an instant. At first as a smudge of gold and red and orange. Then it became clearer as the colors parted to reveal the darkened home of the Underworld's god. Hidden between wispy clouds, spires reached the dark sky, cracked and foreboding. Rocks burrowed up the walls and the smell of sulfur was nauseating. Part of the fortress maintained a gothic style, with gargoyles and medieval dripping from its ramparts. On one side, however, was a long stretch of a building that Cali thought resembled more of a worn-down hospital. *Or mental asylum,* she mused with a grimace.

The source of the lights became apparent as the *Archeon* picked up speed on approach. Another river, filled with boiling fire and flame, crept to the edge of the castle. There seemed to be no discernable horizon outside of flames disappearing.

Cali stood at the helm with James as Blythe attempted to steer the vessel's course, but it was useless. Two other rivers were on their right. The final one lay behind and out of sight, but the wails and screams could be heard vividly from their place in the boat.

"Don't look down," James said in a warning voice.

Cali immediately looked down from her side of the boat and stumbled back with a gasp.

But as she did, the boat seemed to levitate on its own. They cleared the black river that now poured into the very depths of an abyss below like an endless waterfall. Another river poured out beside them, and Cali could see shapes and figures in the water. *People —dead people*. She tried to manage her breath and looked back at the fortress in front of them before she threw up.

"I told you not to look down."

"When has anyone not looked when someone says that?" She didn't look at James for fear of what a sudden movement would do to her stomach. Taking a steadying breath, she leaned against the rail. "Where are ... where are they going?"

James's arm brushed beside her as he looked down. "Wherever the judges send them," he said. "And Pluto makes sure they get to where they're going next."

Goosebumps formed on Cali's arms. Her mind drifted to where she might go when she ... *Don't think like that, not now.* Instead, she checked the fastener on her belt, just where her sword sat. She kept finding herself resting her hand on the hilt, even though she had only had it for a short time. It felt a part of her somehow.

"Slow down," James directed Blythe.

Cali looked up and saw they were coming in close—and fast—to the side of the fortress. They were headed towards a small stone staircase that was attached at the base of the building. The bottom of the stairs had a single post with a rope blowing in the wind. Nothingness hung below the stairs.

Cali threw a worried glance at Blythe.

James took a step back from the rail. "B, slow down."

"I can't!" Blythe heaved against the rudder, but it wouldn't budge.

Cali reached for the side of the boat, but it was too late. The front hit hard against the staircase, pitching them forward onto the floor of the boat. James landed on Cali, knocking her breath out for a moment.

James scrambled off her. "You okay?"

"I'm fine." Cali groaned, doing a quick once-over as she stood. Her stab wound ached, but otherwise she felt stable. Bending her head back, she took in the massiveness that was the fortress to the devil. She wasn't sure if it was the aftereffects of the water, or the natural feeling of hopelessness that occurs when faced with an enormous challenge, but she couldn't help but think this mission—this specific challenge—was impossible. *How in the world will we find a Key of Ymir in this place?*

"Not just for that, Cali." James interrupted her thoughts as he grabbed the flailing rope and pulled them to the stairs. Cali swayed as the boat jolted against the stones again. He avoided her eyes as he tied them to the helm. "What I said on the river, about you, about what I thought. It wasn't—"

"It wasn't you, I know," Cali finished for him, her breath feeling knocked out again. His brows furrowed, but she interrupted him before he could go on. "Maybe it was a good thing. We needed to clear the air, or whatever." She found it hard to meet his piercing stare.

"Cali—"

"She said it doesn't matter." Blythe brushed herself off and surveyed his knot to ensure it met her standards. "Can we have this emotional breakdown later? We are currently alive in the dead world. Let's stay that way, ok? Let's see what the map says about finding this oh-so-powerful key, shall we?"

"Let's go then." Cali stepped over the side of the boat and cringed as her boot connected with the slick surface of the stone. She had to use the post with the tether to ensure she didn't fall back and did her best not to look down. Even without looking, from the smell and the taste of the air, she knew it was blood that soaked the stairs. Blythe pushed her forward, stepping up beside her.

James followed them and the three made their way up the

stairs to a solid, black oak door. "Assuming this is the shadow keeper's door, Pluto's going to be closer to the top, I would think." He shaded his eyes and looked up at the spire. "He has a big ego, so it would be best if we at all possible can avoid meeting him."

"I've heard he has a big—" Blythe began but Cali was faster.

"You said he probably knows we're here," she said. "With it being so ... quiet do you think it could be a trap?" She ignored Blythe's glare as she rested her hand on the doorknob of the Underworld lair.

"Let's assume yes."

James pushed the door open as Cali hesitated. It creaked on hinges that sparked with the movement and showed the way to a spiral staircase that led up. From a first look into the dark spire, there seemed to be no other doors, just stairs. Cali finally met James' gaze before he ducked into the dark. She followed, trying to swallow the last bit of fear as she made her ascent.

***

The staircase wrapped up for ages, and Cali was sure her burning thighs would topple her down the stairs again. She had the vague thought that it would have been better to bring Ike, the idiot son of Icarus, along for this journey. *At least he could have flown us part of the way before making a pass at one of us.*

She winced and held her side. Pain seared through the wound and bone, but she kept moving. Sulfur and the putrid smell of rot drenched them as soon as they entered. Besides the pain, the odor nearly knocked her back down the stairs. Cali kept thinking that, as her eyes adjusted, her nose would adjust to the smell too. There was no such relief. There was also no relief from the muffled cries and wails of the river souls. They echoed down the spire like horrible whispers of despair. Cali rubbed her temples, then her left ear, as she tried to numb the throbbing there. Then she put a finger to her other ear, blocking the sound as she moved up the stairs. It did no good—she was just left to her thoughts in the silence of her head.

"It's a bit strange this keeps going up with no end, no doors, right?" she gasped. She teetered and her hands shot out to brace herself against the stone. "Does the map say anything about how many stairs there are?"

"Nope, just keep going," James said.

He and Blythe kept a good pace up the stairs. Cali, on the other hand, gasped for air and steps behind them. Twice James and Blythe had stopped at the small, red light of a small window in the rock. They conversed over options before moving on and Cali would focus on slowing her heart rate down.

"Great," groaned Cali.

"Should have taken training a bit more seriously," Blythe taunted.

"I must have missed the never-ending staircase training day."

"You, okay?" Blythe asked. "Lookin' a little tired there, Mixie."

"Side ache," Cali snapped and dug her fingers into the stone to pull herself up the next couple of steps. "No thanks to you."

"It'll leave a good scar; guys dig scars. Right J?"

"Sure," James said absently. He leaned over the map, his brows scrunched together. Cali could see the sweat forming on his brown from the awful mugginess of the place. They were all drenched in it. But he seemed to make it look good, the way his shirt ...

Get a grip, Cali. She guiltily shook the thought away.

"The map shows that the Key of Ymir is with Pluto." He stopped and pointed to a place on the map. Cali heaved herself up the step to see. She was surprised when she noticed a faint outline of an actual map, or rather a layout. Rooms, diagrams, and ancient Greek words swayed on the page, moving around the sheet like they were alive. Where James pointed was a room with words on it. Cali assumed this was the 'riddle' he mentioned before. The words moved, as if pacing, across the room. "Whether that's on his person or where he keeps things I don't know. I can't tell if it's ... moving or not. So we have to find where Pluto would keep his most prized possessions."

"Which from here looks like it's in his bedroom, nice." Blythe tapped the paper where the outline of the room was.

"Yeah, but how do we get there? How come it doesn't say how many steps are left?" Cali asked. She could see where they stood on the map, in the spiral stairs, but that was it. For all they knew this could be a layer of hell that went on forever. And they didn't have that kind of time. James was staring at her with a chagrined look on his face.

"What?" Cali demanded.

"So, you can both see the map now?" James questioned.

Cali and Blythe exchanged a look. "I guess," Cali replied. Blythe added, "But it's still kind of fuzzy."

James shook his head as he folded the Map of the Void and placed it back in his jacket pocket. He mumbled something under his breath that Cali didn't catch.

"I guess you don't have to be the *Keeper of the Map* anymore, eh J-J?" Blythe taunted. James didn't respond, only turned to continue up the stairs. "Ah, buddy, c'mon."

"Leave him alone, B," Cali retorted. "He can keep reading it—I don't care."

"Yeah, but *I* might care," Blythe retorted, catching up with James. Cali strained try to and keep the pace as they continued to go round the spire. "I want it."

"Blythe, stop being so—"

"So what?" Cali glared up at Blythe as she spun on her. "I got us to Erebus, and you just *happen* to be on James' side because you think he's ho..."

"Shut up, both of you."

"She started it." Cali took the next step where Blythe stood. "And I'll finish—"

"Seriously, you two, shut up, and look."

Cali followed his gestured hand to a different section of the winding stone. Bending with the curves of the rock was a solid piece of wood, carved intricately with skulls and bones. Cali felt the hair on her arms stand up as she stared at the door. James put a finger to his lips, emphatically looking between them, which Blythe responded to with a middle finger. He didn't have to tell Cali that—she felt it even as her breath held.

He gripped the white handle and pushed in.

Chapter Twenty – Two

"Whoa."

Blythe expressed the view of all three as they stepped into the large, bright, and colorful room.

"You can say that again," Cali said, also in awe, as she stood next to her surveying the space they walked into.

Blythe obliged, "Whoa."

The room they entered was a stark contrast to the outside world and the dark stairwell they came from. It had a very retro-modern look. It was part library, part art exhibit. Bright colors splattered the wall in lines and geometric shapes, standing out against the white bookcases that lined the walls. The strange thing about the books was all their bindings were facing inward so that the only part seen were the leaves inside, making the white stand out even more. Massive abstract paintings by Kaszmir Malevich, Pablo Picasso, and others Cali was not familiar with hung between the shelves. There was a single window between two shelves that stretched from a small seat to the ceiling. Cali was used to the faux windows, as all the bedroom windows on the Farm had held some sort of illusion behind them. But this window day was set in a cartoon fantasy land. It was by far, to Cali, the most disturbing thing in the room, even with the oversized picture of the Scream staring at them. Large double doors opened in front of them, showing a darker room beyond.

"Okay, so this is unexpected," James said, gathering himself. He adjusted his pack and sword before crossing the room. "Through there. Be ready for anything."

James led the way through the double doors into the next room. This room was smaller than the library. With the leather couches, bar cat, and fireplace, Cali felt a strange coziness to the space. Off putting, however, were the animal heads of various species and seemingly various monsters littering the wall and every open space.

"Nice man cave," she mumbled, brushing her finger against a tusk.

"There." James pointed to their left, where an awning led to another room. He pulled the map from his pocket and opened it. "It's the—Cali, don't touch that." Cali jumped, retracing her finger from the stuffed animal's head on the side table. "Blythe." He nodded toward the doorway.

Blythe retrieved *Nordfos* and moved forward, edging the wall before she peered through. She looked back with a jerk of her head.

James waved forward, and Cali growled at him. "I know what a head nod means." He gave her a semi-apologetic look as they crossed through to the doorway.

The room attached to the man-cave gave Cali a strange feeling of peace. She hated it. The simple, modern look of the office space felt too normal. A large desk sat in the center. A balcony stretched out behind large windows and overlooked the five rivers of the Underworld. Cali got a small glimpse through the window as they passed. She shivered as she realized how high they were.

"Blythe," James said, surveying the room and then the map. "There's a hall with an adjoining room just beyond the door. Go check it out and make sure the hall is clear." He eyebrows pulled as he assessed the room. "It's too quiet up here—I don't like it. Be careful and quick." Cali waited for her own instructions, but he shook his head. "You'll stay with me."

"Why does she get to go with you again?" Blythe raised an eyebrow.

"Because I haven't tried to kill her," James said.

"Yet," hissed Blythe in Cali's right ear. She snorted, turned, and disappeared through the door.

James ran his fingers through his curls, sweat making it slick, and crossed the room to the desk that sat at the center.

"I'm not going to try to kill you."

"I didn't think you would," Cali said.

"About before—"

"Nope. Let's not do this again."

He paused while rummaging through the desk and looked up at her. "I just wanted to apologize."

"How about we both apologize when we're out of this mess?" Cali moved to the single cabinet behind the desk, avoiding running into James as he did the same.

"Deal."

Cali rifled through a box of papers and pictures. She flipped through the pictures quickly, stopping for a moment on one.

"Hey—look." In the picture were five gods and goddesses,' by the way they stood. They all had smiles on their faces. She recognized two of them and held the picture up. James came over and looked at it. "It's Auto, Tash, and three others. They look ... happy. It's weird, I'm not sure I like it."

"You don't like being happy, or them being happy." James raised an eyebrow at her as he handed the picture back.

"It's not that. It's just weird." Cali folded the picture and snuck it into her pocket. "Do you recognize the others?"

"Besides Auto and Tash? I only recognize Freya," James said. "I don't know the others."

"Freya?" Cali yanked the picture back out and looked at it. "Which one is she?"

"That one." He pointed out the tall blonde near the center. Beautiful didn't begin to describe how she looked—and fierce. Something about how her head angled, the proud chin mixed with the kind, understanding eyes, made her look unshakeable. She kept her hands at her sides, even though the man beside her wrapped his arm around her shoulder. The man's face was tucked into the mess of hair that lay across her shoulders. Flowers laced a crown on her head as she turned from the man, her gaze nearly meeting Auto's own unnervingly powerful stare.

James said something muffled, and Cali looked over at him. "What?"

"I said you look like her."

Cali could feel her cheeks begin to flush and she quickly ducked her head. "I don't think so."

"You have her eye's—well," he glanced at her, still holding several books from the desk in his hand. "Eye, I mean."

Cali gave a short laugh. "Gee, thanks." He shrugged. "I'm sure Griffin appreciated your compliments."

Awkwardness filtered between them, mixing with silence. He cleared his throat and went back to sifting through the desk. "Mine and Griffin's relationship is ... complicated," he said evenly, although Cali knew with a pang that she had struck a nerve.

"We'll get her back—all of them."

"I know," he said after a moment.

Silence filtered between them as they each picked an area to rifle through. Cali peered into a small box then slammed it shut again. *Those were not real eyeballs*, she repeated over and over in her head – even though she knew the round white shapes were exactly that. "How big is the key?"

"I mean, probably the size of a regular key."

"Would he really keep it unprotected in his office?" Cali asked and tried to avoid looking at the several other small boxes on the shelf she stood near that she imagined were filled with similar body parts. She hesitated before grabbing the next box. "Would he really leave his office unprotected? Or did we just get lucky?"

"There's no such thing as luck," James replied grimly. "Being here at all is a risk— having it quiet, even more so." He fiddled with a low drawer that was jammed. "Let's just hope Blythe gets back and—"

"Well, well, well," a voice interrupted. James whipped around; his sword pointed at the sound. "If it isn't the consequences of your own actions coming back to get you."

***

Cali peered around James' shoulders to see the speaker; a middle-aged man that looked like a washed-up rockstar. Oily brown hair hung in a shag to his shoulders, and dark eyes creased with liner danced with temptation. A black leather jacket with studs and snake-skin boots completed his overt-80's ensemble. Beside the man stood two charcoal black soldiers. Their entire bodies seemed to be made of soot and their fingers left black smudges across Blythe's neck as they squeezed. A gag was tight over her mouth, cutting into her cheeks as her teeth ground together.

"This is something indeed." *Nordfos* swung lazily in the man's grip as he sauntered forward. "The son of Balder and, what's this ..." He took a step forward and was in front of Cali in an instant. The coy smile on his face froze as James' blade stopped him in his tracks. Still, he kept his gaze on Cali. They roved Cali hungrily, mad behind the glossy smudged makeup. "And who are you, little one?"

"Cali," Cali said. She felt James move closer to her, but it didn't help the feeling of fear eddying in her chest.

"Charmed, I'm sure." The face remained unchanged. "Let me rephrase: *what* are you?"

"A demi?"

He frowned.

Cali tried again, "A demigod?"

"Hmm ..." The man touched a finger to her cheek. "Well, you *know* that isn't true, don't you deary?" He stepped back and sighed. "Do you know who—*what*—I am?"

"Pluto," Cali guessed. Her ear pulsed painfully as Pluto dipped his head in a mock bow. "What do you mean?" she said, ignoring the break in her voice. Terror twisted her gut and mixed with a strange sensation—the tingling from before, in Rome and in Varsna. It began to edge into her veins.

She swallowed hard. "What do you mean, I'm not a demigod?"

A smile crept across his face. "Want to find out?"

Chapter Twenty – Three

Pluto spun on his heel before Cali could find out anything. "I'm sure you have just so many questions for me." Pluto rubbed his hands together with excitement. He turned when he reached his desk and looked around with a furrowed brow. "You put *everything* back where it was? That's disappointing. A bit OCD are we?"

"What do you want from us, Pluto?" James' voice cut over the devil's in a fit of confident anger. "Either take our souls or let us go. We don't need games."

"You came here, little mama's boy." Pluto crossed his arms and threw on a pouting face. "And if you're so desperate to be soulless, I can rid you of what little there is left in you." He snapped his fingers, summoning one of the guards besides Blythe to move on them. The guard seemed to split in two and create another as they went for James first.

"Wait!" Cali stepped between them as James decked the charcoal guard in the face. She wasn't sure if James' invincibility still worked in the Underworld, and she didn't want to risk it. The two others moved around to him. "We just came to find out … well, what did you mean about me?"

"Redirection to help a friend, interesting ploy—but I'll bite," Pluto said, waving a dismissive hand to no one. "How could I refuse you, *Immixtus?* When there are so few of you left."

He turned back to Cali and grabbed her hand. James struggled against the guards who held him, but they held his arms back. He pressed it to his lips before she could pull away. "Truly, an honor." He let go of her hand, but Cali felt frozen in place. Her mind buzzed with the words he had said. *You're no demi.*

"Enough!" James leveled one of his captors to ash. The other remained unfazed as it dug its gangly nails in. But James side-stepped out of the grip, knocking into Cali.

Pluto caught her in his arms, and she yelped as she tried to pull herself from him. James' sword was at Pluto's throat in an instant. Both Cali and the devil froze.

"Charming."

"James, wait." Cali wasn't sure if she meant it as a warning or a plea, but he didn't respond to either as the blade traced the exposed skin.

"Yes, *James*," Pluto echoed. He let go of Cali's wrists and she stumbled forward and away from him. "Leave the Immixtus alone."

"What are you talking about?" Cali interrupted before James could protest. From behind Pluto's stud-jutting jacket she could see Blythe struggle against her own bonds. Blood seeped over her brow. Cali tried to focus on it, instead of the word that Pluto had said.

"Hmm?" Pluto looked at her innocently.

"Don't—" James growled.

"I'm not an *Immixtus*," Cali hissed. She recalled the crudely sketched pictures by Maechon, as well as the information he gave her about the Faytes, about how the gods feared them above all others—about how the reason for their fear was because their power was unknown. Because they were monsters. *I am not a monster.* Shivers ran over her skin, but she stared back at Pluto with forced confidence. *I am not a monster.*

"Oh!" Pluto blinked. "Oh, you ... you really *don't* know."

Pluto grinned. "And here your boyfriend is *still* trying to keep you in the dark."

Beside her, James' sword wavered as it lowered from its position. Blood trickled from the small mark on Pluto's neck, but the god didn't seem to mind. Cali knew James' eyes were fixed on her face, but she didn't—and wouldn't—give him the satisfaction of meeting his eyes.

"That's not very nice. Especially after Rome." Pluto turned to James with a mischievous look on his face. "I bet that little Furie told you not to, didn't she? Tash still tries to flex that power I'm surprised I don't see a leash. She does so like her leather."

Cali couldn't focus. *Tash is a Furie? I'm an ... Natasha is a Furie and I'm ...* Her brain wouldn't complete the thought. "Is he telling the truth?"

She could feel a warm liquid begin to seep at the edge of her deaf ear, but she ignored it. Her veins felt like they had been shocked with ice, and yet she felt warm. Too warm. *I'm going to freak out – I think I'm going to have a panic attack.* The ground beneath her boots seemed to shift and groan. Inside her, buried deep, something snapped. She clenched her fists; her nails bit into her palms, and she turned on James.

"Is he?"

His face reflected the answer he couldn't say. Or wouldn't say. "You knew about this?" *I can't breathe.* Tears stung her eyes, but she refused to let them fall. Instead, a hand went to her chest as she tried to remember how air filled her lungs.

"I ..."

"Ugh, we don't have time for this." Pluto rolled his eyes and made a gagging noise. Cali blinked the tears away before facing him. "I can just rip the Band-Aid off and tell you now. Get the show really on the road. I was beginning to feel dissapo—"

A thunderous boom filled the room, rattling the desk and

shelf. Pluto's face became serious. He threw a nod to the remaining ash guards, who had begun to advance to the balcony. They froze in place. Blythe was still gripped by the throat in one of the steely hands. James, blade still in hand, turned to face the newcomer, although he dragged his eyes slowly from Cali. She refused to look at him.

On the balcony, just under the awning, stood a tall, pale woman with crisp blue eyes and raven hair that whipped around her face. She wore fitted black and sheer clothes, topped off with a deep blue cape. She reminded Cali of Erinyes in the way she carried herself, stoic and tall, but there was something different in this haunting woman; something darker. Cali cringed as the woman sauntered into the room.

"Nyx!" Pluto raised his arms as if greeting an old friend as the goddess stalked into the room.

She said no word of welcome, eyeing the captives one by one. Her sharp eyes rested on Cali.

"What brings you this fine way on such a night? Erebus send you? Because I must say I know exactly where his boat is if he wants it back, but I also have to say I'm hurt he doesn't come by himself and—"

"Quiet, fool," Nyx said, her eyes flashing. Her voice remained calm as she stopped in front of the God of Hell, but her eyes continued to watch the demi's.

"Wow. That's a nice way of greeting someone you haven't seen in about, oh, two-hundred years." Pluto crossed his arms and threw the mange of hair behind his shoulders. "On that note, what *are* you doing here, Nyx? Chaos sending the magnanimous and heroic general here, to my home. I'm not sure if I should be flattered or insul—"

"Your false flattery will get you nowhere, Hades," Nyx said, her eyes narrowing as she spun on him. Cali could see the flash of a silver curved blade, hidden just inside the folds of the cloak.

She instinctively went for her sword, but one of Pluto's guards grabbed her wrist. James caught her eye and shook his head, his own lowered blade ready.

"Um, it's Pluto *actually*. Perhaps you should get my name right if you want to insult me."

Nyx bared her teeth. "I'm here for your guests, *Hades*."

"Well, you'll have to be more specific, Nyx." Pluto shrugged off her annoyance with a look of confusion. "I get 150,000 people and some a day, that's about 120 a minute. Every second someone—"

"Give me the demi's, caretaker, or I will take them by force." The curved blade was in her hand and dropped just at Pluto's neck. He remained unfazed. "And then we will be on our way, without any mess or fuss."

"We?" Pluto flicked his gaze towards the awning of the balcony and frowned. "Oh, you mean that we?"

Cali looked toward the balcony, where half a dozen kaoti lingered in the sulfur smoke. Next to them stood the familiar, and foreboding, figure of Erinyes. "So, the rumors were true," Pluto purred. "You really have crawled back to mommy dearest. After how she treated you last time? I thought better of you."

"What you think, does not matter. What matters is what's coming." Nyx's eyes strayed to Cali's hand as it rested on her sword. Then her eyes moved up, catching hers, daring her to react. Cali kept still as the goddess crossed to her. "I'm still taking them with me."

Cali's body reacted before she realized it. With a quick flick of her wrist—in a move she had seen Blythe do many times—she relieved one of the charcoal guards of his hand. He howled in rage, and she sprung forward. Nyx easily blocked Cali's blade. Sparks flew as the steel connected, and Cali heard her name—a warning—being called. But all she could focus on was the dark pits that were the goddesses of Night's eyes. Stars seemed to twinkle in their depths. But the darkness. It beckoned to Cali. drawing her in. She had to get out. She had to get away from it and the feeling bubbled up in her chest against her throat against her skin.

Her eyes closed.

Then Cali pulled back. The blades sparked against each other as she brought it around again. Nyx easily side-stepped in a swift move and brought the tip of her blade to Cali's throat, drawing a single drop of blood. With her other hand, she gripped Cali's sword arm, bending it back. Blood already seeped from the soft touch of the blade. From the corner of her eye, Cali saw James, restrained against four charcoal guards. She also saw, through the black dots forming in her vision, the outline of Erinyes. The Furie paced, straining against some invisible force that would not allow her passage into the room. kaoti shrieks filled the air.

Cali felt herself fading—the spark that triggered in her felt far away now.

"Very few draw their weapon against the goddess of night and survive," Nyx hissed. But there was intrigue, not hate, behind the now black eyes Cali struggled with her free hand to pull the vice-like grip from her throat and dropped her sword to go for Nyx's tightening fingers. "Not quite strong enough to follow through. Such a pity to have to kill you—Chaos could have used you well."

"Ladies, ladies, please." Pluto was beside them in an instant. He raised his hands, beckoning Nyx to release her prey. "Although I generally try to not break up fights between women, I just had the blood cleaned off the floor from the last party I had, so can we just pause a moment, take a beat?"

Nyx glared at Pluto; their faces so close that they nearly touched. Pluto stood his ground. Nyx spun on her heel, stepping back and releasing Cali in the same movement.

Cali choked on air. Her vision began to come back as she

gingerly rubbed her throat, but the voices around her sounded far away. She could hear James from beside her as he said her name, but she didn't respond. As she straightened, she caught Blythe's subtle smirk of approval. In another circumstance, Cali would have felt pride. But they were still trapped. And she had failed to find the strength within her to win. Her sword lay at her feet. The kaoti were rattled, and froth formed at their gaping mouths. *We failed.*

Nyx stalked to the desk and rummaged through the papers there. "You'll give me your captives. Chaos is losing patience after the incident in Rome."

She's looking for the map. Cali dared a quick glance at James, who was covered in the soot from the guards. He caught her look and tilted his head; apologetic guilt creased his face. But Cali was more interested in the contents of his jacket and ensuring those contents did not come to the light.

"She may not have received what she wanted, but she learned of a greater weapon. We both know a prophecy, a promise, cannot be denied for long," Nyx continued. She edged close, sauntering like a tiger waiting to strike if provoked and turned to face them. "Besides, they'll serve a better purpose with her than here."

Blythe bit through her gag and spit out a curse. "I'll tell you where you can put your prophecy, you spineless, cowardly piece of—"

A black hand covered her mouth before she could continue. Nyx turned slowly to stare at Blythe. She crossed the room in an instant—so fast that Cali could barely comprehend how she moved. A single dagger appeared in the goddesses' hands.

Pluto darted forward.

"Of course, of course. Chaos always gets what she wants." Pluto again inserted himself between Nyx and her prey, his voice smooth and charming. Nyx paused her dagger from its place at

Blythe's forehead as Pluto crossed to her. "But let me have a win, why don't you? You already get to deliver prizes, and I want to have a chance to impress the beast. Let me bring them."

Nyx cocked her head, assessing him with twinkling eyes. "I thought the King of the damned was neutral."

"Even Switzerland must know when it's time to play the favorite?" Pluto pouted.

"Why would I trust you to deliver?"

"Why wouldn't you trust me?"

A sharp laugh broke from Nyx.

"Fine." Pluto frowned and crossed his arms like a child about to throw a tantrum. Then his face went hopeful. "For an old friend?"

"For an old friend?" The night goddess paused as if considering. Cali saw a flicker of a smile cross the red lips. "Fine," she said after a moment. "You have until midnight to bring them to Chaos after you're done playing with them. Otherwise, I know where you live, *Hades*. You may run *this* Hell, but surely a stint in the Nif would remind you that everyone has their own version." She leaned in threateningly and Pluto nodded solemnly. "It will also remind you that *anyone* is replaceable, even the devil."

"And Ruby's boat ...?"

"I sank it." Nyx whipped around. "My brother deserves it for allowing them to take it." Her coat flashed around her heels as she replaced her sword and strode to the balcony. "One hour." Cali watched as the sound of the crack rippled, and the kaoti and the Goddess of Night disappeared. Erinyes eyes never left Cali's until she too vanished into the smoke-filled air.

Silence filled the room. Pluto stood, a hand in his hair and another raised in a wave.

"Well," he finally sighed, turning back towards his captive guests. "*That* could have gone better. But it definitely could have gone worse. Mottie, dear, how about we make our guests comfortable? 'Suppose we don't have much time."

Mottie, one of the gray-ash guards, disappeared through the door. Pluto nodded to the guards, who released Blythe and James. Cali tensed and stepped back as the large beings ambled away from their captives. They melted into each other and became three guards. Each took a post near their master.

Blythe had already begun hurling curses at everyone, demanding her bag, weapons, and a fight. The guards closest to her simply turned and left through the door.

"There's no need to—"

James ignored Pluto's words as he stalked after the guard with his sword. He yanked it from the guard's hand and severed its head before it could even turn around. Then, James pointed the tip of the blade at Pluto, who remained in the same spot he had been in, a single eyebrow raised. "There's no need to do that," Pluto huffed. "They listen to what I say. They wouldn't have harmed you—besides, they aren't even alive."

"For some reason, that makes me trust you even less."

"That's just rude," Pluto continued, unfazed. He tapped the tip of the blade with his finger. James hissed but lowered the weapon by several inches. "And here I am, trying to help you."

"What's your game, Pluto?" James demanded.

Cali stepped up beside him to face the devil-god but still kept a distance from James. "Why would you try to help us?" she asked.

"Because I know what Chaos is looking for from you," Pluto replied. "And I know what you are looking for from me." He gave Cali a wink and she bit her cheek to keep from snarling at him.

"So, what do you want?" she asked again.

"You. I want to talk to you. Alone."

"No," James took a step forward. A fiery sword appeared in

front of him.

"Give me mine back, you piece of shit, and I'll show you what real fire is!" Blythe made a move on the guard, but Pluto snapped his fingers. The guard took the hit from Blythe, returned his own sword to its sheath, and stepped back. "Just talk, eh?"

"You're not doing this," James snarled. Cali was unsure if this was directed at her or Pluto. "This isn't the time or place—"

"Oh, and there's a better time and place?" Cali snapped. From the time Pluto had said the words about who she was, something inside her seemed to make sense. At least, began to make sense. Whatever murmur or ripple or thing moved beneath her skin, in her chest and bones—she felt Pluto could answer it. More than that, she knew he would answer with only the truth. Still, the worry and fear behind James' eyes made her hesitate. Only briefly.

"If she wants the truth, she'll find some of it with me," Pluto's voice changed, becoming dangerous. James' jaw tightened and the grip on his sword tensed. "Perhaps you wanted to be the one to tell her? That doesn't really matter now, though, does it?"

Cali looked between the ashen guard and the fiery sword he held. In an instant, more like it could be upon them if James didn't stand down. "I want to know what he has to say," Cali said, her voice lower than before.

James dropped his defense and stared at her, stricken. He seemed to sense her resolution, and accusations, for he returned his sword to its sheath. *Good*, Cali lifted her chin to emphasize her resolve, even as she dragged her nails against her palms. *Now for the truth.*

"I'll talk to him. Alone." Pluto beamed. "For five minutes—and *only* so long as you tell the truth." She narrowed her eyes at Pluto, even though her heart began to hammer in her chest.

"You don't even know if he'll tell the truth," James began.

"Because she's got the truth this far?" Blythe muttered, rubbing her jaw where the hand of the guards had dug their fingers in. She still eyed the guard and his sword with disdain.

"Exactly," said Cali with a sigh. "Thank you, Blythe."

"Brilliant," Pluto said, rubbing his hands together. "Persephone will mend your wounds and keep you company until we get back. She's hardly a healer, but she dabbles ... in everything, really." He gestured a sweeping hand to the door where his two guards stood as if nothing had occurred. The one with the sword stepped back, the fire disappearing from his hand. "Gentlemen, would you bring our guests to the drawing-room? Thank you ever so much. Everyone, play nice while we're gone."

The doors swung open, but the guards remained at their post, motionless and void, waiting for a command. Blythe looked between James and Cali before she shrugged and headed through the doors to a drawing room beyond. Cali could make out a beautiful young woman, lounging on a couch near a fire. The woman looked up as Blythe entered and plastered on what Cali took to be a fake smile.

"Cali," James attempted one last time to plead with her.

She shook her head, "Go. I'll be fine." He met her eyes—an unspoken apology bleeding out. *I know.* "I'll be fine," she said again.

Without another word, he turned, and walked through the doors. Cali watched as the guards pulled them closed, leaving her and Pluto alone in the room. Panic rushed through her veins—ice cold and calculating. She wanted to run through the doors to safety. *You wanted the truth, Cali, now get it.*

Pluto stood for a moment staring at the closed doors, then he turned to Cali with a grin.

Chapter Twenty – Four

"So, good ol'Auto and Tash thought it would be best to keep you in the dark?" Pluto braced his hands in front of him against his desk. Even behind the black eyeliner, his eyes were filled with cunning and fire. On the other side, Cali stood, shifting from foot to foot. "They really haven't changed much, have they? Always lying, always secrets, all for the greater good." He threw his hands up in dramatic emphasis. "I'm honestly shocked they let you train with the others, letting you think you were a demigod. When all along, you were so very much more. It was probably Tash's idea, Auto never really was one for ideas. Also, given your shared histories—"

"I'm not here to talk about them," Cali interrupted as he opened his mouth for a perceived monologue. "Tell me what I want to know, or I'll walk out those doors."

"And go where?" he purred with a raised eyebrow.

Cali wouldn't let him see her flinch.

"What makes you think I'm ..." She couldn't say the word aloud. "Something other than a demi?"

He stepped around the desk to where she stood and towered over her. Whips of alcohol and sulfur filled the surrounding air, and she tried to hold her breath as he studied her.

"You, my dear, dear girl, *are* an Immixtus." Pluto began to circle her. "And I must say, *huge* fan of your work. Not the part in Varsna—gives me too much paperwork. The part where you switched the map in Rome, though," he made a quick chef's kiss gesture, "Even though it did cause Chaos to send her minions to threaten me and *then* to steal my souls and destroy the Farm. Brilliant, truly." He paused at Cali's stunned face. "What? Now you're not so chatty?" His smile grew. "Would you feel more comfortable if I looked more like someone else? How about this!"

His voice changed to a low, dulcet British tone. Before Cali was now the figure of a tall, very handsome young man. His dark skin shone against the bright lights in the room, and he smelled of smoke and forest. A charming smile, with kind brown eyes, looked down at her so sincerely that Cali felt flushed. It was a bit uncomfortable how good-looking he appeared.

"No, I think that this is worse," she stammered, trying to avoid the dark eyes.

"Would you prefer I look like your male friend?" Pluto smiled cheekily.

"No." Red heat crawled across Cali's chest and neck.

"It makes you uncomfortable?"

She glared at him. "Yes."

"Good" —he smirked— "If I don't make you feel a little uncomfortable, then I'm not doing my job." He gave a low laugh as he turned and waved a hand forward towards a door that had opened on the other side of the room. It looked like it led to complete darkness. "Come, I want to show you something."

"No, just tell me what I need to know. Stop wasting time."

He cocked his head. "Down here, there is nothing but time." Cali's brows furrowed in confusion. "Every hour is a day, and every day feels an eternity. You've already been gone a week; in case you're wondering."

He turned and disappeared through the doorway.

Cali stared open-mouthed after him. *A week?* Her friends

could all be dead at this point. She cursed herself, glancing over her shoulder at the doors. *Find out, find out ...*

She took a step. Then another. Then followed the devil through the door.

***

Darkness circled her, and for a moment, Cali thought her heart was going to beat out of her chest. It was too quiet. Instinctively, she turned around towards the now-closed entrance.

"Don't be afraid," Pluto whispered from beside her.

She whirled around and faced the direction of his voice. Thankfully, lights flickered on, and she could see his handsome, smiling face. A disturbing comfort in the dark.

The lights continued to whir to life every couple of feet and revealed a long hallway. Walls of glass lined the corridor all the way to the end, where a single door stood. Cali slowly looked over her shoulder and realized the door she had entered from was gone.

Pluto flicked his gaze down to Cali's side. "You won't be needing that, darling." Cali followed his look. Her knuckles were bone-white in their grip on her sword. She nearly unsheathed it, but, with an unsteady sigh, she let it click back into place on her belt.

He began to walk, and she followed, warily darting glances on either side of her. She unsuccessfully stifled a gasp, passing each window. Behind every pane was a human. Some held several, but all centered around some brutal, horrible, or traumatic event. Several simply held a man crying at his desk as he looked out the window beside his cubicle—his eyes glazed with hopelessness and despair. Others were so graphic that Cali had to look away.

"What is this place?" she asked.

"This," Pluto gave a broad sweep of his arms, "This is the Hall of Pane." He threw a sly smirk over his shoulder at her. "Get it? Pane—pain? Each person behind the glass has some sort of sordid history with guilt and—"

"I get it," Cali interrupted. Her gut churned and she clenched her fists to keep from going for her sword. "You get off on other people's pain and put it on display like a museum." He spun on her, and a look of hurt flashed in his eyes. Still, she crossed her arms and met his gaze. "Why did you bring me here?"

"I don't send them here," Pluto said with a huff, ignoring her question. He went to the closest window and traced a finger against it. The housewife beyond dipped her chin back as she took a pill, then swallowed it down with a martini. "They are all, each and every one, judged. And it is my job," his voice darkened, "my life, to ensure their judgement is carried out." He turned back to Cali. "Do you understand?"

"No."

He shrugged, and the easiness returned to his face. "What do you know of the Morai?"

Cali's mind traced back to the crude images Maechon drew for her and the explanation he provided. The first of the Immixtus. The cursed children of Zeus and Frigg. The gods feared them almost as much as Chaos. *And who doesn't want to be feared?* The thought rippled so quickly through Cali that she started.

Pluto seemed to sense her change and his eyes narrowed. "Well?"

Cali took a sharp breath. "I know that there are three of them and that they are the children of Zeus and Frigg." She paused. "I know that they are often referred to as the Faytes because ... well, because they bind fate to someone's life and whatever fate they bind can't be changed."

"Possibly," Pluto mused. He rubbed his chin in thought as he stopped before her. "Zeus, like many of his children after him, was ashamed of what he created with that Norse—"

"Because he was afraid of them," Cali hissed, angered at the slight against her kind. *My kind.* She ignored this thought as well. "Because all the gods feared them—including you."

Pluto nodded. "Including me." With a tip of his head, he motioned Cali toward the door. "You are an Immixtus, Cali, whether you want to face that truth or not," he continued as they began to walk again.

Cali wasn't sure if it was the hum of the lights or her mind that made her head begin to ache.

"It's not possible," she breathed. "You can't know that."

"Denying something doesn't make it less real—as wishing for something makes something more so. This whole 'manifestation' bullshit kids are into these days." He hesitated as if waiting for Cali to interrupt. She didn't. Too many thoughts swirled in her brain to sift through to form a question. "For the last twenty years I heard whispers of another mixed child. I was one of the few who did research and found out the old-fashioned way: Hermes. Huge gossip; watch out for that fellow. There was talk that when his son escaped, a Furie was sent to kill him *because* of said child. It wasn't hard to fill in the blanks, even with Zeus trying to hide the mess. I mean, after the accident, I kept tabs."

"What accident?" Cali blurted out, finally blinking him back into focus. The door stood before her. If she reached her hand out, she could open it and leave this place.

"I think you know what accident," Pluto said. He tilted his head in the direction of her scarred face, his eyes sparkling with knowing.

Instinctively, Cali brushed her fingers against the raised skin.

She traced the lines to her ear, which throbbed painfully. "The ..." Her mouth went dry as the nightmare wrapped itself around her memory. "There was a waterfall ... and ..." She blinked several times, stunned as if ice had been poured over her head. "That was ... *real*?"

Pluto again nodded. "You meant little to me besides mere sport after that—besides waiting to see if you'd survive till your eighteenth birthday." Cali stared at him. "When I heard the famous Farm was attacked, and that *you* commandeered Erebus ship, I had to meet you in person."

"How does this...none of what you're saying proves I'm an Immixtus," Cali snapped. She pressed her hand against her forehead and took a slow breath in, then out. She thought of Maechon telling her about the history of the Moirai. About their history. Had he been trying to warn her? And then there was Blythe's nickname ... had everyone known? "My mother was Freya, and my father was ... was ..." *Was who?* Before now, Cali never allowed herself to claim the Norse goddess as her parent. But now, with her mind reeling, she felt there was no doubt. But her father ... Natasha had never told her about him and Cali, in her stupid fear and resolve to just keep training as if nothing bad would really truly happen, had never asked.

She looked up at Pluto with pleading eyes, hopeful as if he could somehow fill in the gaps. "I don't know who your father is," he admitted. "But I do know for certain that you are a child of gods, Cali. And not just any: Original gods.

"Wha—what does that mean?"

"Only original gods—those created directly from Chaos—can make their own such chaos as an Immixtus," Pluto said, his voice dropping to almost reverent tones as he stared at Cali. "That is why Aliax and Miriam hid you. Those that created you wanted you dead, and they wanted—"

"To protect me," Cali breathed, her voice hitching at the

words. Pain wracked her body as she tried to recall her parents' faces. "Why are you telling me this?"

Without another word, Pluto turned on his heel, opened the door, and stalked into his office beyond.

Cali blinked at the suddenness of the light and the change in the air. Behind her she heard a scream and, not turning back, she stepped back into the office. The door shifted closed and then melted into the wall.

"Hey—why are you telling me this?" She followed the devil across the room to the balcony, where he stopped and looked out over his kingdom. Sulfur again filled her lungs from the fires that surrounded the fortress. Her eyes stung from the fumes, and she gripped the rail, willing herself not to look down. "You don't owe me the truth. So, why tell me now?" She looked down, and then immediately swallowed the bile that rushed to her throat. "What if I don't believe you?"

He laughed from his post beside her. "You believe me." The hair on her arms began to singe from the heat of the fires below, but she met his gaze. "I want something from you."

She frowned. "What?"

A dark smile played at his lips, and fire lit behind roguish eyes. "Call it generosity," he continued. "But I am going to give you exactly what you came for." He grabbed her hand and, before she could react, pressed it against his chest, just where the neck of his shirt revealed his glistening skin.

She flinched but didn't pull away. Beneath his shirt, she felt his heart, the heat of his skin, and something else. His smile grew as she shot her eyes from his face to his neck. "Yes," he purred. Releasing her hand, he pulled the strand of leather from around his neck and revealed a small, rusted key. Cali swallowed hard as she watched him untie it from his neck. "Yes, I will give you the Key of Ymir—along with the truth. If you will do me a favor in return."

"You've already given me the truth," Cali said, barely able to formulate the words as she stared at the key.

"But I haven't given you the key yet." Her eyes shot to his face. "Do me a favor, Immixtus. Just one."

Don't do it, Cali. "What do you want?" she asked.

He tapped a finger on his lips. "Not yet—but in time." He held the Key of Ymir between them, and Cali watched as it dangled there, taunting her. "What do you say, Immixtus? Do a little deal with the devil?"

Cali snatched the key away so fast that he blinked. "Deal."

"Perfect." The dangerous smirk flitted across his face again. "Let's join your friends again, shall we?"

Cali hesitated. The Key of Ymir was cool in her hands. It was so small, with the two prongs of it caked in rust. She looked up as Pluto walked away. "Why are you helping us?"

He didn't turn to face her as he stopped, but his head tilted so she could hear him. "Like I said before Cali, this is my life," his shoulders shifted, straightening even as his voice dipped into sadness, "and it is my home. I do not want Chaos taking that from me."

Cali nodded, even though he couldn't see her acknowledge him. With a final look out at the world of the dammed, she turned and followed him inside.

Chapter Twenty - Five

Even before Pluto opened the door, Cali could hear Blythe's curses. In the palm of her hand, Cali held the key to solving their problems. *Or at least one of them.* She wasn't quite sure of the lore behind the key and how it worked, but she imagined it must be very powerful if Chaos would disrupt time and place for it, like in Rome.

Pluto held the door wide for her to enter the room, the roughish grin never leaving his face. The room was a small library with soft-toned lounge chairs and shelves lining the wall. A larger coffee table sat near a smoldering fireplace with four chairs surrounding it. *Cozy.*

James stopped pacing and spun on her. With relief, Cali noticed his sword back in place at his side. Blythe barely glanced up from her lounge chair, where she sat playing chess with a beautiful young woman. *Nordfos* rested on the coffee table beside her, close enough for Blythe to grab her if needed.

"Cali! What took you so ..." James' voice trailed as he took in the new Devil standing beside Cali. Cali winced but otherwise kept any discomfort to herself as she stopped beside Blythe. "What happened?" he growled darkly.

"Whoa." Blythe leaned her head back and stared up at Pluto's handsome face as she took a knight from the woman. She smirked at him and Cali. "Guess we know what took you so long."

"Don't feed into it," the young woman huffed, twirling a piece between her fingers. She was gorgeous. Her golden hair dropped like soft waves around her face and bare shoulders. A small line began to form between her brows as she studied the chess pieces. "How come you never look like this when I'm around?"

"Because I hate you, darling Persephone," Pluto responded in his same charming tone. He rested a stiff hand on the back of Blythe's chair and scowled at Persephone.

And here I thought they were madly in love, Cali mused as she fiddled with the key in her hands. James was beside her in an instant.

"What happened?" His eyes searched her for a sign of injury, then went to Pluto, then back to her again. Worry laced his expression, but Cali also saw a hint of anger behind his eyes. *Like he has the right to be angry.* "Did you find out what you needed?"

"You mean, did I find out why Blythe insists on calling me Mixie?" The worry and anger vanished with a flash of guilt. "Yeah, he told me what I needed to know ... I think."

Beside her, Pluto huffed out a laugh, which only seemed to rile more.

"You had no right," he hissed. "I would have told her—"

"Would you have?" Cali demanded. She straightened to meet his gaze, even though she remained inches beneath him. "Would you have told me? Or would you have just let Natasha and Auto and everyone else continue to lie to me?"

"It wasn't supposed to be a lie."

Cali gave a short, bitter laugh. "And what was it supposed to be?" She raised a finger at him, the key still clenched in her fist. "And don't pretend it was to keep me safe. Because look where we are now."

"Hey!" Pluto barked, fake hurt crossing his bored face. "You know" —he placed a gentle hand on Cali's shoulder, which made James' nostrils flare in rage — "at the risk of sounding like I agree with this poor, young demi, I think at this point, there *is* in fact a time and place for this argument."

Cali lowered her hand, the key still digging into her soft flesh, and let her anger and pride drift away. Beneath her skin rippled something that felt like an earthquake of emotions. If she just allowed that feeling to keep going, she could—

No, no focus Cali—save your friends. Focus. As if sensing her emotional change, Blythe moved to her feet. She leaned her knee into the couch and stared with bored eyes.

"Not to be a buzzkill," she drawled. "But aren't we still prisoners here?"

"He's letting us go," Cali replied and lifted the key.

Blythe gave a low murmur of wonder, and James just stared.

"He's letting us go?" he demanded, his wary eyes darting back to Cali. "Why?"

"Apparently, not even the devil is completely evil," Cali shot back.

"And you trust everything he says?"

"More than I trust you!"

Her words struck home, and he blinked. The key still wavered between them, and he reached for it, but she pulled away. "You don't even know how to use it," he murmured, eyes flashing.

"I'll figure it out," Cali hissed back.

"Why are you letting us go?" His question was directed to Pluto, but his eyes remained trained on Cali.

"Let's not waste time on minor details." Pluto waved a hand dismissively.

"You are letting us go seems like a major detail," James said through gritted teeth. "The only way you'd let anyone leave here is ..." Realization dawned on James' face as he grabbed Cali's arm. She didn't pull back as he searched her face. "You made a deal with him." Not a question, really. Fear rippled through his eyes. "You just found out what you are, you don't even know what your power—"

"I *could* have known though if you would have just been honest with me for once."

He let go of her arm as she jerked back. "I—"

Pluto clapped his hands to bring them back. "Alright, alright, *children*, I really don't have time to work through all of these issues in group counseling. Let's get this show—"

A smile quirked onto his face as the familiar crack of thunder filled the room. Persephone looked up from her People magazine in a bit of annoyed surprise. Blythe groaned and straightened.

"Oh, well, look at that! They're early!" Pluto plastered a look of shock on his face "Who would've thought?"

"You knew they'd come back early," Cali snapped.

James and Blythe were going for their weapons.

"Well, look at the bright side. At least you have the key." The devil shrugged. "I said I would let you go. I can't very well let them know I'm *helping* you do that. No one changes that much." He winked at Blythe. "Oh, and let's make it convincing—"

James punched Pluto square in the face. The Lord of the Underworld took a step back., Another hit followed, and blood spurted from his nose.

"James, enough." Cali grabbed his arm to hold back another blow.

"Rude!" Pluto said, one hand cupping his nose as blood began to flow. "And I was going to show you the way."

"Running out of time!" Persephone said in a sing-song voice.

"Come on James, we have the key, let's go." Cali pulled him in the direction of the doors Pluto nodded to at end of the room.

"C'mon—"

"James, listen to Mixie" *Nordfos* hummed in Blythe's hand, her eagerness evident. James jerked his arm from Cali without looking at her. His fingers wrapped so tight around the hilt of his sword that Cali wouldn't have been surprised if his fingers left imprints, but he followed Blythe to the doorway at the other end of the room.

"James—" Pluto was in front of her and grabbed her chin so fast that Cali was unable to react. "What are you—"

In a movement so fast Cali could barely blink, he kissed her. She stared back at him in shock as he pulled away, a grin on his face. "*Respice finem.* You owe me one."

"If I ever figure out what my powers are I'm going to come back and kill you."

"Promises, promises." Pluto's eyes twinkled. "In here!" He shouted over her shoulder as he let her go. "They're escaping—"

***

Cali caught up with James and Blythe as they sprinted down the halls. She pulled out her sword and dug it into the waist of a charcoal soldier that stepped toward her from the shadow. On the other side of her, James and Blythe dealt with their own situation.

Behind them, the screams of the kaoti threatened to close in. Cali tried to ignore the dread and repulsion from Pluto's threat and kiss as it mixed with the pulse of fear, and she raced down the hall. She had no idea what his Latin meant, but she tried to push it from her mind as she followed close behind James.

Two guards stepped out from a hall to the right, but before they could even lift their fiery swords, Blythe lifted *Nordfos* and decapitated the first in an instant. James and Cali reached Blythe as she dismantled the head from the second. Ash flew through the air, covering them all in soot and dust.

"We can't just keep doing this," Blythe gasped. She whipped a hand across her brow, making the black spread across her forehead and face. "We have the key—let's use it."

"How?" Cali could feel its coolness in her fisted hand. She uncurled her fingers.

"Well, keys usually unlock doors—"

"Blythe!" James roared. He grabbed Blythe's shoulder and whipped her around him as another coal soldier hurtled towards them.

Cali's sword was out and through the soldier before he could bring his own weapon around. Ash burst around them as she pulled her blade out, coughing through the soot.

"Where—where will it take us?" Cali gasped.

A scream rippled down the hall, making the corridor shudder. "I think we should focus more on running." James gestured for them to move down the hall the soldiers came from.

The walls around them were bare stone and seemed an endless maze, pulling them deeper and deeper into the realm of the Underworld Keep. Cracks rippled through the stone, giving a view of the outside hellscape of red, orange, and grey. *We're going in circles.* Cali looked over her shoulder as they stopped at a split in the hall. James ran a hand over his curls and cursed in several colorful languages that she didn't understand, but she knew what he meant. *We're lost.* The ground beneath them rumbled and tiny, splintered cracks began to form beneath her feet.

"That can't be good," Blythe muttered. "Aren't there any damn doors in this place?"

"Maybe someone with a map could—"

"I'm already looking!" James snapped back at Cali before she could finish.

She glowered at him but stopped talking. Instead, she focused on the rock that continued to crack beneath her feet. It seemed to spread back down the hall that they came from. Her heart lurched in her chest as she saw the shadows that filled the space they left. It crawled like a mist – reaching out to them ...

"James—" Cali breathed.

"I see it, I see it." James gave the map a desperate shake, flipping it over as if it would provide some insight into where they would go next.

The rumble grew, drowning out his words. A fracture appeared at the edge of the awning in the hallway they stood under. It slithered like an arachnid of darkness to them and webbed out towards the shadow.

"We have to keep moving," Blythe hissed.

With another curse, James agreed, and they bolted to the right.

"Door, door!" Blythe skidded to a stop where, to their left, stood a black-wood door with a single lock. Cali didn't see a handle, but it didn't seem to matter to Blythe who, in an instant, grabbed her hand with the key still clasped tight and slammed it into the lock. With Blythe's cold hand still covering hers, Cali turned the key and felt it click into place. Together, she and Blythe shoved it open. She could sense the darkness as it closed in at their heels.

"Go—go!" James pushed them through the doorway.

Cali cried out as her shoulder popped when she pulled the key loose, only just holding on to their salvation.

With a shudder, the door swung close behind them and left them in the void.

Chapter Twenty – Six

THE SMELL OF SMOLDER still filled her lungs as she inhaled, but the scent was different from the sulfur of the Underworld. This stench was potent, skunk-like, and made Cali feel a strange sense of calm. She blinked, but the darkness didn't go away. *What the ...*

She blinked again. Her arm moved slowly, and even her fingers felt strange and stiff as she curled them into fists and rubbed her eyes until she saw stars. Lights began to flicker in the dark as she opened her eyes.

Where am I? She wasn't sure if she asked aloud or not. Her thoughts felt disjointed from her mind, and she placed her hands on either side of her temples as if to convince herself that she remained sane and present. With unsure hands, she patted herself down. *Okay, I'm here—I don't know where I am, but I'm here.*

The stars didn't fade, and neither did the darkness. As she squinted into it, she realized it looked like the sky at night, with wisps of clouds and stars huddled in space. Her dry throat burned as she swallowed, but she ignored the pang of thirst and tried to focus.

"Where are we?" she croaked.

"You are in my home."

The calm dissipated in an instant. Cali took a sharp breath

as the stars and sky seemed to rise up and reveal a round room. Books lined the shelves that covered the walls and led up into the sky that lingered above. A staircase wrapped around the wall. One doorway stood at the base of the stairs that Cali faced. A wrinkled old woman leaned against the frame and stared at Cali with black, unfeeling eyes. A matted pink fur coat wrapped around the woman's bony frame. Beneath, Cali could see a too-low-cut white gown with newspapers and fabric swatches haphazardly sewn to it. Smoke rippled off the end of a cigarette that she held at the end of her wrinkled fingers.

"Your ... where am I?" Cali demanded. She still held the Key of Ymir in her grip but dropped the hand, holding it close to the hilt of her sword. "Who are you?"

"I think the question is," the woman took a long drag of the cigarette she held between her fingers and then flicked the ash, "who are you?"

Cali frowned. *More mind games.* The woman took a step forward and Cali took one back. "Don't," she growled, then looked around. "Where—where are my friends? What have you done with them?"

The woman laughed, deep and throaty. "This has nothing to do with them." Her voice sounded like she smoked a pack of cigarettes every day, and she smelled like it too. She tossed the cigarette to the floor. "This has to do with you."

"Me?" Cali's heart dropped. "What does this have to do with me?"

The woman remained silent as she pulled another pack of cigarettes from her pocket. A spark flickered at the tip as she pressed it to her lips.

Cali slowly wound the strap of the key over the hilt of her blade. She rested her clammy hands across the cool copper. "Who are you?"

"My name is Postverta." Postverta's black eyes swirled with

smoke as she took another few shuffling steps forward. She raised a hand as Cali began to pull out her sword. "There will be no need for that. There is plenty enough bloodshed in your future without you taking my life in my own home."

After a moment of hesitation, Cali clicked the sword back into place by her side. Still, she kept her hand on the hilt as Postverta met her at the center of the room. *Postverta, Postverta ... I've heard that name before.* She tried to remember the many names strewn throughout Maechon's books. Postverta cocked her head, as if she could see Cali's mind work.

Then she remembered.

"You're an oracle," she gasped, and took a step back. "I thought—"

"You thought all of the oracles were dead," Postverta replied, bitterness laced her tone. "And many—most—maybe all, are. No thanks to you," she pointed a shriveled, bony finger at Cali, "Ophelli could have been one of the greats, had not fate intervened and sent the Furie there to kill her."

Sweat dripped down Cali's back. Panic began to edge into her veins as Postverta closed in on her. Besides the door behind her, there were only the endless stairs to nothing. No escape. "I told that Furie at the Farm to heed my warning, but no. She just had to test her little theories and put you in the middle of trouble. See, *I* am not an oracle, so I don't heed the future—"

"Ah yes, you tend to stay a little too focused on the past, don't you, Postverta?"

Slowly, Cali pulled her gaze from the fathomless eyes of Postverta to Natasha. The Furie stood, dressed to the teeth in black and brown leathers. Her muscles rippled as she crossed her arms and surveyed them from her post at the door. Soft shadows traced the outline of her body as she stalked into the room, almost as if she was a shadow from a dream, or ...

"This isn't real," Cali breathed. "I'm not here."

Natasha gave Cali a tense once-over. "I suppose that is a matter of perspective."

"Don't." Anger replaced the shock and, reality or not, Cali would not forget the lies this woman fed her. "You ... you lied to me."

"Perspective," Natasha said, her lips twitching in a smile at Cali's growl of irritation. "I omitted certain truths—"

"Let me guess, try to and keep me safe?" Cali snapped. Her fingers began to tremble as they wrapped tighter around her sword. "Or was it to keep others safe from me?"

There it was. The truth.

Postverta threw a side-eyed warning at Natasha. "You do not have very much time, Furie." Her black eyes searched the ceiling as a sound like thunder rolled through the clouds there. "They're going to find me soon."

"We will be but a moment, Postverta," Natasha replied, and the old woman hobbled toward the stairs and sat on the last step. Her shaking fingers twisted another cigarette out of the case. "Postverta owed me a favor," Natasha said to Cali. "Which is why you and I are able to meet here. In her mind."

"In her mind?"

"Postverta is one of the first oracle..."

"I'm NOT an oracle!" Postverta screamed, and the room shook.

Natasha rolled her eyes. "One of the first *seers*, specifically of the past." She gestured to the room. "This is part of her past, and one of the places she has been hiding from Erinyes."

"At peace until you showed up!"

"You owed me a favor, Postverta," Natasha coldly reminded the goddess of the past. She turned back to Cali. "I had her summon your mind and mine here for us to meet."

Cali's own mind fizzled and everything around her went gray. She blinked, and the room came into focus again.

"Easy." Natasha grabbed her shoulder. "Too strong of emotions and she might not be able to keep you here."

"Why am I here?" Cali demanded. "Where are James and Blythe?"

"James and Blythe will hardly even realize you're gone. To them, this will be the exact moment you stepped from the Underworld into Tartarus. Trust me."

"You're asking me to trust you?" Cali snorted.

Natasha's eyes narrowed. "Yes."

"Why didn't you tell me I was an Immixtus."

The room stilled. Even the sweet smell of cannabis and smoke seemed to freeze at Cali's words. Natasha's lips formed a thin line as she took another step towards Cali, leaving just several feet between them. "Believe me or not, I was trying to protect you," she said. The silver in her eyes flashed with emotion that Cali couldn't place. "Just like Aliax and Miriam tried to protect you."

"Don't bring them into this," Cali said through gritted teeth. "You should have told me."

"Maybe."

"No, you should have." Cali hesitated, recalling the words Natasha said moments before. "Wait." She ran a hand over her forehead. "You knew we were in the Underworld." She met Natasha's cool gaze. "You knew I had the map." Natasha gave a slow, single nod. "And you knew I'd go after them." No response. "You knew I'd have to go to the Underworld and that we'd have to go to Tartarus? So, all that you've said about keeping me safe. That's crap."

"Perhaps," Natasha said, again keeping her answers vague. Cali grit her teeth. "When you lied about Chaos having the map, I realized you had more spirit than I gave you credit for. But regarding the truth of who, of *what*, you are ..." For the first time since Cali met Natasha, she saw nervousness cross her face.

"You have to understand Cali. The first Immixtus'—the Faytes. They disappeared so long ago that they remain legend, but the truth of their actions remains. What they were and could do was horrible and powerful. They let their power consume them. We ... I was worried that—"

"That I would do the same," Cali finished for her. Her nails dug deep into her palms, but she held Natasha's fiery gaze. *She thinks I'm a monster, that's why she didn't tell me.* "I'm not like them." *I'm not a monster.* She swallowed the lump building in her chest.

"That's your choice, Cali," said Natasha.

A beat of silence passed.

"Tick tock, tick tock," Postverta sang from the corner, her smoke-filled voice filling the air.

Cali dipped her chin and looked at the red crescent-shaped scars on her right hand. "Why did you bring me here, Natasha?"

"Because you do have a choice Cali." Natasha stepped closer. The edges of her frame began to tremble as if she would disappear with the slightest breeze. Her small black braids shifted against her forehead, where a vein throbbed. "No matter what happens going forward. You get to have a choice in your actions, in how you respond, how you wield your power."

"But I don't have any power!" Tears began to betray her words and her voice cracked.

Natasha brushed a hand against her cheek. "Look a little deeper Cali, open the door. You'll find what you need."

"What do you mean?"

Natasha gave a pained smile. "Find the prophecy, and you'll find out who you are."

"Prophecy? What prophecy? What does that even mean?" The ground beneath Cali's feet shifted, and the sky dropped. Natasha began to fade. "Wait—Natasha, what do you mean? You can't just say—"

"Time's up!"

Natasha kept her silver eyes on Cali. "There's more to everyone than meets the eye, Cali."

Cali opened her mouth, but it did nothing to stop the inevitable. The Furie, Postverta, and the room disappeared.

Chapter Twenty – Seven

"Cali? Cali wake up! Come on—come back to me!"

Someone held her shoulders and shook her. It was still so dark.

Come back to me.

Slowly, she opened her eyes. Gray desert stretched for miles. All around them were rolling dunes of gray sand. The air was still and made everything feel far away and hopeless. Cali's insides twisted with the words from Natasha. And the truth the devil had given her. The discussion seemed a strange dream that barely clung to her memory.

I'm an Immixtus.

Her eyes focused on the blurred face of James, who stood in front of her and held her from tipping over as she startled back into consciousness. She blinked several times. His ocean-blue eyes stormed with anger and worry as he studied her face.

"Wha—what happened?" she stammered, her voice coming out hoarse and distant.

Relief flooded James' face. "You're back."

"Thought we lost you, Mixie," Blythe agreed from her post behind James. Her pale face was pulled, but Cali couldn't be sure if it was in concern or her regular irritation. "Where'd you go?"

"I ..." Cali frowned. The strange meeting with Natasha

echoed in her mind like a dream before waking up. *Was that even real?* "I don't really know?" She looked at James' hands on her shoulders, still gripped tight as if she might disappear. He caught the look and let go, taking a step back as he did. "Was I not ... here?"

"Well, some of you was here," Blythe said and stepped beside James to study her. "The rest of you was just like this—" She made a dramatic show of seizing her body and rolling her eyes back into her head, then stopped as quickly as she started with a smirk. "You had your soul pulled."

"My—what are you talking about?"

"Soul pulling," Blythe repeated, as if it was obvious. Cali stared at her confused. "It's when a soul is—"

"It's something only a few and very powerful gods can do." The relief washed from James' face and replaced itself with caution. "They can summon a part of you to them if your mental shield is down and bring you to a place in time or history. They can also send part of their own self-soul to a place."

"Like Chaos did in Rome," Cali murmured in disbelief. "That's what happened to me?" He nodded. "So, it wasn't real—or was it?"

"It was as real as we are now, in a way." He paused. "Where did you go Cali?"

"I don't really know," she admitted. "Natasha was—"

"Natasha was there?" Blythe and James asked simultaneously.

James added, "What did she say? What did she want?"

Cali rubbed a finger at her temple and traced her scar to her throbbing deaf ear. "She just wanted to talk, I guess."

James looked unconvinced. "Natasha wouldn't have risked pulling you to her just to talk." Frown lines creased his forehead as he thought. "Was anyone else there?"

Cali nodded. "A woman—ish. Postverta?"

"*Shit*," Blythe mumbled in mild awe. "Natasha made you go to that kook?"

"You know her?"

"Of her," James answered for them both. "Postverta is said to be the grandmother of many of the oracles. She went into hiding after she tried to help several Immixtus escape death." Cali and Blythe stared at him. "She was unsuccessful. Zeus and Odin killed the children anyway." The pit began to form in Cali's stomach again and she bunched her fists. The key remained a cool reminder of danger in her hand. "She's been in hiding ever since. Almost as long as the Faytes have been. What did she say?"

"She didn't say much," Cali replied. "She apparently owed Natasha a favor, which is why we were able to meet in her 'mind-palace' or whatever - wherever we were." She sighed and looked out over the gray plains that surrounded them. "She knew where we were going, that I had the map, that I would do this – and didn't try to stop me, or any of us," she looked between her companions, "she said there was a prophecy." *And that I am a monster.* That part Cali left out, but from the look in James' eye he seemed to have guessed what she might have said.

"A prophecy?" Blythe groaned. "I hate prophecies—it's so ... cliché."

James remained quiet; his lips formed a thin line.

"What are you thinking?" Cali asked him. "Do you know what she meant?"

He shook his head. "Not entirely." She noticed beads of sweat beginning to form on his brow and something like pain—*pain*—crossed his face. "What I do know is this: we need to keep going and find the others. We may not be able to save the world right now, but we can save our friends. We need to finish this."

To emphasize his remarks, he pulled the map from his inner pocket and unfolded it. His fingers trembled, and he straightened it out so they could all look at the swirling figures and pictures on the old parchment.

"Are you alright?" Cali asked, worry lacing her words as he shifted his weight from one foot to the other.

He scowled at her. "I'm fine."

"But—"

"That way." He pointed towards the horizon, where a gray-hazed sun hung low in the sky. Mountain ranges peaked in the distance. "According to the map, that's where the Door of Cronus will be. With the mountains, there would be plenty of space to hide out and keep prisoners."

"And monsters," Blythe added.

James ignored her. "Chaos would keep them close to the door as her route of escape—if she ever got the power of the key back, that is." He glanced at Cali's clenched fist. She hesitated, then offered it out, but he shook his head. "Keep it. We won't need it until we get to the door anyway." A subtle wince crossed his face as he turned towards the desert spread before them. "Ready?"

Cali looked between them and nodded. "Let's go save our friends."

***

They walked for what felt like hours—and it very well could have been. It was hard to tell because the Tartarus sun never wavered or shifted from its position. Everything it touched was dead and withered. There were a few trees along the desert route they took toward the mountains that loomed ahead. Each tree stretched bone-white branches to the sky, desperate for some sort of life or water. Cali understood the feeling. Her small canteen held just a small amount of water, and she tried her best to ignore the pang of hunger. Even though the sand made for a slow pace, they were getting closer to the mountain ranges. They reached far higher than they looked in the distance, their jagged edges becoming clearer with each step.

James still marched in front of them, keeping his eyes focused on the higher land. He kept silent, whereas Blythe took up a different form of coping. She kept *Nordfos* out and ready, keeping a pace or two behind them as she swung her blade around. *How nice that she can just be so calm about all this.* Cali couldn't stand it. She kept walking and was left to ruminate on her thoughts in the silence of James and the swish of Blythe's blade. She was left to build on her anxiety about the fact that she was potentially walking to her death—or the death of her friends. And she had the words of Natasha and Pluto swirling in her head, too. She replayed their words over and over until she almost forgot who said them. *A promise to Pluto and a prophecy from Natasha.* She also replayed the last few months in her mind, and she still found it hard to believe her life had changed so dramatically. *I still can't believe this is real.*

"I think the same thing, sometimes."

Cali started. "I didn't realize I said that out loud."

James gave a small huff of laughter then went back to silence. He kept his head tilted away from her, as if to avoid talk or eye contact. But she couldn't stand it.

"I thought there were supposed to be monsters in Tartarus?"

Blythe snickered from behind them. She pulled out one of her daggers and lazily flicked it between her fingers while *Nordfos* rested in the other hand. "Well, you're here, aren't you, Mixie?"

"Ha, ha." Cali quickened her pace, so she almost matched James' stride. "I mean, would they know we're coming?"

"Maybe." He kept his eyes forward. Sweat beaded down his brows and soaked his shirt. Their jackets were abandoned a mile or so back, but he looked like he was burning up. "Probably. We should just assume they know, and work based on that information. We stay together, stay alert—"

"And stay alive," Blythe added, with a flourish of her blade.

"Do you think ..." Cali paused as she adjusted her sword, the key wrapped carefully and right around the hilt. She was going to say, *Do you think they are still alive after all this time?* Instead, she bit her lip and stopped talking. She fell into silence alongside James as the steady *swoosh* of Blythe's blades rang behind them.

Beside her, James' steps seemed to falter, but he kept his shoulders back. She studied him, his posture, the way his muscles bunched as he rolled his shoulders and tightened in his jaw, and the way his curls stuck to his sweaty forehead and the blood that trickled down the cut in his arm.

"You're hurt!" She gasped and stopped in her tracks. Grabbing his forearm, she tried, and failed, to pull him around to face her.

He jerked from her touch. "It's nothing."

"James, you're hurt," she said and quickened her pace to get in front of him, causing him to stop before running her over. "How? I thought you couldn't ... how?"

"It's this place, Mixie," Blythe said, peering around James' shoulder at the wound. She prodded the torn sleeve of his shirt at the cut with her dagger, causing James to let out a hiss of air.

"Don't do that," Cali snapped, then turned back to James. "What does she mean?"

"Tartarus was the perfect prison for the monsters because it was the place created to drain power, but not kill," he said, keeping his eyes fixed on the mountains instead of her face. "It made it the perfect prison for Chaos, too. Not so perfect that they didn't still have to harness some of that power into the gifts."

One of which we are bringing to her right now. Cali brushed her fingers against the hilt of her sword. "So, you can be hurt," she murmured as James sidestepped her and continued past. She stepped in beside him, with Blythe taking up her position just behind. "But you—we can't die?"

"Oh, we can die, Mixie," Blythe snorted. She tapped *Nordfos* just lightly enough to draw a sliver of blood from Cali's neck. "It'll just be really, really, hellishly slow. And then we'll probably just end right back up with your new boyfriend."

Ignoring her comment, Cali turned her attention back to James. "We should wrap it with something," she said. When he looked at her, confused, she pointed to his arm. "The wound—it looks shallow, but it could still get infected."

He laughed, and she nearly tripped over her feet at the sound. "I think getting an infection is the least of our worries right now." Nodding towards the ever-approaching mountains, his features returned to their cooled composure. "I'll be fine. I'm just not used to the painful side of living. Or at least the physical. I'll be alright."

"You better be," Cali muttered.

His head tilted as he studied her. "Is that concern I hear?"

"Maybe," she snapped without much bite. "Probably more than you deserve for lying to me all these months."

Any amusement on his face vanished. "I suppose that's fair," he replied coldly. "The Fayte's never seem to give us what we deserve in life." His eyes widened. "I didn't mean it like that."

Cali pursed her lips. The face of Ophelli, imprinted on her nightmares and waking hours, flashed across her mind and the unintended insinuation. It was an accident; she knew logically, but she couldn't shake the feeling of blame—and that she deserved some sort of punishment for her actions, or lack of, in the girls' death.

James said something, and she cocked her head. "What?"

"I'm sorry," he repeated, quietly. His eyes darted to Blythe, who pretended not to listen. "For everything. For failing to help you in Varsna, for failing to protect you from the things that haunt you, for not telling you about who you are and failing as...as your leader. I should have protected you."

A hollow pit formed in Cali's stomach and her throat closed back the tears that threatened to choke her. She swallowed. *So, we both feel our failures too deeply*. "My actions in life are my own, by Fayte or otherwise," she said, with some difficulty keeping her voice even. "They aren't your failures as a leader, James."

"Then for failing as your friend," he murmured. He stopped and stared down at her. The despairing wind brushed some of his curls across his eyes. Cali blinked back the salt stinging her eyes. "I know that apologizing will not make up for the things I didn't tell you, but when we are through this, I will tell you everything you ask—everything you want to know. Although I don't know much about this prophecy. We'll figure it out. I promise."

"That's a pretty big promise," she said after she found her words again. "It means we all have to get out of this."

"We are all getting out of this," Blythe said, coming up beside her and slinging an arm over her shoulder. The dagger—the same one she stabbed Cali with—dangled between her fingers. "And for what it's worth Mixie," she schooled her features into looking almost apologetic as she looked at Cali as intently as James did, "I," she paused and sniffed as if close to tears, "I don't care about your feelings enough to apologize."

Cali rolled her eyes. But the effect worked. The tension broke. And they were at the base of the mountains. *And we will get through this together*. Cali held James' eyes for a split second more, a silent promise confirmed, before they turned to the mountains and their fate.

Chapter Twenty – Eight

The quiet was deafening as they weaved through the base of the mountains. To Cali, they looked more like cliffs, with sharp inclines and jagged rocks pointing in all directions down the slopes. Ice crusted some of the taller peaks. No grass or trees or life of any kind could be seen. But there was *something* here. Cali could feel it in her bones. Like an ache on a too-early, cold morning. The gray sun still beat down on them, but she found herself wishing she'd brought her jacket along as they crept forward. Every scatter of rock or small breath or sound made them freeze. Each of them already held their sword, and the girls flanked James as they moved forward around each bend.

"What are we looking for?" Cali said, barely breathing the words out.

"The Door of Cronus," James replied. "It's the only way in or out for those banished here."

"But Nyx and Erinyes—" They all paused at the sound of rocks sliding down the slope behind them. After several heartbeats, Cali continued, her voice quiet. "If the others are trapped here and Nyx and Erinyes and the kaoti all come and go—can't she?"

James brushed his hair from his face as he pulled the map out and studied it. "Nyx and Erinyes were not banished here, so they can come and go as they please." His frown deepened and he looked at the area they stood in. "The kaoti are Chaos' most recent creations—created now that the prophecy predicting her escape is almost up. She created them from human souls, knowing that they would be outside of the realm of her or her monsters' banishment."

"So, they can attack and kill anyone they want because of a clause in some Realm law?" Cali demanded, annoyed and shocked. James shrugged.

"Semantics," Blythe whispered. "James-ey. Any luck?"

James put the map away with a scowl. "This map is less than helpful at times. It looks like there may be a different way in from behind—" Blythe snorted, and even Cali pursed her lips to keep from untimely laughter. "I suppose I could just leave you both here and figure this out myself."

"Ugh, we may die. Take a joke!" Blythe groaned, and Cali hid her laugh behind her hand.

James shook his head, but Cali caught the faintest hint of a smile.

He nodded for them to continue, and they resumed weaving between the rocks and ledges a few more feet. Cali used the time to re-braid her matted hair so that it would stay out of her face. It had become another nervous habit she acquired and, even though she was nowhere near as good at braiding as Griffin, it did the job.

She followed James, keeping her eyes on his back, as they rounded a ledge.

The air around them remained still and quiet.

"There!" Blythe pointed to their left.

At first, Cali couldn't tell what they were looking at. The bend dumped into a pass between the mountains. A gap between the peaks to their left led to two pillar-like rocks. The pillars bridged each other, precariously balanced. Several feet behind them, Cali could see the smooth face of the mountain.

On the flat surface of the rock, just at an angle as the clouded sun hit, she saw a crude drawing of a sickle in the stone. Blythe looked triumphantly at her find. "Cronus Gate or what?"

"That hardly looks like a gate," said Cali. She tilted her head and squinted at the supposed door. *It looks just like a part of the mountain.*

"I doubt the gate-door thing is going to actually look like a door, idiot," Blythe said, annoyed. "That has to be it."

"She's right. Not about the idiot part, but...anyway" James said from his post behind the map. "Let's try the key just to be—"

Before he could finish his sentence, a familiar scream filled the air. Cali's veins rippled to life, ready for action. But another part of her—maybe her human part—flared with fear. She licked her lips, willing the fear away, and placed both hands over the hilt of her sword. *I will not be afraid—I've made it this far.* The screams reverberated off the canyon walls. But no kaoti appeared. Just their voices echoing from all directions.

"They may not have seen us yet," said James, with less optimism than Cali liked. He jerked his head to the right where, in the bend of the next corner, several gaps in the mountain face created an overhang. "There—let's go."

"Is that where they are?" Cali said in a low voice as she jogged beside her companions.

"The map isn't showing anything very specific anymore," James said as he eyed the ridges. "But if legend is correct, there are caves and catacombs in these mountains. That's our best bet—but we can't risk an open attack. We have to find cover."

The air changed in an instant. The wind whipped up and caused the sand to swirl into a storm. Cali covered her mouth as they stumbled forward as the gravel pelted her. With one hand over his mouth and nose as a shield, James turned back again and pointed to where a massive lizard-like skeleton lay on the ground just at the base of the overhang. It looked like it had died crawling out of its cave. *Or was killed coming out?* Cali tried not to think about whatever might have killed a creature of that size—and what could be lurking in the depths of the cave beyond it.

"There!" James shouted above the storm. "To the cave—go!"

The storm continued to grow, and the wind shoved against them as they stumbled forward. The sand became so thick in the air that Cali could barely see in front of her, much less if Blythe and James were beside her.

"Keep going!" she heard James roar.

Her eardrums rang with the sounds around her as the storm and kaoti screamed in tandem. She shook her head to focus and lurched forward, sword still in hand. It grew darker, and she realized she must have entered the mouth of the cave. Steady throbbing pulsed behind her damaged eardrum and even her sight seemed gone. As she tried to blink away the sand and stinging tears, panic began to crawl over her. Even the comfort of her sword seemed lost as she tried to regain control of her senses.

"Watch out!"

"James!" Cali cried out as she fell through the Earth.

James reached for her, but it was too late.

Darkness took her.

***

Cali's head hit the ground hard. Shocked that she remained conscious, she did a quick mental assessment of her body. Her body screamed in agony as it tried to bring in air. The pain came next. Gasping, she lay on her back, dug her fingers into the soil and spit out the dirt building in her mouth. As the dust settled around her, she managed to pull herself to her side.

She tried to focus her eyes and head as the ringing echoed in her skull. The sound of another groan near her made her turn her head, with some difficulty.

James propped himself on his elbows, then pushed himself to his knees. With a strangled groan, he made it to his feet and straightened. That was when Cali noticed the jagged rock protruding from his side. She rolled to her stomach and winced as she pushed herself to a shaky, all-fours position. *James.* James' eyes glazed and focused on the object embedded in his skin. Cali groaned as she rocked back to her haunches. Three stunned pairs of eyes looked back at her from the edge of, what Cali could only imagine was a steep drop.

"James," Cali choked out, still spitting mud and blood. The taste of copper filled her mouth and she gagged. She struggled to push herself to her feet as her knees screamed in pain and, without looking, she knew blood soaked her pants. At the very least, she was in one piece.

The two humans and the massive faun still stared at her in wary surprise at the sudden intrusion. They hadn't moved in the seconds Cali and James hit the ground floor of the drop. She didn't recognize their faces, so she wasn't sure if they were captors or captives. The three exchanged looks between themselves and spoke, but she couldn't hear what they said.

She shook her head and blinked. "Who ... are you?" *Sword, sword, sword.* She glanced to her right, where she could see the bronze hilt in the red dirt, and she pulled her gaze from the blade to the three watching her.

The faun moved first. He pulled from his belt a massive bat and began to stalk forward. *Okay, so bad not on our side.* Cali spit out more blood as she stood, hunched slightly as her lungs ached for more air. James still stood, swaying as he gripped the rock, confusion evident on his face.

The faun rushed him.

"James!"

Cali got there first.

The faun male was almost twice her size, and it felt like crashing into a mountain as she hurtled into him. He remained upright, but his advance paused as he narrowed in on her as his new target. The other two, a young man and woman, now followed their companion and brandished an axe and a large sword. Both came at Cali and the faun with snarls on their faces.

Cali tried to pull herself from the faun, but he wrapped his free hand around her neck, holding her fast. Her sword lay useless several feet behind her.

He pulled her into the air with little effort and brought the bat around. She brought one fist into his face, striking hard between yellow-red eyes as she'd learned in combat from Bear. The other hand, twisted against the pain in her shoulder, gripped the hand at her throat. She needed air—her lungs screamed and already darkness fuzzed her vision.

She struck again, and again, to the same point in his face. The fauns taunting blood-filled smile slacked when James slammed into him. The grip released from her throat, and she jerked back as they all went down.

Cali's knees ached, landing painfully. She tucked away from the faun and James and rolled to her sword. The hit from the girl's axe radiated pain to her shoulder as Cali brought her blade up to meet the blow. The girl towered over her, lips curled back in a snarl, as Cali remained on her knees. Ducking around her own blade, Cali kicked out and swiped the girl's legs out.

The girl was on her feet at the same time as Cali and leaped at her, dagger raised. Cali dodged the blow to her face and blocked the other hit from the axe. Muscle memory from training helped with footwork, but the girl before her fought with a fierceness that Cali had never seen on the Farm. There was strength in each hit, and feral emphasis to kill with each blow. *She's a demi,* Cali realized.

The young man, almost forgotten by Cali till now, lunged at her. Cali blocked the blow and stepped back, trying to place distance between them and herself.

The girl hissed, baring her teeth as she crouched opposite. Her companion did the same, although he seemed to lack the same energy as the girl. They circled each other like wolves, ready to pounce. Cali hefted her sword in her blood-soaked hand. The hilt was slick, but the wrapped leather from the key made it easier to grip. Cali and her opponents barely had a chance to look up when Blythe came barreling down through the hole Cali and James had fallen through. *Nordfos* impaled the shocked young demi male before he had a chance to react. Blythe stood there, on top of her fallen victim, covered in blood. In her other hand, she held the head of a kaoti. Even with the peril of the moment, Cali felt a pang of admiration and jealousy at her fearless friend. *Always so dramatic.*

Blythe, as if hearing Cali's thoughts, gave her an impish grin, her white teeth standing out among the dark red blood that dripped down her face.

"Having guests and not inviting me?" Blythe panted. "I hate missing a party."

"And yet, you seemed dressed for the occasion anyway," Cali replied through her teeth.

The girl with the axe let out a guttural scream as she lunged at Cali, the sharp double edge narrowly missing Cali's ear. Dipping back, she swung around to block the blow, but the butt of the dagger came up and smashed her in the face as their weapons locked. Stunned, she felt her left knee give, but she ducked and tumbled before the dagger could finish the job with its pointy end.

Blythe growled and went low. The girl had better sense and skill than her companion and dodged Blythe's approach. She rained a volley of blows, which were responded to in kind. Cali sprang back to her feet. Even with the ringing in her ear and fainted breath, she lurched forward and came at the demi girl from behind.

The girl blocked the attack with her dagger without looking. Blythe let out a scream of rage as the girl cut into her sword arm. Cali's heart slowed as she saw Blythe hit the ground. The ringing stopped—her breathing leveled. And something clicked inside of her.

Something—that hidden thing—awoke.

Open the door, Cali.

And she did.

Her opponent swung around to face her fully, bringing her dagger around fast towards Cali's face. Ducking, Cali felt as if she had lost control of her body but gained control of something else. A dark desire crept into her, overpowering her pain and daze. Focus resolved itself. Cali let herself slip into the feeling she had in Rome—that feeling Chaos had teased out and that Cali had allowed to remain afraid and dormant within. It crawled over her like a comfortable embrace, like a feral readiness.

Cali felt a surge of strength as she slammed her blade into the axe and pulled it around. She dragged the steel up the length of the shaft and sliced up the arm of the girl. The demi girl cried out as Cali relieved her of her axe, and then grabbed the hand with the long dagger that remained. The skill became matched—even with dagger against sword. It became a deadly dance between them. The moment came. A faltering step in the movements gave an upper hand. Cali brought her sword up into the girl's chest and cracked against her ribs.

The seconds dragged on to eternity as Cali pulled herself back into focus. The girl's pupils expanded, then dilated as blood spurted from her lips. Words, barely audible, whispered in a language Cali didn't know as the girl gasped beneath her steel. Cali's eyes focused on the face. She had been able to kill kaoti easily enough, if that even is what it was considered given. They were already dead—the souls of the dead stolen by Chaos—but the crunch of her blade against this flesh and bone was startling. Worse still, Cali hadn't known she had a fight like this in her and this win. That desire to win, to kill … it felt *good*.

Cali stepped back slowly, and time seemed to stall. Her eyes never left the girl's face. The light faded from the demi's eyes, and Cali felt drawn to the other face, to the girl in Varsna. *This is not that place.* The girl tipped sideways as Cali withdrew her blade, and she fell to the ground without another sound.

"Cali?"

Cali's swayed as she tried to refocus her gaze on the person in front of her. *I killed her.* Cali couldn't tear her gaze from the unblinking, frozen stare. *I killed …*

Blythe snapped her fingers again. She then began to rip part of her shirt off at the hem and wrapped her bleeding arm. "Didn't know you had that in you—and to think you let me stab you."

"I didn't mean to kill her," Cali said faintly. She hadn't known what she was doing. *But did I?* Each pulse of her heartbeat echoed in her veins. And slowly—so slowly—she closed the door she'd opened.

"Don't think she would have thought twice about it," Blythe continued, tying a knot in her makeshift bandage for her wrist. Cali held her tongue in commenting on how little this did in helping, given her body was covered in would-be scars. "These must be Chaos' recruited demi's." She nudged the dead girl with her shoe. "This must be a Norse. Think that other one was too, maybe?" Cali followed where Blythe pointed to the young man she had impaled. "We'll have to watch out for them now besides the kaoti. Hey, you got dibs on the axe? Cause I'm totally taking it."

Blythe continued to talk as she relieved the corpse of her former axe and snapped it to her own belt with some pride. She then patted the rest of the body down to see if she could find any other trinkets. "And a dagger for you." She held the girl's rusted dagger, hilt first, out to Cali. Making a face, Cali began to shake her head, but Blythe shoved it into her hand anyway. "Spoils of war, Mixie. She ain't needing it anymore."

Cali hated the feel of the dagger in her hand, but still, she slipped it into her belt beside her sword.

"We have to keep going." She wiped the sweat and blood from her face as she turned to James. He stood over the faun male, the jagged rock that had been in his side he now held in his hand, like a savage trophy. Blood pooled down from the wound that it left. Beside the faun were two kaoti, one still twitching violently. Black blood also pooled on the rock. *He'd used it to kill them*, she realized as she staggered to him.

Blythe stood up from ransacking the young girl and studied James with an edge of concern. "You okay there, buddy?"

Cali reached James just as he pitched forward. Blood seeped through his fingers as he gripped the open wound at his side, and he let the rock go. She winced but dug her heels in to keep them both from falling as she braced him up.

"It's fine." James straightened, pushing himself off her even though it took great effort. "Are you alright?"

"James, you are not fine. You're seriously hurt."

He stepped back, searching her face. "Cali?"

"I'm fine." Without looking, she already knew she looked less than fine. Her nose and ear trickled blood down her face and neck, and if she didn't do something about the dirt in her wounds, she would get an infection. *But I'm alive, I'm alive, and I have the key.* And her adrenaline, or whatever that feeling was made her feel ... invincible. It had wafted away with the life of the girl. Now she felt hollow.

"The key?"

"Still got it," Cali said, her fingers instinctively resting on where she had tied it against her hilt. She placed the sword back at her side. "We have to stop this bleeding." She grabbed James' arm to keep him from stepping back again and put her hand on his over his wound. He winced but didn't pull away.

"We don't have—"

"You're going into shock," Blythe surmised.

"Besides that," Cali added before he could protest. "You'll have less time if you bleed out before we find the others."

"Here." Blythe handed her a ripped-up t-shirt, which Cali grabbed without looking back and began tearing into strips.

"Blythe, you better be wearing a shirt when I turn around," Cali muttered more to herself as she wrapped most of the shirt over the wound as Blythe also passed her a thin rope. James tried to laugh, but it came out as a groan. "Another laugh. Wow. Maybe you need to come down here more often?"

"They say laughter is the best medicine. I thought it would help with the pain," he said between clenched teeth. "It doesn't."

"I don't think they meant with things like this." Cali wrapped a rope around his chest and waist several times before knotting it in place. "Hopefully that'll do for now." She looked up at him. His eyes sparkled, daring her to ask again if he was fine.

"We need to keep going." James stepped back from her and turned to a dark tunnel behind him. "The kaoti came from this tunnel, which I imagine is exactly where we now need to get to."

With her eyes adjusted to the dark, Cali could now see the entrance to the tunnel and the black stretch beyond as it weaved further into the ground. The crudely cut walls were lit with wooden stakes in the red-veined rock. It was a strange atmosphere change from the gray dusty land above.

"Looks like we found the catacombs," Blythe said, hefting *Nordfos* into her hand as she stood beside them at the entrance.

"We just walk further in?" asked Cali. She threw a glance behind her and then up. All that remained behind was a steep drop to nowhere, and above she could just see the swirl of gray dust. *Forward.*

"Unless you see a way out from here." James' voice strained, but he turned to face them with a resolute frown. "You still have the key?" Cali nodded. "And you both are still able to keep going?" *Are you?* Cali didn't ask this aloud but nodded again along with Blythe. "Then our best option is to go forward." He turned on his heel and walked into the entrance to the catacombs.

Blythe exchanged a wary look with Cali before they followed.

After a few moments of heavy silence, filled with shaky breathing from all three, James spoke again, "We must be close if we've run into some of Chaos' demi's and kaoti."

"God, I hope that doesn't mean you think we're walking into a trap." Cali wiped some of the blood and sweat from her palms to her pants and rotated her hilt. "I don't know if we can take another attack like that."

"Speak for yourself," Blythe muttered.

"I was," Cali whispered back. She eyed the rock walls around them as if they could hear her. Logically, she knew that wasn't possible. *But there is something wrong—alive and wrong about this place.* She shivered and stepped closer to Blythe. "And I don't doubt your resolve in a fight, but James is bleeding out—"

"I'll be fine," James snapped. "What we should worry about is the adrenaline wearing off. It'll get a lot more painful."

"Great." Cali groaned. "So, we could all die from blood loss before we can get to our friends."

"You'll have some nice battle scars," Blythe pointed out.

"Girls dig that. And they'll match your old ones. It's like a prize for winning."

"And losing is dying ... with scars?"

"Something like that."

Cali rolled her eyes as they continued. It seemed an endless maze of corridors and tunnels, some lit, while others were dark and murky. James seemed to be struggling to keep his pace, so Cali didn't mention retrieving the map. The cave's coolness should have felt like a relief from the outside heat, but it just made Cali feel as if she had stepped into a frigid nightmare.

"It feels like we're going in circles," Blythe hissed after several minutes passed of slow moving. "Also, is no one else worried we haven't had any surprise guests?"

"I'm worried about that too," James said. "But I can't read the map anymore, so ..." He froze.

"What?" Cali and Blythe asked simultaneously.

"Are you okay?" Cali tensed with anticipation; she could feel her heart hammering in her blood and head as she tried to peer over James' broad shoulders.

"I'm fine. The air ... it's different." He gently touched the blood-soaked bandage and Cali could tell pain creased his face. "I think we are getting close to something."

"Or just right back where we started," whispered Blythe.

Cali kept her sweaty grip on her blade. She watched as sweat dripped down the back of James' neck. *He does not look good.* Biting her lip, she shifted her blade from one hand to the other. James moved forward again, and she followed, Blythe at her side.

I have to say something—he needs a healer. She wondered if they found a door down there, could force James to go through it to safety? To whatever island the surviving demi's hid on. Her thoughts drifted to what it felt like to be safe and, distracted, ran right into James' back when he stopped.

"Careful," he murmured, bracing her with one arm and himself with the other against the wall so they both wouldn't fall over. He raised his hand, and Cali and Blythe moved in behind him. They stood motionless, barely breathing, as James edged his way around the bend before them.

From what Cali could see around James' hunched form, they made it into a more open area. Torches provided light in the deep cuts in the rock and revealed paths of dirt and precarious bridges of wood. The rope bridges swung over deep holes in the earth, reaching into fathomless black. Where they came in was close to one of the pits and Cali tried not to look down as she craned her neck to take in the expanse of the underground fortress Chaos had created for herself. Glimpses of gray light flickered above, but she couldn't see the sky. *We're below one of the mountains.* Cali's blood froze as she took in the hundreds of undead beasts that milled in the space. The steady hiss and groans of the kaoti filled the cavern.

James pressed them back against the shadow of the wall. "I think we've found them."

Chapter Twenty – Nine

"Doesn't seem to be any urgency anywhere," Blythe noted from her squat position. They remained at the mouth of the cave, just out of sight of the kaoti's eyes and clung to the shadows as they tried to plan their extraction and escape. "Either these guys didn't get the memo that their friends are dead, or they don't care."

"Clearly, they have the numbers going for them," Cali whispered. She watched as a large kaoti crossed a creaky walkway, shoving one of its own over the edge. The horrible scream faded before the creature hit the ground. "Maybe they don't know?"

"I highly doubt that," James muttered. "We made far too much noise for no one to realize we were here."

"Well, let's just pretend we're lucky," Blythe hissed back.

Cali frowned. "I don't think just luck will get us out of this." She pointed to a corner of the catacombs, several feet above them, just in her eyeline. "Is that the only way out?" she murmured to James.

He pulled the map, hemmed in blood, from his pocket.

"Ew." Blythe gagged and Cali elbowed her into silence.

"There are ..." He let out a low breath as he clutched his wound and focused his attention on a point on the map. "There are several openings in the rocks, beneath the caves. This whole place wasn't on the map before—it's a maze."

"But can we get through it?"

He folded the map. "We don't really have a choice. The lines are fading."

"Okay, well now that's decided, how do we stay long enough to get this over with?" Blythe demanded. "Split up?"

Cali bit her lip. "That can't be an option."

"That's not an option," James agreed.

Blythe unsheathed a dagger from near her ribs. "Even if we are lucky and it's not a trap," she growled in a whisper as the shuffle of feet came close, "there is no way we are getting through all of these tunnels without someone noticing."

"No, it's not an option," Cali hissed back. "We stay together and get out together, or not at all." Her eyes flicked to James. *We promised.* She moved to look back into the weaving bridges and ledges. "If we can manage to get across, do you think—"

"Heads up." Blythe plastered herself against the wall of the cave, pulling Cali with her. James already remained hunched in the shadows, but Cali knew it was because of pain, not fear of being seen.

The gray light flickered out as darkness filled the cavern. It was strange darkness—and cold. Cali peered around the edge and could see the shadow shape that caused the light to flee. It swept from a large door onto a walkway several yards across from where they hid. As the wood creaked shut, Cali could make out the muffled sound of screams. *Human* screams. Tortured screams. She swallowed the bile in her throat as she watched the figure.

Unlike Erebus, this darkness pulled inward. A woman at its center. Her black hair slicked back against her too-pale face. Any other distinctive feature was dissolved in the dark that enshrouded her. A feeling of death emanated in the cave now that pulled at Cali. A weight pressed against her chest—her bones ached. She felt it. The fear of what could not be seen. Like waking from a nightmare.

Chaos.

Beside Chaos walked Nyx. The Goddess of Night and the general to Chaos roved every inch of the catacombs they strode through. Power—undiluted and horrible—radiated from both women as they reached the other side. Several paces behind stalked another goddess. Strangely less terrifying in comparison to the two she followed. But the smoke of her darkness trailed her still. *Erinyes.*

Cali dug her nails into her free hand so hard that she could feel the blood oozing down her palm. The Furie paused, her head cocked to one side and her eyes shifted.

Frozen, Cali held her breath as the Furie searched the darkness. For a moment, Cali thought she looked directly at her. Then Chaos spoke. Cali couldn't hear what she said, but it snapped Erinyes' gaze away and, with a shake of the Furie's head, the three reached the other side of the bridge and the entrance of a tunnel opposite.

"I thought you said she looked normal, like a kid?" Blythe asked as Chaos' shadow drifted into the tunnel. "That was not normal looking."

"Obviously she changed," Cali said. Her breath clouded in the fresh cold air around them. She looked up at the door Chaos came from. With the return of the dim light, she could just make out the intricate carvings on the door itself. Even from the distance, she could see the monsters that gripped the crushed bodies of humans and fauns. "She's holding them in there."

Blythe nodded. "I heard it too. Seems as good of a place as any to store unwanted, tortured demi's."

"Did you see how the kaoti scattered when she came out?" James whispered beside them. He reined in his pain and studied the layout of the cove. "There are still too many for us to take. But if we had a distraction, we could—"

"Say no more." Blythe moved before either James or Cali could respond. She flipped the dagger in her hands and held it, hilt first, to Cali. Cali felt her side itch and glowered at Blythe as she realized what the weapon was. "To remember me by," Blythe said with a flourish.

As Cali wrapped her fingers around the hilt, Blythe pulled her in and kissed her hard. "And for you ..." Before he could react, Blythe leaned forward and kissed James as well. "Gods, I've wanted to do that for *for-ever*. Peace out, a-holes."

"B—no!" James tried to grab her but was too late as she burst into the opening.

Cali blinked. "If she doesn't get killed here," she growled. "I will kill her when she gets back."

"She'll be fine. It's Blythe after all," his voice trailed off as screams ripped through the pit and adjoining tunnels. It was hard to make out where they were coming from as the voices echoed through the walls, tunnels, and walkways around them. The kaoti sprang into action, disappearing into the underground like ants. James glanced at their target location. "Whether that's Blythe's distraction or not, let's move."

Keeping low, James and Cali sprinted across the closest walkway and took the closest, rickey stairs to the next level up. *Don't look down, don't look down.* Her breath felt lodged in her throat as she eased along the side of the rock to the next landing and walkway.

Then they reached the door. James put his hands on either side and slowly shoved it open. The hinges groaned and sputtered at the effort. He jerked his head towards the small opening, and she slipped through. He strained against the door before following her, letting the door slam closed behind them.

Chapter Thirty

Gray-white light flooded the room, making Cali squint for a moment as her eyes adjusted to the sudden brightness. She took in the massive cave in front of them. It spread wide, then narrowed beneath the overhang of the mountain, almost like a teardrop. A pair of large cracks ran through the ceiling and floor that led to the far end of the cave. The crack from both ceiling and floor met at a peak, revealing a tricky, but doable, escape over crumbled rocks at the pointed end of the cave. She tried to peer into the shadows of the overhang, straining to see who had screamed. Three kaoti hurled themselves from the shadows at them. Their screams echoed in the chamber, and she stepped back.

James' sword was through the skull of the first to reach them before Cali could even bring her own weapon up. She sidestepped as James brought the body of the creature, sword still impaled in its neck, straight into another.

The third went for Cali, its sickle reaching for her injured shoulder. Ducking, she spun her sword round her back and up. The crunch of bones and steel in its chest made her wince. It screamed but remained upright, bloody teeth and bulging eyes inches from her face. She tried to pull her sword out in time, but it struggled beneath her blow. Cali pulled Blythe's dagger from where it stuck in her belt and, with a quick flip of her fingers and overexertion in her free arm, she slammed it into the temple of the creature. In another move, she pulled it out and severed the head. The eyes lulled back as the head dropped to the ground; the body followed shortly after.

"Dammit, Blythe," Cali muttered, looking at the dagger in her hand. One fell swing from the piece had rendered the kaoti headless, and the same blade had at one point been embedded in her own side. She made a silent promise to herself that if … no *when* they made it out of here, she would pummel Blythe.

James removed Cali's sword from the twitching kaoti's body, wiped it on his pants, then handed it back to her with a grim look on his face. "You okay?"

Calo nodded, grabbing his offered hand as he pulled her to her feet. "Are you okay?" His face had grayed, and his eyes were rimmed with pain. The makeshift wrap on his wound was covered in blood.

He pursed his lips and nodded. *Liar*.

She rolled her shoulder to ease the pain as she took her sword back from him. Carefully, she replaced Blythe's dagger at her side. Movement from the shadows beyond caught her eyes and she tensed. James' jaw tightened. His sword ready.

"James?" a soft panicked voice, just notes above a whisper, echoed across the cave. The sword went lax in James' grip as he stepped toward the speaker. A mixture of relief and some other emotion Cali couldn't pin rushed through her veins as she followed James towards the sound of choked sobs.

Blood matted the Norse beauty's golden curls, and a gash just below her eye was just beginning to turn purple. Mixed with the mud and blood were tears that now streamed down the desperate Griffin's face. "James … I can't believe you're … you're here I …" Sobs made the words incoherent, and Griffin covered her face.

"Griffin." James stepped forward, and Cali sensed hesitation as she lingered just behind him. Griffin didn't move. As they came closer, Cali could see the reason. Cuffs dug deep into her wrists, connected by chains that led off into the darkness behind her.

"They just left us ... us here for days. For days ... they just ... left us ..." Griffin gestured behind her where Cali could make out the figures of the others. It was still too dark to make out who or how many there were. "They ... she ... she left us!"

"We're here now." James paused just before reaching Griffin. He held a hand up to pause Cali as well. "Cal, go cut the chains quickly. We can get out from here to the surface to get to the gate."

The door rattled. Behind it, Cali was certain Chaos would be aware of the pandemonium Blythe made of her prison-hole. As she looked at the dagger Blythe had given her, Cali found herself hoping her potential friend made it out safely. She hoped they all made it out of here safely. Not looking back at the reunion between her friends, she stepped into the shadow.

"The Door of Cronus?" Griffin asked. From the corner of her eye, Cali could see her pull James close for a harsh, quick kiss as he grappled with his knife. "You ... you found it? You would have to have the key then? If Chaos finds out—finds *it*—she could free herself from this place for good!"

"Don't worry about that right now," James said. He pressed the tip of his blade to the shackle and cracked it in one swift move. "Let's just get you out of here first."

"You're hurt?"

"Hardly," James said through gritted teeth. "We'll get out of here, and I'll be fine. We'll all be fine."

Cali heard the final shackle fall from Griffin's wrists as she moved through the shadow to her friends. Her eyes began to adjust to the dark beyond the beams and she saw a dozen or more demi's chained together. *Not all of these demi's came from the Farm.* She took in the familiar and unfamiliar faces as she inched forward. Her eyes landed on a scrawny, mangled young man.

"Maech!"

Maechon knelt, hands behind his back, with wild eyes staring back at her. A gag covered his mouth and Cali could see his hands were tied to his ankles behind him. After only a week, he looked even more emaciated than normal. His normal afro hair was matted around his face, making him look feral.

"Maech ... it's okay." She crouched next to him, her bloodied hands shaking from the aftermath of her ordeal, and from the anticipation that this horror may be over soon. Her hand drifted from the too-sharp blade Blythe gave her to the one she relieved from the demi girl. Beside Maechon lay Roro, her mouth also gagged and tied in a similar fashion to Maechon. Cali realized, as she began to pull the gag away, that all the demi's were tied in a similar manner.

"It's okay," Cali said looking up at their frightened, wide-eyed faces as she used the demi girl's dagger to pry the chain loose from Maechon. He began to sputter on air as he struggled to speak. "We're going to get you guys out of here. It's gonna be fine."

"No. No. C-c-cali—" Maechon shook his head and grabbed her wrist with the first hand she had freed. His grip was vice-like, and his eyes seared desperation. "I-i-i-it's a ... it's a—"

Cali's blood went cold. *Wrong.* Something was wrong. She made sure the key was wrapped tight around the hilt of her sword as her shaky fingers broke the final cuff holding him.

"No, it's okay Maech. We have the key. We can get out." She pointed with the rusted dagger to the dangerous exit where the cracks met the earth. "It's going to be fine."

"Cali!" Maechon's eyes filled with panic and frustration as he used his arm to continue to shake her. The other captives were also shaking their heads, their eyes as wild as Maechon's.

The hidden door inside began to creak open. *Wrong, wrong, wrong.* Pivoting on her heels, still crouched, she turned back to James.

Griffin wrapped her arms around him, and he stood stiff, brushing her curls as she shook with sobs against him. He caught Cali's eyes and froze. Slowly, he placed his hands on Griffin's shoulders and began to peel her away.

Griffin's head tilted to look at Cali through her mess of gold curls. Slowly, the lips curved into a smile.

"Wait." Cali's voice sounded distant as she stared at the two. *Wrong, wrong, wrong.* Maechon held her arm so tight she thought he might break it. The pain didn't faze her though, and she felt herself try to stand, although the whole moment felt surreal. "Wait!"

Griffin pulled herself from James as she bent her head back to look up at him.

James stared down at her in confusion, and Cali could see his lips begin to form a question, but it was too late. Griffin pulled his dagger from its sheath below his left arm. With her other hand she shoved James backward. Surprised, James stepped back. Griffin shoved again, harder this time, pushing against his chest and his open wound.

Cali stepped forward as James stepped back again. She wasn't sure if she screamed aloud or if it was just in her head. In horror, Cali could only watch as he doubled over from the pain of his wound and fell back. His eyes met hers just as he tipped out of sight into the crevasse of darkness.

***

No.

Something in this air was playing tricks on her mind. The horror, her tiredness and exhaustion—this wasn't real. Of all the real things that Cali had discovered to be true, this could not be one of them.

Griffin stood, back from her, staring into the darkness of the pit. The dagger she pulled from James hung limp in her grasp as her shoulders rolled back.

"Cali," Maechon's voice was muffled beneath the sound of the blood rushing in her head. His hand clasped around the dagger in Cali's hand.

Cali whipped around, bending his wrist so that he squeaked out in pain. They stared at each other, wide-eyed. Her grip relaxed and he nodded, before silently moving across the ground to the other captives sprawled around him.

A loud crash from outside the door reminded Cali that they were not out of this yet. Her body didn't seem to want to react. She watched as Maechon cracked open another chain with Blythe's dagger in tow. Digging her finger into the dirt, she willed herself to stand.

Cali shakily made it to her feet, using her sword to balance her, and then turned to face her friend. She heard the rattle of chains and stifled sobs of the other captives behind her as she watched Griffin's curls rustle in the damp wind from the outside. Cali reached inside herself, searching. *Open the door Cali.* At the time, she hadn't realized what Natasha meant. Her mother always told her to keep the peace, keep calm, and keep the bad feelings hidden behind the door inside. So, Cali had kept it closed her whole life. She never allowed the door to open more than a crack, had never seen what lay beyond, she knew what it was. *The bad things ... the power.* She wouldn't open that door. She wouldn't open that door.

The ground shivered beneath her feet as she straightened and loose rock and dust dropped from the sides of the cave. *Open the door, Cali.*

"I know what you're thinking," Griffin said, her voice barely a whisper. "Loveable Griffin? Who would have thought right?"

"Griffin," Cali's voice cracked, "what did you do?"

A cold hand touched her forearm. Beside her, Cali could make out the doe-eyed face of a young girl. She didn't recognize her, but she did recognize the look. Fear. The desire to run.

"They're going to come for us," the girl whispered as she pulled at Cali's arm. Behind the girl, the other captives, freed by Maechon, stood at the ready. They looked at her, their trembling savior. Cali ran her fingers over the key, catching Maechon's eye. He came up to her as she unwrapped it from the hilt. The demi girl melted into the shadow with the others, wide-eyed and frightened. Cali could feel it all—their pain, their fear, their hopelessness.

"I feel it too, you know. The fear," Griffin said, her voice clearer. "But even with the key, you only have a part of the piece's – the other is down there." She pointed to the crevasse where James, and the map, had fallen.

Maechon stood next to her now. His hand brushed hers. Cali slipped the key from her fingers to his, squeezing his hand shut around it. He shook his head, but she turned her attention back to Griffin.

"Why?"

"Be more specific."

Cali dug her nails into her palms. "Why did you ..." She hesitated, "kill James?"

"It's not an easy feat, being nice to people all the time. Being ... perfect." Griffin slowly turned from the crack in the earth to face her. If she felt any guilt regarding her actions, it didn't show on her face. Instead, her eyes were glazed with madness. "It's also boring. Strangely, people trust you *less* if you're nice. They think you're lying to them or want something. Did you know that? And yet, you didn't see this coming."

Maechon grabbed Cali's wrist.

"Go!" she hissed as she shook him off. Several demi's scrambled to where the crack from the surface met the ground and disappeared into the gray light beyond. The others remained, waiting and unsure. Maechon stayed beside her, is mouth opening in protest. "Go, Maech—get them to safety."

His throat bobbed as he contemplated her words before he too turned and led the others through to the desert.

"Those are probably the two that'll make it to the gate," Griffin said, she teased the dagger between her fingers. "I'm assuming that's Blythe making the ruckus outside. Seems like the three of you really got over your faults pretty quickly. At least James sure did."

Cali felt her heartbeat in her fingertips, pulsing and churning something inside. She was going to erupt. She was going to take this whole place down with her, with or without Prominent power. The door to her hiding place...it was opening. It shook the ground beneath her feet. Whatever lingered behind it wanted out. *Now.*

"So, you ... you're with Chaos now?" Cali ground out. Her sword felt slick in her sweaty grasp, but she just gripped it tighter. *Why? Why, Griffin? You were my friend.* She said none of this aloud even though her mind screamed the words.

"I suppose that's one way of looking at it," Griffin said with a shrug. "But it hasn't just been now, Cali."

The Earth beneath Cali's feet pulsed as she spoke and she wondered if it was her, or the monsters beneath her feet. "What?"

"Nyx found me first, at the orphanage, before James did." At his name, Griffin's lips tightened, just briefly. "Nyx and Chaos, they're connected. And Chaos—they told her not to kill me.

Because I was special. Because I was powerful."

"You...you can't be that shallow, Griffin," Cali almost screamed. "Chaos is killing demi's. They destroyed the Farm and killed gods—"

"And how do you know that?" Griffin asked, taking a step forward. Her eyes roved Cali with fervent energy. "Tash told you? Auto maybe?"

"Pluto said she takes souls from the Underworld."

"And why would they do that?" Griffin smirked. "Yes, I know you and Tash have become very close. Like you and James."

Cali blinked. "What are you saying?"

"The truth."

"What, and Chaos has given you that truth?" Cali growled.

"The truth of the prophecy, the truth of what we are destined for," Griffin hissed. "Chaos didn't even *want* the humans to be here. That was Prometheus and his little sluts doing. They turned on us gods thinking they could do better and look at what they've done to the world."

"So," Cali said slowly, her voice hitching, "your truth is, Chaos wants to destroy the world."

"Humans—mortals. They had their chance and look what they've done!"

"Zeus, Odin, the other Realms—they won't just let you take out the human race," Cali said with less optimism than she felt. She knew nothing about the Realms besides what Maechon said. She assumed they might not want or like Chaos destroying them.

"The other Realms won't have an option," Griffin said with a small, bitter laugh. Her red-rimmed eyes danced with madness. "Because they'll be gone too."

They'll be gone too.

"Chaos isn't just taking out the humans, Cali." Griffin continued, a swagger in her voice. "She's taking them all out. Every.

Last. One." She dug the tip of the knife into her finger, drawing blood. "Unless, that is, they find a place with Chaos. Like me."

"Griffin ..." *That's not possible,* Cali was going to say, but staring at Griffin, and the bodies of the kaoti strewn out near the door. "Why?"

"They all had their chance."

"But why are *you* doing this, Griffin? Destroying the world – this," Cali gestured broadly. "This can't be the reason."

Griffin shook her head. "It doesn't matter."

"It does, and you know it!"

"This is my place, Cali," Griffin said after a pause. "Chaos sees my talent, my potential. She sees me more than being the child of Loki."

"That's not good enough," Cali said, quietly.

"It's as good as you'll get from me."

Before Cali could press further the heavy wood door opened, releasing into the quiet the screams of the kaoti and a more ominous roar from beyond. Blythe stood, a hand gripping her side with gashes across her body. She swung the door closed behind her as she lumped forward.

She groaned as she reached the two. "Who died?"

"Blythe!" Cali leapt forward; sword drawn alongside her dagger.

Blythe, though injured, was still fast and side-stepped the dagger that flew past her into the door.

"Good to see you too, Griff," she said, pausing to straighten herself and hold *Nordfos* in both hands. "Not really the greatest welcome for a rescue party."

"Always glad to see you B," Griffin said with a smile. The three young women stood for a moment, sizing each other up. Blythe looked over at Cali with a frown.

"She's with them," Cali spit out, her steel drawn in defense. "It's a trap."

Blythe cocked her head as if considering this, then looked at Griffin. "Damn, who would've thought."

"Well, clearly you don't. I don't know how you bypassed the kaoti, but they…"

"Oh, those guys, yeah they're a bit distracted by Hecter the Friendly Hecatoncheire." Blythe lowered her sword as she crossed over to where Cali stood.

"You let the Hecatoncheire out?!" Griffin's voice shrilled. "You've always been an idiot, Blythe."

"Oh chill, your new kaoti pals are fine, plenty more where they came from." Blythe moaned as she grabbed her hip. "James get the crew to the gate?"

"Maechon took them," Cali whispered.

"Maechon standing right behind you?" Blythe nodded and Cali whipped her head around. Maechon stood frozen in his tracks as he had retraced his way back to the cave.

"Maech!" Cali hissed.

He glared back at her. "I c-c-can hel—"

Blythe straightened and walked towards them. "So, where's James?"

"He's dead."

"Who?"

"James."

Blythe's face darkened and her eyes flashed. She turned, slowly and steadily, to Griffin.

"You," she seethed through clenched teeth. *Nordfos* glimmered in the shadow as it pointed at Griffin.

Rocks began to crumble down around them and Blythe, already weak, lost her footing and fell to her knees. Maechon rushed past Cali to her side, but as he did so, something hit them. He fell alongside Blythe.

Cali couldn't hold her sword as she caught herself before hitting the ground. Pain reeled through her body as her open wounds reminded her of their presence. From the corner of her eye Cali could see kaoti on top of Maechon. It tore into his already worn jacket, and he scrambled to push it off. Cali reached for her sword, which fell inches away from her fingers, but a boot slammed into her wrist. It crushed it into the ground, grinding further as she cried out in pain. The rusted dagger in her left hand slipped from her grasp.

"I don't think so, Cali." Griffin cursed. Beside her, Maechon grabbed Cali's sword and relieved the kaoti of a good portion of its face. He then stabbed Griffin's shin.

The cave rattled, and the ceiling began to drop dust and rock down on them. Cracks spread like spiderwebs across the red and gray rocks and ricocheted. One appeared near the door to the cave, large enough for some kaoti to sneak through.

"Hector's coming, we gotta go." Blythe appeared by their side as Griffin stumbled back. She pulled Cali to her feet, and they moved toward their exit.

Maechon handed Cali back her sword, hilt first, but his face showed reluctance as he pointed to something behind Cali. Cali turned without looking and slammed her sword into the oncoming kaoti. Blood spurted across her fingers as she yanked her blade free.

"W-w-we gotta run," Maechon grabbed her elbow and pulled her around to join them.

"Go!" Cali spat out the words. The feeling inside her had erupted. "Go, run! I'm behind you."

She drove her sword into another kaoti as she backed alongside Blythe and Maechon. In a swift move, she dipped, scooping the rusted dagger from the ground, and slammed it into the temple of the next dead creature to reach her. Beside her, Blythe beheaded another, a grin on her face. The look faded to one of horror as she glanced over Cali's shoulder. From the corner of her eye, Cali saw it before it happened. But even then, she knew she couldn't have stopped the moment.

"No—Griffin!" Cali stared in frozen panic at where Griffin stood.

The Norse demi held Maechon by the scruff of his hair, forcing his head back as he kneeled before her. She had somehow made it around them, blocking their escape. Blood poured from the wound at her thigh where Maechon had done his damage, but she still held her position. Blythe and Cali stood motionless.

The dagger—James' dagger—pressed against Maechon's neck.

"Go ahead," Griffin taunted. Her eyes were wild against the soot and blood that covered her face. "I wouldn't hesitate. Cali knows it."

"I do now." Cali tried to keep her voice even against the chaotic screams and rocks that rained down. She weighed the sword and rusted dagger in each hand, wondering if she could reach her friend in time. "But you don't have to do this, Griff. Let him go—"

The door heaved beneath the Hecatoncheire pressing to get through. The wood began to splinter below the arms that beat it down. Cracks rippled up from underneath Cali's feet, splintering as they reached where Griffin held Maechon.

"Griff, let him go." Blythe's voice was low and shook as she held out an open-palmed hand toward Griffin as if she were a feral animal. Blythe's other hand gripped *Nordfos*. "It's Maech. Come on—"

"Maech," Griffin sneered. He squirmed beneath her as her nails dug into his scalp, his face contorted, but he remained silent as the blade pressed against his throat. Blythe and Cali tensed. "Everyone's out there protecting little, mister know-it-all from harm. It's people like him, he's the reason Chaos is doing this—we're better than this, than him! I'm better."

"People—he's a demigod too, Griff, just like you," Cali begged.

"He's a *damaged* demigod. We all walk around it on eggshells, don't we?" Griffin pulled the knife so close to Maechon's throat that the blood began to seep through his skin. Blythe looked ready to rip her head off. "I'm saying the fact he can't even form a sentence without breaking down in the middle? He's ... shut up, Maechon—He's broken. Like you ... you're not like us. You're an ... abomination ... broken, just like him! Broken people like this can't be fixed. A broken world can't be fixed!"

"How can you think this is the only way of fixing a broken world?" Cali asked, clenching down on the power rippling at the edge of her sanity. Her weapons felt useless in her hands. "How can you believe this is right, Griff?"

It seemed that Griffin was trying to stem Maechon's fear with her power, as her fingernails dug into his skin and sweat beaded her forehead with concentration. But the power of Tartarus left her too drained. Cali, on the other hand, felt like she could tear the place apart.

The arms of the Hecatoncheire were almost through. They were running out of time.

Griffin's head tilted, and her eyes slightly glazed, as if she saw something the others could not. She murmured something, too quiet to hear.

Then the doors shattered. Cali glanced towards them as they splintered through the cave, bracing herself for what would come through. Her eyes turned to Griffin, whose face went stone cold. The knife in her hand changed positions.

"One more step to perfection."

"No!" Cali cried. She stepped forward, hand outstretched, knowing it was already too late.

Chapter Thirty- One

Griffin's dagger made quick work.

Blood spurted from Maechon's mouth, and his agonizing scream got lost in the cries of the kaoti that fled through the cavern. The arms of the Hecatoncheire ripped apart any unlucky enough to cross its path. Cali stared, stunned, as Griffin let go of Maechon's hair, pushing him forward as she did so. She stared back at Cali with dead eyes. Blood still dripped from her fingers.

Blythe rushed to catch Maechon as he pitched forward, his face was covered in tears and blood. kaoti ran around them as the rocks fell, ignoring them in their own plight for safety. The deep chasm widened beneath them as the cave shook. Cali wasn't sure if it was due to the damage the monster was causing at the shattered doorway or if it was something stronger. Rocks and boulders plunged around them.

The Hecatoncheire roared with rage as it leveled its gaze on Blythe.

"I guess we both didn't see that coming."

All three looked up at the dazed smile on Griffin's face. Her bloody fingers dropped her dagger, however there was another blade protruding from her chest, right near her heart.

The fallen demi girl's rusted dagger. Cali hadn't even realized she had thrown the blade, but it had met its mark. She and Blythe hauled Maechon up and scrambled out of the dust and stone. Griffin swayed, then lost her balance and tumbled backward into the same chasm she had sent James down, the dagger buried in her chest.

With the Hecatoncheire closing on them, the three made their way to the crack that opened into the gray desert. They dodged falling rock and scattered kaoti as they reached the gap of light in the cave and navigated Maechon around the cracks with some difficulty, but finally, they broke into the gray dust.

Once in the open, Cali could still hear the Hecatoncheire behind her, but she also let herself hope that the demi's—or at least one—had enough faith that they would make it to the door before they closed it. She missed the comforting feeling of the key in her hand—the comforting feeling of hope.

"Stay with me, Maech!" she begged as Blythe tore some of his shirt and shoved it into his mouth. "We're almost there."

"We are not!" Blythe snapped. She heaved Maechon up between them from her position on his right. Throwing a glance over her shoulder, she stumbled, almost taking them all down. "Cal—

Cali didn't need to turn to know what else followed them. Black shadows began to creep up from the depths of the cracks that raced across the ground at their feet. The cracks seemed to continue to grow as they moved forward, weaving between the canyon to where Cali hoped to gods the door was. She knew, with the feeling that crept over her skin, what followed this darkness. *Keep going, keep going ...* She willed her legs forward.

"We have to make it to the door."

"And if they left without us?"

"They'll be there!" Cali tried to brace Maechon's head as it lolled back. "He's losing too much blood—"

"He'll make it!" Blythe said through clenched teeth. "Where is the door?"

"Here!" a voice screamed from their left.

Both whipped around and saw one of the former captive demi's waving wildly at them. Her mouth moved, but Cali could only hear some of the words as Maechon's shoulder kept blocking her good ear.

"What did she say?" Cali asked.

"She says we've got company." Blythe heaved Maechon up higher, and they tried to quicken their pace. "Keep moving."

Keep moving, keep moving. Cali looked back to where they had come. They had rounded a corner, away from the sight of the cave. Kaoti still screamed around them, but overall, they had a straight path to the girl demi, and hopefully, to safety. *Safety.*

As if hearing her heart's hope, darkness swept over the gray sky like a cloud. The misty shadow rolled out like waves across the sand. The cracks continued to spiral out around them, like spiderwebs leading deeper into the powerful mystery that was Tartarus. Looking ahead, the girl disappeared behind the large pillar of rock that they had seen before where the sickled door stood.

"That key had better work," Cali mumbled more to herself as she pulled Maechon forward. She tried to ignore the pain and rage emanating over her own body as she heaved him upright.

"Maech, open your eyes," Blythe said, desperate as she used her sword hand to touch Maechon's face. "Maech!"

"There! Look—" Cali pointed ahead. Several yards before them stood a flat part of the canyon, just beyond the pillars that they now crossed. It was almost completely smooth save for the intricate engravings in old Latin and the crudely engraved sickle at the center. From its place at the center, the sickle seemed to be radiating some sort of smoke. The young girl was nearly jumping up and down with fear as she waved the key in her hand. Cali saw no other trace of the other demi's. "It worked ... I can't believe—"

"Hurry!" The girl clamped a hand over her mouth, her eyes

wide with horror.

Cali knew without looking that the darkness was behind them. She felt Blythe's hand begin to slip away from its position around Maechon, but Cali somehow moved faster. Pulling away, she stepped back from them both., nearly fell backward, but used the tip of her sword to dig into the ground and steady herself.

"Keep going!" she hissed as Blythe turned halfway to her, Maechon still drooping in her arms.

"What are you doing?" Her eyes looked past Cali, then directly met Cali's gaze. For the first time, Cali saw fear behind Blythe's eyes. "Cali—"

Cali whipped around. The place where the skin had been ripped from her palms burned as she grasped her blade and swung blindly. No. Not blind.

The kaoti howled, screaming its pain to the dead wind as its human eyes rolled back in its head. The head split beneath Cali's blow, and it dropped to the ground. Feet beyond the body stood the General of Chaos army, Nyx. Her scattering kaoti formed a chaotic wave of madness around her as they rushed both in fear and to where the door to freedom stood. Just behind Nyx's shoulder, hidden just barely in the shadow, Cali could make out the features of another. *Erinyes*. Her stomach tightened.

The darkness emanating from Nyx hovered but went no further than Cali's feet.

Cali felt it could not go further, even though it lapped around her feet with effort. *Her power is also faded here*, Cali thought as she rolled her shoulders. She gripped her blade in both hands as she faced the two. The Hecatoncheire could be seen behind them, ripping apart scattered undead. But Nyx kept her focus on Cali. The blue eyes sized her up from where she stood, several feet away. Erinyes' lips were pulled back, her teeth bared, and in her hands, she held two identical black swords. But still, no

Chaos. *Show yourself*. Cali was surprised by the will to face the beast behind this madness. The pain in her chest, the image of Ophelli, of James ... her parents, who were still alive out there somewhere, who hid this from her.

Show yourself!

No. The answer rang clear in her mind. Chaos would not face this battle. This was her game; she would let others be her pawns. The hilt of her sword felt slick with the blood and sweat of her palms. It reverberated beneath her skin—or maybe that was the earth beneath her feet.

Behind her, Cali could hear a muffled crack. The Ket fit the lock; the door opened. The demi's—her friends—would be safe. She won.

"You think you can stop what's coming," Nyx said, as if guessing her thoughts. Her hands folded before her, empty of weapons. "You may escape today, but fate has already told us that the end is coming, just like the prophecy said. It's destiny. Why fight it, Immixtus?"

"Destiny can eat shit," Cali hissed through bared teeth.

"Destiny is what saved your life when the Furie tried to end it all those years ago," Nyx responded coolly. Beside her Erinyes growled. The Furie rocked on her black boots, ready for action. "But Autolycus is not here to save you now, Immixtus. Now your path is all on you, as are the choices you make. The gods know you are here, that you survived. You will not be welcome in any Realm of theirs. They'll never accept you."

"Oh, and you will?"

"Yes."

It was a dumb question; Cali knew it. And she got the response she knew would happen. But no. Cali's desire wasn't acceptance—she knew that. It was the lesson her parents, Aliax and Miriam, had drilled into her since childhood. Cali needed no one's approval. But she did want the truth. Something in her, though, was tempted by the possibility of what lies Chaos could give, or what veiled truths lay on the other side. But then she thought of Griffin. That was a truth she couldn't ignore. Griffin, what she had done – and become - for a part of Chaos' world.

"I think I'll pass."

Nyx shook her head. "Why have more bloodshed needlessly? Haven't you suffered enough?"

"Yes, I think I have," Cali replied. "But I prefer chance over your stupid version of reality."

She could feel the rush of the air as the door pulled open behind her. It creaked beneath the weight of the stone, and she struggled to stay on her feet as the wind rushed grit and sand around her. She would face this threat, alone. *This* would be her destiny. Saving the few friends she had—*yes*, she felt good with this word now for the people in her life. This would be her fate. *To die for friends ... that seems like a good idea.*

"Erinyes is not allowed to kill you yet, Immixtus," Nyx said, barely reacting to the weapon in front of her. "But know that I do not need you intact to be useful—"

Nyx looked over her shoulder with narrowed eyes. Cali used the moment to her advantage and leaped forward, closing the space between them, blade raised. She moved fast. Nyx's eyes lowered to meet her as she struck. But Cali's weapon connected with another blade. Both silver and black steel were locked before the general. Erinyes' eyes danced madly; her mouth pulled into a tight smile, revealing her white teeth. Smoke simmered from her blade as it edged up to Cali's wrist.

"Not quite fast enough, child," Nyx sighed. With a snap of her fingers, the kaoti flinched to attention and began to pour around them. Still locked against Erinyes, Cali risked a glance over her shoulder towards the gate. It remained open.

Nyx turned on her heel straight for the Hecatoncheire as if

Cali's attack meant nothing. The surrounding darkness around her pulled away as she moved and covered the creature, pulling it down into the darkness. Cali, unable to turn to see if her friends had made it through, barely had time to step back from Erinyes' second blade that came for her neck. She just narrowly missed as she ducked back, and brought her sword back around towards Erinyes, twisting her wrist around as her feet worked mechanically beneath her.

Rage and that strange security from that dormant feeling inside made her strong., She could feel it. Numbing her body, allowing her to move fully into the dance Instinct rushed through her veins, untapped and raw in its power. Her feet moved, and she ran her blade around again, coming back hard. Erinyes, for her part, continued to do her own dance, although her smile faded as Cali continued to hold her own against the double blades.

"So, you're the reason I'm here." Cali panted. "You're the Furie who tried to kill me as a baby?" Erinyes' smoldering blades braced Cali's between them, forming an X. "What? No cryptic, Latin comeback?"

For a brief moment, Cali wondered if she could reach Blythe's dagger at her side, but Erinyes hit her again. Cali blocked the blow and nicked the goddess' knuckles as she did. The black eyes narrowed, the only sign that Erinyes felt the hit.

"Always just blindly obeying Chaos' orders then? Killing innocent children? Tearing apart famili—"

"*Du vet ingenting om kaos*!" Erinyes hissed. Spit flew from her mouth as she leaned close to Cali's face. "*Din skjebne er døden, og jeg vil sørge for det.*"

"Uh ... okay." Cali recognized the language as Norse. Her father, the lover of inspirational and wise quotes, used to say things to her in this language. Cali never understood what he was saying, and he would never translate it back for her. It had always bothered her. It bothered her when Erinyes had spoken first in Varsna It made her skin crawl. She tried to claw at the dark place, will the power or whatever it was in her to the surface, but she wavered.

The Furie matched Cali's movements with her quick, silent steps and heavy blows, pressing her back. Cali brought her blade up fast, and then round again, ducking as a black smoking blade brushed her forearm as she circled back. Erinyes broke the space between them, coming close to Cali as she spun around. Cali lost control of her sword, and Erinyes pressed her advantage. Dropping one of her black blades as it held high over Cali's head, she smashed her fist into Cali's face. Cali staggered back, her sword loose in her hand, blood spurting from her nose. Her resolve, her adrenaline-driven anger, faded. As she struggled to focus her gaze. Her head swarmed, buzzing with the noise around her.

Cali's blade connected with Erinyes' again, driving it towards the ground as the steel scraped against each other. Sparks and smoke flew around them at each hit. Cali stepped back, but this time her body betrayed her, and her heel caught on a rock on the ground. She pitched backward, landing on her rear. She struggled back as Erinyes towered over her.

The Furie's breath was labored. Sweat and blood dripped from her face and hands. Sword still in hand, Cali raised it as Erinyes brought her blades down.

She felt a cold rush come over her body, like when she had seen Auto for the first time, or when she took the first jump into the lake at Foloi Forest when she was a little girl. It had been too early in the season for a swim, her mother said, but she had gone anyway. She had been fearless then. Now that fear flooded her veins, clouding out any trace of power or strength. Her breath caught as her parents' faces flashed through her mind. *So, this is it.* She felt her own sword pressed down to meet her and she closed her eyes.

***

"No!"

Cali's eyes flew open, immediately recognizing the voice.

Natasha stood over Cali; her blade interlocked with Erinyes'. Cali's own sword lay inches from her right hand covered in blood. She pushed her head up to look behind her and saw a large revealing crack of bright sunlight break across the gray world. The light revealed figures. Centaurs, demi's, and the fauns intermixed in battle with the kaoti, daring them to take a step through the gap. Cali tried to blink the fog away from her brain as she pushed herself to her elbows and stared up at the locked swords before her.

"Erinyes," Natasha said, her muscular arms tight as she pushed her opponent's weapon away from Cali. "Do not think for a second I will not use this blade to strike you down as well sister. You have seen me do it before. I would do it again without hesitation."

Sisters? Cali stared up at Natasha with a look of awe and shock at the announcement. Cali always knew Natasha was a Furie, it had never been hidden truth. But the connection was lost till now. Erinyes stared at her sister with unbridled hatred. Foam built in her mouth as she stepped back. She rolled her shoulders as she pointed her sword at Natasha's face, hissing as she did so.

The two last Furies faced and circled each other.

"You are correct." Nyx appeared in her shadow, just behind where Erinyes stalked. Her black hair whipped around her face as she watched them. "We do not have our full potential here, and neither do those who come with you. We do not need to fight, Alecto. We have both been around long enough to know that destiny will be fulfilled, whether we all die here, or later."

"That is no longer my name," Natasha said, her voice even., She caught Cali's eye and nodded for her to stand. Cali scrambled to her feet, getting up behind Natasha and holding her sword. Her hand shook, and she nearly dropped it from the blood on the hilt. "Where is your master? Where is Chaos?"

Nyx's face remained impassive as she folded her arms in front of her.

"At this time, it is not Chaos' battle. And this is no longer mine. That is how the Faytes have worked it. How the prophecy was planned all those years ago to end all things." The night goddesses' black eyes narrowed. "You know this."

Natasha brandished another dark blade as she placed herself between the goddesses and Cali. "Still holding on to prophecies—a little outdated for our time, don't you think?"

"We shall see if you believe in destiny or not." Nyx cocked her head as if amused. "In the end, it won't matter." Her face grew paler. "Erinyes, *fullføre dette*."

The kaoti overwhelmed the rescuers, and from the corner of her eye, Cali could see Arastoo yelling for a retreat through the gate. She could also see the bodies, both of kaoti and those from the Farm, both ones she had tried to save, and ones who were now trying to save her. *We have to get out of here.* She blinked through the blood and sweat threatening to blind her. *We can't win this.* Her heart hammered. Natasha whispered something, so soft that Cali almost mistook it for the wind.

"I'm not leaving you," Cali said, realizing as Nyx stepped away what Natasha intended to do.

"Go, now," Natasha commanded. She turned her head just briefly to catch Cali's eyes. Cali opened her mouth to protest, but something grabbed her from behind. She struggled, cursing and lashing out, but Arastoo held firm. He pinned her arms to her sides as he rushed her away from the battle.

"No!" Cali screamed. "No, stop—"

Cali kept her eyes on Natasha as Arastoo lifted her from the ground and pulled her to the gate. Nyx gave one last nod in Cali's direction before she disappeared into the shadows she created. The Hecatoncheire came alive with focus. Its dozens of arms flew around, some used almost as legs to propel it towards the fray outside the gate. Erinyes also moved forward and towards her sister; blade raised high.

Natasha was faster than her sister. But just barely. The two were locked in a battle of skill and steel. It was mesmerizing to watch. Skill matched skill, hate matched hate. *No, no, no! Run!* Cali tried to scream but the air from the world beyond the gate rushed around her, taking the words from her mouth before she could shout her warning. Nothing could stop her from seeing what happened next.

The Hecatoncheire's focus remained on the gate, but as he passed the Furies in their deadly dance, he reached out a hand and grabbed Natasha's leg. The stumble from Natasha was all Erinyes needed to find her ground, and the sword in her hand moved quickly as it sliced at the neck, and in the fell blow, removed Natasha's head from her body.

Shock rattled Cali's brain and she went limp in Arastoo's arms. The gray world of Tartarus, the kaoti, the Hecatoncheire and all the monsters he represented seemed to fade as her vision blurred. With each hoofbeat from the centaur, Cali's head pounded.

"The key—now!" Arastoo shouted to a demi who waited at the gate for them.

As she reached up to grab the small key, a kaoti grabbed her. Its teeth bared into her before she could even scream. They crossed the threshold of the massive stone door, and Cali reached out and yanked the key from its lock. She felt her shoulder pop, and her brain went fuzzy, before darkness closed on her like the gate of Tartarus.

Chapter Thirty-Two

"James!"

Cali sat upright in her bed. She immediately regretted it.

Her stomach churned, she leaned over, and threw up in the waste bin. For a moment, she thought she was in the Underworld again. Dark spots filled her vision and sparkling lights were behind her eyes. She would see the judges soon and be placed in the farthest, darkest pit of Hell for her failure. It would be no less than what she deserved. She swallowed as she thought of this, or tried to, but it felt papery and rough. The torture had begun then. Tilting her head from the wastebasket, she lay on her back and closed her eyes.

A fan lulled lazily above her head and her eyes fluttered open. The pain in her chest overcame the ache in her bones, and tears squeezed their way out of the corner of her eyes. Natasha would not be there this time to tell her things would only get worse. Not that Cali needed to be told that anymore. Blinking several times, Cali sighed, pushed herself to her elbows, and sat up. Dull, faded-orange wallpaper lined the hotel room she was in. The only other things besides the bed and wastebasket were outdated 70s curtains and a single picture of a vulture that hung crooked on the wall.

They were in the new safe zone, Gozo, an island off Italy, near Malta. It had been three weeks since the battle of Tartarus. Arastoo had brought the few who'd survived to the island through the door. The Key of Ymir was safe with Autolycus.

Auto.

He hadn't spoken to her in weeks since they had arrived, and Cali didn't blame him. Instead, he spent his time on the beach, or in his room. Arastoo, Bear, and the remaining centaurs were trying to keep things normal and had already built a routine of tasks around the island that included training, cleaning, and meditation. The demi's were resilient but traumatized. Even though they knew and prepared for this, nothing had equipped them for what they had faced at the Farm or in Tartarus. They were frightened that their leaders were shattered, that Natasha was dead, and that Auto refused to take charge.

A strange change occurred as Cali began to heal. She healed ... quickly. And she could feel it as it happened. The muscles and flesh pulled and stitched themselves back together. It felt no worse than growing pains now. She could still feel the cracked ribs and bruises, but her body worked to put her back together, even without the healer's help. But the pain she felt in her body ran deeper than the superficial cuts and scars.

She trudged out of her room and stared into the day as her hearing gradually came back to her. Not that there was much she wanted to hear, or see, on this tiny, abandoned island. The abandoned hotel, although whitewashed and cracked, still had some elegance against the blue sky that taunted its beauty at her sadness. The ocean shore stood several feet away from where they stood and surrounded them on all sides within about a mile each way.

Garwin stood outside her bedroom, talking to Seeny. She'd lost one of her yellow eyes and now had a patch over the other. She darted a look at Cali as she joined them.

"Cali, you're up!" Garwin gave her a half-smile as she exchanged a somber good morning.

"Auto still out there I see." Cali nodded thanks for the cup of coffee Garwin handed her.

He and Becca, the final healer of their group, had worked tirelessly to heal those who had been injured, and for that Cali was thankful. Becca's skill as a healer lessened without the help of her sister. But she was able to mend the bones, set, and heal the wounds. However, she had not been able to restore all. Seeny's eye was still gone, Mauricio would always walk with a limp, and Maechon would never speak again. Blythe, who was also injured, never left his side. It seemed to Cali that she was not the only one who was attempting penance.

"I should go talk to him," she mumbled. She inhaled the coffee and stared out to Auto's silhouette against the sand.

"You can try," Garwin said, following her gaze. "All he does is stand there."

"Then we'll just stand there in silence," Cali muttered.

She made her way down the crumbled walkway to the beach. The sand bent under her feet as she made her way to Auto's side. They stood there for a moment in silence, both looking out at the crash of gray and blue waves. Cali blinked several times, trying to rid herself of the memory—the eyes—those colors brought up. So many painful last looks; so many dead pairs of eyes floated around in her dreams. *Don't think about it,* she chided herself. *Focus on now.* This was not the journey she would have anticipated herself going on when she had been with her parents in the Foloi Forest those three months ago. She took a shuddering breath as the memory of the dead washed over her.

"I would have done anything for you." Auto's voice snatched her from her thoughts.

"What do you mean?" she asked cautiously.

He wouldn't look at her.

"When I held you in my arms that day on Asgard," he continued, so softly that Cali had to tilt her head to hear his words. "I swore to ... those I loved that I would care for you. But looking into your eyes even then, I knew I would do anything to keep you safe."

Cali stiffened. Her eyes widened with confusion at his words, and her mind raced at the thought they produced. She knew Freya was her mother, and Pluto divulged her other parentage had been Olympian. But he had provided little more in his perpetually teasing conversation. And Cali had tried to rid herself of her curiosity about this till the right time.

"I'm not your father." He looked down at her, a strained half-smile crossing his face. "I don't know who he is." His eyes grew distant. "But for Freya I would have moved mountains—"

"You loved her?"

Auto didn't respond but stared out at the ocean again.

"What happened?" Cali asked.

"She was afraid you would be found out, so I took you away," he said solemnly. A spray from the waves knocked into them. "After the accident, after the waterfall—even though the Realms thought you were dead, I told them you were dead." He paused and wiped his eye. "They wouldn't allow me home. That was when Tash found me. The *gods* only considered us useful again when murmurs of Chaos' return began to churn across the Realms."

"You saved me." Cali recalled her dream—her forever nightmare—of the runner in the North. Who ran across ice, cold, and snow to get away from the threat of the darkness that followed. The runner who threw himself over the ice-glazed waterfalls. That was always the moment in the dream that Cali would wake. Covered in a cold sweat of her own, she would run to her parents' room. Then she got older, but the dream remained, and she depended on her parents less—even though the fear remained with it. "You were the runner."

Auto nodded.

After a moment, she spoke again. "I don't understand why they want me dead. Even if I am a ... mixed god, I have no real power." He threw her a small, knowing look, which she chose to ignore. "I'm not even the best fighter here. I couldn't even save the people that I cared about."

"You're something they cannot control, and can't understand, even in your perceived *lack of power*.," Auto said. "Zeus and Odin cannot touch the Moirai now; they are too strong. You, whether you believe it or not, are getting stronger. You're a threat."

"But they won't be able to kill me?"

"Possibly, no. But that won't stop them from trying." Auto crossed his arms and turned to study her. She turned to face him, following his pose. "The greatest threat to the gods are things they cannot, or do not, know—and things they cannot control. That could be another god, or a prophecy."

"Natasha said something about that—I thought she was joking."

"Natasha never joked," Auto said, almost smirking. "But there is a prophecy."

Cali waited.

"I don't think it's the time."

"Are you kidding me?" Cali looked back at the small hotel littered against the white sand and sky. Auto shook his head and remained mute. "Fine then." *I'll ask Maechon.* "Isn't this a demi safe zone given by the gods? Don't they know I'm here?"

"Well, yes and no," Auto glanced at the waves that now lapped at his feet. "You see...we are surrounded by water. The god of fish ..." The wave kicked up and slapped at his clothes, covering him to his waist in water. "*Poseidon* has allowed us to be here without the others intervening."

"Poseidon?" Cali looked out to the water. "Why?"

"Because he wants something, obviously." Auto glared at the

wave as he looked himself over. He nodded for Cali to move away from the edge and up the beach again. Cali stepped in beside him.

"What does he want?"

"A box."

"Okay? Like, he wants me to make one?"

"You're a carpenter now? Can you walk on water too?" Auto pushed himself on his crutch and made his way across the sand. Cali wrinkled her nose at his comment. "This is not the kind of box you can make. At the beginning of the Silent Treaty the gods exchanged gifts to ... to ... damn this god-damned sand!" He let out a slew of curses as they reached the grassier part of the beach, but still almost knocked himself over in the process. "They exchanged—"

"Gifts, yeah, like the key," Cali recalled.

"They were a key, a box, and a stone, I think."

"You don't know what the third item was?" Cali asked.

"I only know what I know," Auto snapped. *So, no.*

They reached the sidewalk that led to the dilapidated hotel, and he straightened. A few demi's milled around, as if in a daze, going about their tasks and chores assigned by Bear and Arastoo. Some would catch her eye as she passed, then look away just as fast. Cali tried not to let it bother her. She believed—or more wanted to believe—it was the trauma of battle and loss that caused the haunted looks. But she now knew better. Her secret, hidden even from her, was out. Everyone on the island knew what she was. *Immixtus.* Even though she couldn't hear it said, she knew they murmured it to each other like a curse. Her small group of friends had shrunk further, and even those she had saved, like Mauricio, Roro, and Garwin, looked at her with fear.

"As we do not have the map anymore," Auto continued. She kept pace beside him as they made their way up the walk. "But we do have the key. Not that Posey knows that. He does know the box was given to Odin—"

He nodded at Mauricio, whose arm hung in a cast on his chest, as he limped by. Auto remained quiet until he'd passed. "The box is on Asgard, in the catacombs."

"Why is this important and not going after Chaos, since she has the map?"

"This is *about* Chaos," Auto insisted gravely. His voice grew quiet. "These items are not just mere gifts of representation. They are powerful items; containing the balance of life and death and reality between them."

"What is she going to do with them?" Cali asked as she ran her fingers through her hair. "Why is Chaos so obsessed with these items?"

"Chaos is bound to the power of Tartarus so that it drains her. It keeps her at bay of gaining her full power. But the gifts contain the binding that she needs to be free—to be fully herself."

"And then she can take over the world." Cali thought back to Griffin's claim that Chaos wanted to cleanse the world of humans and Realms; to hit the restart button. She rubbed her arms, even though she was quite warm. Some of what Griffin said made sense. The world was a messed-up place. Humanity and gods alike had seen to that. But total destruction—*is that fair*? She was jolted from her thoughts by Auto staring at her. Her stomach tightened and they paused just outside his door.

"Why are you telling me this?"

Auto reached into his pocket as he leaned on his crutch and pulled out the leather strapped key. She swallowed hard as she looked from the key to his worn face.

"I did not want to ask so soon." Auto held the key out to her but extended his hand no further. He wanted her to reach for it. "Poseidon is fickle, and ever-changing, like the sea he claims. You may not be safe here long, even with his promise of protection." He sighed. "I want to protect you, but—we do not have a Totem tree to protect those who are here and…it just isn't safe."

Cali understood. He wasn't afraid for her safety. He was afraid for the demi's. With all his resolve to be dismissive of them all, he knew the safety of the many outweighed her own. He knew she was a threat. That if Poseidon chose to, he could let the other Realms come for her.

"Why not then?" Cali's voice cracked at her attempt to lighten her anxiety. His hand pulled back, but her own shot forward and grasped it. He met her stare as he released it into her sweaty hands.

"I'm sorry."

"Where am I supposed to go?" Cali ignored the apology and the heaviness in her chest. The hidden place inside began to rustle, like a stirring animal, ready to pounce. "Just … jump through time and hope I land in Asgard?"

"That would be unwise." Several demi's who had been out for a run on the beach made their way past them, their chatter covering the quietness of the walkway. "But North, yes. That would be a start. And back farther than whispers of Immixtus have reached, I think. Odin is not as charming as this century has made him out to be. You'll have to be fast, quick…to be able to get the box. I believe." He leaned against his door. "I believe Maechon may have knowledge of a route."

Cali looked at the runners as they stretched together, laughing quietly, and talking amongst themselves. "Maech … If I ask him Blythe will find out."

"What others choose to do is not up to you. However, I believe Blythe may truly kill you if you chose this task by yourself." Auto smirked, his beard pulling at the ends. Then his face fell. "I didn't mean for any of this to happen."

"It doesn't matter much now," Cali said as she wrapped the key around her neck. "I can do this. I mean … what else am I gonna do? Wait for some damned gods to come and kill me for doing nothing but exist? I think I'd rather die on my own terms."

"That's the spirit." He pushed his door open and stepped into his room.

"Auto," Cali called after him. "Thank you for saving my life."

His head turned, but he didn't look at her. "I am sending you to your potential death, and yet—"

"I mean, before all of this," she murmured. "I know you are the runner from my nightmare. I know you saved me." He stiffened; a hand gripped the doorframe. "I know what you lost for me, and I—"

"Sometimes when we lose something, we gain something else in return – it's balance." He paused and added, "Cali." He finally put his ice-cold gaze on her and she shivered. "Happy birthday."

Chapter Thirty-Three

"You must be out of your damn mind!"

Blythe stood, cross-armed and scowling, in the middle of Maechon's small room.

Maechon had been discharged from the medical ward—a former indoor pool—three days ago and was recovering in his own room. Blythe visited daily. She had even gone with a small party to the mainland to collect needed items and brought back several tattered library books about learning Sign Language. Maechon, being gifted in memory and quick adaption to languages, immediately caught on to his new language. Cali had learned Sign Language as a child, as her parents had been unsure if she would lose her hearing completely, but she was far from being fluent. Not to be outdone, Blythe worked hard to keep up. She'd quickly learned the curse words so that she could now use them when frustrated with learning the language.

"You don't have to come," Cali shrugged. "How is he?"

"Unlike you, he's not deaf," Blythe snapped in annoyance as she pulled her hair back from her face and put it into a bun. Maechon looked up at both morosely as they stood in front of him. His physical wounds seemed to be healing rather nicely, but his face was still bruised, and he looked skinnier than ever. A book lay open in his lap, his cracked glasses sitting on the end of his nose.

"So, you have a plan then?" Blythe asked, plopping down on a chair beside the bed.

"A loose plan."

"Great." Blythe groaned, pulling her feet up on the bed to rest them beside Maechon. "All this for a box huh? What's so special about it? And why do we have to go to the Asgaard to get it?"

Maechon signed something, but Blythe frowned and shook her head. "Slower." Maechon complied.

"We *should* be able to get there because we're only half gods. The rules don't apply I guess."

"A little too many risky verbs in there, Cal."

Maechon nodded solemnly in agreement with Blythe's observation.

"Also, need I remind you, *we*," Blythe gestured to herself and Maechon, "are half-gods. *You* are a god-god. Mixie. We would actually die."

"We don't know that for sure." Cali sat down beside Maechon on the bed before she fell over. She tried to hide the thought that gnawed at her. The potential that she, as a god, may be immortal. *No.* She buried her fingers in her knees and winced as she felt the almost healed scars send pain through her legs. *Concentrate Cali, one thing at a time.*

"I'm not asking you to come along. But we have just as much of a shot at this as anyone. I can't just ... sit here and wait for Poseidon to change his mind and let the gods kill me."

Blythe stared at her for a moment. "Well, I'm obviously coming," she said. "You're far too emotional to make good judgments, and I'm the only reason you got out alive last time. Let's be honest, Cal, you make every mission way more complicated than it has to be."

Cali opened her mouth to protest, but when Blythe raised an eyebrow at her, she closed it again. At least Blythe was consistently, horrendously honest.

"Fine." Her ambitious feeling of pulling this off dwindled as she realized Blythe could be right. But the little spark of resolve remained. She had lost her friends. She had lost her mentor. She had lost her parents. Although they were alive, this somehow made it worse for her. Knowing they were out there ... Cali shook the thought from her mind. She had worked hard to push the feelings of homesickness away. She would do this. *I can do this.*

"No, you're not coming, end of story!" Blythe shook her head as Maechon made loud gestures. They both stood, facing each other. Although not as built as Blythe, he stood about a good foot above her. He shook his head vehemently and pointed at himself, then them, then made a circle around with his fingers, finalizing his motion with a fist. "No, Cali!"

"I can't stop him from coming." Cali sighed as she stood up. "Besides, Becca said there wasn't more she could do ... at this time. But I don't think ... are you up to it Maech? Our missions don't really have the best track record."

"I'm coming," Maechon signed firmly.

Blythe groaned and flopped back on the bed, staring at the ceiling.

"Then let's do this and get it over with," she muttered, closing her eyes. Maechon patted her knee sympathetically.

"Okay," Cali said. She rubbed her fingers over the key. "Then let's gather what we might need, and I guess meet back here in an hour?"

"Oh Captain, our captain."

Without another word, the three dispersed to gather what little they could for their travel north.

***

"Last chance to bail," said Cali as they stood in the empty room. Each one wore several layers of long-sleeved shirts, thin jackets, and tattered boots. Greece was not a great place to find winter gear; especially on an island like this. Cali couldn't help but grin as she took in their rag-tag appearance.

"And miss our chance to see a yeti?" Blythe strapped *Nordfos* to her hip and another blade just below her left arm. "I don't think so."

Maechon also nodded resolutely.

Cali lifted her chin and put the key into the lock. She let her mind clear, even with her heart racing, and thought of the place Maechon had described in the North. Her mind shifted, as if pulling the location from memory.

She turned the Key of Ymir and it clicked.

Frost crept over the handle as her fingers touched it. Blythe and Maechon stepped up beside her as she turned the knob and pushed the door outward. The icy wind hit them before the view did, blasting them fully in the face. Snow peppered around them as they stared in wonder at the frozen forest on the other side.

"Cool!" Blythe murmured. She sidestepped Cali and moved into the North beyond the door.

Cali pulled her jacket closer. The cold did not make her shiver. There was something about the look of this place that made her anxious.

"Forward." Maechon signed.

They moved forward into the snow, their boots leaving soft imprints on the ground. Cali pulled the key from the lock as she did and closed the door behind her.

"It's so... magical!" Blythe smiled. Cali and Maechon stared at her, open-mouthed. She shrugged. "What? I can't enjoy things too?"

"I didn't say anything," Cali said, with a laugh.

Maechon raised his hands defensively too and grinned.

A rush of wind swept up around them and there was a thud. Turning around, only trees stood where the door had been. "So ... I guess we're staying here for a bit then," Cali muttered as she rubbed her arms. She let one hand drop to the sword at her side and her fingers traced the hilt. Something felt ... *off.*

Blythe tilted her head back and caught a snowflake on her tongue. "I don't think this is Asgard."

"Auto said we couldn't just land in Asgard," Cali replied. "Something about magical new portals being created and sending off alarms for the gods." She surveyed the area. "We were supposed to be close though. Maech?"

"This isn't the place I was thinking of," Maechon signed, a crease forming on ins forehead.

Cali and Blythe exchanged a look. "So, where are we?" Cali asked.

Maechon tapped his fingers together. "We are... North."

"Well, that's helpful."

"It's fine, B," Cali interrupted Maechon's obscene gestures. "We're North, we have the key, we'll figure it out."

Blythe shook her head before and then bent down and ran her fingers through the snow.

Cali turned to take in the new land. Trees scattered out around them, creating a hedge of deep, green foliage and low visibility. The sky was clouded and scattered light flakes down on them. It seemed to add to the quiet. Cali tentatively touched her left ear, tracing the scars there. *I've been here before.*

Something hit the side of her face, and she yelped. Blythe laughed aloud and held another snowball in her hand. She sent it toward Machon this time.

Maechon attempted to return the volley from Blythe, but he was unlucky in his aim. Their laughter faded as Cali walked through the snow. A few steps from where they entered was a frozen solid river and trees gathered on the banks of the other side. She walked down the slope. To her right, there was a low rumble. She walked the edge of the river towards it. Out of the corner of her eye she saw the fluttering of wings. An owl was spooked up and sat, staring at her. The rumble of the falls now matched the beating of her heart. The owl ruffled its feathers, cooing softly.

Cali peered over the edge at the frozen waterfall. Water broke free in places, but otherwise it was a solid chunk of ice all the way down. It was a steep drop. A drop few, if any, would survive. Panic surged through her. With one hand on her sword, she spun to her companions.

"Guys, we have to—"

The blunt end of the weapon smashed into her face. The surprise made her step back. She grabbed at the air as she fell back.

Cali couldn't see his face, but the dark blue eyes followed her as she disappeared over the edge and into the icy falls below.

***

The man with the one-eye patch dragged her by the hair across the snow, away from the edge, leaving a trail of Cali's blood on the snow behind him.

Cali struggled beneath his visceral grip, both of her hands wrapped around the massive fingers threaded through her hair and digging into her scalp. To her right, even with her blurred vision from the hit to her head, she could see Blythe's effort against three men twice her size. *Run, run!* Cali tried to call out to her—but she found it difficult to form a sentence, much less focus on a thought. *Maech—where's Maech?* She couldn't see him through the throng of horses that her captor pulled her through.

The one-eyed man halted before one of the younger men on horses—someone he referred to as *fylltegn*. He said something else Cali couldn't hear, mostly over the ringing in her ears.

The young man looked down at her from his steed, cool hate behind his eyes. "*Hvem er du?*"

Cali blinked. Her head throbbed and she could feel the warm, sticky blood tracing down her neck. "Wh—what?"

The cold eyes narrowed. "Who, and *what*, are you?"

Unsure of the weight the truth could carry, and remembering Auto's warning, Cali hesitated. "We," she began slowly, "we are just travelers. We," *think, Cali, think,* "got separated from our village—our group."

The face remained impassive, and Cali could tell by the look on his face that he wasn't buying it.

She tried again. "If you could just—" she began but was interrupted when the leader suddenly dismounted and strode over to her.

Instinct told her to step back, and she tried, but the vile-smelling man holding her tightened his grip. The younger man stopped in front of her, his piercing gaze assessing her face, her arm, then to the sword in her grasp. *No, no, no.*

He grabbed the sword, but Cali held firm. Cocking his head, he tsked and gently removed each of her fingers from the blade's hilt. Cali could do nothing but watch as he unwrapped the key and held it in his hand.

"That—" She struggled to find words as the roots of her hair pulled tighter. "That's just a key."

The ice-blue eyes met hers in a flash of amusement and another emotion she couldn't decern. Without a word, he wrapped the Key of Ymir around his neck, turned on his heel, and remounted his horse.

"*Bind dem*," he commanded the man holding Cali fast, and then turned to the rest. "*Raskt.* Quickly—we leave now."

"Leave? Wha—wait!" Cali struggled against the man's grip, straining towards the leader as he turned his horse away. "Where are you taking us?"

The leader of the Vikings turned to her, a grim smile on his face. "North, little demigod. I am taking you north."

About The Author

Hope Forsman is native to Minnesota, but spends most of her time in England, in a garden, or in daydreams. When she is not writing, she is reading, out for long walks (on the moors), dancing (under a full moon), or gardening (wherever dirt can be found).

Immixtus is her debut novel – the first of a series of Cali and her demigod friends mission to save the Realms.

Made in the USA
Monee, IL
02 June 2023